LUX
OPPOSITION

LUX

OPPOSITION

A Lux Novel

BOOK FIVE

PLUS SEE WHERE IT ALL BEGAN . . .

prequel novella *SHADOWS* included!

from #1 *NYT* bestselling author

JENNIFER L. ARMENTROUT

Entangled Publishing, LLC
2614 South Timberline Road
Suite 109
Fort Collins, CO 80525
Visit our website at www.entangledpublishing.com.

Edited by Liz Pelletier
Cover design by Liz Pelletier and Heather Howland
Text design by E. J. Strongin, Neuwirth & Associates, Inc.

Ebook ISBN 978-1-62266-265-4
Hardcover ISBN 978-1-62266-733-8
Paperback ISBN 978-1-62266-264-7

Manufactured in the United States of America

First Edition August 2014

10 9 8 7 6 5 4 3 2

To every reader who stumbled across *Obsidian* at some point and thought, *Aliens in high school? Why the heck not? I've read weirder stuff.* And then ended up loving Katy and Daemon and crew as much as I do. This is for you. Thank you.

1

{ Katy }

Back in the day, I had this plan for the off chance that I was around for the whole end-of-the-world thing. It involved climbing up on my roof and blasting R.E.M.'s "It's the End of the World as We Know It (And I Feel Fine)" as loud as humanly possible, but real life rarely turns out that cool.

It was happening—everything about the world as we knew it was ending, and it sure as hell did not feel fine. Or cool.

Opening my eyes, I inched aside the flimsy white curtain. I peered out, beyond the porch and the cleared yard, into the thick woods surrounding the cabin Luc had stashed in the forests of Coeur d'Alene, a city in Idaho I couldn't even begin to pronounce or spell.

The yard was empty. There was no flickering, brilliant white light shining through the trees. No one was out there. Correction. *Nothing* was out there. No birds were chirping or fluttering from leafy branch to branch. Not one sign of any woodland creatures scurrying anywhere. There wasn't even the low hum of insects. Everything was silent and still, sound-less in a totally creeptastic kind of way.

My gaze fixed on the woods, glued to the last place I'd seen Daemon. A deep, throbbing ache lit up my chest. The night we'd fallen asleep on the couch seemed like ages ago, but it had only been forty-eight hours or so since I'd woken up, overheated, and nearly been blinded by Daemon's true form. He hadn't been able to control it, although if we'd known what it signaled, it probably wouldn't have changed anything.

So many others of his kind, hundreds—if not thousands—of Luxen, had come to Earth, and Daemon . . . he was gone, along with his sister and brother, and we were still here in this cabin.

Pressure clamped down on my chest, as if someone were squeezing my heart and lungs with vise grips. Every so often, Sergeant Dasher's warning came back to haunt me. I'd seri-ously thought the man—that all of Daedalus—was riding the crazy train into Insanity Land, but they had been right.

God, they had been *so* right.

The Luxen came like Daedalus had warned, like they had prepared for, and Daemon . . . The ache pulsed, ripping the air right from my lungs, and I squeezed my eyes shut. I had no idea why he left with them or why I hadn't seen or heard from him or his family. The terror and confusion surrounding his disap-pearance were a constant shadow that haunted every waking moment and even the few minutes I'd been able to sleep.

What side would Daemon be standing on? Dasher had asked that of me once, while I'd been held at the very real Area 51, and I couldn't let myself believe that I had that answer now.

In the last two days, more Luxen had fallen from the sky. They'd kept coming and coming like an endless stream of fall-ing stars, and then there was—

"Nothing."

My eyes popped open, and the curtain slipped from my fingers, softly falling back into place. "Get out of my head."

"I can't help it," Archer replied from where he sat on the couch. "You're broadcasting your thoughts so damn loudly I feel like I need to go sit in the corner and start rocking, whispering Daemon's name over and over again."

Irritation pricked at my skin, and no matter how much I tried to keep my thoughts, my worries and fears, to myself, it was useless when there was not one, but two Origins in the house. Their nifty little ability to read thoughts got real annoying real fast.

I picked at the curtain again, watching the woods. "Still no sign of any Luxen?"

"Nope. Not a single glowing light crashing to Earth in the last five hours." Archer sounded as tired as I felt. He hadn't been sleeping much, either. While I'd been fixated on keeping an eye on the outside, he'd been focused on the TV. News all across the globe had been reporting nonstop on the "phenomenon."

"Some of the news stations are trying to say it was a massive meteorite shower."

I snorted.

"Trying to cover up anything at this point is useless." Archer sighed wearily, and he was right.

What happened in Las Vegas—what we had done—had been videotaped and blasted all over the internet within hours. At some point during the day after the absolute obliteration of Las Vegas, all the videos had been pulled down, but the damage had already been done. From what the news copter had captured before Daedalus had shot it down, to those on the scene who recorded everything with their camera phones, there was no stopping the truth. The internet was a funny place, though. While some people were blogging that it was the end of times, others took a more creative approach to everything. Apparently, there was even a meme created already.

The incredibly photogenic glowing-alien meme.

Which had been Daemon phasing into his true form. His human features were blurred to unrecognizability, but I knew it had been him. If he'd been around to see that, he would've really gotten a kick out of it, but I didn't—

"Stop," Archer said gently. "We don't know what the hell Daemon, or any of them, are doing or why at this point. They will come back."

I turned from the window, finally facing Archer. His hair, a sandy brown color, was cut close to the scalp, typical military style. He was tall and broad-shouldered, someone who looked like he could throw down when it counted, and I knew he could.

Archer could be downright deadly.

When I'd first met him at Area 51, I had believed he was just a solider. It wasn't until Daemon had arrived that we discovered he was Luc's implant within Daedalus and also, like Luc, an Origin, a child of a Luxen male and mutated, hybrid female.

My fingers curled inward. "You really believe that? They will come back?"

Amethyst eyes flicked from the TV to mine. "It's all I can believe at this point. It's all any of us can believe right now."

That wasn't really reassuring.

"Sorry," he replied, letting it be known he'd picked up on my thoughts yet again. He nodded at the TV before I could get ticked off. "Something's going on. Why would that many Luxen come to Earth and then just go silent?"

That was also the question of the year.

"I think it's kind of obvious," said a voice from the hall. I turned as Luc entered the living room. Tall and slender, he had his brown-colored hair pulled back in a ponytail at the nape of his neck. Luc was younger than us, around fourteen or fifteen, but he was like a little teen mafia leader and, at times, scarier than Archer. "And you know exactly what I'm talking about," he added, eyeing the older Origin.

As Archer and Luc locked eyes in a battle of the stare-down, something they'd been doing a lot of during the last two days, I sat on the arm of a chair by the window. "Care to explain out loud?"

Luc had a certain boyish quality to his beautiful face, like he hadn't quite lost the roundness of childhood yet, but there was a wisdom in his purple eyes that went beyond a handful of years.

He leaned against the doorframe, crossing his arms. "They're planning. Strategizing. Waiting."

That didn't sound good, but I wasn't surprised. An ache formed between my temples. Archer said nothing as he went back to staring at the TV.

"Why else would they come here?" Luc continued as he tilted his head, gazing at the curtained window near me. "I'm sure it's not to shake hands and kiss babies' cheeks. They're here for a reason, and it's not good."

"Daedalus always believed they would invade." Archer sat back, clasping his hands over his knees. "The whole Origin initiative was in response to that concern. After all, the Luxen don't have a history of playing nice with other intelligent life-forms. But why now?"

Wincing, I rubbed my temples. I hadn't believed Dr. Roth when he'd told me how the Luxen were actually the cause of the war between them and the Arum—a war that had de-stroyed both of their planets. And I'd thought Sergeant Dasher and Nancy Husher, the head bitch in charge of Daedalus, were crazy freaks.

I'd been wrong.

So had Daemon.

Luc arched a brow as he coughed out a laugh. "Oh, I don't know, might have to do with the very public spectacle we put on in Vegas. We know there were implants here, Luxen who aren't that fond of humans. How they communicated with the Luxen not on this planet is beyond me, but is that really important now? This was the perfect moment to make an entrance."

My eyes narrowed. "You said it was a brilliant idea."

"I think lots of things are brilliant ideas. Like nuclear weapons, zero-calorie soft drinks, and blue jean vests," he replied. "That doesn't mean we should nuke people, or that diet drinks taste good, or that you should run out to the local Walmart and buy a jean vest. You people shouldn't always listen to me."

My eyes rolled so hard they almost fell out of the back of my head. "Well, what else were we supposed to do? If Daemon and the others hadn't exposed themselves, we would've been captured."

Neither of the guys replied, but the unspoken words hung between us. If we'd been captured, it would've sucked donkey butt and then some, but Paris, Ash, and Andrew would probably still be alive. So would the innocent humans who had lost their lives when everything went to crap.

But there was nothing we could do about that now. Time could be frozen for short periods, but no one could go back and change things. What was done was done, and Daemon had made that decision to protect all of us. I'd be damned if anyone threw him under the spaceship.

"You look exhausted," commented Archer, and it took a moment for me to realize he was talking to me.

Luc turned those unnerving eyes on me. "Actually, you look like crap."

Gee. Thanks.

Archer ignored him. "I think you should try to sleep. Just for a little while. If anything happens, we will get you."

"No." I shook my head just in case my verbal cue wasn't enough. "I'm fine." The truth was I was far from being fine. I was probably one step away from going to that dark corner in the room and rocking back and forth, but I couldn't break down, and I couldn't sleep. Not when Daemon was out there somewhere, and not when the whole world was on the verge of . . . hell, turning into a dystopia, like one of those novels I used to read.

Sigh. Books. I missed them.

Archer frowned, and it turned his handsome face a little scary, but before he could lay into me, Luc pushed off of the doorway and spoke. "I think she needs to go talk to Beth, actually."

Surprised, I glanced at the stairwell in the hall outside the room. The last I checked, the girl had been sleeping. That was all Beth seemed to do. I was almost envious of her ability to sleep all of this away.

"Why?" I asked. "Is she awake?"

Luc ambled into the living room. "I think you two need some girl-talk time."

My shoulders slumped as I sighed. "Luc, I really don't think this is the time for girl bonding."

"It isn't?" He dropped onto the couch beside Archer and kicked his feet up on the coffee table. "What else are you doing besides staring out the window and trying to sneak past us so you can go off into the woods, look for Daemon, and probably get eaten by a mountain lion?"

Anger punched through me as I flipped my long ponytail over my shoulder. "First off, I wouldn't get eaten by a mountain lion. Second, at least I'd be trying to do something other than sitting on my ass."

Archer sighed.

But Luc just smiled brightly up at me. "Are we going to have this argument again?" He glanced at a stone-faced Archer. "Because I like it when you two get into it. It's like watching a mom and dad have a marital disagreement. I feel like I need to go hide in a bedroom or something to make it more authentic. Maybe slam a door shut or—"

"Shut up, Luc," Archer growled, and then he turned his glare on me. "We've been down this road more times than I care to even think about. Going after them isn't smart. There will be too many of them, and we don't know if—"

"Daemon is not one of them!" I shouted, jumping to my feet and breathing heavily. "He hasn't joined them. Neither would Dee or Dawson. I don't know what's going on." My voice cracked, and a swell of emotion rose in my throat. "But they wouldn't do that. *He* wouldn't."

Archer leaned forward, eyes glittering. "You don't know that. We don't."

"You just said they'd be back!" I fired at him.

He didn't say anything as he cast his gaze back to the TV, and that told me what I already knew deep down. Archer didn't expect Daemon or any of them to come back.

Clamping my lips together, I shook my head so fast my ponytail turned into a whip. I turned away, stalking toward the doorway before we did get knee-deep in this argument again.

"Where are you going?" asked Archer.

I resisted the urge to flip him off. "I'm going to have girl talk with Beth, apparently."

"Sounds like a plan," commented Luc.

Ignoring him, I rounded the stairs and all but stomped up them. I hated sitting around and doing nothing. I hated that every time I opened that front door, Luc or Archer was there to stop me. And what I hated most of all was the fact that they could stop me.

I might be a hybrid, mutated with all that special Luxen goodness, but they were Origins, and they could kick my butt from here to California if it came down to it.

The upstairs was quiet and dark, and I didn't like being here. Wasn't sure why, but the tiny hairs on the back of my neck rose every time I came up here and walked down the long, narrow hall.

Beth and Dawson had commandeered the last bedroom on the right the first night here, and that's where Beth had holed herself up since he . . . since he left. I didn't know the girl well, but I knew she'd been through a lot when she was under the control of Daedalus, and I also didn't believe that she was the most stable of all hybrids out there, but that wasn't her fault. And I hated to admit this, but sometimes, she kind of freaked me out.

Stopping in front of the door, I rapped my knuckles on it instead of busting up into the room.

"Yes?" came the thin and reedy voice.

I winced as I pushed open the door. Beth sounded terrible, and when I got an eyeful of her, she looked just as bad. Sitting up against the headboard with a mountain of blankets piled around her, she had dark circles under her eyes. Her pale, waiflike features were sharp, and her hair was an unwashed, tangled mess. I tried not to breathe too deeply, because the room smelled of vomit and sweat.

I halted at the bed, shocked to my core. "Are you sick?"

Her unfocused gaze drifted away from me, landing on the door to the adjoined bathroom. It didn't make sense. Hybrids—we couldn't get sick. Not the common cold or the most dangerous cancer. Like the Luxen, we were immune to everything out there in terms of disease, but Beth? Yeah, she wasn't looking too good.

A great sense of unease blossomed in my belly, stiffening my muscles. "Beth?"

Her watery stare finally drifted back to me. "Is Dawson back yet?"

My heart turned over heavily, almost painfully. The two of them had been through so much, more than Daemon and I had, and this . . . God, this wasn't fair. "No, he's not back yet, but you? You look sick."

She raised a slim, pale hand to her throat as she swallowed. "I'm not feeling very well."

I didn't know what level of bad this was, and I was almost afraid to find out. "What's wrong?"

One shoulder rose, and it looked like it had taken great effort. "You shouldn't be worried," she said, voice low as she picked at the hem of a blanket. "It's not a big deal. I'll be okay once Dawson comes back." Her gaze floated off again, and as she dropped the edge of the blanket, she reached down, put her hand over her blanket-covered belly, and said, "We'll be okay once Dawson comes back."

"We'll be . . . ?" I trailed off as my eyes widened. My jaw came unhinged and dropped as I gaped at her.

I stared at where her hand was and watched in dawning horror as she rubbed her belly in slow, steady circles.

Oh no. Oh, hell to the no to the tenth power.

I started forward and then stopped. "Beth, are you . . . are you pregnant?"

She tipped her head back against the wall and squeezed her eyes shut. "We should've been more careful."

My legs suddenly felt weak. The sleeping. The exhaustion. All of it made sense. Beth was pregnant, but at first, like a total idiot, I didn't understand how. Then common sense took over, and I wanted to scream, *Where were the condoms?* But that was kind of a moot point.

An image appeared in my head of Micah, the little boy who'd helped us escape Daedalus. Micah, the little kid who had snapped necks and destroyed brains with a mere thought.

Holy alien babies, she was carrying one of them? One of those creepy children—creepy, dangerous, and extremely deadly? Granted, Archer and Luc had probably been one of those creepy kids at one time, but nothing about that thought was reassuring, because the newest batch of Origins that Daedalus had whipped up were different than the ones Luc and Archer had popped out of.

And Luc and Archer were still kind of creepy.

"You're staring at me like you're upset," she said softly.

I forced a smile onto my face, knowing it probably looked a little crazy. "No. I'm just surprised."

A faint smile appeared on her lips. "Yeah, we were, too. This is really bad timing, isn't it?"

Ha. Understatement of the lifetime.

As I watched her, the smile slowly slipped off her lips. I had no idea what to say to her. Congratulations? That didn't seem appropriate for some reason, but it also seemed wrong not to say it. Did they even know about the Origins, about all those kids Daedalus had?

And would this baby be like Micah?

God, really? Did we not have enough to worry about right

now? My chest tightened, and I thought I might be having a panic attack. "How . . . how far along are you?"

"Three months," she said, swallowing hard.

I needed to sit down.

Hell, I needed an adult.

Visions of dirty diapers and angry, red little faces danced in my head. Would there be one baby or would there be three? That was something we never thought about when it came to the Origins, but the Luxen always popped out in threes.

Oh, holy llama drama, *three* babies?

Beth's gaze met mine again, and something in those eyes caused me to shudder. She leaned forward, her hand stilling over her belly. "They're not coming back the same, are they?"

"What?"

"Them," she said. "Dawson and Daemon and Dee. They're not going to come back the same, are they?"

About thirty minutes later, I walked downstairs in a daze. The guys were where I'd left them, sitting on the couch, watching the news. When I entered the room, Luc glanced at me, and Archer looked like someone had shoved a pole up some very uncomfortable place.

And I *knew*.

"Both of you knew about Beth?" I wanted to hit them when they stared blankly back at me. "And no one thought to tell me?"

Archer shrugged. "We were hoping it wouldn't become an issue."

"Oh my God." Not become an issue? Like being pregnant with an alien hybrid baby wasn't a big deal and would just, I don't know, go away? I dropped into the chair, placing my face in my hands. What next? Seriously. "She's going to have a baby."

"That's usually what happens when you have unprotected sex," Luc commented. "Glad you two talked, though, because I so did not want to be the bearer of that news."

"She's going to have one of those creepy kids," I went on, smoothing the tips of my fingers over my forehead. "She's going to have a baby and Dawson is not even here and the whole world is going to fall apart."

"She's only three months along." Archer cleared his throat. "Let's not panic."

"Panic?" I whispered. The headache was getting worse. "There are things she needs, like, I don't know, a doctor to make sure the pregnancy is going all right. She needs prenatal vitamins and food and probably saltine crackers and pickles and—"

"And we can get those things for her," Archer replied, and I lifted my head. "Everything except the doctor. If someone draws her blood, well, that would be problematic, especially given what's going on."

I stared at him. "Wait. My mom—"

"No." Luc's head whipped toward me. "You cannot contact your mom."

My spine stiffened. "She could help us. At least give us the general idea of how to take care of Beth." Once the idea popped into my head, I latched onto it. I was totally honest with myself. Some of the reason why it seemed like such a great idea was because I wanted to talk to her. I *needed* to talk to her.

"We already know what Beth needs, and unless your mom has the low down on how to care for pregnant hybrids, there's not much more she can tell us that Google won't." Luc pulled his feet off the coffee table and they thumped on the floor. "And it will be dangerous to get in contact with your mom. Her phone could be monitored. It's too dangerous for us and her."

"Do you really think Daedalus gives two craps about us right now?"

"Is that something you want to risk?" Archer asked, meeting my gaze. "You willing to put all of us in danger, including Beth, all based on a hope they have their hands full? You willing to do that to your mom?"

My mouth screwed shut as I glared at him, but the fight leaked out of me like a balloon deflating. No. No, I wouldn't risk that. I wouldn't do that to us or to my mom. Tears pricked my eyes and I forced a deep breath.

"I'm working on something that will hopefully take care of the Nancy problem," Luc announced, but the only thing I'd seen him work on was the fine art of sitting on his butt.

"Okay," I said, voice hoarse as I willed the headache to go away and for the edges of bitter panic to recede. I had to keep it together, but that dark corner was looking better and better. "We need to get stuff for Beth."

Archer nodded. "We do."

Less than an hour later, Luc handed over a list of items he'd searched down on the internet. The whole situation made me feel like I was in some kind of twisted after-school special.

I wanted to laugh as I folded the piece of paper into the back pocket of my jeans, but then I probably wouldn't stop laughing.

Luc was staying behind with Beth in case . . . well, in case something even worse happened, and I was going to go with Archer. Mainly because I thought it would be a good idea to get out of the cabin. At least it felt like I was doing something, and maybe—maybe going into town would give us some clues to where Daemon and his family had disappeared.

My hair was tucked up under a baseball cap that hid most of my face, so the chances I'd be recognized were slim. I had no idea if anyone would, but I didn't want to take that risk.

It was late afternoon, and the air outside carried a chill that made me grateful I was wearing one of Daemon's bulky long-sleeve shirts. Even in the heavily pine-scented air, if I breathed in deeply, I could catch his unique scent, a mix of spice and the outdoors.

My lower lip trembled as I climbed into the passenger seat and buckled myself in with shaky hands. Archer passed me a quick glance, and I forced myself to stop thinking about Daemon, about anything I didn't want to share with Archer, which was pretty much everything right now.

So I thought about belly dancing foxes wearing grass skirts.

Archer snorted. "You're weird."

"And you're rude." I leaned forward, peering out the window as we traveled down the driveway, straining to see among the trees, but there was nothing.

"I told you before. It's hard to not do it sometimes." He stopped at the end of the gravel road, checking both ways before he pulled out. "Trust me. There are times when I wish I couldn't see into people's heads."

"I imagine being stuck with me the last two days has been one of them."

"Honestly? You haven't been bad." He glanced at me when I raised my brows. "You've been holding it together."

I didn't know how to respond to that at first, because since the other Luxen had arrived, I felt like I was seconds from shattering apart. And I wasn't sure what exactly was keeping me together. A year ago, I would've freaked out and that corner would've been my best friend, but I wasn't the same girl who had knocked on Daemon's door.

I would probably never be that girl again.

I'd been through a lot, especially when I'd been in the hands of Daedalus. Things I'd experienced that I couldn't dwell on, but the time with Daemon, and those months with Daedalus, had made me stronger. Or at least I liked to think they had.

"I have to keep it together," I said finally, folding my arms around me as I stared at the rapidly passing pines. The needled branches all blurred together. "Because I know Daemon didn't lose it when I . . . when I was gone. So I can't, either."

"But—"

"Do you worry about Dee?" I cut him off, turning my attention fully on him.

A muscle thrummed along his jaw, but he didn't respond, and as we made the quiet trip into the largest city in Idaho, I couldn't help but think this wasn't what I really needed to be doing. That instead, I needed to do what Daemon had done for me.

He had come for me when I'd been taken.

"That was different," Archer said, cutting into my thoughts as he turned toward the closest supermarket. "He knew what he was getting into. You don't."

"Did he?" I asked as he found a parking space close to the entrance. "He might have had an idea, but I don't think he really knew, and he still did it. He was brave."

Archer cast me a long look as he pulled out the keys. "And you are brave, but you are not stupid. At least I'm hoping you continue to prove you're not stupid." He opened the door. "Stay close to me."

I made a face at him but climbed out. The parking lot was pretty packed, and I wondered if everyone was stocking up for the coming apocalypse. On the news, there'd been rioting in a lot of the major cities after the "meteorites" fell. Local police and military had locked it down, but there was a TV show called *Doomsday Preppers* for a reason. For the most part, Coeur d'Alene appeared virtually untouched by what was happening, even though so many Luxen had landed in the nearby forests.

There were a lot of people in the store, their carts stacked high with canned goods and bottled water. I tried to keep my gaze down as I pulled out the list and Archer grabbed a basket, though I couldn't help but notice no one was grabbing toilet paper.

That would be the first thing I grabbed if I thought it was the end of the world.

I stuck close to Archer's side as we headed to the pharmacy section and started scanning the endless rows of brown bottles with yellow caps.

Sighing, I glanced down at the list. "Couldn't this crap be in alphabetical order?"

"That would be too easy." His arm blocked my vision as he picked up a bottle. "Iron on the list, right?"

"Yep." My fingers hovered over folic acid and I picked it up, having no idea what the hell that even was or what it did.

Archer knelt down. "And the answer is yes to your earlier question."

"Huh?"

He looked up through his lashes. "You asked if I was worried about Dee. I am."

My fingers tightened over the bottle as my breath caught. "You like her, don't you?"

"Yes." He turned his attention to the oversize bottles of prenatal vitamins. "In spite of the fact that her brother is Daemon."

As I stared down at him, my lips twitched into the first smile since the Luxen had—

The boom, like a sonic clap of thunder, came out of no-where, shaking the rack of pills and startling me into taking a step back.

Archer stood fluidly, his shrewd gaze swinging around the crowded market. People stopped in the middle of the aisles, some hands tightening on their carts, others letting go, the wheels creaking as the carts slowly rolled away.

"What was that?" a woman asked a man who stood next to her. She turned, picking up a little girl who had to be no more than three. Holding the child close to her breast, she spun around, her face pale. "What was that—?"

The clap of sound roared through the store again. Some-one screamed. Bottles fell from the racks. Footsteps pounded across the linoleum floor. My heart jumped as I twisted toward the front of the store. Something flashed in the parking lot, like lightning striking the ground.

"Dammit," Archer growled.

The tiny hairs on my arms rose as I walked toward the end of the aisle, forgetting all pretenses of keeping my head down.

A heartbeat of silence passed, and thunder blasted again and again, rattling the bones in my body as streaks of light lit up the parking lot, one after another after another. The glass window in front cracked, and the screams . . . the screams got louder, snapping with terror as the windows shattered, fling-ing glass at the checkout lanes.

The streaks of blinding light formed shapes in the parking lot, stretching and taking on legs and arms. Their tall, lithe bodies tinged in red, like Daemon's, but deeper, more crimson.

"Oh God," I whispered, the bottle of pills slipping from my fingers, smacking off the floor.

They were everywhere, dozens of them. Luxen.

2

{ Katy }

Everyone, including me, seemed to be frozen for a moment, as if time had been stopped, but I knew that hadn't happened.

The forms in the parking lot turned, their necks stretching and tilting to the side, their steps fluid and snakelike. Their movements were unnatural and nothing like the Luxen who had been on Earth for years.

A red truck squealed its tires as it spun out of a parking space, spilling smoke and the smell of burned rubber into the air. It whirled around, as if the driver planned to plow through the Luxen.

"Oh no," I whispered, my heart thumping heavily.

Archer grabbed my hand. "We need to get out of here."

But I was rooted to where I stood, and I finally understood why people rubbernecked car accidents. I knew what was coming, and I knew it was something I didn't want to see, but I couldn't look away.

One of the forms stepped forward, the edges of its body pulsing red as it raised a glowing arm.

The truck jerked forward; the shadow of a man behind the wheel and a much smaller body beside it would be forever etched into my memory.

Tiny sparks of electricity flew from the Luxen's hand as a brilliant light tinged in red curled down its arm. A second later, a bolt of light radiated from it, snapping into the air, smelling like burned ozone. The light—a blast straight from the Source of what had to be the purest kind—smacked into the truck.

The explosion rocked the store as the truck went up in flames, flipping over into the line of cars next to it. An inferno poured out of the busted windshield as the truck crashed down on its roof, tires spinning aimlessly.

Chaos erupted. Screams shattered the silence as people ran from the front of the store. Like a herd, they pushed into carts and other people. Bodies went down on hands and knees, and the screams pitched louder, mingling with the cries of young children.

In a stuttered heartbeat and in the blink of an eye, the Luxen were in the store and they were everywhere. Archer yanked me around the end of the shelf, pressing our bodies against the sharp edges. A teenage boy raced past us, and all I could think was how red his hair was—like scarlet—and then I realized it wasn't his hair color but blood. He made it to the body-wash section before a burst of light hit him in his back. The boy went down, face-first and unmoving, as a charred hole smoked from the center of his spine.

"Jesus," I gasped as my stomach roiled.

Archer stared, eyes wide and nostrils flared. "This is bad."

I inched to the edge of the aisle and peered around, my stomach flopping when I saw the woman who'd been holding the small girl minutes before.

She was standing in front of one of the Luxen, her mouth

gaping open, seemingly frozen in fear. The little girl was pressed back against the rack of supermarket books, huddled into a small ball, wailing as she rocked back and forth. It took me a moment to realize what she was shrieking over and over again.

"Daddy! Daddy!"

The man was lying in a pool of blood at her feet.

Energy crackled along my skin, snapping against Archer as the Luxen reached out and placed a hand on the center of the woman's chest.

"What the . . . ?" I whispered.

The woman's spine straightened as if someone had dropped steel down the center of her back. Her eyes widened, pupils dilating. The shimmery white light radiated from the Luxen's palm, and then draped over the woman like a waterfall. When the light reached her pointy-toed high heels, it faded off, seeping into the floor. Suddenly, the woman's head kicked back and her mouth dropped open in a silent scream. Her veins lit up from within, a glowing white network across her forehead, filling her eyes, and then down her cheeks and throat.

What was happening? I could feel Archer pressing against me as the Luxen stepped back from the violently trembling woman. As the light receded from her veins, the color leached from her skin, and the light surrounding the Luxen pulsed like a heartbeat. It all happened at the same moment—the woman's skin wrinkled and creased like she was aging by decades within seconds, while the Luxen's form shifted and warped. The woman's body crumbled and caved into itself, like all her life force was sucked right out of her. As she folded like a sheet of paper, skin gray and features unrecognizable, the Luxen's light pulled back, revealing its new form.

It was identical to the woman, same tan skin and pert nose. Light brown hair fell over bare shoulders, but its eyes . . . they were an unnaturally brilliant blue, like two polished sapphires had been placed on its face. Eyes like Ash's and Andrew's.

They're assimilating DNA. Archer's voice floated among my thoughts. *Rapidly. I've never seen it done or known it was possible.* There was a level of disturbed awe in his tone.

It was like *Invasion of the Body Snatchers*, the Luxen version. It was also deadly, and it was happening throughout the supermarket. Bodies were hitting the floor everywhere.

"We need to go." Archer's hand tightened around mine as he pulled me back against him. "Now."

"No!" I tried to dig in. "We—"

"We don't need to do anything but get the hell out of here." He hauled me around the end of the shelves, tugging me toward him until I was plastered against his side once more.

I struggled as he guided me down the aisle. "We can help them."

"We can't," he gritted out.

"You're an Origin," I snapped. "You're supposed to be the badass alien test-tube baby, but you're—"

"Running? Hell, yeah. Origin or not, there are dozens of Luxen, and they are powerful." He pushed me around the rows of toothpaste. In his left hand he still carried the bin full of pills I'd already forgotten about. "Did you not just see what they did?"

I slammed my hand into his stomach, pushing him back as I tore myself free from his grasp. "They're killing people! We can help them."

Archer snapped forward, his face contorting in frustration. "There is no Luxen on this Earth who can take on DNA like that. These are stronger. We need to get out of here, get back to the cabin, and then get the—"

A scream made me whip around. From the end of the aisle,

I could see that the Luxen who'd taken on the woman's appearance was staring down at the small girl, her lips curled into a mocking smile.

No. No way could I leave the girl. I had no idea what the Luxen planned, but I doubted it involved a test run at motherhood. I glanced at Archer, who cursed under his breath.

"Katy," he growled, dropping the bin. "Don't."

Too late. I took off, my legs and arms pumping as I darted into the next aisle and ran toward the front of the store. The clap of thunder came again as I reached the display of paperbacks, and the parking lot lit up as more Luxen arrived, over and over again, thunder cracking until I thought my heart would implode.

I skidded around the end of the aisle.

The Luxen froze in front of the little girl, and then its head tilted toward where I stood. Brilliant eyes locked onto mine. Rosy red lips parted. The coldness in its stare was like stepping out in subzero temps. There was nothing human in the stare, not even a hint of compassion, just cold calculation.

I knew in that tiny second as we stared each other down that this was the beginning and this was also the end. The Luxen were truly invading.

Swallowing the bite of icy terror, I lunged forward, grabbing the girl from behind. Her scream bounced through me and she went crazy, kicking me in the leg. I clamped my arms around her, holding her as tight as I could as I started to back up.

The Luxen rose like a pillar of water. Little bursts of energy crackled along its arms. It stared at me like it could see right into my insides. Each word it spoke rolled off the tongue like it was learning English at breakneck speed. "What are you?"

Oh crappity crap.

I learned two things pretty quickly. The Luxen could sense

that I wasn't riding just the human friendly skies, and by the way it drew back, raising a hand, I figured that wasn't a good thing. I also learned it had no idea what a hybrid was.

The little girl in my arms squirmed, managing to wiggle an arm free. Swinging on me, she knocked my baseball cap off, and my hair spilled down my back. The Luxen stepped forward, lips peeling back to bare its teeth.

Not good.

With my arms full of a kicking and screaming child, I knew when to retreat. Spinning around, I took off down the nearest aisle. The scent of burned flesh and plastic was strong as I rounded the corner, kicking rolls of bread out of the way. I slid to a halt. Whoa.

Holy naked aliens everywhere.

Even if I wasn't a hybrid and knew to check out the peepers to see if someone was an alien undercover, it would be quite easy to pick out the Luxen right about now, considering they apparently had no modesty issues when it came to being completely naked.

Dumbly, I realized I was seeing more male and female flesh than I ever wanted to see, but as I turned, spying Archer coming to my side, a bigger concern took hold.

We were surrounded.

"Happy?" Archer gritted out, his amethyst eyes burning bright.

At least six Luxen were staring at us, trying to figure out exactly what we were. Three were in human form, standing next to the crumpled bodies of those they had assimilated. The other three were in their true forms, their bodies tinged in reddish-white light. Behind us, the female Luxen from the front of the store appeared.

Not a single one looked like it wanted to hug and love us.

My heart kicked against my ribs as I knelt down slowly, looking into the tearstained face of the little girl. "When I let go, you run," I whispered. "You run as fast as you can and you don't stop."

I wasn't sure if she understood me, but I prayed she did. Exhaling roughly, I let her go and gave her a little push toward the gap between two aisles. The child didn't disappoint. Spinning around, she ran for the space, and while I wished I could do more for her, I stood.

One of the glowing Luxen glided forward and then stopped, head cocking to the side. The rest of them, the ones in their true and human forms, all looked toward the woman who I'd snatched the kid away from.

This is going to end badly. Archer's voice intruded. *Is it assuming too much that if I tell you to run, you will?*

I took a deep breath. *I'm not going to leave you.*

One side of his lips curved up. *Figured as much. Let's go on the offense. Clear a path toward the front.*

During my time with Daedalus, I'd been taught to fight not only in the very human way, but also using the Source. I'd tapped into that training while in Vegas, and while there was a part of me that was confident I could throw down with the best of them, an arctic blast of fear slid its way up my spine.

Without any warning, Archer went all badass.

Snapping forward, he reared his arm back. A ball of pure energy traveled down his arm, erupting from his palm and slamming into the center of the Luxen's bare chest, knocking the alien out of its human form and into the glass door of the dairy section. Containers exploded, sending rivers of milk over the floor.

One of the glowing Luxen shot toward Archer as he whirled and took aim at the naked woman. I pulled from the Source.

The light that whirled down my arm was nowhere near as intense as Archer's, but it did the trick. Arcing across the aisle, it smacked into the shoulder of the Luxen, spinning it around.

I geared up to let loose another bolt of energy when pain burst along my shoulder. One second I was standing, and the next I was on my knees, my left shoulder smoking. I reached around, gently touching my shoulder as I forced myself to stand. My hand came back smudged in red.

Turning around, I nearly took a meaty fist in the face from a Luxen in its human form—a young male. Stumbling several steps, I caught myself and raised my knee. Air stirred around me as I planted my foot in an area I didn't want to look at.

The Luxen male doubled over.

Smiling grimly, I grabbed hold of its brown hair just as it started to shift, warming my hands as I slammed my knee into its nose. Bones cracked, but I knew that wouldn't keep the Luxen down.

And I knew what needed to be done.

Archer let loose another blast as I tapped into the Source. It flowed down my arm, cascading over the top of the Luxen's head as he lifted it, eyes glowing like white orbs.

The next second, I was flung backward like a car had smacked into me. The air cracked with static as I hit the hard floor on my back, momentarily stunned while I stared up at the broken, swaying tray of fluorescent light.

Holy ouch.

Groaning, I rolled onto my side and blinked tightly. The Luxen was also on its back, several yards away. Struggling to my feet, I saw Archer flinging a Luxen into the freezer section. He spun toward me, saw me standing, and nodded.

There was a path cleared, down by the spilled cartons of ice cream. Not a very clear path. Luxen were sprawled on the floor, flickering in and out, down for a moment but not out for the count.

An explosion from somewhere in the grocery store rocked the tall shelves. The freezer doors imploded as Archer and I ran down the aisle, glass shattering inches behind us. Skidding across the slippery floor by the bakery, we reached the front. Around us, humans scurried toward the broken windows, bloodied and shell-shocked.

My heart dropped into my stomach as the parking lot and the buildings beyond came into view. Smoke poured into the air, shooting up in great plumes above orangey-red flames. An electric pole was down on a row of cars with crumbled roofs. Sirens screamed in the distance. A car zoomed across the parking lot, slamming into another vehicle. Metal crunched and gave way.

"It's like an apocalypse," Archer murmured.

I swallowed hard. "All we're missing are the zombies."

He looked down at me, brows rising, and he opened his mouth, but the snack aisle threw up all over the place.

Chips and pretzels flew into the air, along with cheese puffs and foil wrappings. They rained down, pinging on the floor. There was a hole in the middle of the snack aisle now.

"Let's get out of here," he said, and this time I didn't argue.

I was saving all my words for a different battle, because I knew when we got back to the cabin, if we could, Archer was going to push for us to bounce on out of Idaho. I got that it wasn't safe here anymore, and if he wanted to leave, so be it. Considering Beth's condition, it would be smart to get her far away from all of this, but there was no way I was leaving here without Daemon.

Screw that.

We darted down a demolished checkout lane. Archer was

in front of me when I ground to a halt, every muscle in my body locking up as a series of tight tingles traveled over the base of my neck.

My knees went weak as the air leaked out of my lungs. The tingling was there, warm and familiar, a feeling that had been absent for two days. In my chest, my heart kicked into hyper-drive, sending the blood roaring through my veins.

Daemon.

I stumbled around slowly, like I was moving in quick-sand, scanning the destroyed aisles. Light peeked and pulsed through the destruction of the market. Time seemed to slow down, the air thickening until I couldn't drag in enough breath. Dizzy, and too hopeful with the rising tide of tangled emotions, I moved back toward the lights.

"Katy!" Archer's voice traveled from the broken doors. "What are you doing?"

My pace picked up as I neared the collapsed display of candy bars. Snack bags crunched under my feet. My mouth dried and my eyes blurred. The aches and burning pain radi-ating from my shoulder faded into the background.

Wind picked up, whipping the long, loose strands of hair around my face, and I wasn't sure where that was coming from, but I pushed forward, nearing the edge of the destroyed snack aisle.

I stepped to the side, just a foot or two, and looked up the aisle to the end. My heart stopped. My entire world came to a startling pause.

"Dammit!" shouted Archer, his voice closer. "No!"

But it was too late.

I saw *him*.

And *he* saw me.

He stood at the end of the aisle in his true form, shining as bright as a diamond. He didn't look any different than the rest of the Luxen, but every ounce of my being knew it was him. The very cells that made me who I was snapped alive and cried out for him. He still was the most beautiful thing I'd ever seen. Tall and shining like a thousand suns, edges shimmering a faint red.

I took a step forward at the same moment he did, and I reached out to him the way we could, because when he had healed me all that time ago, he'd connected us together. Forever.

Daemon? I called out to him through the connection.

He disappeared from in front of me, moving too fast for even me to track.

"Kat!" Archer yelled. At the same time, I swore I heard my name echoing in my head in a deeper, smoother voice that caused my belly to flip and the strings attached to my heart to pull taut.

Warmth traveled across my back and I turned, coming face-to-face with dazzling emerald-colored eyes; skin that seemed to always be tan, no matter the time of year; broad, sweeping cheekbones; and unruly black hair that brushed equally dark eyebrows.

Full lips tipped up at the corners tightly.

It wasn't Daemon.

A good head and a half taller, Dawson locked his eyes with mine. I thought I saw a flicker of remorse, but that could've simply been wishful thinking. Light rushed from behind his pupils, turning the entire orb of his eyes white. Static traveled across his cheeks, forming tiny fingers of electricity.

There was a flash of intense light, a shocking wave of heat that seemed to lift me off my feet, and then there was nothing.

3

{ Daemon }

The constant stream of voices in my true tongue, along with a dozen other human languages, caused a fierce throbbing in my temples. The words. The sentences. The threats. The promises. The goddamn nonstop chatter of my newly arrived oh-so-extended family members as they discovered something new to them, which was about every five freaking seconds.

Oh! A blender.

Oh! A car.

Oh! Humans sure do bleed a lot and break easily.

Hell, as soon as they opened their eyes, they were seeing something for the very first time, and while the awe as they tinkered with appliances or with human anatomy was a bit childlike, it was also a little on the demented side of things.

The newly arrived were the coldest sons of bitches I'd ever seen.

In the last forty-eight hours, literally thousands of my kind had come to Earth for the first time, and it was like one giant hive. We were all connected, one wavelength to another, little worker bees for the queen.

Whoever the hell that might be.

The connection was overwhelming at times, the needs and desires and wants of thousands all joined together in the forefront of every Luxen's mind. Take over. Control. Rule. Dominate. Subjugate. The only time there was even a measure of relief was when I was in my human form. It seemed to dull the connection, dial it back, but not for everyone.

Striding across the polished wood floors of an atrium in a mansion that could house a militia and still have room for sleepovers, I saw my vision tint red when I spied my twin. He lounged against the wall, near a set of closed double doors. His chin was tilted down, brows furrowed in concentration as his fingers flew over the screen of a cell phone. When I was halfway across the brightly lit room that smelled like roses and the faint metallic scent of spilled blood, he lifted his head.

Dawson took a deep breath as I approached him. "Hey," he said. "There you are. They—"

I snatched the phone from his hands, turned, and threw it as hard as I could. The little square object flew clear across the room and shattered against the opposite wall.

"What the hell, man?" Dawson exploded, hands flying up. "I was on level sixty-nine of *Candy Crush*, you bastard. Do you know how hard that—?"

After cocking back my arm, I slammed my fist into his jaw. He stumbled into the wall, raising a hand to his face. A sick sense of satisfaction twisted up my insides.

He raised his head, tilting it to the side. "Jesus." He grunted as he lowered his hand. "I didn't kill her. Obviously."

My thoughts emptied like a bowl of water being tipped over as I drew in a shallow breath.

"I knew what I was doing, Daemon." He glanced at the door, his voice lowering. "There was nothing else I could do."

Launching forward, I gripped the collar of his shirt and lifted him up onto the tips of his boots. The reasons were not good enough. "You have never had any measure of control when it comes to using the Source. Why in the hell would it be different now?"

The pupils of his eyes started to glow white. He shoved his arms between mine, breaking the hold. "I had no other choice."

"Yeah, whatever." I stepped around him, forcing myself away from my brother before I threw him through a wall and in front of a tank.

Dawson turned, and I could feel his shrewd gaze on my back. "You need to get control of yourself, brother."

I stopped in front of the closed doors and looked at him over my shoulder.

He shook his head. "I'm—"

"Don't," I warned.

Dawson's eyes squeezed shut for a moment, and when they reopened, he was staring at the closed doors, nearly devastated. "How much longer?" he whispered.

Real fear punched me in the gut. It was too much. I knew his defenses were down and he had been put in a bad position. He didn't have any other choice. "I don't know, because . . ."

I didn't have to elaborate. Understanding dawned on his face. "Dee . . ."

My eyes met and held his, and there was nothing else to be said. Facing forward, I pushed open the door, and the constant hum banging off my skull grew stronger as I entered the wide, circular office.

Newcomers were in the room, but it was the one in the seat

with his back turned to me who mattered, the one we'd been drawn to the moment they'd shown up at the cabin.

He was sitting in a leather chair, watching a big flat screen on the wall. It was a local TV news station broadcasting images of downtown Coeur d'Alene. Totally different place than it had been three days ago. Smoke billowed from buildings. Fire covered the west like a burning sunset. The streets were a mess. Complete war zone.

"Look at them," he said, his voice carrying a strange lilt as he navigated the new language. "Scurrying around on the ground aimlessly."

Looked like half of the humans were looting an electronics store.

"They're so helpless, unorganized. Inferior." His laugh was deep, almost infectious. "This will be the easiest planet for us to dominate."

It still amazed me that they'd been out there this whole time, generation after generation since the destruction of our planet, holed up in some godforsaken universe that was apparently not as comfy as Earth.

He shook his head, almost in wonder, as the screen flipped to images of tanks rolling into the city. He laughed again. "They can't defend themselves."

Another newcomer, a tall redhead dressed in a tight black skirt and pressed white shirt, cleared her throat. Her name was Sadi, which was fitting, because I referred to her as Sadi the sadist.

She didn't seem to mind, because in the short time I had known her, the nickname was well earned, and the only other thing I did know about her was that her gaze was usually attached to my ass.

"Actually, they do have weapons," she said.

"Not enough, my dear. This is happening in some of the largest cities in every state, in every country. Let them have their little weapons. We may lose a few, but those losses will not impact our initiative." The chair wheeled around, and the muscles along my back tensed. The human form he'd chosen was that of a trim male in his early forties, with dark brown hair parted neatly and a wide, perfectly straight white smile.

He'd taken the form of the mayor of the city, and he liked to be called by the dead human's name: Rolland Slone. Sort of weird. "Our goal will still be reached. Isn't that right, Daemon Black?"

I met his stare. "I really don't think they'll be able to stop you."

"Of course not." His fingers steepled under his chin. "I hear you brought something with you?"

He posed it as a question, but the answer was already known. I nodded.

Sadi's body angled toward mine with interest as her bright teal gaze lit up, and by the wall, the other one stirred.

"A female?" asked Sadi, who must've picked up the fleeting image that had flickered through my thoughts.

"The last time I checked, yes." I smiled when her eyes narrowed. "But I'm still not convinced you're rocking all the right girl parts."

Sadi's fingers straightened at her sides. "You want to check that out?"

I smirked. "Nah, I think I'll pass on that."

Rolland chuckled as he hooked one knee over the other. "This female. She's not exactly human, is she?"

Sadi pulled her attention from me when I shook my head. A muscle or a nerve or something else equally annoying started to twitch under my eye. "No. She's not."

His hands rested in his lap, one folded on top of the other. "What is she exactly?"

"A mutant," answered Dee as she strode into the room, her long, dark curls spreading out behind her. A sweet smile formed on her lips as she looked at Rolland. "Actually, she was mutated by my brother."

"Which one?" asked Rolland.

"This one." Dee nodded at me as she popped her hands on her hips. "He healed her about a year ago. The girl is a hybrid."

Eyes flicked back to mine. "Were you trying to hide that from us, Daemon?"

"Did I really get a chance to answer that question?"

"True," Rolland murmured, eyeing me closely. "You're a hard one to read, Daemon. Not like your lovely sister here."

Folding my arms across my chest, I shrugged. "I like to think I'm an open book."

"Out of all of us, he's always had little use for humans," Dee said.

Rolland's brows rose. "Except for this girl, I imagine."

"Except for her." Guess Dee was now my own personal speaker. "Daemon was in love with her."

"Love?" Sadi coughed out a surprisingly delicate laugh. "How very . . ." She seemed to search for the right word. "Weak?"

My shoulders stiffened as I muttered, "'Was' being the key word."

"Explain to me this healing and mutation thing," Rolland ordered, leaning forward.

I waited for Dee to chime in, but for once, she appeared happy to remain quiet. "She suffered a fatal injury, and I healed her without knowing that it would mutate her. Some of my abilities were transferred to her, and we were connected together from that moment on."

"What made you want to heal her?" Curiosity colored his tone.

Dee snorted. "I don't think he was thinking with the head on his shoulders when he did it, if you get what I mean."

While I resisted the urge to shoot my sister a look, Rolland stared at me for a moment, and then smiled like he not only got what Dee meant but was also very interested in a whole lot of detail.

"Interesting," murmured Sadi as she flipped a wealth of coppery hair over a slim shoulder. "How tight is this bond or connection between you?"

I shifted my weight, glancing at the silent Luxen male who was still leaning against the wall. "She dies; I die. Tight enough for you?"

Rolland's eyes widened. "Well, that is not good . . . for you."

"Yep," I drawled out.

A slow curl of Sadi's lips made her look hungry. "And does she feel what you feel? And vice versa?"

"Only if it's a near-fatal wound," I answered, voice flat as the floors.

Sadi glanced at Rolland, and I knew they were communicating. Their words were lost in the hum of the others, but the eagerness that suddenly crept over Sadi's face had my fists tightening.

I didn't trust her.

I didn't trust Quiet Dude, either.

"You don't have to trust her," Rolland said, smiling widely. "We just have to trust you."

Dee stiffened. "We can be trusted."

"I know." His head cocked to the other side. "And there was something else there, right? It got away?"

Back to being the ever-helpful minion, Dee nodded as she sat down in an armchair, all but draping herself over it. "An Origin, a product of a Luxen male and a hybrid female. I hope we don't have to kill him. I think he's kind of cute."

"Interesting." Rolland glanced at Sadi, and again, I knew they were getting all kinds of secret squirrel chatty with each other.

Coming to his feet, he buttoned the front of his beige suit jacket. "There's a lot we don't know. These hybrids are new to us," he said, which almost made me laugh. For a race of beings who'd never been to Earth, they seemed to have a lot of knowledge about the layout. There was something more that I hadn't figured out. Something, or a bunch of somethings, had been working from the inside. Seemed important. "We're counting on you and your family, others like you, to aid us in these situations."

I nodded curtly, as did Dee.

"Now. I have things to do." He came around the side of the oak desk, and the Luxen male finally moved away from the wall. "People to meet and to put at ease."

Surprise caught me. "Put people at ease?"

As Rolland strolled past me with Sadi and the Man of Few Words snapping at his heels, he smiled broadly once more. "See you in a little while, Daemon."

The doors closed behind them, reinforcing the fact that I wasn't privy to every thought and whim. There was a lot hidden.

Sighing, I turned to where my sister sat, and for a second, realization poked free. I barely recognized her.

Dee glanced up, her eyes meeting mine.

"Thought you were supposed to be watching her?" I said.

She shrugged. "She's not going anywhere anytime soon. Dawson knocked her into next week, I think."

The back of my neck tensed. "So no one is with her?"

"I really don't know." She frowned at her nails. "And I really don't care."

I stared at her a moment, unthinkable words forming on my lips, but I pushed them down. "I'm surprised you didn't bring up Beth."

She arched a brow. "Beth is weak—weaker than Katy. She'd probably run away the second she saw us, fall, and kill herself, taking out Dawson in the process. I think we need to keep her a secret for Dawson's sake."

"You'll lie to Rolland?"

"Haven't we already been lying to him? Obviously Dawson's keeping that little secret buried deep, just like you have, and so have I. They don't know about Beth and didn't know about Kat until a little while ago."

Pressure clamped down on my chest, and I forced it out of my system when Dee tilted her head to the side to watch me. "If you think that's best."

"I do," she replied coolly.

There was nothing left to say, so I turned toward the door.

"You're going to her."

I stopped but didn't turn around. "So?"

"Why would you?" she asked.

"If her wound festers and she dies, well, you know where that leaves me."

Dee's tinkling laugh reminded me of icicles falling from the roof of our porch back home during the winter. "Since when do hybrids get festering wounds?"

"Hybrids don't get colds and cancers, Dee, but who knows what a charred hole in their flesh does. Do you?"

"Ah, that's kind of a good point, but . . ."

Turning to her, my hands clenched at my sides. "What are you trying to say?"

Her lips curled up. "The worst thing that could happen is her arm rotting off."

I stared at her.

Tipping her head back, she laughed as she clapped her hands together. "You should see your face. Look, all I'm trying to say is that it sounds like there's another reason why you want to go see her."

A twitching muscle moved from under my eye to my jaw. "You were right earlier."

She frowned. "Huh?"

I let the kind of smile that was a lifetime ago pull at my lips. "Thinking with a different kind of head."

"Ew!" Her nose wrinkled. "God, yeah, I don't need to know anymore. 'Bye."

Winking at her, I pivoted around and left the room. Dawson was no longer in the atrium, and I didn't like that I had no idea where he was or what he was doing. No good could come from that, but I really didn't have the brain cells to deal with that on top of what waited upstairs.

I hadn't brought her back here.

Dawson had, and I hadn't been with him when he'd carried her upstairs, but I knew where she was without asking. Third floor. Last bedroom on the right.

Framed photos of the real Mayor Rolland Slone and his family adorned the stairwell, a pretty blond wife and two kids under the age of ten. I hadn't seen the wife or the kids when we came here. The last photo on the second floor landing was cracked, smeared with dried blood.

I kept going.

My steps were faster than I intended, but the upper floors were virtually empty, and as I started down the wide hall with paintings of the lakes surrounding the city covering the forest-green walls, the hum and chatter faded until it almost felt like it was only me in my head. Almost.

Thrusting a hand through my hair, I let out a ragged breath that immediately turned into a swift curse when I spotted the last door.

It was cracked open.

Had Dee left it that way? Possible. My hand fell to my side as I drifted toward the door. My heart jackhammered against my ribs as I reached out, pushing it open. Abnormally bright light spilled into the hall.

A Luxen was in the room with her, bent over the bed, its form completely blocking her.

There wasn't a single thought in my head.

4

{ Daemon }

The edges of my vision tinged in red, and like a ticked-off cobra striking, I shot across the room as the Luxen sensed my presence and straightened. He turned as he shifted into the human form he'd adopted—a male in his early twenties. I think he was going by the name of Quincy. Not that I gave two craps about his name.

"You shouldn't—"

My fist crashed into the space just below his ribs, doubling him over. Before he could fall back on the bed, I gripped him by the shoulders and tossed him to the side.

Quincy bounced into the wall, the impact rattling the framed pictures hanging on it. His blue eyes flashed white, but I exploded forward, punching my hands into his shoulders, slamming him back into the wall again.

I got all up in his face. "What were you doing in here?"

Quincy's lips pulled back over his teeth. "I don't have to answer to you."

"If you don't want to find out what it feels like to have your human skin ripped away, one strip at a time," I replied, my fingers digging through the shirt he wore, "you will."

He laughed. "You don't scare me."

Rage whirled through me, mixing with frustration and a shitstorm of a thousand other emotions. I wanted nothing more than to take it all out on the douche. "You should be. And if you come around her again, if you even look in her direction or breathe on her, I will kill you."

"Why?" His gaze started to move over my shoulder, toward the bed. I gripped his chin, forcing his eyes on mine. His form shimmered. "Are you protecting her? I can sense she's not just a human, but she's not one of us."

"None of that is really important." Skin and bone ground under my grip on his chin.

He wrenched free from my grasp. Laughing, he tipped his head back against the wall. "You've been with the humans too long. That's it. You're *too* human. And you think I don't see it? That the others haven't noticed it?"

My lips curled into a cold twist of a smile. "You've got to be a special kind of stupid if you think being raised on Earth will stop me from killing you. Stay away from her and my family."

Quincy swallowed hard as he met my stare. Whatever he saw in my gaze had him backing down. My smile spread and the white glow went out from his eyes. "I'm telling Rolland," he gritted out.

Letting go of him, I patted his cheek. "You do that."

He hesitated a moment, and then he pushed off the wall. Stalking across the room, he left, and he didn't look back toward that bed. Not once. Brother knew better now. Waving my hand, I watched the door slowly swing shut. The click of the lock thundered through my veins. Locking the door was pointless in a house full of Luxen, but it was such a *human* thing to do.

Closing my eyes, I scrubbed my hands down my face, suddenly exhausted on a bone-deep level. Coming up here might not have been the smartest of all my ideas, but there'd been no way that I couldn't. From the moment I'd stepped back into this house, I'd been drawn to this room, and the lure was just as powerful as the pull from my own kind.

I couldn't even *think* her name.

My walls were down and I tried to keep my thoughts empty, but as I turned toward the bed, it was like a punch in the stomach. I couldn't move or breathe. I stood there as if suspended in air. Two days had passed since I last saw her, but it felt like a lifetime ago.

And it had been a lifetime—a different world with a different future.

Staring at her, I was reminded of going into Area 51 and finding her asleep after months of separation, but things had been different afterward—better, even. I almost laughed to think that being under Daedalus's thumb was a more fortunate outcome for her, but it was true.

She was lying on her back, and it was obvious that when someone who wasn't Dawson brought her up here, no one gave any care for her comfort. She had just been dropped there, like a sack of dirty laundry. She was lucky that they'd placed her on a bed instead of the floor.

Her sneakers were still on. One leg was bent at the knee and tucked under the other leg. The knees of her blue jeans were stained with dried blood. Her right arm was folded at the elbow and her other rested against her lower stomach. The oversize shirt—*my* shirt—had ridden up, exposing an eyeful of pale skin. My hands curled inward, clenching so tightly my knuckles ached.

What had Quincy been doing in this room? Was it curiosity

that had drawn the Luxen? I doubted he'd seen or felt a hybrid before, and these newly arrived Luxen put Curious George to shame. But was it something else?

Christ. I couldn't even think of all the possibilities, because none of them was good. If Rolland continued to value my presence, she'd stay alive, but after spending two days with them, I knew there were worse things than death.

I was standing next to the bed without realizing I'd even moved. I shouldn't be in here; this was the last place I should be, but instead of turning around like I had two functioning brain cells, I sat beside her, my eyes glued to the hand resting just above her navel.

Her hand was so pale, so small. So fragile in spite of the fact she was no ordinary human. My gaze traveled up her arm. The shirt was torn and the material was charred over the shoulder, the navy blue dark with blood.

I leaned over her, placing one hand beside her still hip. Blood had seeped into the white comforter and sheets. No wonder her skin was so washed out. My heart pounded as my gaze crawled across the long lengths of brown hair that had spilled across the pillow.

My fingers burned to touch her hair, to touch *her*, but every muscle locked up in my body when my gaze stopped on her parted lips.

Too many memories slammed into me, and I struggled through them, my pulse ratcheting up. The only thing that seemed to dampen the roar in my veins and the tightening of every muscle in my body was the shocking scarlet swipe under the corner of her lip.

Blood.

I dragged my eyes up, feeling pressure clamp down on my chest as I saw the ugly reddish-purple bruise along her temple. When Dawson had zapped her, she'd gone down, cracking her head on the floor, and that sound still echoed through my thoughts as if taunting me. Truth was it would haunt me. Forever.

Her lashes were thick and unmoving, the skin under her eyes shadowed. There was another bruise along her hairline, but she still was the most—

I cut off the thought, closing my eyes and exhaling slowly. For some reason, I saw Archer's face, his expression as our gazes locked the second after she had gone down. In the bloody chaos and confusion, it had been like time had stopped. Then Archer had started toward her, and I . . . I had wanted to leave her there. I knew I had to leave her there, but someone else had grabbed her.

And I hadn't stopped him.

Opening my eyes, I saw my arm tremble as I lifted her right hand. The moment our flesh met, a charge jumped from her skin to mine, stirring me. Carefully, I tugged down the hem of her shirt, my knuckles brushing across her stomach as I covered her, the contact brief but torturous.

Then I caressed her, and I was fucking lost.

My fingers drifted over her cool cheek, brushing a strand of soft hair back from her face. I don't know how long I sat there, tracing the line of her jaw and the curve of her lips, and I really wasn't aware of healing her, but the bruises faded from her skin and I knew the bleeding had stopped. I wanted to pick her up, clean her, but that would be too much.

It could already be too much, and then what?

Color now infused her cheeks, a sweet pink flush spreading across her face, and I realized she would wake soon.

I couldn't be in here.

Gently, I removed her shoes and then lifted her legs, tucking them under the blanket. There was more that could've been done, *should've* been done, but this . . . this had to be enough.

Closing my eyes, I lowered my head, inhaling the sweet, unique scent that was solely hers, and then I kissed her parted lips. Sensation rushed over me, a jolt of something close to being described as sublime, and I forced myself to lift my head and stand and back the hell away from her before it was too late, even though a dark voice whispered that it probably already was.

There were a hundred ways all of this could play out, and I couldn't see a happy ending with any of them.

{ Katy }

I had to fight my way through the fog of unconsciousness, and my brain was slow to come back online. Lying still for several moments, I was kind of surprised by the fact that I wasn't in any serious pain. There was a dull ache in my shoulder, and somewhere deep behind my eyes, there was a faint throbbing, but I'd expected more.

Confusion swirled inside me as I played back those precious minutes before I landed headfirst in la-la land. The poo had hit the proverbial fan at the market and the Luxen had been everywhere, taking on human DNA at such a rapid pace that it had done something to the humans, killing them. I prayed that little girl had made it to safety, but where was it safe? They'd been everywhere and . . .

My heart sped up as I remembered feeling Daemon, seeing him in his true form, knowing he'd seen me, but then he'd disappeared and . . . and *Dawson* had hit me with a blast from the Source. Why would he have done that? Better yet, why hadn't Daemon come to me?

In the furthest reaches of my consciousness, there was an insidious whisper that spelled out the answer. Luc and Archer had suspected as much, but I couldn't let myself believe that they had been right and that our greatest fear had come true.

Just thinking that Daemon could be different now, could be one of *them*—whatever they actually were—made it feel like a fist had seized my heart.

Taking a deep breath, I blinked my eyes open and immediately sucked in a startled breath, jackknifing up so fast my head felt like it would fall off my shoulders.

Two emerald-colored eyes stared back into mine, framed with heavy black lashes. All at once I was tossed back to last summer, the morning after I'd discovered Daemon Black wasn't quite human—when he'd frozen time, stopping a truck from turning me into roadkill. I'd woken up to find Dee staring at me.

Just like now.

Perched on the foot of the bed, Dee sat with her legs drawn to her chest and her chin resting on her knees. A curtain of dark hair fell over her shoulders in thick curls. To this day, she was probably the most beautiful girl I'd seen in real life, just like Ash, but Ash . . . she was no longer with us.

But Dee was here.

Relief loosened the tense muscles in my back as I stared at her, at the girl who had become my best friend, was still my best friend even after the tragedy with Adam. Dee was here and that had to mean something good, something great. I started to move toward her, letting the blanket fall to my waist, but I stilled.

Dee stared at me, unblinking, the same way she had that morning. But something was off about her.

Throat dry, I swallowed. "Dee?"

One perfectly shaped eyebrow rose. "Katy?"

Unease rose at the sound of her voice. It was different, colder and flat. Instinct warned that I stay back, even though that didn't make sense to me.

"I was beginning to wonder if you'd ever wake up," she said, loosening her arms from around her legs. "You sleep like the dead."

I blinked slowly, glancing around the room. I didn't recognize the green walls or the framed photos of breathtaking landscapes. None of the furniture looked familiar.

Neither did Dee.

Pulling my legs up, away from her, I tried to swallow again as I glanced at a closed door near a large oak dresser. "I'm . . . I'm so thirsty."

"So?"

My gaze bounced back to her, reacting to the sharpness in her tone.

"What?" Her eyes rolled as she unfolded her long, slender legs. "You expect me to fetch you a drink?" She laughed, and my eyes widened at the strangeness of the sound. "Yeah, think again. You're not going to die of thirst anytime soon."

Dumbfounded by her attitude, all I could do was stare at her as she stood and smoothed her hands down the sides of dark denim–clad thighs. Maybe I had really damaged my brain back in the market or woken up in an alternate universe where sweet Dee had turned into bitchy Dee.

She faced me, her eyes narrowing in a way that reminded me of the woman in the grocery store after the Luxen had snatched her body. "You smell like blood and sweat."

My brows shot up my forehead.

"It's kind of repulsive." She paused, her nose wrinkling. "Just saying."

Oookay. I slumped back against the headboard. "What's wrong with you?"

"Wrong with me?" Dee laughed again. "For once, there's nothing wrong with me."

I stared at her. "I . . . I don't understand."

"Of course you do. You're not stupid. And you know what else you're not?"

"What?" I whispered.

Dee's lips curled into a cruel, almost mocking smile that transferred her beauty into something venomous. "You're also—"

She launched toward me, her hand rising, and I reacted without thinking. My right arm snapped up, and I caught her wrist before her palm connected with my cheek.

"You're also not weak," she said, easily pulling her arm free from my grasp. Backing up, she placed her hands on her slender hips. "So you can continue to sit there and look at me like you're half stupid, but we don't have a lot of time to play catch-up, especially since it appears Daemon healed you."

Shaken by her attitude and the realization that I had been blasted with the Source twice and I probably should be concerned by that, I glanced down at my hand. Creases of dried blood marred my palm. I reached back to my left shoulder. The shirt was burned and the flesh tender, but it was in one piece.

I lifted my gaze. "He . . . he was here?"

"Was."

My heart turned over heavily, and then I moved. Forget Dee and her bitchiness or the fact that I apparently smelled. I needed to see Daemon. Flipping off the blanket, I swung my legs over the edge of the bed. No shoes. No socks. What the? Didn't matter. "Where is he now?"

"I really don't know." Sighing, she pulled back the curtain covering the one window and stared out. "But the last I saw, he was heading into one of the bedrooms." The curtain slipped from her fingers, drifting back into place as she faced me with a chilling smile. "Not alone."

I stilled.

"Sadi was following him. Something that she's quickly made a habit of doing. She's probably in the process of attempting to molest him." She paused, tapping her finger on her chin. "Then again, I don't think it's really molesting when it's wanted."

Tiny balls of ice formed in my stomach. "Sadi?"

"That's right. You don't know her. I'm sure you will, though."

I shook my head as my entire being rebelled against what she was insinuating. "No. No way." I stood on shaky legs. "I don't know what your problem is or what happened to you, but Daemon would never do anything like that. Ever."

Dee's gaze sharpened as she eyed me like I wasn't worth the ground she stepped on. "Things aren't the way they used to be, Katy. The sooner you get with the program the better, because right now, you're his weak link. That's *all* you are to him." She took a measured step forward, and I held my ground. "The only reason you're alive right now is because of him. And not because he loves you, because that boat sailed the big old ocean blue the moment we opened our eyes. Thank God."

I flinched at her words, and the ice grew bigger, spreading into my veins.

"And it's about time," she continued, tilting her head to the side. "Ever since you came into his life—our lives—everything has been messed up. If I could take you out right now without killing him, I would. I'd relish it. So would he. You're nothing to us anymore, or to him. Nothing more than a problem we need to figure out how to handle."

I sucked in a breath that didn't seem to do any good. A knot formed in my throat, making it hard to swallow, and I told myself that it didn't matter what Dee was saying. Something was definitely wrong with her, because Daemon didn't just love me; he was *in* love with me, and he'd do anything to be with me. Just as I would for him, and nothing could change that. The commitment we'd made to each other in Vegas may not have been technically the most legal of all things, but it had been real to me—to *us*. But her words . . . they still cut worse than any blade could ever inflict.

Dee's lashes lowered as her features pinched tight. "So . . . ?"

I opened my mouth, but the ball of emotion cut me off for a moment, and when I spoke, my voice was hoarse. "What do you want me to say to that?"

She shrugged. "Nothing really, but I need to take you to see him."

"Daemon?" I tensed.

"No." She chuckled, the sound light and airy, and for a moment, it sounded like the Dee I knew. "Not him."

When she didn't elaborate and I didn't move, she clucked her tongue in frustration and then popped forward. Grabbing my arm in a tight grasp, she all but dragged me out of the bedroom and into a wide hall.

"Come on," she urged, impatient.

I struggled to keep up with her long-legged pace. Barefoot and exhausted and beyond confused, I was feeling more human than hybrid, but when we got to the landing, she'd nearly pulled my arm out of my socket and had my shoulder aching something fierce.

"I can walk. You don't have to drag me." I yanked and slipped free, knowing that she simply let me. "I can . . ." The framed photo of an attractive family on the stairwell caught my eye. The glass was broken and there was something dark and rusty smeared across it.

My stomach roiled.

"You can just stand there?" Her eyes narrowed on me. "If you don't move, I will throw you down the stairs. It'll hurt. You might break your neck. It's three levels. Someone will heal you. Or maybe we'll just leave you like that, alive but unable—"

"I get your point," I snapped back at her, taking a deep breath so I didn't attempt to push *her* down the stairs.

"Good," she chirped, grinning.

For some reason, it was in that moment, as I tried to reconcile the girl who had stood in the kitchen with me a few days ago and made spaghetti with this nasty creature before me, that I remembered Archer. "What happened to . . . ?" I trailed off suddenly, and probably rightfully, wary of bringing up anything that led back to who remained at the cabin.

"Archer? He got away." She started down the steps.

I stared at her back, my heart working overtime.

"I'm serious," she called. "I will throw you down these damn steps."

I took a second to entertain the idea of drop-kicking her in the back of the head. The only thing that stopped me was the fact that I was convinced she had to have an alien insect attached to her somewhere that changed her personality, and her attitude wasn't her fault.

Heading down the stairs, I willed my brain to start working correctly as I took in my surroundings. I was in a big house, the kind that opulence would be envious of. There were a lot of bedrooms and halls, and when we reached the second land-ing, I could see down into the foyer, lit by a crystal chandelier. Like, real crystals.

But down below, I could also see Luxen, all in human forms. None of them looked familiar to me. At least these Luxen had discovered the usefulness of clothing, but as I scanned them, I noticed there weren't any sets of three other than the Blacks. Each one of them was different. My fingers were numb from how tightly I was clenching my hands. The Luxen looked at me the same way Dee had. A few pushed off the wall as we walked past, heads tilting in that weird way that reminded me of a snake. Another stood from a leather chaise longue; all of them appeared to be in their mid-twenties to their forties, though who knew what their real age was.

What I'd seen in the market hadn't been anything like Daemon and Dee had explained to me. What the Luxen had done had been different.

A light-haired woman by the leather chair sneered and looked like she wanted to jump the heavy-looking oak table, straddle my shoulders, and rip off my head. As hard as it was, I forced my chin high, even though my heart was beating so fast I thought I'd be sick.

We walked through a long atrium, and from the darkness beyond the glass walls, I could tell that it was night outside. As we reached the middle, I felt it.

A tingle spread across the nape of my neck.

My heart stopped and then skipped a beat. Daemon was here, behind those double doors. I knew it, and warring hope and uncertainty fought inside me.

The doors opened before we reached them, revealing the kind of office I'd never seen in a home before, and my gaze was drawn to a desk in the middle of the room. A man sat behind it wearing a smile, but what was most shocking was the fact that I'd seen him before, seconds ago.

He was the man in the broken photo, but I knew he wasn't human. His eyes glowed a bright, unnatural blue. He rose fluidly as we stepped into the office, the doors closing behind us, but my attention veered off immediately.

There were other Luxen in the room, two more males and a tall, beautiful redhead. I didn't care about any of them. Standing next to the redhead, to the right of the man behind the desk, was Daemon.

My heart did something funky in my chest as a rush of shivers danced over my skin. Our eyes locked, and I felt dizzy once again. So much rose inside me as I stepped toward him, my tongue forming his name, but my voice was gone. Our gazes held for a second more and then he . . . he looked away, his profile stoic and blank. Heart thudding in my chest, I stared at him.

"Daemon?" I said, and when he didn't answer, when he watched the man behind the desk like he . . . like he was bored with it all, I tried again. "Daemon?"

Like the night the Luxen came, there was no answer.

5

{ Katy }

I still stared at Daemon, completely aware that everyone else except him was watching me. Closely. But why wouldn't he look at me? A razor-sharp panic clawed at my insides. *No.* This couldn't be happening. *No way.*

My body was moving before I even knew what I was doing. From the corner of my eye, I saw Dee shake her head and one of the Luxen males step forward, but I was propelled by an inherent need to prove that my worst fears were not coming true.

After all, he'd healed me, but then I thought of what Dee had said, of how Dee had behaved with me. What if Daemon was like her? Turned into something so foreign and cold? He would've healed me just to make sure he was okay.

I still didn't stop.

Please, I thought over and over again. *Please. Please. Please.*

On shaky legs, I crossed the long room, and even though Daemon hadn't seemed to even acknowledge my existence, I walked right up to him, my hands trembling as I placed them on his chest.

"Daemon?" I whispered, voice thick.

His head whipped around, and he was suddenly staring down at me. Our gazes collided once more, and for a second I saw something so raw, so painful in those beautiful eyes. And then his large hands wrapped around my upper arms. The contact seared through the shirt I wore, branding my skin, and I thought—I expected—that he would pull me against him, that he would embrace me, and even though nothing would be all right, it would be better.

Daemon's hands spasmed around my arms, and I sucked in an unsteady breath.

His eyes flashed an intense green as he physically lifted me away from him, setting me back down a good foot back.

I stared at him, something deep in my chest cracking. "Daemon?"

He said nothing as he let go, one finger at a time, it seemed, and his hands slid off my arms. He stepped back, returning his attention to the man behind the desk.

"So . . . awkward," murmured the redhead, smirking.

I was rooted to the spot in which I stood, the sting of rejection burning through my skin, shredding my insides like I was nothing more than papier-mâché.

"I think someone was expecting more of a reunion," the Luxen male behind the desk said, his voice ringing with amusement. "What do you think, Daemon?"

One shoulder rose in a negligent shrug. "I don't think anything."

My mouth opened, but there were no words. His voice, his tone, wasn't like his sister's, but like it had been when we first met. He used to speak to me with barely leashed annoyance, where a thin veil of tolerance dripped from every word.

The rift in my chest deepened.

For the hundredth time since the Luxen arrived, Sergeant

Dasher's warning came back to me. What side would Daemon and his family stand on? A shudder worked its way down my spine. I wrapped my arms around myself, unable to truly process what had just happened.

"And you?" the man asked. When no one answered, he tried again. "Katy?"

I was forced to look at him, and I wanted to shrink back from his stare. "What?" I was beyond caring that my voice broke on that one word.

The man smiled as he walked around the desk. My gaze flickered over to Daemon as he shifted, drawing the attention of the beautiful redhead. "Were you expecting a more personal greeting?" he asked. "Perhaps something more intimate?"

I had no idea how to answer. I felt like I'd fallen into the rabbit hole, and warnings were firing off left and right. Something primal inside me recognized that I was surrounded by predators.

Completely.

"I don't know what to . . . to think." There was a horrifying burn of tears crawling up my throat.

"This is all overwhelming for you, I imagine. The whole world as you know it is on the brink of great change, and you're here and don't even know my name." The man smiled so broadly, I wondered if it hurt. "You can call me Rolland."

Then he extended a hand.

My gaze dropped to it and I made no attempt to take it.

Rolland chuckled as he turned and strolled back to the desk. "So, you're a hybrid? Mutated and linked to him on such an intense level that if one of you dies, so does the other?"

His question caught me off guard, but I kept quiet.

He sat on the edge of the desk. "You're actually the first hybrid I've seen."

"She really isn't anything special." The redhead sneered. "Frankly, she's rather filthy, like an unclean animal."

As stupid as it was, my cheeks heated, because I *was* filthy, and Daemon had just physically removed me from him. My pride—my *everything*—was officially wounded.

Rolland chuckled. "She's had a rough day, Sadi."

At her name, every muscle in my body locked up, and my gaze swung back to her. *That* was Sadi? The one Dee said was trying to molest Daemon—my Daemon? Anger punched through the confusion and hurt. Of course it would have to be a freaking walking and talking model and not a hag.

"Rough day or not, I can't imagine she cleans up well." Sadi looked at Daemon as she placed a hand on his chest. "I'm kind of disappointed."

"Are you?" Daemon replied.

Every hair on my body rose as my arms unfolded.

"Yes," she purred. "I really think you can do better. Lots better." As she spoke, she trailed a red-painted finger down the center of his chest, over his abdomen, heading straight for the button on his jeans.

And oh, hell to the no. "Get your hands off him."

Sadi's head snapped in my direction. "Excuse me?"

"I don't think I stuttered." I took a step forward. "But it looks like you need me to repeat it. Get your freaking hands off him."

One side of her plump red lips curled up. "You want to make me?"

In the back of my head, I was aware that Sadi didn't move or speak like the other Luxen. Her mannerisms were too human, but then that thought was quickly chased away when Daemon reached down and pulled her hand away.

"Stop it," he murmured, voice dropped low in *that* teasing way of his.

I saw red.

The pictures on the wall rattled and the papers on the desk started to lift up. Static charged over my skin. I was about to pull a Beth right here, seconds away from floating to the ceiling and ripping out every strand of red—

"And *you* stop it," Daemon said, but the teasing quality was gone from his words. There was a warning in them that took the wind right out of my pissed-off sails.

The pictures settled as I gaped at him. Being slapped in the face would've been better.

"Amazing," said Rolland, eyeing me like I imagined all the scientists at Daedalus had done when they first came into contact with the Luxen. "You have adapted many of his abilities. Amazing and yet disturbing."

"I have to agree with that," said one of the male Luxen.

Rolland inclined his head. "We are a higher life-form, and to mix so intimately with something like you is . . . well, an abomination of sorts. You shouldn't exist. Whatever injury you suffered should've taken you."

A muscle started to tick along Daemon's jaw.

"After all, it is the survival of the fittest, is that not what humans say? You were not fit to survive without our interference."

Well, that was all kinds of insulting.

"And yet it cannot be undone, can it?" His gaze flickered to Daemon. "There is so much we are unaware of. All of us were too young when our planet was destroyed and we were split among the universes. We have never been here, and apparently, there is a lot our kind who have been residing on Earth were also unaware of."

Most Luxen didn't know about hybrids. Daemon hadn't until I was mutated, so it didn't take a genius to think those who hadn't been to Earth had no idea. It also made me wonder if they were aware of the weaknesses that existed here—the onyx and diamond shields? Did these things exist on whatever hellhole they'd crawled out of? I doubted they had PEP weapons, the kind the government had created that could nuke a Luxen into the afterlife with one blast.

"We are curious by nature. Did you know that?" he asked, and then he slid a knowing look in Daemon's direction. "I'm sure you did. After all, was that what drew him to you? Or was it more?"

Daemon's lips thinned, but if there was bait dangling in front of his face, he didn't take it.

"Love," muttered Rolland with a laugh.

Dee glanced at her brother. "That was before."

"Was it?" he asked.

A moment passed as Daemon held Rolland's gaze. "It was before."

The thunderous cracking in my chest should've been heard in the nearby towns. I sucked in a sharp breath, and Daemon finally looked at me. His back was unnaturally stiff as his eyes met mine, but it was like he saw right through me.

"I wonder if that's truly in the past," Sadi challenged, and when Daemon outright ignored her, a tension pulled at her features, turning them sour.

The hair on the back of my neck was standing again, but for a very different reason as Rolland's smile grew. "As I said, we are curious creatures. Quincy?" He glanced over his shoulder, and after a moment passed, the other man nodded.

My eyes widened as the other Luxen strolled forward. He wasn't as tall as Daemon, but he was broader, and he walked like he was gliding over water. When he passed Daemon, he sent him a mocking smile.

I took a step back, my hands opening and closing at my sides. I had no idea what to expect from any of them, even Daemon at this point. Horror churned in my stomach.

Quincy was wide like a linebacker, and the look in his eyes sent an icy whirl of wind over me. My feet slipped over the cool wood floor as energy balled low in my stomach. I glanced at Daemon, my heart thumping. His eyes met mine as Quincy stopped in front of me, his striking features stark. Quincy's smile creeped me out as he reached forward. Jumping back, I knocked his arm away.

"Don't touch me," I warned, feeling a rush of static over my skin.

The smile slipped off Quincy's face as his eyes narrowed.

"What is this about?" Daemon asked.

"I'm curious," said Rolland, his voice almost syrupy sweet as his gaze flickered over to Daemon. "Restrain her."

My heart dropped as my gaze bounced between Daemon and the Luxen. There was a moment when Daemon didn't move as he stared at Rolland, and then he pivoted on his heel. I locked up, throat dry, as he stalked toward us.

He cut Quincy a dangerous look as he stepped around me. The moment his hands folded over my shoulders from behind, holding me in place, I thought I'd throw up. Like literally hurl all over the smug-looking Luxen in front of me.

I jerked, pressing into Daemon as Quincy reached for me once more, gripping my chin with cool fingers, but I couldn't shy away. Daemon was an unmovable wall.

Daemon stiffened behind me as Quincy lowered his head so that we were eye level. I never thought I'd ever be in this situation, that instead of Daemon protecting me, he would be allowing some random, really skeevy Luxen guy to get all up in my face. Not since the day at the lake, the first time he'd opened up to me and told me about his brother.

"She feels different," Quincy announced, his hands sliding down my neck to where my pulse beat rapidly. "Not like other humans. Besides sensing something in them, we'd be able to tell by feel." He paused, his gaze flickering up to Daemon. The Luxen's smile turned brittle as his long, tapered fingers circled my neck. "You're very angry."

"Really?" Daemon's hands flexed around my arms. "Remember what I told you before? That statement still stands."

"Is that so?" Quincy hesitated, and then he placed his hand above my chest, the same place I'd seen the Luxen touch in the supermarket.

A low rumble reverberated along my back, and I wasn't sure if it was from Daemon or if it was me shaking so badly. The Luxen's brows knitted in concentration, and then he glanced at Rolland.

"Nothing," he said. "I cannot assimilate her DNA."

My eyes widened in understanding. My God, I'd seen what had happened to the humans after their DNA had been assimilated at a rapid clip. He would've killed me! And Daemon, but at this point, I wanted to knee Daemon in the groin. Anger burned its way through me as I twisted in his grasp, trying to get free, because I needed space, but his grip tightened as furious tears stung my eyes.

"That's an interesting development," Rolland commented. "What else can you two do? We know that if one dies, the other does. She obviously has access to the Source. Is there anything else?"

"She won't get sick. Like us." Daemon's words were short, to the point. "And she's fast and strong."

I sucked in a sharp breath as the blister of something ugly, of betrayal, curled around my heart.

"Remarkable." Rolland clapped his hands as if we'd performed *Swan Lake* instead of just standing there in front of him.

"And that is all?" Sadi asked, looking wholly unimpressed.

"Yes," Daemon answered, and my eyes widened, but I schooled my features blank.

I held my breath, but Dee didn't disagree. Both of them had just blatantly lied by omission. There was more. When he was in his true form, Daemon and I could communicate the way he did with other Luxen. I didn't know what to think about that, but hope sparked deep in my chest. My gaze darted to Dee, but she was staring at the wall as if there was something amazing going on there.

What was really happening here? There was more—

My thoughts careered off, crashing in a fiery glory as Quincy, who wasn't even looking at me but was eyeballing Daemon, slid his hand down my chest, like right *on* my chest. Shock rippled through me, quickly followed by red-hot rage and bitter disgust. Every part of me recoiled.

Suddenly, I was sliding across the wood floor and bumping into an empty leather chair. Startled, I lifted my head and peered through the length of matted hair that had fallen across my face.

The two Luxen were locked in an epic stare-down, and across from me, Dee was no longer staring at the wall, but was focused on her brother. It was so quiet in the room that you could hear a fly hiccup.

And then Daemon exploded like a bottle rocket.

{ Daemon }

Wrath tasted like a pool of blood in the back of my mouth, and I was unable to see or think past it. There were a lot of things I could deal with, that I could force myself to tolerate and I could *wait* on. But him touching *her* like that not only crossed the line, it blew a freaking hole in it.

Shifting into my true form, I felt the immediate bombardment from others of my kind, their needs and wants, rising in a vicious cyclone, but my rage overwhelmed them. Catching Quincy the second before he could shift, I flung him into the far wall, but this time with a hell of a lot more effort than when I found him in her room.

Body say hello to wall.

He crashed into it without changing. Plaster cracked and gave way under the impact. White dust flew into the air. Quincy started to slide down the wall. That was the funny thing about the Luxen. They hadn't realized yet just how weak they were in their human forms.

I was on him before he hit the floor.

Slamming my fist into his chin, I reveled in the cracking sound of his head knocking backward. Nowhere near done, I hauled him up and then practically put him *through* the wall, all the way to the supporting beams.

Then I let go.

Quincy went down, crumpled on the floor, flickering in and out like a squashed lightning bug. Shimmery blue liquid seeped out from behind his head, and as I stared down at him, debating on whether or not I wanted to throw him like a football through a nearby window, I realized just how quiet the room was.

Leaving Quincy, or whatever was left of him, I shifted out of my true form as I turned around. I might have maybe gone too far with that, but there was nothing I could do about it now.

Rolland arched a brow. "Well, then . . ."

Chest rising and falling sharply, I spared him a quick glance before turning to where *she* stood. Her hands were gripping the back of a chair as she stared at me, her gray eyes so big and so wide on her pale face.

Our gazes locked, and I could tell by the stricken look on her face that she wasn't sure what to make of any of this. There was confusion and raw hurt and fury pouring from her, choking the air, choking me.

It took several moments to slow my roll. I got my breathing in check as I forced myself back to Rolland, meeting his curious stare. "I told him not to touch her before and that if he did, I would kill him. I'm not a liar."

Sadi's gaze flickered to where Quincy lay. "He's not dead."

"Yet," I promised.

A look of anticipation, of pure eagerness, swept over Sadi's face as she wet her bottom lip. "Why would you care if he touched her or not?"

There were a thousand endless reasons. "She belongs to me." I could practically feel the daggers she was driving into my back, but I didn't look at her. "No one else. It's as simple as that."

Rolland eyed me intently, and then he pushed off the desk. Straightening, he clapped his hands. "Everyone. Listen up."

I stiffened, knowing this could be real bad.

"You." He motioned to another Luxen. "Get Quincy out of here. Let me know if he wakes up."

Part of me hoped he did so I could beat the shit out of him again.

To Sadi, Rolland pinned her with a sharp look. "Take this young . . . lady over here and make sure she gets cleaned up and that's she *comfortable*."

Oh hell no. I opened my mouth, but Sadi snapped forward, her eyes glittering with malicious pleasure. "Of course," she said, casting a half smile in my direction as she all but bounced past me. I stepped forward to intercept and make good use of the window.

"You," Rolland directed at me, "will stay right here." Then to Dee, he smiled. "It's late. I find that being in this form makes me incredibly hungry. Would you get something for me to eat?"

Dee hesitated, but then nodded. Turning, she shot me a worried look as she hurried out of the room to do Rolland's bidding.

There was a good chance I was going to punch someone else as I watched Sadi force her out of the room. The back of my neck tingled and my skin crawled as the door shut behind them, leaving me with Rolland and some dude whose name I refused to learn.

Rolland strolled around the desk and sat down. "Quincy was quite unhappy with you earlier. Said you . . . went after him because he was in the room with that . . . that girl." Leaning back in the chair, he hooked one leg over the other. He gestured at the damaged wall. "Not that his anger seems to be a problem right now."

I shrugged. "I'm sure he's not the only one. And I don't trust Sadi with her."

His brows rose. "You don't?"

"No."

Folding his hands, he studied me. "I want you to answer a question for me, Daemon Black, and I want an honest answer."

My jaw ached from how hard I was grinding my molars. I didn't need to be in this room. I needed to be wherever Sadi was at the moment, but I nodded.

"Like I said, you're a hard one to read. Not your brother or sister, but you're different."

"People do say I'm special."

He laughed under his breath. "What does that girl mean to you, Daemon? And I do want an honest answer."

My hands curled into fists. Time was ticking. "She belongs to me."

"You've said that."

I forced air into my lungs with a deep breath. "She's mine and she's a part of me. So, yeah, she means a lot, but what I feel for her doesn't change anything here, with you." I met his stare with my own unflinching one. "I support what you are doing."

"Me?" He chuckled. "It's not me you must support. I'm just a . . . busy bee, like you."

Well then.

"Do you still love her?" he asked, flipping the subject. "Do you still want her?"

What he was asking was if I had any *human* emotions left over since their arrival, or was I just as tuned in to the hive as the rest of them. "I want her."

"Physically?"

Jaw aching fiercely, I forced my chin up and down.

"Do you want more than that?"

I chose my words carefully. "What I *want* is a home where my family is safe, and only we can provide that. We come first."

Rolland's head tilted to the side, his gaze never leaving my face. "We do. And soon you will have that safe home for your family. It is already well under way."

I wanted to ask exactly how it was well under way, because all I had seen from them so far was a lot of nasty killing.

Tension-filled silence stretched out between us, and then he flicked his hand at the door. "Go do what you need to do, but please do not throw Sadi at anything. She has her uses that I might want to partake in later."

Not one to look a gift horse in the mouth, I spun around and started for the door.

"Oh. And Daemon?"

Shit. I stopped, turning to him.

The damn smile was on his face, the same smile he'd worn when he addressed the public earlier in the day over the local news. When he'd told the city, or whatever was left of it, that everything would be fine, that mankind would prevail and a whole load more crap he'd actually made sound believable.

"Don't make me regret not snuffing out your life in the clearing, because if you are a *trataaie*," he said, slipping into our native tongue, "it will not be me you will fear, but the *seni-traaie*. You will not only lose your family, but that little girl up there will suffer a very slow and very painful death, and her horror will be the last thing you see. *Inteliaaie*?"

Back stiff, I nodded again. "I am not a traitor and I only answer to our leader. I understand."

"Good," he said, raising his hand. A remote flew from the desk into it. "Remember. No throwing Sadi."

Dismissed with the bite-in-the-ass kind of warning, I left the office and nearly plowed right into my sister as I exited the atrium.

She gripped my arm, her fingers digging into my skin. "What in the hell were you thinking?"

"Aren't you supposed to be getting him a late-night snack?"

Her eyes flashed. "You could've gotten yourself killed in there protecting her."

I stared at her for a moment, searching for something, anything in her, and came up with nothing. I gently removed her hand. "I don't have time for this."

"Daemon."

Ignoring her, I headed through a sitting area and then took

the steps two at a time. When I reached the second landing, I could already hear the shouting coming from the third floor.

Jesus.

Something shattered above me, and I took off, hauling ass. I reached the last door on the third floor in less than a second. Pushing it open, I scanned the bedroom as I wondered how I was going to stop myself from throwing Sadi through something.

The bedroom was empty, but it looked like a tornado had gone through it. The olive-green armchair was toppled over onto its side, one of the wooden legs broken. The white curtains had been pulled down from the window. The dirtied and bloodied pillows were strewn across the floor.

And the shirt she had been wearing—my shirt—rested in shredded tatters at the foot of the bed. What in the hell?

My gaze whipped toward the bathroom door when I heard what sounded like a body bouncing off it, and then a shriek blasted the room.

I kicked open the bathroom door and came to a complete stop. The room was large, the kind that had a separate tub and shower, but this room, too, had seen better days. The mirror above the double sink was broken. Multiple bottles had been tipped open. White cream covered the floor in milky pools.

She stood in front of the large tub, her hair a tangled mess around her flushed face. Gray eyes snapped fire as she stood with her legs spread wide. A trickle of blood ran from her nose. In her hand she held a jagged piece of glass.

And she was only in her bra and jeans—a white bra with little yellow daises on it. Her chest heaved with indignation and fury.

Apparently, Sadi had taken the cleaning thing to a whole different level.

My gaze crept to where Sadi stood only a few feet from her, breathing heavily. Her white blouse was torn. Buttons popped and missing. Her normally coiffed hair looked like she'd been inside a wind tunnel, but the best part?

Fingernail marks were etched down the side of Sadi's face and reddish-blue blood had been drawn. A disturbing level of pride rippled through me.

Kitten got claws and then some.

"She doesn't play nice with others," Sadi huffed out. "So I'm in the process of adjusting her attitude."

"And I'm in the process of getting ready to cut out your heart, bitch."

In spite of everything that was so damn messed up, my lips twitched into a small smile. "Get out."

Sadi turned her hateful gaze on me. "I'm—"

"Get the hell out." When Sadi didn't move, I stalked over to where she stood, picked her up, and shoved her out of the bathroom. She caught herself and started back toward us. "Rolland has a use for you tonight, so if you want to be able to come through for him, don't take one more step toward me."

Her nostrils flared as her cheeks mottled with anger, but she stopped as her hands curled into claws. A second passed and she didn't move from the doorway. Sadi was going to test me—she seriously was.

I slammed the bathroom door shut in Sadi's face and then whipped around. Heart hammering, I saw her again and immediately forgot about Sadi.

She still stood in front of the garden tub, the piece of glass in her hand, and she stared back at me like an animal cornered. In that moment she didn't remind me of a harmless little kitten.

She was a full-grown tigress, and she still looked like she wanted to do some damage. To me. Could I really blame her?

Those eyes of hers shifted the longer we stared at each other, turning wet with a sheen of tears, and that was worse than a kick between the legs.

I was in so deep. *We* were in so deep, and I didn't want her here. I wanted her far, far away from all of this, but it was too late.

Too late for both of us, and maybe for everyone else, too.

Her lower lip trembled as she shifted her weight from one foot to the other, her toes sinking into spilled conditioner or shampoo. An eternity stretched out between us as I soaked her up with my eyes. A collage of memories—from the day she knocked on my front door and changed my life, to the first time she said those three words that made my life what it was—bombarded me. But it was more than just memories. I knew right then I shouldn't be feeling what I was, but every cell demanded her. My blood boiled.

I wanted her.

I needed her.

I loved her.

She took a step back, bumping into the tile ledge surrounding the tub.

"*Kat,*" I said, speaking her name for the first time in days, allowing myself to actually *think* it, and the moment that happened, the seal inside me broke wide open.

6

{ Katy }

The edges of the piece of glass were digging into my palm as I stared at Daemon. After everything that had gone down in the office, and then with that horrible woman, I couldn't catch my breath or stop the tremors racing along my arm. I watched him take a step forward. The look in his incandescent eyes and the intent in his step sent a shiver down my spine. "Don't."

His eyes narrowed.

Too much hurt swelled in my chest, mixing with all the terrible things Sadi had said she planned on doing with Daemon, things that, when he'd been in the office, he hadn't sounded like he'd be against enjoying.

My skin felt raw, my insides flayed open. I wanted to lash out and hurt something, someone. Tears burned my throat. "Are you sure you don't want to leave with your new friend?"

Only a thin sliver of green showed now. "Yes, I'm sure."

"That's not what it looked like earlier. You two—"

"Don't say another word," he all but growled.

I blinked as anger roared through me like a typhoon. "Excuse me? Who the—?"

Daemon was on one side of the bathroom, and then he was right in front of me the next second, causing me to stumble to the side and step in the gooey mess on the floor.

I shrieked. "I *hate* it when you do—"

He clasped my cheeks, and the moment his skin was against mine, my entire brain seemed to short-circuit. The piece of glass fell from my fingers, landing harmlessly on a nearby fluffy bathmat.

He lowered his head until our mouths were so close that we shared the same air. It was all so unfair. From the moment he'd disappeared, all I wanted was to see him again, to touch him and to love him, and now I didn't really know what was standing in front of me.

Nothing since the Luxen had arrived made sense.

He didn't move. Instead, his luminous emerald gaze traveled over my face as if he was committing each inch to memory. There was a warmth that followed his stare, and the throbbing in my nose, where that heinous bitch had slapped me, faded away.

He was healing me. Again. After pushing me away from him and saying that he *loved* me, as in the past tense, and after associating with the worst kind of monsters. I couldn't take it.

"This is so wrong," I said, my voice cracking. "Everything is so messed—"

Daemon kissed me.

There was nothing soft or tentative about it. His mouth was pressed against mine, boldly parting my lips, and he kissed like he was starving. The rush of sensation nearly took my legs out from underneath me. My stomach dipped as a deep sound rumbled from his throat, shaking through me.

The spark of hope in my chest grew stronger, but confusion and anger snapped at its heels like an annoying little dog. Daemon tilted his head as one hand slid off my cheek. His fingers curled into my hair at the back of my head. My heart pounded, and it was too much.

I placed my hands against his chest and pushed.

"Kitten," he growled, nipping at my lower lip.

A breath shuddered through me. "You—"

"She's still outside the room," he whispered against my lips, and then he was kissing me again.

His words were lost for a moment as his other hand trailed down the length of me, settling on the curve of my waist. He tugged me against him, fitting our bodies together, and the feel of it was somehow shockingly new and sweetly familiar. The kiss deepened until his taste was everywhere.

My hands shook as my fingers gripped the soft material of his shirt. A breathy sound escaped me. The tremble traveled up my arms and kept going until every part of my body shook.

"She's gone." Daemon lifted his head away, but I kept my eyes squeezed shut. I couldn't stop shaking. "Oh, Kitten . . ."

I wanted to tell him not to call me that if this wasn't real, but a sob rose in my throat. I clamped my mouth shut, because at this point, tears and breaking down didn't help anything, and there had already been too many tears between us.

Daemon's arm circled around me and his fingers spread across the back of my head, guiding my cheek against his chest. He held me in an embrace so tight I could feel his heart pounding through him.

"I'm sorry," he whispered against the top of my head. "I'm so sorry, Kitten."

"Is . . . is this you?" My voice cracked. "Is this real?"

"As real as I'll ever be." His voice was barely audible, a hoarse whisper like mine. "God, Kat, I . . ."

It felt like my chest had imploded, and I reached up, digging my hand into the wisp of hair at the nape of his neck. My cheeks were damp.

"I'm so sorry," he said again, and for a moment, it was all he seemed to be able to say. He turned so that his back was to the wall, and then he slid down, pulling me into his lap, nestled between his bent knees and the hard expanse of his chest. "I don't know how much I can say or how long I can keep them out of my head."

Keep them out of his head? I blinked back tears as I opened my eyes. "I don't . . . understand what is happening."

"I know." Pain flashed across his striking face as he rested his forehead against mine. "We're connected—all of us. From the moment they came, we've been inside one another's heads. I'm not sure how it works. It's never been like this before. Maybe it's because there are so many of us here, but when I'm in my true form, there's no hiding from it. It's not too bad . . . now. There are things they don't know, that we've been able to keep from them, but I'm not sure how much longer that's going to work."

"Us?" I whispered.

He nodded. "Dawson and me."

I frowned, clearly not remembering him as being a friendly. "But he hit me with the Source." And I was also pretty sure he'd cracked my skull in the process.

Daemon's eyes deepened to a vibrant moss green. "Yeah, and his jaw has been thanked for that. He didn't have a choice, though. Another was heading for you, and he did what he did to stop one of them from killing you."

"And killing you." My thoughts raced to keep up with everything. It was an act—all of this. "Dee?"

Daemon's thick lashes lowered as he shook his head.

"What?" I pulled in an unsteady breath as the crush of disappointment hit me. Her words had stung me, but it had to be worse for Daemon and Dawson. "She's not . . . pretending?"

"No. She's sucked into them. It's kind of like a hive." He shook his head again, and I could see the weariness settling in the lines around his full lips. "I don't know why Dawson and I are able to . . . think for ourselves but not her."

I placed the tips of my fingers against his cheek, feeling the faint stubble. "I think I know."

His brows rose.

"Dawson has Beth," I said quietly, meeting his eyes. "And you have me. Maybe that's it. Just like with the mutation thing. It's something so simple."

"There's nothing about you that's simple."

A faint smile crossed my lips. "I was so scared," I admitted after a few moments. "When you left with them, and then seeing you again like . . . like you were. I thought I'd lost you." Emotion clogged my throat, and it took several seconds to get the words out. "That after everything we've been through, I'd lost you anyway."

"You haven't lost me, Kitten. You could never lose me." He folded me in against him, and when he spoke in a low voice, his lips brushed my cheek. "But I didn't want you here, anywhere near here. It's not safe for you."

The fierce ache in my chest eased a little as his words sank in, but the bitter tang of hurt and fear lingered in the back of my throat. There was still so much I didn't understand, things I didn't think even Daemon understood.

He took one of my hands and placed it against his chest, above his heart. "You really thought I'd forgotten you?"

I dipped my chin, and it was too easy to recall the coldness in his stare. "I didn't know what to think. You . . . you looked at me like you did when we first met."

"Kat." He uttered my name like it was some kind of prayer, and then he pressed a kiss against the skin behind my ear. "I broke every rule of my kind to heal you and keep you with me. I married you and burned down an entire city to keep you safe. I've *killed* for you. Did you think I'd forget what you mean to me? That anything in this world—in any world—would be stronger than my love for you?"

A choked sob escaped my lips as I buried my face in the space between his shoulder and neck. Circling my arms around his shoulders, I clung to him like a needy baby monkey. I squeezed until his low chuckle whispered against my cheek.

"You're strangling me," he said, smoothing a hand up my back. "Just a little."

"Sorry," I mumbled against his shoulder, but I didn't let go. He kissed the crown of my head, and a sigh leaked out of me. God, nothing was okay. Far from it, but *Daemon* was okay. He was himself, and dammit, together we could face anything. We would because we had to. "What are we going to do?"

He tucked the tangled mess of my hair back from my face, exposing my cheek to the path of his lips. "Keep pretending. There are gonna be things I'm going to have to say, maybe even have to do—"

"I understand." My heart dropped anyway. I didn't want to relive the whole office thing again, but I would if needed. I had to.

"Of course you do." He placed a kiss on the corner of my lips. "But it's not something I've ever wanted you to have to understand." His lips followed the curve of my jaw, eliciting a shiver from me. "We'll get out of here, but I can't go without Dee."

I nodded. I would never expect him to leave her behind, even if she had turned into a raging bitch who apparently wanted to throw me down a flight or three of stairs.

"And not before I know what they're planning," he added. "They're up to something big."

"Obviously." I smiled faintly. "The whole invading-Earth part kind of gave that away."

"Smartass." His teeth caught the edge of my earlobe, and the little nip sent a jolt through my entire body.

I gasped, and his answering chuckle was downright wicked and wholly inappropriate given the situation. I drew back, cheeks flushing. "Only you could behave like this with everything going on."

One side of his mouth tipped up as his gaze dropped to my lips and then below. "Well, you are sitting in my lap wearing only jeans and a bra—a cute bra—after kicking some chick's ass. That's hot. And I'm really turned on by that."

The blush traveled to the lacy edge of my bra, because I could tell he was really turned on by that. "You're ridiculous."

"You're beautiful."

"I stink," I murmured.

Daemon chuckled hoarsely. "I can help you rectify that. I mean, I can be *really* helpful in that department."

"Oh Lord, seriously?"

"Hey, I'm supposedly all about the physical." He paused as I stared at him. "Okay, probably not supposedly. When it comes to you, I'm feeling physical pretty much all the time." His hands moved up my bare arms, leaving a rush of tiny bumps behind them.

I tilted my head back. "So besides the obvious me dying equals you dying, the other Luxen think you want to keep me around because you just like . . . ?"

"Having wild, animalistic sex with you?" he suggested.

My lips pursed.

"Something like that." His mouth brushed mine as he spoke, and his hands settled on my hips. "Though after everything in the office, I doubt they'd think you'd be down for that."

"I'm *not* down for that right now, you douche."

An eyebrow rose. "I bet I could change that."

"Daemon." I put my hands on his shoulders. "I think we really need to focus on other stuff." And there was so much. "Do they know about Beth, about . . . ?"

"They don't know about her or Luc. We need to keep it that way." His hands slipped around to my back and slid up to the bra strap.

"But they know what Archer is." I bit down on my lip as two of his fingers dipped under the strap. "Beth's pregnant."

His head dipped to my bare shoulder. "I know."

My jaw dropped. "What?" He didn't answer, because he was too busy *licking* my shoulder— Sweet Jesus. I grabbed a handful of hair and lifted his head. "You didn't tell me?"

He captured my mouth in a deep, searing kiss that almost made me forget what we were talking about and where we were. His kisses had that kind of magical power. "I didn't get a chance to tell you." He hooked his pinkie under one of the straps, easing it down an inch or two. "Remember. Holy alien invasion everywhere."

"Oh. Yeah. That." My lashes lowered as his lips chased after the strap. Tension curled low in my stomach. "Beth's been sick, though. I don't know if it's normal or not. That's . . . that's why we were at the grocery store. We were getting her stuff."

"Archer should've never let you leave that house." Daemon's head jerked up suddenly, swiveling toward the closed bathroom door. His pupils gleamed like diamonds. "Someone's coming."

I stiffened in his arms, heart lurching into my throat.

He turned his attention back to me. Cupping my cheek, he lowered his mouth once more, kissing me deeply and spinning my senses so fast and so furiously that when he lifted his head, I whimpered. Actually whimpered. "Act like you're mad at me. Fight me."

Still lost from the last kiss, I stared at him. "What?"

Suddenly, I was on my back, dangerously close to the broken glass. Globs of spilled conditioner and shampoo splattered. Daemon hovered over me, his hands capturing my wrists and holding them to the floor as one of his legs shoved in between mine.

My chest lurched. "What in the—?"

He dipped his head to mine, voice low. "Pretend I'm Sadi."

If I did that, I might cut him.

My eyes narrowed, but the bathroom door swung open, and a Luxen male—the quiet one from the office—stood in the doorway. Heat swept across my face, partly due to how I was undressed, and partly because of how we must've looked at that moment.

"Everything okay here?" he asked in that strange, lilting way.

"Just spending a little one-on-one time with her," Daemon answered, and my breath caught at the change in his voice. It was back to that smug, mocking way of his that made me want to introduce my knee to an important part of his body.

Over Daemon's head, I saw the Luxen tilt his head to the side. "Doesn't look like it's going too well."

"Well . . ." He flashed a grin. "It would be easier if she wasn't so upset. Isn't that right?" he asked me. "But that's okay. I like the way she *tries* to fight."

"Tries?" I spat, my fingers curled inward. "I'm going to—"

"Shush it," he murmured lazily. And then he moved lightning fast, and from an angle the Luxen could see, he nipped my ear again. I had to bite down on my lip to stop myself from crying out *and* punching him in the gonads.

I was so going to kick his butt later.

Daemon made a show of eyeing me like I was an all-you-can-eat buffet, then glanced at the other Luxen. "Do you mind? Or are you planning to watch?"

The flicker of interest on the Luxen's face turned my stomach. "As alluring as that sounds, I'll need to pass. This time."

Oh, yuck. Wiggling a leg free, I slammed the heel of my foot into Daemon's calf for starting that line of conversation.

"Ouch." He shot me a look.

My lips twitched as satisfaction rolled over me.

"Rolland just wanted to make sure everything was fine," the Luxen said, his cool, crystallized gaze straying to areas I was so not happy about.

Daemon shifted, casually blocking a good portion of my body. "Is that all?"

"No," was the response. "Rolland would like you to attend the press conference tomorrow. And he wants you to bring the girl with you."

Press conference? Bring me? Oh . . . a shiver danced over my skin. I so did not like the sound of all of this.

Daemon managed a smirk. "Sounds like fun."

The Luxen hesitated, and then nodded. After one more way-too-long look in my direction, he backed out of the bathroom. "Have fun."

Neither of us moved or spoke for a good minute after the Luxen had left the bathroom, and then Daemon glanced down at me.

I drew in a deep breath. "I don't like the way tomorrow is looking."

"I don't either."

I wet my lips. "You don't think Rolland knows you're faking?"

"No." He sounded so sure. "I've been more than careful."

"Then what do you think they're planning?"

He shook his head, causing several black waves to brush against his eyebrows. "He videoed a press release earlier. He's pretending to be the mayor . . ."

As Daemon trailed off, he released my wrists and rocked up, his expression far off, and I had a feeling he was thinking the same thing I was. Sitting up, I wrapped my arms around my waist. He looked over and our gazes locked.

"Do you think he's pretending?" I asked. "That he's really pretending to be the mayor, as in . . ." As in working from the inside to take over. "What if there are more like him? Ones who have taken over the bodies of important people?"

He cursed under his breath as he shoved both hands through his hair. "I should've seen it right away. I mean, I got that he was pretending to be mayor, but I didn't think beyond that. They're only killing some people without assimilating them. They're targeting certain people. Same age group. People old enough to have . . ."

"Families," I whispered. And that would be even worse than assimilating those in positions of power, because if they pretended to be mothers and fathers and teachers, they'd be everywhere, and no one would be able to tell, even if there were witnesses. Accounts of the Luxen snatching bodies couldn't stop something this huge.

I looked at Daemon.

The Luxen had already been on this planet for decades and then some, and no one knew.

"Does the TV in that room work?" I asked.

"I think so."

"I think we need to turn it on."

After helping me up, Daemon rubbed his hands up and down my arms, chasing away the chill. "Take a shower, and I'll find something for you to wear."

I glanced at the door, hesitating. Stripping naked with a bunch of Luxen nearby who had no concept of personal space made me want to hurl.

Daemon dipped his head, brushing his lips across mine. "I won't let anyone come in here. You're safe."

You're safe.

Two words I couldn't wait until I never had to hear again. Closing my eyes, I stretched up and kissed him softly. "Okay."

He pulled me in for a quick hug, and then he started for the door. Stopping, he twisted at the waist, and his gaze drifted over me, warming my cold skin. "Kitten?"

"Yeah?"

His eyes were beautiful when they met mine, luminous and clear, and a long moment stretched out between us. "I love you."

7

{ Katy }

Daemon had the TV turned on in the bedroom, volume low, when I walked in with a towel wrapped around me.

He glanced over at me, and his lashes lowered as his gaze moved from the tip of my now-clean toes, all the way to the top of my wet head. "Hey there."

It seemed like he'd forgotten what he was watching, which was one of the world news channels. I hadn't seen any reports since I'd left the cabin.

"Come here." He extended an arm from where he sat on the edge of the bed.

The room had been restored to how it had looked before Sadi and I had gotten into it, with the exception of the curtains and the chair. They still lay in a pile on the floor. The sheets and pillowcases had been replaced.

Holding the towel where it was knotted, I padded over to the bed. I started to sit beside him, but he looped an arm around my waist and tugged me onto his lap. The room was chilly, but his body heat immediately seeped into me. He was like a walking, talking electric blanket.

On the TV, a silvery-haired newscaster solemnly stared into the camera as he spoke. At the top of the screen, there was a live video of an affiliated station in L.A. Filmed from what appeared to be a helicopter circling the distressed city, the snapshots of smoking buildings, bumper-to-bumper traffic on the major highways, and streets crowded with people didn't bode well. Then the tiny screen on the right switched to a live stream of New York City, spitting out the same kind of images.

"Sources believe that the initial strike started in Las Vegas, and we're trying to get confirmation of that." Weariness etched into the lines of the newscaster's face and clouded his tone. "It is now believed that the meteorite shower three nights ago was not, in fact, meteorites, but . . ." He cleared his throat and seemed to struggle with the next words. "But was the first arrival of a widespread . . . extraterrestrial invasion."

"I think he just choked on the word 'extraterrestrial,'" Daemon commented drily.

I nodded. The guy looked like he couldn't believe he'd just said that on national television.

The newscaster glanced down at the papers in front of him, shaking his head slowly. "We're still waiting on Dr. Kapur to see if we can gain any insight into the . . . biology and the possible endgame involved, but at this time, what we do know is that there was a period of silence after the mass arrival and then"—he looked up at the screen, his features tense—"a strategic, targeted attack all across the world, in every major city. There are no definite numbers, but we do expect that the loss of life will be substantial in the areas and the surrounding cities."

I shuddered at the overwhelming horror of it all. Even being what I was and seeing so much in the last year or so, it was almost too much to fully wrap my head around. It wasn't just *my* world that had changed anymore. Everyone's world had changed.

Daemon's arms tightened around my waist as he watched the TV. He didn't say anything, because it was one of those moments where there weren't any words powerful enough to describe what either of us was feeling.

On the television, the man's fingers curled around the sheets of paper in his hands. "What we do know is the attacks on the cities lasted for a few hours, but this . . . this alien life-form has not been seen since."

Glancing over at Daemon, I watched a muscle along his jaw flicker. I had a feeling why they hadn't seen any Luxen. They were no longer in their true forms.

"We also have received word of a very frightening and . . . and frankly disturbing development. There honestly are no words for it, and if you haven't seen this video yet, I will warn you that it may not be suitable for younger viewers." He looked off-screen and nodded. "This was sent in by a viewer in the Miami, Florida, area. We believe it was captured on a camera phone at some point yesterday, during the attacks."

The screen to the right switched to a shaky recording and then expanded, filling the television. My eyes widened.

It looked like whoever was filming had hidden behind a car on its side. A Luxen was on the screen, in full glowworm mode as it stalked a human male who looked like he was in his twenties. The Luxen's movements were as fluid as sculpted water as it backed the human male up against an abandoned city bus. Horror etched into the guy's face as the Luxen launched forward and placed a glowing white hand on the center of his chest.

I knew what was about to happen.

"Oh my God. Oh my God," whoever was filming whispered over and over again as the Luxen rapidly assimilated the DNA of the human male, taking on the physical form and characteristics until there was nothing left of the human but a dried-out husk crumpled on the ground.

The video started shaking more, and then I could tell the person was getting the hell away from what had just gone down.

When the video ended, the newscaster appeared as if he had aged a decade. "We are still waiting on the press conference from the president of the United States, but we have received word that many government figures in the sieged cities will be making statements later in the day."

"How are they doing it?" I asked.

Daemon knew what I was asking. "When we arrived and were brought in by Daedalus, we were assimilated." His hands slid down my arms to my cold hands. He folded his over mine. "We were exposed to a human—the three of us— over a period of time. It took several months, and when we finally shifted into our human forms, we had his characteristics—the dark hair, skin color, facial features. He was like a surrogate, but we didn't kill him. At least as far as I know. Once we were moved out, along with . . . Matthew and the Thompsons, we never saw him again."

Daemon had never gone into this kind of detail before, and trying to fully picture three little toddler-like aliens assimilating a human over a period of time made my brain hurt. How in the world had Daedalus gotten humans to sign up for that?

"So these Luxen are doing what you did but faster—too fast?" I said.

He nodded. "They're doing exactly what we were *taught*

to do." He brought our joined hands to his lips and pressed a kiss against my knuckles. "It's strange. They know so much, too much for not being here, but then there's a lot they don't know. Someone or something had to be working with them from here."

"Sadi?"

His brows rose.

"I don't mean just her, but haven't you noticed? She doesn't move or talk like the other Luxen," I explained. "She's more human. I think she's been here."

The corners of his lips pulled down. "I hadn't noticed, but I try to stay away from her. She's a little bit touchy."

A slow burn of anger blazed through my veins. "I really don't like her."

"I know." He kissed my cheek and then gently lifted me out of his lap. I swayed a bit on my feet, drawing a concerned look from him. "You need to rest. We have a few more hours before the sun breaks and the press conference happens."

I folded my arms over the edge of the towel. "Why does he want us there?"

"That I can't figure out. Rolland says he can't get a read on me, and I can't get one on him, either." Daemon reached behind him, picking up a long shirt. "I was able to find this for you to sleep in."

It was a man's shirt, and I really tried not to think about where it came from when I took it and slipped it on over my head. I shimmied out of the towel, and the shirt almost reached my knees.

"I'll stay with you." He rose, glancing at the door. "I don't think that will raise any suspicions."

Not when they thought Daemon and I were banging our brains out. My cheeks heated, even though it was stupid to be embarrassed over it, but it was like the Luxen saw me simply as Daemon's property and nothing else.

That made me itchy in my own skin and sick to my stomach.

I climbed into the bed and rested on my side. Daemon floated around the room, checking the door and the windows even though we both knew it was pointless, and then he turned off the TV. The bed dipped behind me as his weight settled. An arm snaked around my waist, urging me against his chest and into all his warmth.

He smoothed my hair behind my ear as his breath danced along my temple. My eyes closed when his lips brushed over my skin. "We've been in worse situations," he whispered. "We'll get out of this one."

Had we been in worse? At least with Daedalus we knew they wanted us alive. Alive to do horrible things for them, but that somehow sounded better. With the Luxen, I knew deep down they couldn't care less if we woke up dead tomorrow.

I think Daemon realized that, too.

"We need to get out of here." I stared into the darkness of the room. "Tomorrow, when they take us outside, it will be the perfect opportunity."

Daemon didn't respond, and after a few moments, I squeezed my eyes shut. Tomorrow might be our only opportunity to get out of here, but there was one big thing in our way, one thing that would stop Daemon right in his tracks.

And that was Dee.

{ Daemon }

Dawson looked as antsy as I felt standing outside the room Kat slept in. I wasn't surprised that he'd come to find me in the early morning hours, when most, if not all, the Luxen were asleep, completely unafraid that anyone would attempt to take them out.

People always thought I was arrogant, but hell, nothing touched these Luxen.

Taking them out while they slept was something we'd discussed the first morning we realized they all seriously went nightie-night, but neither of us turned out to be that stupid. We'd be able to take some of them, but there were more than two dozen Luxen on the grounds, and it wasn't just our lives we'd be risking.

"How is she?" Dawson asked, voice low as he nodded at the closed door.

"She finally fell asleep." I leaned against the wall, watching the end of the hall. No one else slept up here, not even Dee, but my guard was up.

"I really am sorry. She knows that, right?" Dawson thrust a hand through his hair, grimacing. "I owe her everything, and—"

"She knows." I shifted my weight. "You know why she was at the grocery store with Archer? Turns out they were picking up prenatal stuff for Beth."

Blood drained from his face.

"She's been sick, and I don't know if it's normal or if it's something more." I thought about those damn kids back at Area 51, but I doubted this was the time to ask Dawson if he knew about them and really freak him out. "Kat isn't sure, either. None of us knows crap about pregnancy."

He squeezed his eyes shut as he blew out a breath. "I know we can't leave without Dee, but . . ."

But how much longer was Dawson expected to stay away from Beth, the girl he loved, the girl who was carrying his child? The girl who needed him right now more than anything?

How long could I wait?

Before Kat had ended up here, I'd been willing to stick around to find out who was leading the Luxen and how he or she planned on carrying out the ultimate strategy, because I knew Kat was safe with Luc and Archer. I'd hated not being with her, freaking drove me out of my mind not even being able to think about her out of fear the others would pick up on it.

But now?

Screw the Luxen.

Screw mankind.

I wanted Kat out. Every cell of my being demanded that I protect her, even though I knew she was hella capable of doing so herself, but I wanted her far away from here. Hell, I'd keep her in Bubble Wrap if it weren't so damn creepy and also inconvenient, considering I had a terrible habit of obsessively popping the damn things until not a single bubble was left.

Getting her out of here was what I wanted, but I couldn't do it. How could we leave with Dee this way? We needed to break their hold on her, but neither of us knew the magic key to doing it. And what would Kat and I be running to? What future waited for Dawson, Bethany, and . . . and their baby?

I didn't know.

In the minutes since I'd told Dawson about Beth being sick, dark shadows of worry had blossomed under his eyes, and I wondered if I should've just kept that part to myself.

Pushing off the wall, I clamped a hand on my brother's shoulder and squeezed. As our gazes locked, pressure circled like vise grips around my chest. It wasn't the first moment the thought popped into my head. Ever since I realized Kat was going to be brought back to the compound, it had been there, on the fringes of my consciousness. I knew it was the same for Dawson.

He shuddered as he placed his hand on my shoulder. "I can't wait much longer."

Meaning sooner rather than later, he would make a run for it, for Beth, with or without our sister.

"I know." Real pain lanced through my chest at the thought of leaving Dee to these things I really didn't want to claim any relation to.

Dawson nodded as he stepped back, lowering his arm. "This sucks."

I choked out a laugh as I glanced at the closed door. "Can you hang here for a few minutes while I find her something to wear?"

"Sure."

I left Dawson by the door and headed into a nearby bedroom where Dee had been pilfering clothes. The room was a mess. Bed destroyed. Dressers turned over and items spilled out. I stepped over bottles of perfume and pictures, and then entered the walk-in closet. Scanning for something that looked like it would fit Kat, I realized there weren't many options. The original woman of the house was obviously a very small woman. Probably never ate a double cheeseburger, based on the size and style of the gowns.

I pulled out a dazzling, glittering blue gown. There was a split all the way up to the hip, and despite everything, I pictured Kat wearing it.

And then I pictured Kat out of it.

That image hit me like a punch in the gut.

Great. Now I would be a walking hard-on all morning. Just what I needed.

Finally, I found a pair of white pants that looked like they'd fit and a short-sleeve black sweater. There was also a pair of flats in her size. After gathering up the stuff, I turned and walked back into the main room, happening to glance down at the nightstand next to the bed.

I came to a complete stop.

Drawers were pulled open. One of them had an adult store's worth of *toys* in it. Man, the mayor and his wife sure liked to get freaky. In the top drawer were other . . . interesting things. Among them was a black box full of sealed wrappers.

Really not necessary, but . . .

I grabbed a handful and slid them in my back pocket.

Nothing like being prepared.

Smiling to myself, I pivoted around and hustled back to where Dawson waited.

"What's up with the shit-eating grin of yours?" he asked.

"Nothing."

He shot me a look that said he knew better. "You need anything else?" When I shook my head, he started away and then paused. "Rolland wants you at the conference today?"

My free hand on the doorknob, I nodded. "He wants Kat there, too."

Dawson frowned.

"We need to be prepared for anything," I told him.

Drawing in a deep breath, he nodded, and I watched him retreat down the hall. Easing into the room, I was surprised to see Kat sitting up in bed. Hair air-dried, it tumbled down in messy waves, then fell over her shoulders and down her arms.

"Is everything okay?" She rubbed her eyes with balled fists.

"Yeah. Found you some clothes." For a moment, I just stared at her as she lowered her hands, tossed off the covers, and stood. My heart thumped.

Sometimes—and it happened at random moments—I was blown away by the fact that she was *mine* and I was *hers*. This was one of those times.

I offered the stolen clothes. "For you," I added, like a complete idiot.

A tired smile appeared on her face as she took the clothes from me. "Thank you."

I watched her shuffle past me and disappear into the bathroom, and I stood there as the water came on. It was still way too early and she could've slept more, but being the selfish ass I could be, I was happy she was awake.

Sucked I wasn't getting to watch her change clothes, though. That would've really given me the picker upper I needed. But then the door opened, and I was still standing in the middle of the room as she stepped out.

Lucky me, the pants I'd given her hadn't really fit.

They were about a size too small, hugging her shapely ass like a glove, and that made me a very happy man.

Kat caught my stare and rolled her eyes. "Thank God these pants are stretchy."

"I'm having inappropriately timed thoughts right about now," I told her.

She crossed her arms under her chest, drawing my attention to another place on her body I might be a wee bit fascinated with. "I'm not really surprised."

"Just thought I'd let you know."

As she walked past me and bent at the waist to place the shoes on the floor, I really got an eyeful, and I stopped thinking. Maybe I was exhausted and I didn't care about getting my priorities straight while the quietness of dawn seeped in. Maybe it was the dress I saw in the closet or all the junk in the drawer. Maybe when it all came down to it, I was a dude and had sex on the brain no matter the situation. Either way, I stopped thinking, and that was a common problem of mine whenever I was around her.

I reached out, snagging her right off the floor, lifting her up with one arm around her waist. A startled sound escaped her lips as I hauled her against my chest, digging my hand through her hair as I pressed my mouth against hers.

I kissed her deeply, taking everything I could into me—her taste, her tongue, and every soft sound she made against my mouth. In the back of my head, I knew this wasn't something I should be doing. Hell, we should be plotting and all that crap, but screw it.

Like always, I wanted her.

Setting her down on her feet, I traced a path of tiny kisses to that small earlobe of hers as I slipped my fingers under the hem of the sweater. Her skin was warm, soft as spun silk. I pulled back, lifting the sweater over her head, dropping it on the floor.

I blazed a new trail down her throat, kissing each of those little yellow daisies, lingering on some more than others. Then, I turned her around, and the air stilled in my lungs.

The scars.

A low, inhuman-sounding thing rose from my throat.

"Daemon?" She glanced over her shoulder.

I swallowed. "I . . . It's okay."

But it wasn't okay.

I hated seeing the scars, even though they were nothing more than a faint pink with smoothed edges, but they would always be a reminder of the pain she suffered and the help-lessness I had felt. Bad times.

Touching her shoulders lightly, I lowered my mouth to just below her shoulder blades and placed a reverent kiss against each of the scars, wishing I could somehow wipe them away, erase the memory of the whole damn thing. Closing my eyes, I moved my mouth to the base of her neck and made myself a promise I would do terrible things to keep.

There would not be another scar on her body.

Not one.

With shaking fingers, I unhooked the tiny clasps and slipped the straps of her bra down her arms. She sucked in a breath as I straightened and eased the length of my body against hers.

Reaching around her, I flicked the tiny pearl button on her pants as I caught her earlobe between my teeth. I loved the little piece of flesh and the sound she made that set my blood afire.

"I can't help myself when I'm around you," I whispered in her ear. "But I think that's something you already know."

The back of her head rested against my chest as I slid my hands up. She bit down on her swollen lower lip. I felt my pulse in every part of my body and I wanted to slow everything down, worship every inch of her, but lust and love were riding me hard.

Truth was, time wasn't on our side. I'd make time later. Damn, I would make so much time, we'd need a straight three months of alone, one-on-one quality time.

Once I had her facing me, I picked her up and sat her on the bed as I took her mouth in a deep, scorching kiss that left me unsteady on my feet. When I pulled back, I could see the burning white glow in her eyes and I knew, just like our heartbeats, that her eyes mirrored mine. I peeled off the damn tight white pants and nearly lost it right there. Glancing up at her, I raised my brows in question.

"What?" She flushed the prettiest shade of pink. "You didn't bring me any undies. And honestly, I'm not wearing anyone else's."

My hands slid up her calves. "I have absolutely no problem with that. Whatsoever. Like, ever. And ever. Forever. You get me?"

A soft laugh parted her lips. "I think I get your point."

"Are you sure?" I kissed the spot behind her knee, grinning when her leg jerked. "Because I could make it a rule."

"I don't think that's necessary."

I chuckled as I pushed back from the bed and shucked off my clothes faster than I ever had. Her gaze dropped, and she gasped as her eyes brightened. A ridiculous amount of pride brought a smile to my lips. "You like?"

Her lashes lifted. "What do you think?"

"I think you like a lot."

With a deep breath, her chest rose. "But we don't have any protection, and considering I about passed out when I realized Beth was pregnant, I think we really need that."

"Got it." Snagging up my jeans, I pulled out one of the foil wrappers. Oddly enough, though, as I glanced over at her, seeing her on the bed, waiting for me, only me, I almost forgot how to put one on.

That would've been awkward.

"Oh my God," she said, laying her head back against the bed. Amused exasperation colored her tone, but she looked like a damn goddess positioned like that. "It's like you have a special skill when it comes to finding condoms. Seriously. They must just fall out of the sky whenever you're around."

I winked as I tore the edge of the wrapper with my teeth. "I have the skills that count, Kitten."

She grinned, and that sexy, heavily hooded gaze of hers worked me right to the edge. I climbed over her, bypassing parts I was so going to take a lot of time on later, over and over again. I opened my mouth, probably to say something outrageously smug and overtly sexual, but whatever I was about to say was lost.

Kat reached up and cupped my jaw, bringing me down for a kiss that wrecked me from the inside out in the most perfect way. Amazed, absolutely blown away by how a single word, a look or a touch, or just a sweet kiss from her could put me right in my place, completely humbled by her.

Then, there really was no talking and no thinking. My mouth was everywhere. Our hands on the move. I found she was ready, and I blasted beyond that moment the second we kissed. We moved together, our hands joined tightly as I lifted up and stared into gray eyes speckled with white light.

I fell in love all over again.

Flickering light played over the walls as our hearts pounded together in tandem. She held on tight, wrapping her legs around me, drawing me in, and I swallowed her cry with a kiss as a shattering whirl of sensation powered down my spine.

I don't know how much time passed, but while I held her close, wrapping every part of my body around hers so there wasn't even an inch between us, I finally closed my eyes. And despite all the shit going down around us, I found peace.

8

{ Katy }

I kept my lips sealed tight as the Luxen male—the same one who'd shown up in the bathroom to check on Daemon the night before—led me away from the vehicle Daemon and Dawson piled into along with their sister.

Police surrounded the fleet of cars, and while that seemed like a normal thing during a war or alien invasion, every officer I saw who wasn't wearing sunglasses was rocking Luxen eyes.

Of course.

When I realized the dark-haired Luxen was steering me toward the tinted-out black limo, tight knots formed in the pit of my stomach. I dared a quick glance down the line of cars and saw Daemon stopped beside a Hummer. The look on his face told me he was seconds from dropping the act and rectifying the car assignments, and that would be bad, very bad.

I gave a little shake of my head and then hurried toward the waiting car's open door. The pressure against the center of my back from the dark-haired Luxen was not on the gentle side, and I all but toppled onto the leather seat. He climbed in beside me as I straightened myself, pushing strands of hair out of my face.

Sitting across from me was Rolland and the bitch, Sadi, whose cheek was completely unblemished. Damn Luxen and their ability to heal. I'd love to see my mark on her face instead of the syrupy-sweet smile directed at me.

The door closed, and I felt like it was a coffin shutting on me.

Rolland sat with one knee hooked over the other, hands folded in his lap like a perfect politician in a navy suit. Beside him, Sadi was dressed like she had been the day before, pin-stripe skirt suit, hair in a neat twist. They looked perfect in a creepy plastic way.

A fine sheen of sweat covered my palms as I glanced at the window, wondering how fast I could summon the Source and bust out a window if I needed to make a hasty escape.

"You're probably wondering why you're riding with us," Rolland stated.

I shifted my gaze back to his, meeting the startling azure eyes. There wasn't an ounce of humanity in that cold stare. "I am."

A slow smile pulled at his lips. "I'm curious about your kind, Katy Swartz, about you and Daemon. He feels such a strong physical connection with you. What do you feel for him?"

The limo started to move, and I figured it was probably best that I was as honest as I could be with Rolland. None of us really knew how much information he actually had about us, what Dee or the brothers might have inadvertently shared with him.

"I feel a strong connection with him," I said, and thinking of how he'd been this morning, that *so* wasn't a lie.

"You were fighting him last night, though." Rolland nodded at the quiet Luxen beside me. "Why was that?"

"I didn't like how he treated me in the office." That was also the truth.

"You love him," Sadi added, and the way she said it made it sound like loving someone was tantamount to walking in front of a bus.

Taking a deep breath, I nodded. "I do."

"And do you think he loves you?" Rolland straightened his tie.

"I did, but . . ." I forced tears to my eyes, which wasn't hard considering the way he'd acted before I knew what was going on. It still burned like a sting from a hornet. "But I don't know anymore. The things he said and . . . and how he acted afterward." I added in a shudder for show. Someone hand me an Oscar. "I don't know anything anymore."

There was a moment of silence, and then Rolland laughed deeply.

That wasn't what I was expecting.

"You're cute," he said finally.

Uh.

He chuckled again. "You sit there, so demure and so small, but you made Sadi bleed a handful of hours ago."

Sadi scowled, and her look promised retribution. My hands clenched in my lap, and I so wanted to scream *bring it* at her. Better yet, I wanted to launch myself across the space and wrap my hands around her thin neck.

"You stood before me and tapped into the Source so easily, and yet you sit across from me like a timid little creature," he continued as he leaned back, stretching his legs out until his calf was pressed against mine.

I stiffened.

His smile spread. "I just wanted to point that out to you."

The limo jarred over a pothole, jostling me against the silent Luxen. Right now, I felt like a mouse that was being stalked by a cat. A very large and very hungry cat. My heart pounded in my chest. Perhaps I shouldn't be mentally writing my Oscar acceptance speech. "Okay."

"I want to know more about the Origin who was with you in the store," he ordered. "Who is he?"

I didn't respond.

Shaking his head with a humored smile, he glanced at the Luxen beside me. Before I could take a breath, a hand encased my throat, fingers digging into my skin and cutting off air. A jolt of panic zipped up my sternum as my eyes widened. I'd taken my last breath before I'd even realized it.

Rolland leaned forward, placing both his hands on my knees. "I want this to be easy and not messy. All you have to do is answer my questions."

I clawed at the Luxen's hand, but he started to shift, and the heat seared my skin, the light blinding me.

"And if you want to keep Daemon alive, you better value your life," he said in a tone that sounded like we were discussing what to have for dinner. "Okay?"

I nodded as best I could.

The Luxen let go and his light receded. Sitting back into the seat beside me, he readjusted his sleeves calmly. Rolland didn't move. Still leaning forward, his hands curled around my knees, forcing a wave of disgust over me.

"Who was he?"

I hated what I was about to do, but it wasn't just me I had to consider. Even though I was protecting Daemon by saving my own neck, I knew I could potentially be tossing Archer and Lord knows who else under the bus.

"His name is Archer. I don't know his last name or if he even has one." My skin crawled.

"And how did you come into contact with him?" Rolland asked. When he leaned back, Sadi shifted from the seat next to him to the one beside me.

Every muscle in my body locked up as her hand replaced his. "Don't lie, Katy." She leaned in, her mouth near my ear. "We know more than you think."

"Because you've been here this whole time?" I asked.

She laughed softly. "Well, aren't you the astute one?" Her sharp nails seemed to dig through the thin material of my pants. "Come on, don't be shy."

I drew in a short breath. "I met him in Daedalus."

"And what would that be?" Rolland asked.

As much as I wanted to shift away from Sadi, I remained where I was sitting. "They are a group within the government that has worked at assimilating the Luxen. They watch over them, keep tabs on them—"

"Control them?"

"To some extent." I sucked in a breath as Sadi extended an arm behind me and leaned in, getting all up in my personal space. "They've done experiments." As I told them about Daedalus, I fought back the urge to sink my nails into her face.

Rolland listened as the limo rolled along. "Thank you for being so forthcoming, Katy. I would've been so disappointed if you'd lied."

"And we would've known." Sadi's hand was somewhere around my navel. "You see, we know about their little weapons and the onyx. Those things may still affect us, but we know they are there. We will be prepared for them."

Confused, I flicked my gaze from her to Rolland. He spread his arms out over the back of his seat, getting all kinds of comfy. "We've had help here. I'm pretty sure you've realized that by now."

Pressure seized my chest as I got a real bad feeling about everything. "Someone like her?"

Her throaty laugh raised the hairs on my arms. "Yes, someone like me. Like your Archer. Oh. And who else haven't you told us about?"

Air leaked out of my lungs.

Rolland tsked softly. "Are you keeping something or someone from us, Katy?"

"She is." Sadi drew a finger up my arm. Tiny bumps chased the disturbing caress. "His name is Luc, I think."

Oh God.

"But that's not all." Sadi looked over at Rolland.

He grinned. "Of course it isn't."

Sadi's finger trailed over my jaw. "There's Beth . . . and the baby."

"Oh dear," Rolland murmured.

I stared at him, my brain refusing to compute the twist.

He tapped his fingers on the back of the seat. "Did you all really think we'd come here without an invite? That humans, with all their intelligence and advancements, wouldn't be the source of their own destruction in the end?"

"After all, naming a serum after Prometheus?" Sadi's breath danced against my cheek. "I mean, isn't that like self-fulfillment?"

Because in Greek mythology, Prometheus had created man out of clay and, disobeying the gods, gave mankind fire, therefore starting civilization. He had been punished for his own ingenuity.

Just like Daedalus, Sadi's voice whispered among my turbulent thoughts.

Horror swamped me as I slowly turned my head toward her. Her eyes, the brilliant blue, they weren't real. Contacts. Just like Archer had hidden his eyes from us, making them appear human. Sadi had gone in the opposite direction, donning lenses that made her look Luxen.

But she wasn't.

She was an Origin.

And not only had she been able to pick up my thoughts the entire time, she would've heard Dawson's and Daemon's, in and out of their true forms.

"Yes," she whispered, her lips brushing the curve of my cheek, sending a shiver down my spine. "You are all so screwed."

The inside of the limo was suddenly too small. "Why?" I gasped out the only thing I could think.

"Why tell you?" Rolland raised his arms idly. "Or why ask you questions? You see, we couldn't figure it out. The two brothers were smart. Even when they were in their human forms, they didn't think anything."

"They are extraordinarily beautiful, and while most aren't blessed with good looks and intelligence," Sadi said, laughing when my jaw clamped down, "I doubted their heads were *that* empty."

"There were things that Sadi could pick up every once in a while—brief flashes of thoughts that raised our suspicions when it came to how honest they were being with us," Rolland went on. "But we couldn't figure it out—what made those two so resistant to our cause when their sister fell into line so quickly. But then you came along."

Sadi tapped a nail off the tip of my nose. "How lucky for us."

"You are the answer. Because you were mutated, an unbreakable bond was formed between you and Daemon."

"And we knew that Dawson was hiding something from us," Sadi added. "Or someone. That would be Beth."

"So now we know that there will be other Luxen out there, some like Daemon and Dawson, who may be bonded to humans in a way that will be problematic to our cause. It's not like the four of you are unique. There has to be more, and that is what today is all about."

Crap. Crap. Crap.

Sadi giggled.

"We need to calm the poor little humans, get them to think that their leaders are protecting them, but you and me, well, we know that's not really going to happen." He smiled that charming smile of his. "But we also need to give a message to any other Luxen out there who may be thinking that our cause is not something they wish to support."

My pulse in my throat felt like a hummingbird trying to peck its way out. "And that's what we are? A message."

"Smart girl," he replied as the limo hung a sharp right.

"She wants to know how," Sadi interjected, and I shot her a dark look. She patted my cheek. "Should we tell her?"

He shrugged.

"You see, there will be Luxen who will be watching, and even through the TV and all the channels it's broadcast on, they will know what we are," she explained. "We will toss the brothers right under that bus you were worried about earlier. We'll expose them as Luxen."

Holy crap.

"Takes care of two things." Rolland leaned forward again. "When the humans see beyond a doubt that the Luxen look just like them and that there are humans working alongside some of them, it will cause panic."

Making it easier for them to take control.

"Exactly," Sadi murmured, tracing my lower lip with her finger.

"And it also sends a clear message to the Luxen that we will not tolerate any who may have the smallest inkling to stand against us." The smile slipped from Rolland's face as his pupils turned to light. "Like I said, serves two interests."

Good God. The panic they would incite would be astronomical. Even if only a small percentage of the world saw the video at first, it would go viral. If there were Luxen out there like Daemon and Dawson, they'd get the message.

There had to be something I could do.

"There is nothing you can do," Sadi said, reading my thoughts.

But there was.

She tipped her head back and started laughing, and I started picturing people twerking—everyone in the limo. Quiet Luxen Dude. Rolland. Sadi. All of them bent over, butts in the air, looking like damn fools.

Sadi drew back, frowning. "What are—?"

Twisting in the seat, I acted without much thought behind it, letting instinct take over. The risk was great, but I couldn't let them reach their destination.

Sadi shouted something as I summoned the Source, pulled from deep within me. Quiet Luxen Dude slammed his hand around my throat as energy rolled down my arm, spinning rapidly as I let the bolt loose.

Air was cut off, and I couldn't breathe, but the bolt of energy had struck true, slamming into the back of the driver's head.

The limo swerved sharply to the right and kept going, speeding up when the driver slumped over the wheel. The car went up on two wheels, and as the grip around my throat tightened, the limo went airborne.

9

{ Daemon }

I didn't like this setup at all. Having Kat in a different car was bad enough, but leaving her with Sadi and Rolland made me want to put my fist through the back of someone's head.

Dee was sitting in the front, next to one of the newcomers, dressed like a mini-Sadi, wearing a pantsuit. God, that made my skin crawl right off my bones. There were at least a hundred things I didn't like about that, and all of them made me want to punch myself in the face.

I was in a punching mood.

That was so messed up after the bliss I'd experienced this morning with Kat. The time spent with her, in her, now seemed like forever ago. There was an odd, desperate edge to my thoughts that I couldn't shake. Like the feel of her lips, and how it almost seemed like it was something in the past.

My brother cast me a long look before shifting his gaze back to the window. He was tense, practically as tight as a bow.

The mayor lived out in the boondocks, and we were still

at least five miles or so from the city. I wanted to tell the guy behind the wheel to hurry the hell up.

Suddenly, the cruiser in front of us slammed on its brakes, and I was jerked forward when the Hummer followed suit. Grasping the back of the seat in front of me, I swore under my breath.

"What's going on?" Dee asked, frowning. "We shouldn't be stopping."

Up ahead, a black sedan veered to the left without any warning, and I saw something that caused my heart to freaking stop on a damn dime. Horror balled in the pit of my stomach.

The limo Kat traveled in swerved into the right lane, and then went up on one side. It clipped a motorcycle cop, and as it spun out, right into the path of another, the rider shifted forms a second too late and smacked against the sedan's windshield. The limo was airborne, coasting several feet before coming down on its roof. Metal crunched.

"Stop the car!" Dawson shouted.

I was already reaching for the door while the Hummer fishtailed to a stop. Throwing open the door, I didn't stop to think what it looked like to the dozen or so Luxen spilling out of their respective vehicles. I didn't care.

Pushing past one in a uniform, I raced toward the wrecked limo. The only way I knew Kat was still alive was the fact that I was breathing, but that didn't mean jack. She could be injured, and the knowledge she could be seriously hurt was enough to nearly take my knees out from underneath me.

Dawson and Dee were right behind me as I rounded the mangled, flickering body of the Luxen who had been on the motorcycle.

A bright white light flared inside the limo.

I skidded to a halt.

The back door blew out from the limo, winging across the road at such a force that it ripped *right* through a Luxen in a police uniform. Like, one Luxen suddenly became two not-so-put-together Luxen.

"Holy halfies," Dawson murmured.

No sooner than those words popped out of my brother's mouth, a blue and red and white form followed the path of the door, zooming across the road and slamming into a pine. The ancient tree rocked. Needles fell to the earth as the blur dropped face-first onto the ground.

Sadi.

My wide eyes swung back to the limo as one small, delicate hand appeared on the asphalt, and then a slender arm followed, revealing the short sleeve of a black sweater.

Kat pulled herself out of the busted opening where the door used to be. Pushing to her feet, she brushed long hair out of her face. Blood trickled from her mouth and her right pant leg was ripped around the thigh, covered with red.

I started toward her. Two words stopped me.

She looked at me, dragging in a deep breath as the white light, tinged in red, powered down both her arms. "They know."

Dawson cursed as understanding rippled over the two of us. Dee shouted as I slipped out of my human form. It was like taking off a jacket. Game over. The only thing I was capable of thinking at the moment was getting those I cared for the hell out of here.

I whipped around, unleashing the Source on the driver before he had a chance to go all special Luxen on our asses.

Our kind wasn't the easiest to kill. We were like alien Energizer Bunnies. We kept getting up and we kept coming. The blow had to be catastrophic to the system. Kind of like with zombies—an analogy Kat would approve of—taking off the head was one way. A blow to the heart was another. One blast of the Source wouldn't always do it.

The driver stumbled to his feet, rearing back to unleash his own little ball of happiness, and I hit him again, and then again, right over the chest.

Multiple hits from the Source would do the trick.

White light flared over the driver, pulsing through the network of veins, and then all the light went out as the driver toppled over like a paper sack in the wind.

Dawson was taking out a lot of pent-up aggression as he went after a Luxen in officer's clothing. Kat had turned back to the limo, arms raised, flipping the crumpled car back on its wheels.

Dayum.

The tall Luxen who hardly spoke rushed out of the car, and I started toward him, easily dodging a blast of light, but drew up short as the long lengths of Kat's hair lifted off her shoulders. Static crackled into the air around her.

A blast of the Source left her hand smacking into the Luxen and launching him into the air. She didn't stop, sending another and another until he crashed back down on the hood. A shimmery, incandescent pool of liquid rapidly formed under the still form.

Oh, parts of my body got all kinds of tingly seeing that go down.

Kat whipped toward me, her eyes glowing from within. In that moment, she looked like a goddess—a goddess of vengeance.

If we weren't in the middle of a fight, I'd have you up against a tree right now.

One side of her lips curled up. *You're such a— Behind you!*

I spun, catching the Luxen's arm.

Trataaie, it seethed, branding me a traitor.

Whatever. Twisting to the side, I gripped the Luxen hard as I lifted it up and tossed it like a Frisbee of Fun. The Luxen whirled through the air, connecting with a telephone pole. Wood splintered. Lines snapped and electricity arced, sending sparks flying.

Kat rushed past me, letting loose on a Luxen who was sneaking up on Dawson while he finished off two others. The newcomer whirled on her, howling as he clutched his shoulder and then charged her.

Baby held her ground.

Dipping to the side at the last minute, she slammed her knee into his midsection and then slapped her hands down on his bowed head. The Source crackled from her palms, cascading over the Luxen in a direct headshot.

Another down.

Damn, she was freaking glorious.

By the side of the road, Sadi was up and stumbling forward. She planted a hand on the hood of a cruiser, holding herself up.

Kat stalked over, determination set in the lines of her pale face. She swooped down, picked up the damaged car door, and swung it like a baseball bat. The door caught Sadi in the chest, knocking her away from the car and down onto one leg.

"That was for being a complete bitch!" She caught Sadi in the back, pushing her forward. "And this is for even thinking it was okay to touch me." The final swing came from the front, snapping Sadi's head into next week. "And that is for even speaking Daemon's name."

Sadi toppled over onto her ass, knees folded under her, and Kat, breathing deeply, turned to me.

Damn, Kitten, you're badass, almost scary, and yet so freaking hot.
She tossed the door to the ground. "I don't think she's dead."
She looks dead.

Her lip curled up. "She's an Origin. I don't even know how to kill one of them, but I really want to find out."

Before I could process that revelation, a Luxen raced from the rear of our little caravan, wanting to get in on our party of awesome ass-kicking. Taking a step back, I looked around and tapped into the power inside me as I spied the perfect weapon.

An intense wave rippled out from me, cracking the asphalt and throwing a cruiser onto its side. Sirens went off as the roll hit the pines lining the road. Two trembled violently and then uprooted. Thick roots hung, dirt clinging to them, and the scent of rich, old soil filled the air.

Get down! I sent the message, and Kat and Dawson hit the ground like pros.

The pines flew across the road like a giant clothesline, catching and picking up the line of glowing figures, carrying them across the road into the other thick stand of pines.

Lowering my arms, I shook out the tension creeping up my shoulders and stepped forward. A few looked like smashed bugs on a windshield, covered in shimmery liquid. They wouldn't be getting up again any time soon, but the others would.

Kat climbed to her feet. Straightening, she pointed at the limo. Rolland was wiggling out, still in his human form. "Kill them!" he shouted, then got all repetitive in our native language.

There were at least seven or so standing, and as I darted toward Dawson and Kat, I knew the odds weren't looking good. We were doing some damage, taking a few out here and there, but there were still many left. Too many.

During it all, Dee stood there. She didn't get in on the fight, didn't come to our aid or theirs. She stood by the side of the road, her hands balled into fists, watching the remaining Luxen surround us. I raised my hand as I reached out to her. She had to join us. There was no way. No matter how strong the pull, we were her real family.

But she didn't move as the others drew closer.

Dee?

She looked at me and shook her head, taking a step away. I couldn't believe it. Weight pressed down on my chest as I stared at her. She couldn't be making this choice. There was no way.

The Luxen were closing in.

This is bad. Dawson's voice floated through me. *This is real bad.*

It was, but we weren't going down like this. I wrapped my hand around Kat's and she squeezed back, causing light to pulse up my arm. I pulled her closer as Dawson moved to stand in front of her. Wasn't that either of us thought she couldn't handle her own. But ultimately, we were stronger than she was. We could take more hits, and there were definitely some major hits coming our—

What sounded like a hundred large-winged birds descended on the forest surrounding us. We turned, just like the other Luxen did, as six dark-colored helicopters crested the tall pines.

They tilted as they neared the road, doors open on all except one, which circled around, sliding the doors open.

I'd seen the movie *Black Hawk Down* a few times. I knew what I was watching.

Ropes flopped over the edge, spinning down to the road. Within seconds, soldiers appeared at the doors of the helicopters, dressed in all black, faces hidden behind protective headgear. Some went for the ropes, rapelling down. Others knelt at the edges of the helicopters, aiming weapons that reminded me of a small rocket launcher.

It was the same weapon strapped along the backs of the soldiers racing down the street—PEP weapons, pulse energy projectiles. Weapons deadly to Luxen, hybrids, and Origins.

Oh hell.

{ Katy }

Every part of my body ached. Things went from *oh crap* to *FML* in a matter of seconds. We were seriously screwed every which way from Sunday.

The brothers, slipping into their human forms, pushed me back against a wrecked cruiser as soldiers dropped to the street. We didn't have a chance. Not with so many soldiers coming down like rain all around us.

Daemon's hand tightened around mine as one of the Luxen reared, sending a bolt of the Source at the nearest helicopter. The energy hit just below the propellers. Sparks flew as the helicopter veered sharply, spinning out of control and into the pines. The impact shook the ground, and the wave of heat from the fireball forced me farther back against the cruiser.

A soldier went down on one knee, hoisting his weapon. There was a blue flare at the end of the muzzle, and then light shot out, much like the Source, but it was a brilliant sheen of blue. It smacked into the Luxen, lighting him up as if he had been struck by lightning. There was a vibrant pulse, a whitish-red, and then the Luxen fell backward. As the glow dimmed from the Luxen, it was obvious that there was no life left.

All hell broke loose.

Pulses of PEP streamed across the street, as did the light from the Source. Both sides were going down quickly, toppling like a row of dominoes.

"Jesus," Daemon grunted as he pushed me to the side.

I hit Dawson's chest as a stray beam of PEP rolled into the cruiser. He pushed me around the hood and kept pushing, but I dug in my heels, straining around the cruiser so I could see Daemon.

He was moving among the abandoned cars, blue and white light flashing across his form.

"Dee!" he shouted.

My eyes scanned for his sister, finding her farther up the road near a rapidly retreating Rolland. He was heading for her, narrowly dodging blasts of light. My heart jumped in my chest as a PEP explosion hit the ground only a few inches from his feet.

"Daemon!" I started toward him but was grabbed from behind.

"You're going to get yourself killed!" Dawson yanked me against his hard chest, and as I struggled to get free, he lifted my feet clear off the ground.

I grasped his forearms, kicking out. "Let me go!"

Dawson kept pulling me down the side of the road as Daemon vaulted over a sedan, racing toward his sister. Dawson turned, and near the limo, the flashes of light were almost blinding.

"Good God," Dawson muttered in my ear. "Look at them."

For a moment, all we could do was stare. He lowered me to my feet, his grip loosening. We shared the same objective, maybe morbid, fascination.

One by one, the Luxen charged and were picked off by a blast of PEP from the soldiers who had formed an almost impenetrable line.

The Luxen were well aware of the weapon, but they didn't seem to grasp the fundamental fact that all it took was one blast. But as far as I was concerned, they could keep running straight at the soldiers all they wanted. Have at it.

However, two soldiers streamed up the middle of the road, in between the cars, searching down the Luxen who seemed to have an ounce of common sense and were making a run for it.

One of the soldiers was heading straight for Daemon, who had caught up to Dee and had her by the shoulders, shaking her. Rolland was by the side of the road, too close to them. A cluster with nothing but bad things written all over it was about to go down.

All I could think about was getting to Daemon.

I slammed my foot into Dawson's, startling him into letting go, and I broke free, racing up the side of the road, his curses following every one of my steps. Pain lanced my leg as I darted between a Hummer and a cruiser.

The soldier went down on one knee, leveling the gun.

Up ahead and in front of the soldier, Dee yanked herself free from her brother, her face contorted. "No!"

"Please—" He grabbed for her again.

"No. You don't get it!" She shoved him, and he stumbled, more out of shock than from her strength. "For once, I don't *hurt*. I don't *worry*. I want this."

Blue light pulsed at the end of the muzzle, but I couldn't pull any more of the Source. I was drained, wiped out. I pushed with everything physically in me, more than willing to go hand to hand.

I was no more than three feet from the kneeling soldier when the other soldier abruptly stepped out in front of me. Skidding to a stop, I lost my balance and landed on my butt.

The end of a PEP weapon was planted in my face.

"Don't move," came a muffled voice from behind the helmet.

Blue light flared from the other weapon, and horror zinged through me as I cried out. Daemon whirled around, shielding his sister even as she pushed free from him once more. The PEP blast shot through the cars, forging the distance between the gun and where Daemon and Dee stood, striking its target in the chest.

Behind them, Rolland was knocked back, flipping in and out of his human form. His head kicked against the road as he bellowed. The glow surrounding him throbbed once, and then there was nothing.

The soldier hadn't been aiming for Daemon—and Daemon stared, his eyes wide, chest rising and falling sharply.

Dee hesitated, and then she turned, shifting into light and disappearing among the thick pines. Blue light bounced off the tree trunks, following her retreat. Daemon started to twist around, to go after her, but stopped when he saw me. Out of the corner of my eye, I saw Dawson being guided toward where I was still sitting.

"I told you to stay put," he gritted out without taking his eyes off the soldier with the gun trained on me.

"Looks like that worked out well for you," I shot back.

The other soldier now had Daemon rounded up, herding him back to where we were. When he reached us, he slowly bent down.

"Stand still," the soldier barked.

Anger rolled off Daemon as he continued on, shooting the

soldier a look that screamed to try to stop him. The finger on the trigger spasmed as Daemon wrapped his hands under my shoulders and hauled me up. He pulled me into the shelter of his arms, angling his body so that very little of me showed.

A muscle thrummed along Dawson's jaw. "Well, crap."

Chopper wings beat at the air, and within seconds, another Black Hawk crested the pines, easing down in the middle of the street a couple yards from us, kicking up wind and causing my hair to whip out from underneath Daemon's arm as I pressed tighter against him.

Exhausted and beat up, drained like a twisted sponge, I knew we were done. The three of us. If they opened fire, it would be over. A sick feeling crawled up my throat. I wanted to close my eyes, but that seemed like a coward's way out.

There was the sound of metal grinding, and then the door to the helicopter slid open, slowly revealing who was kneeling inside, staring at us. Waiting. Like always.

Nancy Husher.

10

{ Daemon }

There were moments in my life when I seriously couldn't believe things could get any more fucked up than they already were, especially with Dee running off to join the damn Luxen circus.

But each time, I was proven, yet again, how wrong that thought was.

Nancy stared down at us with dark eyes, her face devoid of any emotion, a total blank slate.

Dawson swore and started to shift, but Nancy spoke before he could do something that would end with a lot of explosions and general mayhem.

"If you want to live," she said, voice clipped, "you'll get in this damn helicopter. Now."

We really didn't have much of a choice. Either we put up a fight and got taken down with one of their weapons, or we got in the helicopter. Then what? We were out of the frying pan and smack-dab in the middle of the fire. But one option most likely involved dying now, while the other was probably dying later. Later gave us some time to figure a way out of this latest mess.

I shot Dawson a look that said, *Simmer it down*, and for a moment, I thought he was going to say to hell with it, but his shoulders squared, and then he hoisted himself up into the helicopter.

Turning to Kat, I met her eyes, and the wariness in her gray gaze, the exhaustion and pain, were tinged with fear. It cut me deep seeing that and knowing there wasn't anything I could do at this moment to change it.

I bent my head and brushed my lips across hers. "It'll be fine."

Kat nodded.

"How cute," Nancy said.

My lip curled as I turned my gaze to her. "Remember how it ended last time you thought you had us under control?"

A flicker of anger crawled across her otherwise stoic face. "Trust me. It's not something I've forgotten."

"Good," I growled, hoisting Kat to where Dawson waited just inside. He pulled her toward him as I leaped in, crowding Nancy. The woman backed up, dropping down onto a bench as she met my stare. "But this time will end differently."

"Will it?"

I got all up in her face and lowered my voice so that only she could hear as the chopper propellers blocked out my words to anyone else. "Yeah, because this time, I will make sure you're dead."

Nancy stiffened as I drew back and reached for Kat. My brother handed her to me, and Nancy said nothing. Instead, she tipped her head back and closed her eyes. The woman had bigger balls than I did, all things considered.

I tucked Kat against me as Dawson sat on her other side. Two of the soldiers jumped in, taking the seats beside Nancy.

One leaned back, motioning with his arm to the pilot to take us up.

The moment the bird left the ground, Kat squeezed her eyes shut. A shudder rocked her as she balled her fist into my shirt. Her heart was pounding too fast. She wasn't a huge fan of flying, so being in a copter probably had her one step from full freak-out mode.

Keeping my eyes trained on Nancy and her little minions, I lifted Kat up and sat her in my lap. I wrapped my arms around her, curling one hand against the back of her head, positioning her so that her heart rested against mine.

One of the soldiers propped his gun between his legs and reached up, pulling off his helmet. Shoving a hand through his sandy-brown hair, he worked out a kink in his neck as he opened his eyes.

Amethyst.

Freaking Origin.

Obviously one of Nancy's successful products, like Archer and Luc. I couldn't pick up jack shit from the guy, but I hadn't picked up anything from Archer before he revealed what he was. The same with Luc. I always knew there was something off about the kid but could never put my finger on it. And Sadi had felt like a Luxen to me.

Another Origin talent, I assumed, seamlessly blending into something that they weren't. There was a lot about them I didn't know, and right now, didn't give a crap about.

Lowering my head, I kept a steady watch on the three across from me as I spoke into Kat's ear. I talked absolute nonsense. The last *Ghost Hunters* show I'd seen and how I wanted to check out the abandoned asylum one day. I told her about the time I'd convinced Adam that I'd seen the Mothman one night when I'd been out scouting for Arum. Then, I reminded her that with Halloween only a month or so away, we needed to find us Gizmo and gremlin outfits. I talked to her about anything, trying to keep her mind off the fact that we were winging through the air, heading to God knows where. It worked to an extent. Her heart rate slowed a little and she loosened her death grip some.

No one talked during the ride except what I was saying to Kat. Wasn't like you could really hear anything unless you were right up on someone. The drone of the helicopter traveled through our bodies, making it feel like we were in a steel drum.

I had no idea how long we were in the air. Maybe an hour or so before the copter started to tilt to the side, and I was almost positive Kat started praying under her breath. Any other time I would've laughed, but wariness settled into every cell.

What were we about to face now? Being locked up? As I watched Nancy open her eyes and smooth her hands across her black pants, I doubted she wanted to keep us alive. Her obsession with breeding Luxen and hybrids to create the perfect race could only go so far. She had a huge bone to pick with us. After all, we'd broken out, taking down a lot of soldiers; had a hand in destroying an entire city; and had exposed what we were before the Luxen came.

Hell, what we did might've had something to do with why the others chose this time to arrive.

Then again, if she wanted us dead, it would've been an easy feat to carry out on the road outside of Coeur d'Alene, so I had no clue what she was up to.

The helicopter landed, and the doors were drawn open immediately. As Kat leaned away, I got my first glimpse of the outside. All I saw was a tall chain-link fence, and beyond that, a gray mountain in the distance. Maybe the Rockies?

One soldier climbed down, motioning us out. Dawson went and then Kat. We kept her between us, and the moment my feet hit the ground, I grabbed her hand. Getting a better look around, I didn't like what I was seeing.

It was obvious we were at a military base, a huge one that spread as far as I could see. Row after row of bunkers and planes and tanks and other major inconveniences when it came to forming an escape plan. Up ahead, there was a wide and tall U-shaped building.

And a whole crapload of soldiers.

Some dressed in fatigues. Others wearing black like the soldiers on the road. I had a feeling they were extra special.

"Welcome to Malmstrom Air Force Base," Nancy said, stalking past us. As we passed the lines of soldiers, I expected them to salute Nancy. They didn't. "The whole base is under lockdown. No one gets in or out, including the Luxen."

My eyes narrowed on her back.

God, that woman had a bull's-eye on her head. Not just for what she did to Kat, but also for my brother, for Beth, and for every other life her twisted hands had touched.

I didn't get off on the idea of snuffing out someone's life, even someone like her. But damn if I wasn't looking forward to the moment when I paid her back tenfold for everything.

"Why did you bring us here?" Dawson demanded.

Nancy kept walking at a rapid clip. "You'll find that the base is wired to deal with your kind."

Meaning there was weaponized onyx and diamond and a ton of other delightful little things that Daedalus had whipped up over the years.

"That doesn't answer my question," Dawson replied.

Nancy stopped in front of double steel doors. We obviously weren't going in through the main entrance. She turned to the side, looking back at us, and for the first time since I'd known the woman, I saw something in her dark eyes I'd never seen before.

I saw fear.

What the . . . ?

The steel doors opened, metal grinding as they spread wide, revealing the brightly lit tunnel and one person standing in the center. Hands shoved in the pockets of faded, ripped-up jeans.

Kat recoiled in surprise, bumping into me.

"It's about time you guys got here. I was getting really bored." Luc rocked back on the heels of his boots, grinning widely. "But I think you're missing one, Nancy."

Nancy stiffened as she drew in a deep breath through her nostrils. "Dee left with the Luxen. She's under their control."

The smile slipped off his face. "Well, that sucks."

"Sucks" didn't begin to cover it, but I had no idea what to do with any of this. I shook my head as I stared at him. "What the hell is going on, Luc?"

He arched a brow. "How about a thank-you first? Maybe? I mean, I did get your asses out of trouble, didn't I? I really would like a thank-you. Maybe a hug? I'm feeling kind of needy."

"Where's Beth?" Dawson stepped forward, seeming to forget that Nancy was *right* there. Not that he appeared to care. "Please tell me she's not—"

"Calm down," Luc replied, pulling his hands out of his pockets. "She's doing well. She's actually here. I'm sure one of these helpful . . . people"—he gestured at the soldiers in fatigues outside the doors—"that I really don't know what the hell their job is can take you to where she's at."

Dawson started to turn as one of the soldiers stepped up. I lurched forward, grabbing his shoulder. "Wait a minute," I cut in before my brother could run off blindly. "What in the hell are you doing here with her, Luc?"

Luc's smile returned. "It's okie dokie smokie, Daemon. No need to Hulk out on anyone. You're safe here. Nancy won't be a problem. Will you?" he asked the tight-lipped woman.

She looked like she had something really uncomfortable shoved up a really awkward place.

Her lack of response didn't soothe me, but even if she had said no, I wouldn't have been convinced. I didn't budge. Neither did Kat, but Dawson was ready to go Road Runner on us.

Luc sighed as he raised his hands. "Look, this is not a trap, a test, or a drill. Archer's here, too. He's waiting for us, actually, and I'm more than willing to explain everything to you, but I'm not doing it standing here. Not when I found a Lunchables just a few minutes before you guys showed up, and I'm ready to make myself a delicious buffet of ham and cheese on crackers."

I stared at him.

"What? It's the kind that has Oreo cookies included," he replied. "That shit is banging."

"God, you had *so* much potential," Nancy muttered under her breath.

Luc turned violet eyes on her and spoke in a voice that was barely audible to those around us. "And you are really wearing on my last nerve. I don't think you want that, do you?"

Holy crap if that woman didn't turn as white as a sheet of brand-spanking-new paper. I glanced back at Kat, seeing if she'd noticed, and her wide eyes told me she had.

I still hesitated.

"The Lunchables also comes with a Capri Sun," Luc added. "Fruit punch. That Lunchables of Awesome isn't joking around."

Man, no matter what I did or decided from here on out,

there was a risk, and I never knew where I stood with Luc. I don't think anyone did. The fact was that we really didn't have much of a choice.

My gaze settled on Luc. "If you're screwing with us, I swear to—"

"God, Jesus, and the Holy Ghost that you're going to kill me or whatever," he cut in. "Got it. And although I might not appear appropriately threatened, I am. So, kids, can we move this group along?"

Drawing in a shallow breath, I let go of Dawson's shoulder. The soldier waited until Dawson joined him. Nancy stepped aside, allowing them both to pass through. I didn't like it, but he had one focus—Bethany. He didn't look back, not once.

Just like Dee hadn't looked back.

Thinking of my sister slammed weight down on my shoulders, and I let out another breath as I reached for Kat's hand. She was already there, threading her fingers through mine.

"All right," I said. "Let's do this."

Luc clapped his hands together as he pivoted on his heel. We headed down the tunnel, veering off to the right, when Dawson had gone in the other direction. The place reminded me of Area 51. Wide halls. A lot of closed doors. Strange antiseptic smell.

In some ways, it was better than being with the other Luxen. At least this was the enemy we knew and all that jazz.

Luc kneed open a set of double doors and caught one side with his hand. Nancy followed him in, and like he'd claimed, at one side of a long table was a Lunchables. Archer sat at the other side, his legs kicked up, arms folded behind his neck.

When the door shut behind us and only Nancy had come in, I knew something really strange was up. Before, the woman had traveled with an entourage.

"You're okay," Kat breathed out as she broke free, limping around the side of the table. "I've been so worried."

Archer pulled his long legs off the table and rose. A second later, he enveloped Kat in a hug. "I told you to stay where you were. But oh no, you didn't listen." He looked over her head at me. "I totally told her to stay."

Luc scowled. "Why didn't I get a hug?"

He was ignored.

"Sorry." Kat's voice was muffled. "I had to, you know?"

"I get it. But damn, girl, it might not have worked out so well," Archer replied. "Could've all gone to shit, and then who would take me to Olive Garden so I can try out the endless breadsticks?"

Kat laughed, but the sound was thick and choked.

I stood where I was, telling myself that the ugly heat invading my veins was indigestion and not jealousy. Totally not that, because Archer had nothing on me.

But did he need to hug her that long? And that hard? Come the hell on.

Archer's purple gaze met mine over her shoulder. *Yeah. Yeah, I kind of do.*

My eyes narrowed. *I still don't like you.*

Grinning, he pulled back, relinquishing his embrace, and then reached for a chair. "You look like you're about to fall down. Why don't you grab a seat?"

Kat did look worn out as she eased into one of the metal folding chairs. "What's going on, guys? Why are you all here and with *her*?"

Archer glanced at me again as he sat. "Where's Dee?"

The pressure increased as I moved to the seat beside Kat. As I sat, tension flickered across Archer's face, gathering around his eyes. "She . . ." I shook my head, at a loss as to how to explain what was up with her.

His hands clenched together atop the table. "She's not . . . she's not *gone*, is she?"

"No," Kat spoke up. "She's not the same. She's kind of batting for the other team right now."

Archer opened his mouth, but as he sat back, he snapped it shut. I wasn't sure how much they knew about everything, but I couldn't get into that stuff until I knew what the hell was going on here.

I turned to Luc, arching a brow as I watched him stack slices of cheese and ham on a cracker. "What's going on?"

"Nancy's going to play nice," he said, nudging the cheese onto the center.

She had sat next to Luc and looked like she wanted to start breaking things. Her gaze met mine. "Trust me, if I had a choice right now, you'd all be dead."

Luc tsked softly. "Now, that isn't very nice."

I didn't understand. As Luc chomped down on his snack, I leaned forward. "What's stopping you from taking us out?"

"Let's just say everyone has an Achilles' heel, and I found hers." Luc set about making another cracker. "It's not pretty. Not something even I wanted to stoop to. But oh wells."

That didn't tell us jack.

Kat shifted closer. "How did you all end up together?"

"I made it back to the cabin. And after I told Luc what went down at the store, we considered hitting the road," Archer explained. "But we didn't get the chance before Daedalus showed up."

Nancy's lips formed a tight line.

"She thought she had us." Luc plopped a mini Oreo on top

of his ham-and-cheese cracker, and well, that was just sick. "But—"

"You said you were working on that," Kat said, glancing at a silent Nancy. "A way to deal with Daedalus? You found something?"

"I'm a very well-connected person," Luc said around a mouthful of junk. "When they kicked down our door and Nancy strode in as if she was the biggest, baddest thing this side of the country, I proved just how well connected I am."

"How?" I watched Nancy.

"Like I said, everyone has an Achilles' heel. Nancy's is pretty obvious." Luc stabbed a straw through his Capri Sun. "There's only one thing that she cares about in this whole entire world, that she'd throw her family in front of a tank for—if she even has a family, because I'm pretty sure she was hatched from an egg—and it's those baby Origins."

"Baby Origins?" I repeated.

"Micah? Those?" Kat asked.

Luc nodded. "Yep."

"Fun fact is that most of the hybrids and older Origins, the ones who left with her to retrieve you guys, aren't really thrilled with the Daedalus treatment." Archer smiled, but there was no humor. "The ones who were loyal, well . . ."

"Bastards," Nancy hissed. "Do you know how long it took to cultivate something that was so loyal and so tested—?"

"*Something?*" Kat's voice rose. "See, that's why you're so messed up. The hybrids and the Origins, they aren't a *something*. They are living, breathing people."

"You don't understand." Nancy turned a dark look on Kat. "You've never created anything."

"And you have? Just because you forced two people to have children and then ripped them away doesn't mean you created anything." Anger tightened Kat's lips. "You're not their mother. You aren't anything but a monster to them."

Something akin to pain flickered across Nancy's face.

"Either way, they mean a lot to her, and I know where they're being kept," Luc explained, finishing up his last cracker. "Tell them what the bigwigs wanted, Fancy Nancy."

She gripped the edges of the table. "After the arrival of the Luxen, I was told to dismantle the Daedalus project."

"Dismantle?" whispered Kat, and I already knew what she meant. I think Kat did, too, but didn't want to believe it.

"I was told to clear out the program, erase everything," Nancy explained.

"Oh my God," Kat murmured.

I closed my eyes. Dismantle. Erase everything. In other words, she'd been given an order from someone higher up than her in the food chain to wipe out any proof of the program. "They wanted you to kill them?"

She exhaled noisily as she nodded. "Plausible deniability, they said. That the public couldn't know that we had not only been aware of alien life-forms but had been working with them for decades."

"Jesus." I rubbed a hand across my brow. "Not just the kids, right? Every Luxen who was in there of their own free will? The ones who were allowing you to do tests? And even the ones who hadn't assimilated to your standards?"

"Yes," she responded.

"Of course, she had no problem wiping them out. They are expendable after all, at least according to her. But those Origins?" Luc shook his head slowly. "She couldn't do it."

My brows rose. Did the woman have a heart somewhere in her chest?

Luc laughed as he picked up on my thoughts. "No, Daemon,

she doesn't have a heart. Not in the way a normal person would grow attached to a classroom full of little freaky, and yet oddly adorable, kids. She didn't want all of her work to go to waste, so she moved them out of Area 51, and she thought she had them hidden."

"But she didn't?" Kat tucked her hair behind her ear.

He shook his head. "As I said, I'm pretty damn well connected. I know where they are and I know how badly Nancy wants to return to them when this is all over, given that any of us are still alive, and cultivate the little freaks into big freaks."

"Like I did with you?" Nancy asked.

Luc flipped her off. "Nancy knows that if she harms one hair on any of our bodies, even looks at us in a way that I find annoying . . ."

The casual indifference that he always rocked slipped off his face like a mask falling away. He leaned forward, his eyes glowing like purple diamonds, as Nancy turned to him.

In that moment, I was seeing the Luc who caused grown men to piss themselves, the Luc I didn't want to be on the wrong side of, and that Luc was downright disturbing-looking as his features sharpened.

"She knows I will have every single one of them killed in seconds," he said, his voice low. "And if my people don't hear from me, even if I can't make it to a phone in time, they are all going to die. And then Nancy has nothing."

Good God.

Kat stared at the kid like she'd never seen him before.

There was no doubt in my mind that Luc was capable of doing something like that. As messy and wrong as it was, he'd do it, but I also didn't believe that he'd ever let those kids fall back into Nancy's hands.

And I wondered if she really believed that. Then again,

what choice did she have? "Why didn't you just kill her?" I asked.

"We kind of need her," Archer explained. "At least, we need the government, someplace safe until . . . well, hopefully there's an 'until' and not a forever. We also needed to get you all out and we—"

"As freaking awesome as we are," Luc threw out, slipping back into the not-so-disturbing Origin mafioso.

Archer sent him a bland look. "Going up against that many Luxen would prove difficult. Right now, she's a necessary evil."

"And boy, do we mean evil." Luc grinned.

Sitting back, I thrust my hand through my hair. Looked like Luc had Nancy on a leash. There was so much running through my head.

"What now?" Kat asked, drawing my stare. "We need to get Dee away from them."

That made me want to get her name tattooed on my freaking forehead.

"And we need to find a way to stop what is happening, what—"

And that made me want to lock her in a closet or something.

"What you need is rest and probably something to eat," Archer jumped in, glancing at me. "Both of you. That is the priority."

"There are things that are going down. Stuff I'm sure Nancy will be happy to share with you, but that's for a different day." Luc reached over, patting Nancy's hand like she was a small child. "But there's something else she does need to tell you."

Nancy's jaw jutted out.

I smirked. "I doubt there's anything she can tell me I'll give a crap about."

"Actually." Luc drew out the word. "I think you and Katy will care about this."

Kat tensed. "What now?"

"Tell them," he goaded, and when Nancy didn't speak, he said in a hard voice, "Tell them the truth."

Oh shit. My stomach took a drop off the deep end. "The truth about what?"

Nancy's lips pursed.

Archer stood, folding his arms like he was about to be the muscle in the room, and I really didn't like where any of this was heading. "What the hell? Just spit it out." My patience was reed thin.

Nancy took a deep breath and then squared her shoulders. "As you know, Daedalus worked on many serums before we had any amount of success, and in some cases . . ." She paused, looking pointedly at Luc, who smiled brightly. "The successes proved to be failures in the end. There was the Daedalus serum, which was given to Beth and Blake and so on."

Kat drew in a sharp breath at the name of the bastard I hoped was rotting in a special corner of hell. I hated the mere mention of him in her presence. Kat had taken him out, in defense, but I knew that what she'd had to do still got to her.

"Then, of course, there was the Prometheus serum," she said, her eyes lighting up like a kid catching the Easter Bunny hiding eggs. "The serum that was given to the men you mutated."

"You mean the men you forced to be mutated?" I challenged.

"The *volunteers* you mutated were given the Prometheus serum, just like the hybrids that the most recent batch of Origins were created from," she explained, surprising me.

"Wait," Kat chimed in. "You were just testing out that serum when we were there."

Luc shook his head. "What she means is that humans who were accidentally mutated on and off throughout the years were given the Prometheus serum in test batches. Not ones like Daemon mutated, but people like you and Beth and anyone else out there who was healed by a Luxen."

Confusion poured into me. "So you were testing the Prometheus serum for the first time on forced mutations?"

"Like I said, they *volunteered*," she corrected.

I was about to volunteer my foot upside someone's head. "Okay. This is great info, but basically useless to me."

A smirk graced Nancy's lips for the first time since our lovely reunion. "The Prometheus serum is different from the Daedalus serum. It ensures that the mutated human, that the hybrid, is not connected to the Luxen."

My head cocked to the side. "Okay?"

"When you healed Kat, and Dr. Michaels alerted us when she fell ill, we didn't use the Daedalus serum."

Kat stiffened. "What? He said—"

"Do you think he really knew what we were handing him?" Her dark gaze fixed on Kat. "He believed what we told him and that was it. He was given the Prometheus serum, which is what was given to you." Her attention flicked back to me. "It was the same thing given to those you also mutated, Daemon."

"No." I leaned forward. "That doesn't make any sense. When Kat was shot—"

"You got sick. Thought you were dying? Oh, save us from the dramatics." Her eyes rolled. "It's because you truly bonded with her on an emotional level. You love her." She spat out the L word like it was an STD. "Yeah, we've figured that out. The whole true want and need crap."

"Well, yay for you, but I was dying."

She shook her head. "You were weakened and you were

ill, but if she had died, you would've survived. You would've gotten better. Life would've gone on. You just didn't get to that point because obviously someone else healed her."

Kat gasped.

I stood. The floor under my feet seemed to shift. I locked my knees together. I was rocked through and through, almost unable to believe her.

Nancy took a deep breath. "Your lives aren't joined like you think they are. If one of you dies, the other will feel it—feel everything, down to the last breath, the last heartbeat—but the other one will take another breath and their heart will beat again."

11

{ Katy }

After that little bomb was dropped on us, no one really had anything else to say. We'd reached our limit when it came to lies and chatting it out with everyone.

My brain was on overload, running circles around what Nancy had just told us, what Dee was doing, where my mom and friends were, if Luc really had control over Nancy, and what the future held for all of us.

I was done.

Daemon was done.

Archer made a pit stop on the way to showing us our room. Rapping his knuckles on the door once, he eased it open without waiting for an answer. Luckily none of us was scarred for life.

Dawson was standing at the foot of the bed, near where Beth sat. We were probably interrupting something, but the smile that transformed Beth's face as Archer stepped aside and we walked in caused me to trip over my feet.

Daemon glanced back at me, brows arched, but I was

focused on Beth. She . . . she looked *normal* sitting on the bed, cross-legged, hands resting in her lap. Weariness still marked her pretty face. Her skin was too pale and the shadows under her eyes stark, but her gaze was clear and focused.

"I'm so happy to see you guys," she said, placing one hand on her lower belly. "I was so worried."

"We're doing well," Daemon responded, glancing at his brother. Although we were standing in front of his brother and Beth, who appeared unharmed, tension radiated off of Daemon. "And everything is fine with you all?"

His brother nodded as he sat beside her. "Yeah. Beth's been to the doctor on base already." He curved a hand around her knee. "They seemed to have experience with this. Kind of weird, but I guess it's a good thing."

Daemon shot a look in Archer's direction, and then his gaze settled on Beth. "The doctor treated you right?"

"She—Doctor Ramsey—was really kind and said that . . . well, the pregnancy is progressing as it should. She said that I needed to rest and I have to start taking vitamins." Pausing, she gestured at a dresser. On it were three large bottles that were like the ones Archer and I had tried to obtain for her. She followed my gaze. "Thank you for going out that day. You risked a lot. Again."

I blinked, not realizing at first that she was talking to me. I shrugged. "No biggie. I wish we could've gotten them for you then."

"It was a big deal," Dawson corrected. "You and Archer could've . . ." He trailed off as his brother stiffened. "Yeah, you know what could've happened."

"But nothing bad happened, did it?" Archer leaned against the door, folding his arms. "It worked out in the end."

"We're all here." Beth's brows pinched as she ducked her

chin. "Well, almost all of us. Not Dee. I'm . . . I'm sorry." She peeked up at Daemon, who was now staring at the wall behind the bed.

"We're going to get her back," I said, and dammit, we had to. We just needed to figure out how.

"So . . ." Archer cleared his throat. "Do you guys know if it's a boy or a girl?"

The change of subject couldn't come at a better time, and I swore Dawson's cheeks colored a little. "We don't know," he said, turning to Beth. "The doc said something about an ultrasound?"

"This week," she replied, resting her cheek on his shoulder. "They want to do an ultrasound. It might be too early to tell."

A small smile appeared on Archer's face. "If it's a boy, you should name him Archer."

I giggled.

Daemon faced the Origin. "They should name him Daemon."

"Daemon 2.0? I don't know if the world can handle that." Dawson laughed under his breath, shaking his head. "Honestly, I don't think that's something we've really thought about at this point."

"No," she agreed. "But I guess we need to."

Their eyes met then, and it was like they forgot that anyone else was in the room. It was just them. I understood the kind of connection they had. I had it with Daemon, but I wondered if we looked as love-struck as they did.

"You do," Archer commented softly.

Ah, well, that was kind of embarrassing.

"Yes, it is," he added.

I shot him a look over my shoulder as Daemon growled, "Get out of her head."

Archer grinned. "Sorry. Can't help it."

Rolling my eyes, I didn't intervene as the two of them started bickering, and then it was time to give Beth and Dawson some privacy. After leaving their room, we were given a room that reminded me too much of the ones back in Area 51. So much so, I couldn't repress the shudder that worked its way down my spine.

"There's basically a town on this base," Archer said from the doorway. "Houses, a school, shops, and even a medical facility. There's a mess hall one level up. I grabbed you some sweats earlier and stashed them in the dresser."

Daemon nodded as he scanned the room, his gaze dipping over the wall-mounted TV, the door that led to a bathroom, and the single dresser and metal desk.

"Is it really safe here?" I asked, trying to comb my fingers through the mess that was my hair.

"As safe as any place is right now. Definitely the best place for Beth, all things considered."

Yeah, having a medical facility nearby was good for her.

Daemon folded his arms. "Will Luc really kill those kids?"

"Luc is capable of anything."

Sitting on the edge of the bed, I stretched out my aching leg. I couldn't picture Luc doing that. Not because I didn't think he would, but because I just didn't want to believe he'd do such a thing.

"And he'd really hand those kids over to her in the end?" he asked.

Archer lifted one shoulder. "Like I said, Luc is capable of anything, especially when it comes to getting what he wants. Lucky for all of us, he wants us alive." He pushed off the doorframe. "There's a lot more to discuss. So I'll be back later."

As he started to leave, something struck me, seizing me up. "Wait. Did you bring any of our stuff with you?"

He nodded. "I brought everything that appeared important, including those papers."

Those papers. I let out the breath I didn't realize I was holding. The papers were our marriage certificate and fake IDs. Although the marriage wasn't technically real, it was legit to Daemon and me.

"Thank you," I said.

He nodded. With that, Archer stepped out and closed the door behind him. I strained to hear a lock turning, but when that didn't happen, my shoulders sagged with relief.

Daemon turned to me. "You thought we'd be locked in here, didn't you?"

My gaze traveled over his striking face, lingering on the faint shadows forming under his eyes. "I really don't know what to think. I trust Archer and Luc, but I've trusted a lot of people and that turned out bad. I hope that doesn't make me crazy."

"I think trusting anyone makes us all a little crazy."

I watched him move around the room, stopping in front of the dresser and inspecting what was inside, then moving to the desk. He raised a hand and rubbed his fingers through the mess of dark brown waves. Each step was filled with strain.

Knowing that his thoughts must be with his sister, I felt an ache in my chest for him. I knew how it felt to lose someone who was actually still around. Not an hour went by that I didn't think of my mom. "We'll get Dee back. I don't know how yet, but we will."

He slowly lowered his hand, but his shoulders tensed as he turned to me. "If we really are safe here, you'd leave this to go into a nest of vipers to get my sister out?"

"Do you really have to ask that question? You know I would."

Daemon walked to where I sat. "I wouldn't want you to put yourself in danger."

"I'm sure as hell not staying behind if you run off to go find her."

One side of his lips kicked up, and it was amazing how a simple half smile could twist my insides. "I didn't think you would, and I wouldn't leave you here. Where I go, you go, and vice versa. You're not getting rid of me for any length of time that easily."

"Glad we actually agree on that." Not too long ago, Daemon would've tried to shelter me, but I think he'd learned that didn't work out very well.

This was the first time in days that we were together and could speak openly with each other, and as I watched him, I knew there was something beyond his sister on his mind. With as many things as we had to stress over, it would be like looking for an apple in a pile of apples.

"What?" I asked.

Our gazes collided and held, and I drew in an unsteady breath. Those emerald eyes, which were such a bright, unreal green, never failed to catch my attention. Daemon was beautiful in a way that didn't seem possible, but that beauty ran deep, beyond the skin that really wasn't his true form, and into the very core of his being. When I first met him, I hadn't believed that. Now I knew better.

His thick lashes lowered. "Just thinking about what Nancy said about the serum—about us."

"About us not being connected like we thought we were?"

"Yeah."

"This is good, though." I smiled when he looked up. I didn't know what to think, other than that our lives really not being joined together had to be good news and that it didn't change anything between us. "I mean, don't get me wrong. I'm ticked that Nancy lied to us, that she tested something so volatile on me, but it's . . . it's okay. I know I can kick some butt and tap into the Source, but you are stronger than me. I'm the weaker—"

"You're not weak, Kitten. You've never been weak, before or after the mutation."

"Thanks for that, but you know what I mean. Let's be realistic. I'm a liability to an extent when it comes to fighting. I can only go for so long before I tucker out. You really don't."

"I get it." He thrust his hands through his hair again, frowning.

I searched his face. "Then, what?"

"It's just that . . ." Daemon knelt down in front of me, his brows knitting together. He reached out and draped his hands over my knees. "It's just that since the moment I realized what healing you meant, or what I thought it meant, I never thought I'd face a day without you. That I'd never have to worry about going on if you weren't there. And I'm not trying to make this into some kind of *Romeo and Juliet* bullshit, but now I know there's a chance of that and it . . . it fucking terrifies me, Kat. It really does."

I blinked back a sudden rush of tears as I cupped his cheeks. The slight stubble tickled my thumbs. "The idea of you not being there terrifies me, too."

He leaned in and pressed his forehead against mine. "I know it's good news, and I know it's stupid. I should be more scared of dying in general than not, but—"

"I know." I closed my eyes and pressed my lips against his. "Let's just not die on each other, okay?"

Daemon's chuckle teased my lips. "I like that plan."

"You won't let anything happen to me," I told him, resting

my hands on his shoulders as I drew back. "And I won't let anything happen to you."

"That's my Kitten," he murmured as he looked me over. "Speaking of not letting anything happen, how are you feeling?"

"Tired. Some sugar would be nice." For some reason, eating sugar helped after using the Source. It always reminded me of Harry Potter.

"I'll make sure Archer grabs some of that when he comes back." He stood and then climbed on the bed so he was sitting behind me. "But for now . . ."

He grabbed my hips and tugged me back against his chest.

"What are you doing?" When his right hand slid onto my upper thigh, my breath caught. "Oh."

His deep laugh rumbled through me. "Believe it or not, I'm not thinking inappropriate thoughts."

I turned my head to look back at him, eyebrow raised.

The wicked half grin turned my heart to mush. "Okay. Ninety-nine-point-nine percent of the time I am thinking something that would turn the tips of your ears pink."

"And you're not now?"

His lips pursed. "Yeah, all right. A hundred percent of the time, but I actually do have totally appropriate reasons for touching you."

"Uh-huh." I rested my head against his cheek. And then I felt his hand slide over the top of my right thigh. "What are you doing?"

"Taking care of you."

Heat from his fingers radiated out over my thigh. "You don't need to do this. It's just a scratch."

"More like a flesh wound, and you've been limping around since it happened. I should've done it while we were in the helicopter, but I was too busy keeping you from throwing yourself into the cockpit."

"I wasn't *that* bad." A small smile pulled at my lips. "But thank you for that. I was afraid I'd hurl all over you."

"I'm glad you didn't," he replied drily.

Once the dull ache in my thigh eased until it was nothing but a memory, I started to pull away, because healing me could take its toll on him, but instead of letting me go, he scooted off the bed with me in front of him. The moment his feet hit the floor, he scooped me up in his arms.

I let out a startled yelp as I swung wide eyes on him. "Whoa. What are you doing now?"

"Still taking care of you." He started toward the bathroom, his eyes heavily hooded, but there was a mischievous tilt to his lips. "I've just realized we both could clean up."

That was the truth. Once again, I was spotted with grime and dried blood, and so was Daemon.

He took us into a surprisingly large bathroom, gently putting me down in front of a tub. It wasn't as big as the one back in the mayor's mansion, but it still seemed abnormally large.

Flicking on the low lights, he turned to me, wiggling his fingers. I stepped toward him. He grinned. "Closer."

I made it another foot.

"Lift your arms."

Telling him I was capable of undressing myself was on the tip of my tongue, but nervousness swallowed the words. I lifted my arms and he pulled off the ruined sweater, stopping to ease my hair out before dropping it onto the floor. He didn't speak as he flicked the tiny pearl button on the pants and then tugged them off.

I placed my hand on his shoulder to balance myself as I snagged a leg free. A flush swept from my cheeks down my entire body. No matter all that we'd shared together, I was still shy around him. Not sure why, but maybe it was because he didn't seem to have a single flaw while I had a very human body full of them.

The last remaining piece of clothing also hit the floor, and then I was standing there completely in the buff, with him fully dressed. I folded my arms across my chest as he reached around me, turning on the water.

Warm steam immediately poured into the bathroom. As he straightened, his lips brushed the curve of my cheek, sending a shiver down my spine.

I'd never seen a guy get undressed as quickly as Daemon, and before I knew it, I was face-to-face with his corded pecs. My gaze drifted down tightly rolled abs and then it moved lower—

Two fingertips pressed under my chin, guiding my gaze up to a pair of startling green eyes that seemed to carry a sheen of white behind them. "Eyes up here, or I'll start feeling like man candy."

My cheeks heated, but I laughed. "Whatever."

He winked after he drew back the curtain. "After you."

I'd never showered with a guy before. Obviously. But even if I had, I don't think it would even remotely touch showering with Daemon Black.

My hands trembled as I stepped under the hot spray of water. A second later, he was in the tub, too, and it suddenly didn't feel very big at all.

His hands were gentle, the pressure barely there as he turned me so my back was against the spray. Drawing in a stuttered breath, I lifted my head. I expected him to kiss me and do something that would most definitely make my knees go weak, but that's not what he did.

His eyes locked with mine, and he carefully scooped the soaked strands of my hair over my shoulders. Then, his hands skimmed up my upper arms and coasted over my back.

His arms folded around me, drawing me against his chest, sealing our bodies together. I squeezed my eyes shut as a different kind of need slammed into me. The rising swell of emotion went beyond the physical, and as he held me so tightly that there was no space between us at all, I knew it was the same for him.

I don't know how long we stood like that, just holding each other as the water beat down on us, but there was something intensely powerful between us that transcended words.

My knees went weak when he dropped his cheek to the top of my head and somehow managed to hold me closer.

God, I loved Daemon. I was *in* love with him as much as I had been the very first time I recognized what that burning sensation was, what that almost electric shock every time we touched meant.

It was hard looking back and thinking about all the time we'd wasted fighting what was between us, fighting each other, especially when the future looked appallingly short, but I couldn't focus on that now, because we were together. It didn't matter how many hours, days, months, or years we had stretched out in front of us; we'd always be together.

This kind of love was the real deal, stronger than a whole planet full of psycho aliens and an entire government.

We stood together for a long time, wrapped around each other, before we actually made good use of the shower—good, *appropriate* use of the shower. But bathing with Daemon was like . . . well, bathing with Daemon. We finally climbed out, dried off, and changed into the sweats and oversize cotton shirts, which weren't so oversized on Daemon. The white shirt stretched taut over his shoulders, followed each dip of his abs. My skin was overly sensitive even though there'd been no shenanigans going down in the bathroom.

I'd found a comb and sat in the middle of the bed untangling all the knots, while Daemon turned on the TV, settling on a news station. Tossing the remote onto the foot of the bed, he sat behind me.

He took the comb from my fingers. "Let me do this."

I made a face but sat still as he started to work the comb through my hair. I glanced at the TV, saw another city in ruins, and then looked away. I didn't want to think about that, because I didn't know where my mom was or how my friends back home were faring during all of this.

Daemon was surprisingly apt at combing out the knots. "Is there anything you can't do?" I asked.

He laughed. "You know the answer to that."

I grinned.

Once he was finished with my hair, I felt the edge of the comb poke me in the lower back. Brows raised, I glanced over my shoulder at him. "What?"

He leaned in, kissing me softly. The edges of his damp hair brushed my cheeks as he slanted his head, deepening the kiss until my heart was pounding.

I placed my hand over his chest, above his heart, and felt it match the rhythm of my own. My gaze lifted, and our eyes met. Somehow we ended up stretched out across the bed, my back curled against his front.

"I'm not finished healing you," he said, voice gruff. His fingers trailed around a tender spot along my temple.

I closed my eyes, letting him do what he wanted. After all, it made him feel better. But the healing warmth slowly turned into something else when the tips of his fingers slipped down my arm, under my shirt, and across my stomach. There was nothing between his skin and mine.

"You've been using the Source a lot." His hand flattened against my lower stomach, his pinkie finding a way under the loose band on my sweats. "It's had to have worn you out."

Another finger traveled under the band, and I wasn't sure I was that worn out. My entire consciousness was focused on his hand—the weight and warmth of it, the exact positioning.

"Kitten?"

"Hmm?"

His voice was deep and smooth. "Just seeing if you'd passed out on me."

"I'd never do such a thing."

He was quiet for a moment. "You know what I've been thinking?"

With him, it was anyone's guess. "What?"

"I was thinking about when all of this is over, where we are going to go." Half of his hand was under the band now. "What we are going to do."

"You have any idea?"

"I have lots of ideas."

A hot, sweet feeling swept over me. "I bet you do."

Daemon chuckled as his thumb moved in a slow, idle circle under my navel. "I was thinking college."

"You think there'll be colleges around after all of this?"

"I think so."

The tips of two fingers delved low, causing my breath to catch. "Why do you think that?"

"Easy answer." He dropped a kiss on my cheek. "If you've taught me anything, it's that humans are resilient, more so than my kind. No matter what, they'll keep forging on. So I can't believe that there won't be colleges and jobs or anything like that."

My lips curved into a small smile as I decided to play along. "College would be good, I think."

"I think you mentioned University of Colorado before," he said, his fingers creeping farther south, causing the muscles in my lower stomach to clench. "What about that?"

I remembered the first time we'd talked about the university, and I'd been so worried that I'd been overstepping relationship lines. Seemed like forever ago. "I think that's perfect."

"I'm sure Dawson and Beth would like it there." He paused. "So would Dee."

"Yeah, she would." Especially if Archer would be around, but then, we kind of needed to get Dee's head on straight first. "Maybe . . . maybe I could get my mom to move out there, too."

"Of course," he murmured, and I bit down on my lip hard enough to taste blood as he managed to get his knee between mine. "Your mom has to be there, because we're going to do it."

My eyes widened. "Uh, I'm not sure that's something I want my mom to be a part of."

Daemon's laugh tickled me. "Get your mind out of the gutter, Kitten. We're going to do a real wedding. The whole thing—bridesmaids, best man, the pretty white gown, and the ceremony. Even a reception. Everything."

My mouth opened, but there were no words. I got caught in the fantasy of a real wedding—of my mom being there to help me get into a beautiful Cinderella-type gown; of Dee and Lesa standing beside me; of Dawson, Archer, and even Luc as best men. Then there was Daemon in a tux, and damn, that was something I wanted to see again.

And there'd be pictures taken and pot roast served at the reception. There'd be a DJ playing questionable music, and then Daemon and I would have our first dance as husband and wife.

My heart kicked around in my chest, and I hadn't realized until that moment how badly I wanted that. I was such a girl and I didn't care.

"Kitten?"

"I like this," I whispered as my chest squeezed. "Talking about this, I mean. It feels normal. It feels like we have a—"

Daemon had leaned over me, capturing my mouth with his. The kiss reached deep down inside me, lighting up every cell. "We do have a future."

I stopped thinking as his lips returned to mine, and he eased me onto my back. The rest of the world, all the concerns and dangers, faded away until it was just the two of us. He did crazy insane things with his hand, and there was this rush of sensations that tossed me around like I was riding a wave. And when I came back down, I pushed him onto *his* back.

Daemon's brows flew up as I hovered over him. "What are you—?"

He got with the program pretty quickly, and the edges of his body started to glow that luminous whitish-red as his hand curled around my damp hair. Before his lashes drifted down, his eyes were like rough diamonds, and the expression was sort of awed, even though I really had no idea what I was doing. But he seemed to love it, and I think it was because he loved me.

Later, we lay facing each other and we were quiet. I traced the line of his bottom lip, working up the nerve to ask him something I'd been curious about. "Why did you leave with them when they came?"

His eyes were closed, face relaxed. "When they came out of

the woods, I could hear everything they were thinking, what they wanted. It was the same for Dawson and Dee. We were immediately connected. And at first, it was overwhelming. I wanted to go with them." He paused, opening his eyes. Our gazes locked. "It was like I forgot everything except them. They became *everything*."

I couldn't even wrap my head around that. "Do you hear them now?"

"No. If anything, it's a low hum way in the background." He paused. "It's not the first time something like that has happened. When a lot of us are around one another, it can get hard, because it's like a million-way radio. It's why we never liked being in the colony. When there are so many of us, we all are connected, almost like one being, and you're influenced into things you don't want. You're not an individual. You're a *whole*. I just didn't know it could be as strong as it was when they came."

"But you beat it," I reminded him, because he sounded almost disappointed in himself.

"Because of what I felt for you. Same with Dawson, and obviously any other Luxen who is connected to someone else, but Dee . . ." He trailed off, shaking his head. "Those who came, they are different from the rest of us. I know that's obvious now, but they . . . they're so cold. No empathy or compassion." A sigh shuddered through him. "I don't remember my parents, but I can't believe they were like this. I guess we aren't like that because we've been around humans. That lack of compassion and empathy makes them dangerous, Kat. More than I think we even realize."

As I smoothed my thumb along his jaw, he turned his head, placing a kiss on the center of my palm. "They have to have a weakness, though. Everything in the universe has a weakness."

Daemon captured my hand, threading his fingers through mine. "In every colony, there is an Elder who pretty much rules over the group. I know that out of those who have arrived, there has to be one who is kind of like . . . like their sergeant. Their queen in a hive. Taking out that person won't end this, but it will weaken them—the hold they have over other Luxen."

Like Dee.

"Any idea who that is or where that person is?" I asked.

His lips kicked up on one side. "No. Rolland kept it pretty hidden, and now that makes sense. Because of Sadi, he knew better than to share that little piece of information. Damn Sadi. I had no idea she was an Origin, but I think she's not the only one who's been pretending and hiding out among the Luxen."

I frowned. "Who else?"

"It's something I never really noticed until I was leaving the colony, when I came for you. Strange thing is, I never trusted this guy. There was also something off about him, and he said some off-the-wall stuff when I left. Things that didn't make sense then, and I didn't really put anything together until Archer revealed what he was—you know, the eye coloring." He rolled onto his back, exhaling slowly. "Ethan Smith."

It took me a moment to remember who he was. "He's the Elder from the colony back home?"

He nodded. "His eyes are just like Archer's and Luc's."

"Holy crap," I breathed. Sitting up, I folded my legs under me. "But if he is an Origin, and if the Origins somehow helped get the rest of the Luxen here, the question is why?"

Daemon's gaze shifted to mine. "That's the question of a lifetime, right? Why would some of the Origins be working with the Luxen?"

12

{ Daemon }

Kat looked like her brain hurt.

I couldn't blame her. There was so much being thrown at us, I felt like I needed to be wearing catcher's gear.

The whole thing about Ethan kept tossing around in my head as we lay in bed together, trying to get some sort of rest before Archer returned and most likely dumped even more messed-up news in our laps.

I could tell that even though Kat was quiet in my arms, she wasn't sleeping. Like me, there was too much to dwell on. Thinking about Dee made me want to slam my face through a wall, so I'd rather figure out what the hell Ethan could have to do with the Luxen invasion.

The thing was, it truly was the million-dollar question. Why would the Origins and the Luxen work together? It was something I asked Archer after he showed back up with bags of clothes. When he tossed Kat a chocolate bar, I frowned, wondering just how much he picked up on.

Archer raised a brow at me. "Enough to know you picture

knocking my head off my shoulders whenever we're around each other."

I smiled at that while Kat looked up from unwrapping her candy bar. "What?" she asked.

"Nothing," I said as I peered into one of the bags and found jeans in my size. That was weird on a disturbing level.

"Back to your question. About Origin and Luxen." Archer propped himself against the desk and folded his arms. "I honestly have no idea what could be gained by that, other than the typical joining powerful forces for world domination and blah, blah."

"That's cliché," I said.

"And too obvious," he agreed.

I glanced over at Kat. The look on her face as she devoured the bar, as if she tasted heaven for the first time and was seconds away from having a mouth-gasm, made me wish Archer wasn't in the room.

His smile went up a notch.

And it also made me wish he'd get the hell out of my head. "Did you know about Ethan?" I asked, refocusing.

He shook his head. "We're not like you alien freaks, where we mind-meld or know where the others are at every given second."

"Last I checked, you're a part of our alien freak family, so . . ."

Kat snapped off a tiny bar and offered it to me. I shook my head, and she popped it between those lips of hers. "So you've never met Ethan or heard of him?" she asked.

"There're a lot of Origins I never came into contact with or haven't seen since they were transferred to other bases. Daedalus has many set up throughout the world in very powerful positions. If even a few of them are working with the Luxen, we're really in trouble."

"Like we aren't already?" I pointed out.

"Yeah, well, here's the problem with that. We can pretend to be human or Luxen or even hybrid. We can read your thoughts. You've already had your happy ass burned by one you thought was a Luxen. Probably even twice if you count this Ethan you're talking about, which makes trusting what you think you know or see a real big problem," Archer explained. "Let's say a handful of Origins who are politicians, doctors, or members of the military are really working with the Luxen. It'll turn into a cluster—"

"So what do we do?" Kat scooted off the bed and tossed the wrapper in the trash. "I mean, we can't be just screwed. There has to be something we can do."

A hard tension crossed Archer's face. "Something is being done about it."

Kat stopped in the middle of the room, her expression a mixture of hope and foreboding. "What?"

Archer glanced over at me, and that one look told me simple words weren't going to explain anything, and I was so picking up on his vibe that this wasn't going to be a good thing. "Why don't you two get changed and meet me out in the hall," he suggested.

Her little hands balled into fists. "What aren't you telling us?"

"It's not that I'm unwilling to tell you." He pushed off the desk and headed for the door. "It's just something I think you guys need to see to believe."

"Well, that's not unnecessarily mysterious or anything, but whatever." I stood and reached for the sweats I was wearing. Archer was still at the door, and I arched a brow. "Unless you want to see me in all my glorious nakedness, I'd suggest you go now."

Archer's eyes rolled. "No, thank you."

Kat and I got changed quickly, and the fact that her jeans fit her perfectly had me picturing the all-too-familiar punching-Archer-in-the-face daydream, but she looked good, more like herself in the dark denim and lightweight gray sweater. Her hair had dried in soft waves, and she looked like we were going out to grab something to eat or maybe a movie.

What we were doing was so far from that fantasy it was freaking sad.

Our eyes met after I hooked the button on my jeans. "Are you ready to do this, whatever 'this' is?"

She nodded. "I'm almost half afraid to see what he wants to show us."

"I feel you. At this point, anything is possible." I stopped at the closed door and extended a hand to her. When she took it, I hauled her toward me. Wrapping my arms around her waist, I lifted her up and gave her a good squeeze.

Her soft laugh that danced in my ear was too rare. "You're squishing me."

"Uh-huh." Putting her back down, I dropped a kiss to her forehead. "No matter what, don't forget our plans." It felt important to remind her of them.

Her eyes were a soft gray as she stared up at me. "The wedding plans?"

"Those." I leaned down and whispered in her ear, "Because when we get shown something absolutely messed up, which I'm sure we're going to, I'm so going to start focusing on those plans and lifting up your wedding gown and getting down on my knees."

"Oh my God," she whispered, and when I pulled back with a chuckle, her cheeks were bright red. "You're . . . you're . . ."

"What?"

She shook her head and swallowed. "A lot to handle."

I smirked as I opened the door. "After you, Kitten."

As she walked through, I landed a nice swat on her behind that caused her to jump and spin around. Kat shot me a dirty look, and I grinned, totally unrepentant. It was the little things in life that kept me happy.

Archer ignored that, which meant he must value certain parts of his body. We followed him down the hall and then down a stairwell and into another corridor. Up ahead was a set of glass double doors and what looked like a NASA-level command center inside.

"What's this?" I asked.

"What you think it is." Archer's smile didn't reach his odd eyes when I glared at him. "It's the base's command center. They're hooked up to satellites, missiles, and all kinds of fun things in here."

Kat scrunched her nose but remained quiet.

Archer opened the door, and I wasn't surprised to see Luc sitting in a chair at the front, legs kicked up on a white ledge, crossed at the ankles. He had a fruit punch box in his hands.

I shook my head.

Nancy was near the front, arms crossed over her narrow chest, her face tight, like she was sucking on something sour. A man stood next to her in full military regalia with enough shiny buttons and badges to tell me he might be a problem.

The room was staffed with military folk all wearing headsets and wired in to whatever the hell they were doing on the monitors in front of them. A few looked our way when we walked in. None of them seemed surprised. There was a huge monitor on the wall in front of Luc.

I turned my gaze back to the man with steely gray eyes and short, light brown hair. "Who's this douche?"

Kat's eyes widened, and it sounded like Luc choked on his laugh as he spun around to face us. "God, I knew there was a reason I liked you."

"Yay," I muttered.

Nancy did not look amused as the man faced us, his shoulders squared. "This is General Jonathan Eaton, the *highest*-ranking officer in the United States Air Force," Nancy said, her words clipped and like little punches. "Perhaps you could show some respect."

I arched a brow. "Sure."

I had to give it to General Whatever His Name Was. There wasn't a single flicker of any smidgen of annoyance as his gray eyes settled on me. "I know you don't have a very . . . high opinion of members of the government," he said. "But I can assure you, right now, we are not your enemy."

"I reserve the right to decide that," I said, glancing up at the screen. From what it looked like, it was a distant aerial view of a major city. I could pick out the tops of skyscrapers and a blue blob that might be an ocean.

"That's understandable," he replied, drawing my attention. "Let it be known, I've never had any problems with your kind."

"I never had a problem with yours," I said. "Not until you basically kidnapped us, started doing horrific experiments on us, ripped my family apart, and became a general pain in our asses."

A slight flush of pain stained Nancy's cheeks, but she remained quiet.

The general, however, did not. "Many of us were not fully aware of what Daedalus was carrying out or how they were acquiring the Luxen and hybrids. There will be a lot of changes in the future."

"He's one of the big guys who put the smackdown on Daedalus." Luc folded his arms behind his head, and I had no idea where his fruit box had gone. His slippery gaze slid over to Nancy, and a chilling grin tilted his lips. "I think he's kind of cool."

"That means a lot to me," the general replied drily, and Archer's cough sounded suspiciously like a laugh. "We may not see eye to eye or think along the same lines," he said to me, "and I will never be able to say anything that will make up for what was done to your family or to those you care for." With that, he passed a stern look in Nancy's direction. "Those who were responsible for the more unsavory aspects of Daedalus will be punished accordingly."

Kat gaped at him.

"Wait." I moved closer to her—not that I was far away in the first place. Now I was practically standing on top of her. "That's all great that you love yourself some Luxen, but why in the hell would you trust any of us right now? Why would we trust you?"

The general tilted up his chin. "I know you don't think you and your brother are the only Luxen to ever mutate a human you care deeply for. Matter of fact, I think you also realize that there are many Luxen out there who would do anything to protect the human or humans they care for. I know that bond is stronger than the influence of those who have recently arrived. I know that for a fact."

"How?" Kat asked.

"Because my daughter and her husband are here on the base," he said, looking at me. "And yes, he is a Luxen."

I could feel Kat's eyes on me as I watched the general. For some screwed-up reason, out of everything, that had to be the most shocking shit I'd heard. I laughed. I couldn't help it. "Your daughter is married to a Luxen?"

Nancy's lips pursed, and I thought her cheeks might cave in.

"They've been married for five years," he said, and as he folded his arms, the dark blue uniform stretched over his shoulders.

"Your daughter is married to a Luxen, and you're okay with what Nancy was doing to them? To us?" Anger flashed across Kat's face.

A long look of chagrin settled in his eyes. "As I said, there were things we were unaware of."

"That's not an excuse," she said, and damn, I knew she was about to get a wee bit feisty.

His lips twitched as if he wished to smile. "You remind me of my daughter."

Nancy turned her cheek, and I swore her eyes rolled.

"I know there is nothing I can do to change what has been done in the past other than ensuring it will never happen again. And I will." He drew in a breath. "But right now, we have an unprecedented global disaster on our hands. That is all I can focus on."

"Global disaster." Luc arched a brow. "That sounds so incredibly dramatic and like there's—" A muted beep cut him off. He reached into his pocket and pulled out his cell phone.

Luc dropped his sneakers onto the floor, his expression stark as he shot to his feet. "Got something I need to take care of."

He headed for the door without a backward glance, his free hand curling into a fist, and warnings fired off, one at a time. I'd never seen Luc look so . . . so unsettled.

It's okay. Archer's voice filtered through my thoughts. *What he has going on right now has nothing to do with any of this.*

Call me paranoid if that doesn't mean shit to me, I sent back at him.

The general is legit, Archer replied, his gaze locking with mine. *And like I said, what Luc is dealing with has nothing to do with it.*

I still wasn't 100 percent on board, so I draped my arm around Kat's shoulders just in case. My gaze flickered over the general and Nancy. I wasn't sure what was really going on there. "Where's the other one?" I asked. "Sergeant Dasher?"

Nancy turned to me. "He's dead."

Against my side, Kat stiffened. "How?" she asked.

"In a fight with the Luxen just outside of Vegas." Nancy's dark eyes narrowed on us. "That should make both of you happy."

"I can't say I'm going to lose any sleep." I held her gaze until she looked away. Dasher may not have been a complete sociopath like her, but he was on my To-Kill list.

At least I could mark his name off.

"General Eaton." A voice traveled from a man near the large monitor. He was standing, arms pressed to his sides. "We're five minutes out."

Five minutes out from what?

No sooner was that thought finished than the image on the monitor zoomed in and the tops of buildings became clearer, as did congested streets. Some areas were nothing but blobs of gray smoke.

"What is this?" Kat asked, stepping forward and out from underneath my arm.

I glanced at Archer, and at once, I knew this was what he wanted us to see. "What's going on?"

The general strode down the middle of the room, past the lines of smaller monitors and people pecking away at their computers. "This is what we are doing to stop the invasion."

I turned my gaze back to the screen. Man, I had a real bad feeling about all of this.

"Four minutes," another guy up front announced.

Yep. When people started counting down, no good shit came from that. Kat had asked for clarification, but as I stared at the twinkling lights of the city, an idea began to take form in the back of my head.

"What you see on the screen is Los Angeles," the general explained. "There was a significant number of invading Luxen there, all who have taken human form, mostly government officials and others in positions of power. They have rapidly assimilated the human DNA of those who are around the age necessary to have a family. We have people in there who've been keeping us up to date, but as of yesterday night, we've lost complete control of the city."

"Oh wow." Kat folded her arms around her as she stared at the monitor.

"We've also lost Houston, Chicago, and Kansas City," Nancy interjected. "That we know of at this point. The only city we've been able to hold without any Luxen is D.C., but the invaders are amassing tremendous forces around the city—Alexandria, Arlington, Mount Rainier, and Silver Spring are all almost completely under their control."

Damn.

"And we don't know of any Origins inside D.C. who might have joined forces with the invading Luxen," he added. "We're hoping that's not the case, but we have to plan for it."

"Three minutes."

My gaze landed on the back of the man counting. "What happens in three minutes?"

Kat turned around, her face pale, and I knew her mind was going where mine was, and none of this was heading to a pleasant place.

"We have to stop the Luxen by any means necessary that will result in minimal human casualties." The general's shoulders rose as he drew in a deep breath. "Obviously, that limits what we can do."

Archer pushed off the wall, gliding closer, as if he expected me to lose my shit when my suspicions were confirmed.

"The president of the United States, in conjunction with the secretary of defense, has approved a test strike of an EMP over the city of Los Angeles."

I stared at the general.

"EMP?" Kat said, her eyes wide.

"Electromagnetic pulse weaponized in the form of several nonnuclear e-bombs," he explained, and my stomach dropped to my feet. "It will work just like a PEP weapon once the bomb detonates around a three-hundred-foot elevation, but on a more widespread level. Expected loss of human life is nominal, limited to those with heart disease or other disorders that might be susceptible to an electric pulse of that magnitude . . . and currently those whose lives are dependent upon life-support systems."

"Two minutes, elevation at seven hundred feet," came from the front, followed by a static-filled voice announcing the location over a radio signal.

Archer was now standing near me.

"Most humans will experience a burst of pain and momentary paralysis," he continued as Kat turned back to the screen. "The EMP will act as a lethal, immediate kill weapon to any Luxen, hybrid, or Origin within the strike zone."

Holy shit.

I got the necessity of it—they had to do something against the invading Luxen—but my sister was out there somewhere, hopefully nowhere near L.A. And there had to be innocent Luxen and hybrids there, even Origins, and they had no clue what was coming their way.

"Innocents will die in this, both human and Luxen," the

general said, as if he could read my mind. "But we have to sacrifice the few to save the many."

I turned back to the screen as it flickered rapidly for a second before evening out. The image had zoomed in once more, enough that I could track movement on the ground.

"That's not all it does," Archer said quietly. "The EMP was designed for a different purpose."

The general nodded. "Originally, it came to creation as a weapon of mass destruction that would limit the loss of human life. The EMP irreversibly damages any and all electronic devices and power sources."

Holy shit.

That was all I was capable of thinking.

"That's everything," Kat whispered. "That's absolutely everything in the city—phones, cars, hospitals, communications—everything."

"One minute, elevation at four hundred feet."

"It will virtually knock L.A. back into the Dark Ages." Archer stared at the large screen. "You're about to see history be made again, but the kind of history that can never be rewritten."

"You can't do this," I said.

Kat was shaking her head. "You can't. There're people there who need electricity—there are innocent people, and their whole way of life is about to be ended. You can't—"

"It's obviously too late," Nancy snapped, dark eyes firing. "This is our only option to stop them. For there even to be a tomorrow where mankind is safe."

I opened my mouth, but the broken radio transmission fired up, counting down from twenty seconds, and there wasn't any way to stop this. It was happening, right in front of us.

Moving closer to Kat, I continued to rivet my eyes on the screen, on the cars traveling the freeway, trying to exit the city. There could be Luxen in those cars, good ones and bad ones. There could be humans with heart conditions. There were also hospitals somewhere on that screen, people whose next breath would never come.

And then it happened.

Kat smacked her hand over her mouth as a flash of blinding light caused the image on the screen to wobble for a moment or two, and then the picture settled. Everything looked as it had seconds before, except none of the cars moved on the freeway. Nothing moved, actually, and . . .

The entire city had gone dark.

13

{ Katy }

Oh my God, I felt like I needed to sit down or I was going to fall over.

I couldn't tear my gaze from the screen. Nothing was happening. Of course not. Millions of people in L.A. were currently stunned. And out of them, how many would never get back up again? Hundreds? Thousands? I couldn't believe what I'd just witnessed.

A voice crackled over the radio, declaring a successful drop of the EMP bombs. No one in the room cheered. I was glad they hadn't, because I was sure either Daemon or I would've ended up with onyx being sprayed in our face.

"We'll be initiating a scan for any electrical pulses," the man who had been counting down earlier announced. "Two minutes and I should have the data."

General Eaton nodded. "Thank you."

"Luxen and their many spinoffs emanate an electrical response," Nancy explained, but I already knew that. That was why the PEP and EMP weapons were so dangerous.

They fried us on a massive level.

Daemon wrapped an arm around my shoulders, dragging me against his side. When I placed my hand on his chest, I could feel his body hum. He was angry, like me. The fury swirling inside me caused a rush of static to pop across my skin. There was so much frustration, because I knew our options were limited, but this . . . ?

The magnitude of what had just happened went beyond the loss of life. Today, whatever the date, would go down in infamy as the day the City of Angels just *stopped*. Nothing would work there the same again. All of the electrical grids, the networks, and the complex infrastructure that was so beyond my realm of understanding were all gone.

"There's no recovering from that, is there?" I asked, and my voice sounded hoarse.

Archer's jaw was set. "It would take decades, if not longer, to rebuild to what it was."

I closed my eyes, floored by the ramifications of this.

"There is no activity," the man announced. "Not even a blip."

Daemon stiffened beside me, and I pressed my hand against his chest. There had to be a lot of innocent people who had perished.

And this was only the beginning. I knew it. They would do this to more cities, all around the world, and more innocent people would die and the world would become . . . holy crap, life as we knew it would become a freaking dystopian novel like I'd thought before, but for real.

Pulling away, I turned and faced General Eaton. "You can't keep doing this."

His deep gray eyes met mine, and I knew he had to be thinking, *Who in the hell is this chick to think she can even say anything?* and maybe I didn't have a right. Hell, in the grand scheme of things I was a nobody, just a freak of nature, but I couldn't stand here and not say something as they literally destroyed the world one city at a time.

"You're obliterating millions of people's way of life, and that's not even taking into consideration the people who were killed when those bombs were dropped," I said, voice shaking. "You can't keep doing this."

"This wasn't a decision that came lightly. Trust me when I say there were and will be many hours where sleep will be lost," he replied. "But there is no other way."

Daemon folded his arms across his chest. "What you're doing is basically committing genocide."

No one responded, because what could they say to that? It *was* genocide, because those bombs were going to wipe most of the Luxen off the planet.

Archer scrubbed a hand along his jaw. "The thing is, guys, what other option do they have? You know as well as I do that if the invading Luxen aren't stopped, and if the Origins who are working with them aren't rounded up, it will take just weeks before they have complete control of the whole planet."

"Maybe not even that long," Nancy commented as she dropped into an empty chair. Her expression was as impassive as ever, but I wondered if she feared that wherever the Origins were holed up was near one of the cities where bombs would be dropped. "If the Origins are in on this—"

"They are," I said, thinking of Sadi and the Elder Daemon had mentioned. "Some of them are."

Her cool, dark gaze landed on me. "Then there truly is no other option. The Origins were created as the perfect species, with cognitive abilities beyond anything ordinary humans are capable of. The Origin—"

"We get it," snapped Daemon. His eyes glimmered like cut emeralds. "Maybe if you hadn't messed with Mother Nature and create Origins—"

"Hey," muttered Archer. "One standing right here."

Daemon ignored him. "Maybe if you hadn't done this, the Luxen wouldn't have come."

"You don't know that," she said, shoulders bunching. "They could've—"

"What I do know is that they are working with the Luxen," he said, cutting her off. "And it doesn't take a giant leap of logic to think that they had something to do with the Luxen coming here. That shit is on your hands—on Daedalus."

"Which is awfully ironic, don't you think?" Archer said, and when Daemon shot him a blank look, I thought for a second he might roll his eyes. "Daedalus was the father of Icarus in Greek mythology. He built the wings Icarus used to fly, and the dumb kid got too close to the sun. The wings melted and he plummeted back down to Earth, drowning in the sea. Kind of like his invention was his own downfall. Same with Prometheus."

Daemon stared at Archer for a long moment and then turned back to Nancy. "Anyway, no matter how you guys spin it, this mess is on your hands."

"And we are trying to fix it," General Eaton responded. "Unless you all have something we haven't thought of, there is no other option."

"I don't know." I pressed my fingers to my temples. "We really could use the Avengers right about now."

"Screw that. We need Loki," Daemon retorted.

General Eaton arched a brow. "Well, unfortunately, the Marvel universe isn't real, so . . ."

I started to laugh, because I was seconds from doing the

crazy laugh and never stopping, but then Daemon blinked as if something had smacked him upside the head.

"Wait," he said, thrusting a hand through his unruly hair. "We need the equivalent of Loki."

"I'm not really following that train of thought," I said.

He shook his head. "There is something we can use, that I know we can use."

General Eaton inclined his head as Archer's gaze turned razor sharp. His lips thinned, and I knew he was peeking in on Daemon's thoughts. Whatever he was seeing, he didn't look like he was a big fan of it.

When Archer spoke in an awed whisper, he confirmed my suspicion. "That's crazy insane, like completely senseless, but it might work."

Daemon sent him a killer look. "Gee, why don't you go ahead and tell them what I'm thinking."

"Oh, no." Archer waved his hand dismissively. "I don't want to steal your thunder."

"I think you already did, so—"

"Come on," I jumped in, impatient. "Tell the rest of us who don't have nifty mind-reading abilities."

Daemon's lips twisted into a semblance of a smile. "There is one thing that the invading Luxen really have no defense against."

"Well, obviously the EMP weapon," Nancy commented mulishly.

His nostrils flared. "Besides something that destroys everything as we know it on Earth."

She looked away, focusing on the monitor as if she were bored with the whole conversation. I wondered if anyone would get mad if I spin-kicked her in the back of the head.

"The Arum," Daemon said.

I blinked slowly, thinking my brain just went kaput on me. "What?"

"The invading Luxen know of the Arum. That much I picked up, but there was something else I learned from them," Daemon explained. "They have no experience with them."

"But they know of them," General Eaton said. "You just said that."

"Yeah, but from my personal experience, knowing of the Arum and hearing about them are totally different than actually dealing with them, especially if you've never seen one face-to-face before—and they haven't. The Arum were long gone, on their way here, and these Luxen went in the opposite direction. Even if they'd seen one before, they were just children then."

A few of the officers in the room, the ones at the mini-monitors, had turned in their seats and were paying a lot of attention to Daemon.

"The first time I faced off with an Arum, I would've died if Matthew . . ." He took a breath, and the others might not have noticed the flicker of pain, but I saw it, and my chest ached. Matthew, who had been a father figure to all of them, had betrayed them, and I knew that would cut deep for a very long time. "If Matthew hadn't been there, someone older and more experienced with the Arum, I would've died. Hell, many times over before I got the hang of fighting them."

"The Arum were created by the freaking laws of nature to keep the Luxen in check and fight them," Archer said, excitement thrumming in his voice. "They are the only true predator of the Luxen."

A tiny spark of hope flared in my chest, but I didn't want to give it too much room to grow. "But the Origins will know how to fight them."

"They will, but there aren't thousands and thousands of them," Daemon said. "And there's no way they can teach the Luxen that quickly how to defend themselves. Hell, I doubt they even think the Arum will be a problem. Luxen, by nature, are arrogant."

"Gee, really?" I muttered.

One side of his lips kicked up in a sexy, smug half grin as Archer snickered.

"Origins are probably more arrogant, you know," Daemon said. "The borderline stupid kind of arrogant."

The smirk faded from Archer's face.

"Wow. I feel like Morgan Freeman should be doing a voice-over right now, like, 'Their weakest link is something already here,'" I said, and when several sets of eyes settled on me with identical looks of confusion, I flushed. "What? It's from *War of the Worlds*, and I think it's totes appropriate for the situation."

A real smile crossed Daemon's face, and in spite of everything, my insides melted into goo whenever he smiled liked that, because it was so incredibly rare. "I love how your brain works."

There's that love-struck thing you were wondering about in Beth and Dawson's room. Archer's words floated through my head, and I cringed. Heat enveloped my cheeks as I cleared my throat. "Do you think this will work?"

"How many Arum are here?" Daemon directed the question at the general and Nancy.

One of the biggest things that had surprised us over the years was the fact that Daedalus had been working with the Arum to keep the Luxen in check, for whatever gross, nefarious reasons.

Nancy's lips pursed. "We don't have exact numbers, not like with the Luxen who have been assimilated. Many of the Arum went dark when they came here."

"Went dark?" I frowned.

"They went underground," General Eaton explained. "Moving from city to city. They're damn hard to keep track of."

"And you guys were more concerned about us and the cool things we could do." Daemon smirked. "Nice."

"So how many do we know are here?" I asked before the conversation went downhill.

"A few hundred worked for us," Nancy said.

"Wait." Daemon's eyes narrowed. "That's in the past tense." Oh, no.

General Eaton looked like he wanted to strip out of his jacket. "Many of them left when the Luxen arrived."

"Many?" scoffed Nancy as she smoothed her hands down her legs. "All of them did. None of us should be surprised. They aren't the most loyal of all creatures."

That tiny spark of hope started to fizzle out when Archer spoke up. "But they are still here, on this planet."

"So what?" Nancy challenged. "You're going to get them to help?"

A mysterious smile trekked across Archer's face. "Not me, but I know someone who owes someone else a really big favor."

Nancy rolled her eyes. "Even if you could get them to help, it would be pointless. There're too many spread out and—"

"Actually, if I may speak up," came a voice from the middle of the room. It was a middle-age woman with dark blond hair pulled back into a tight, neat bun. She was standing, her hands clasped behind her back.

General Eaton nodded for her to continue.

"Most of the invading Luxen landed in the United States with manageable numbers overseas. We think this is due to the amount of Luxen we already have here in the States. As you know, we've been tracking movement over the last ten or so hours. Many of the invading Luxen have been moving east, toward the capital. If our suspicions are correct, they will be joining forces there and becoming a sizable unit," she said, glancing toward Daemon and Archer. "Some have integrated themselves into the cities we've already lost, but if we were able to make a strike against D.C., we'd take out many of them."

"And that is what we are planning," General Eaton said.

"But you're planning to drop an electrical-whatever bomb on the nation's capital," I stated, hands clenching at my sides.

"Actually, if an even more sizable mass of Luxen does appear, it will be several e-bombs," Nancy said. "Enough that most of Virginia, Maryland, and even the I-81 corridor in West Virginia would be hit."

"Jesus," I whispered, squeezing my eyes shut. That's where my mom and my friends were. "What are you doing to the cities already lost—Houston, Chicago, and Kansas City?"

"Over the next twenty-four hours, EMPs will be dropped." Empathy bled into his voice. "Those cities are gone, Miss Swartz. Most of the Luxen have taken on human form and they have killed the humans they've found not suitable. There is little to no contact coming out of them from any source that we trust. I pray for whatever humans are left in those places."

"All right. Those cities are gone, but nowhere else so far. What if we can stop them?" Daemon said. "What if we can do the same thing without killing innocent people on both sides, and without destroying the cities to the point they'll be unlivable?"

Nancy choked out a laugh as she shook her head in disbelief.

"Think about it," Archer jumped in. "You're going to have millions of Americans completely displaced in just those three cities, not counting L.A., and the more you do this, the more refugees you're creating. The States would go under."

A muscle flexed along General Eaton's jaw. "Do you think this is not something we have thought about or have begun preparation for? Right as we speak, we're planning for an even worse outcome than losing the major cities. We're planning for a complete loss in case the EMPs fail in some manner."

The general described the precautions they were taking, moving computers and other valuable electronic-based equipment into underground bunkers stocked with nonperishable items, and he droned on until I felt like I really was going to hurl.

If I thought the invading Luxen were bad, I'd had no idea. We truly were on the verge of a catastrophic disaster.

"We can get the Arum," Archer said. "I know we can."

My heart toppled over. Could we really get the Arum? I doubted it would be easy, and I almost couldn't believe it when General Eaton said the magic words. "If you can get the Arum to fight, then we will hold off on neutralizing the force outside of the capital."

"Thank you." I almost jumped. I almost hugged the dude, and I was glad I didn't, because that looked like it would be all kinds of awkward.

"But we don't have a lot of time. We've got about six days, maybe seven, and then we have to go to the EMPs," the general said. "I'll need to make a lot of phone calls."

"This is ridiculous." Nancy stood, throwing her hands up. "I cannot believe you're even thinking of allowing *them* to—"

"You forget your place, Husher. Like always," snapped General Eaton. He drew himself up to his full height, pouring authority into the air. "I, just as the president of the United States, am willing to vet out different tactics."

General Eaton continued to dress Nancy down, and I thought I'd be happier to see that happen, but I ended up experiencing a mad case of secondhand embarrassment and I seriously wished I wasn't around to see it.

Daemon, on the other hand, looked positively gleeful as I moved to stand next to him while Nancy did the walk of shame.

Archer started talking about different ways the Arum could maim and kill the Luxen in less than five seconds flat, a conversation I never thought I'd hear Daemon taking part in so enthusiastically.

Eventually, Nancy left to probably go rock in the corner somewhere and plot her revenge, and General Eaton started making phone calls. It was then that my stomach decided to announce that it could use massive quantities of food.

Surprised that I could eat after seeing and hearing what I did, I pressed the heel of my palm against my belly and smiled sheepishly when the boys looked down at me. "Sorry?"

Daemon's lips tipped up. "Hungry?"

"Maybe. A little."

"There's food in the mess hall near your rooms," Archer said. "I thought I told you guys about that."

"We didn't have time . . ." I trailed off and started imagining dancing naked babies so I didn't think about why we didn't have time.

Archer's brows rose. "The hell?"

Cheeks flaming, I turned to Daemon. I needed to get out of there before Archer got a peep show. "I think I'm going to go get something to eat."

"Okay." He brushed his lips over my forehead. "I'll meet you back at the room."

I didn't look at Archer as I spun around. Leaving the boys

in the control room, I hurried out into the hall. Not only did I need to get food in my tummy, I needed something else to do that felt normal. I considered visiting Dawson and Beth again as I climbed the empty stairwell and entered the wide corridor on the main level. As I rounded the corner, I stumbled to a surprised halt.

Luc stood up ahead, a few doors down from where Dawson and Beth were, but he wasn't alone. A girl was with him, maybe around his age or a year younger. She was a tiny thing, and he all but dwarfed her. Ridiculously slender, her denim-clad legs were as thin as my arms. Her hair was like spun gold and she was stunningly pretty, with a heart-shaped face full of faint freckles and eyes that were a warm chocolate.

And I'd seen her before.

Back when Daemon and I had gone with . . . with Blake to meet Luc for the first time. She had been on the stage, as beautiful and fluid as a dancer, and then later, she'd poked her head into Luc's office, and he'd gotten all frownie face about it.

But she looked different now.

A very pretty *human* girl, but there were dark smudges under her eyes, her cheekbones were sharp, face gaunt and pale, and her entire appearance was overly frail, as if it was taking everything in her to be upright on two feet.

She wasn't really standing on her own, either. Luc's hands were wrapped around her upper arms, almost as if he was supporting her weight. I didn't need to be a doctor to know that she bled some serious illness into the air around her. Not a cold or flu, but something bad.

Something that reminded me of my father.

I bit down on my lip. Luc seemed unaware that I was there as he smoothed his hands up and down the girl's arms. "It's going to be okay now," he said. "Just like I promised."

A wan smile turned her lips up. "Do you have any idea what's going on out there? I don't think anything will ever be fine again, Luc."

"I don't care about that right now," he said in typical Luc fashion. "Remember what I told you about that new drug?"

"Oh, Luc." She wrapped bony, pale hands around his wrists. "I think we're beyond the point of anything working—"

"Don't say that." Strength and determination poured into his voice. "It will work. It has to work. Or I'll kick its ass."

The girl didn't look convinced, but her smile spread as she leaned forward, sliding her arms around Luc's waist.

Luc closed his eyes, and his lips parted as he let out a slow breath. "Why don't you go in there and get some rest, Nadia." He drew back, smiling down at the top of her head. "I've got some things I need to take care of, and then I'll be back. Okay?"

I so knew he was totally aware of me, and yet I didn't feel bad for eavesdropping, considering how many times he'd peeped on us.

She glanced over to where I stood, her curious gaze starting at my toes, and when she reached my face, recognition flared in her big eyes. She hesitated for a moment, and then ghosted into the room.

Luc closed the door behind him and faced me. Once more I was struck by the wisdom in his odd purple eyes and the set of his face, as if he was much, much older than he appeared.

"Who is she?" I asked.

"You heard me say her name."

"That's not what I meant." I glanced at the closed door. "I remember her. She was at the club, dancing on the stage."

He cocked his head to the side. "I've killed people for just looking at her, and you want to know who she is?"

Luc could do that in the blink of an eye, and he could also

make me squawk like a chicken if he wanted to, but I wanted to know who this girl was to him, and I seriously doubted he would mess with me. Or at least I hoped not.

Shoving his hands into his pockets, he strolled up to me. "After everything you've seen and heard, you really want me to tell you about her?"

I crossed my arms. "Right now, I would like to think about anything other than what I just saw and heard."

He was silent for a long moment as he studied me, and then he leaned a shoulder against the wall. "Nadia just got here from Maryland—Hagerstown, to be exact. I called in some favors when I got to this base."

The kid had more favors owed to him than a gambler had debt. "Of course."

A slight grin appeared. "I've known Nadia for a couple of years, met her when I first visited the Wild and Wonderful West Virginia. She was a runaway—abusive home, a father who would make you sick."

The moment those words formed, the worst-case scenario took form.

"What you're thinking doesn't even touch what really went on," Luc said, voice hard. "Don't worry. He got his just deserts in a very slow and painful way."

My heart skipped a beat at the cold, grim smile that appeared on his face. I didn't even need to ask what he did. I knew.

"She was young and living on the streets when I met her, so I took her in. Paris wasn't too keen on it. She's human after all, but there's something . . . Well, Nadia is special." A far-off look crept onto his expression.

"Is she your girlfriend?"

Luc let out a dry laugh. "No. I'd never be that lucky."

My brows rose, and I couldn't stop myself from thinking it. He was in love with her.

If Luc picked up on the thought, he didn't acknowledge it. "Two and a half years ago, she started getting bruises all over her, would end up worn out easily, and couldn't keep any food down. It's a cancer of the blood, a label with too many words that don't matter." His eyes narrowed. "It's fatal."

I closed my eyes. "Luc, I'm . . . I'm sorry."

"Don't be," he said, and when I looked at him again, he was staring right back at me. "Your father died—a lot of people die from cancer. I get that. But Nadia won't."

"She's why you wanted the Prometheus serum." From the moment I saw her, I'd been putting two and two together. "Luc, they said it didn't work for—"

"It works on *some* diseases and *some* cancers. They didn't get a chance to roll the drug through every sickness out there," he interrupted, and I snapped my mouth shut. "As messed-up as Daedalus was, they did do a few good things. And hopefully, this will be another karma point for them."

I wanted it to be the case. I didn't know the girl, but after losing someone to cancer and losing all contact with my mom, I knew how hard loss was. It never went away, but stayed with you like a faint shadow that was thicker some days than others.

"I hope it works," I said finally.

He gave a curt nod. A moment passed and then he said, "So you guys want to use the Arum to fight the Luxen?"

I blinked. "Does it ever get old being a know-it-all?"

Luc chuckled. "Not one single time."

My look turned bland.

"Using the Arum is one hell of a Hail Mary, you know that, right?"

I sighed. "It is. Archer said he knew someone who was owed a favor. I'm going to take a wild guess and say it was you."

He laughed again as he tipped his head back against the wall, looking like a teen boy lounging outside of a classroom. "Yeah, one of the Arum does owe me a favor." A winsome grin appeared. "And his name would be Hunter."

14

{ Daemon }

"Hunter?"

Luc sighed and repeated, "Hunter."

"The douche who was at your club?" Luc and Kat had come and found me in our room, and I didn't like where this was going.

"Hmm." Luc tapped a finger on his cheek as he glanced at where Kat sat on the bed. "There were two douches there. He was one of them. So you were—"

"Funny," I said.

"I thought so." Luc flashed a grin as he dropped down beside Kat. "Do you know that saying, beggars can't be choosers?"

My eyes narrowed. "I'm never the beggar."

"Guys." Kat tucked her hair back behind both ears. "So what do you not like about this Hunter guy?"

"Let's see." I pretended to think about that. "He's an Arum for starters."

Her gray eyes rolled. "Other than that?"

"Does there need to be another reason?" To me, that was good enough for my rabid dislike of the guy.

Luc nudged Kat with his arm. "It doesn't matter if he likes Hunter or not. The Arum owes me a favor, and if anyone knows where all our natural-born killers are currently holed up, he'll know."

"And we can trust him?" she asked.

I snorted. Trusting an Arum? Yeah. Right.

Luc ignored me. "He wouldn't dare screw around with me, not when he has so much to lose."

Something ignorant was on the tip of my tongue, but it faded away like a memory just out of reach. I thought about the woman I'd seen with him at the club—a human woman. There had most definitely been a relationship between the two.

I about vomited in my mouth at the thought of that.

"I've already talked to him," Luc said, stretching his arms above his head like a cat in the sunlight. "He's gonna meet us in Atlanta."

"Atlanta?" Surprise colored her voice. "And how are we supposed to get there?"

"Probably gonna have to drive." He shrugged. "There're no planes in the air, not since ET phoned home and then shot down a commercial jet."

Kat paled. We hadn't heard that news yet.

"So, yeah, I don't suggest flying the unfriendly skies. I've already looked it up," he continued. "It's gonna take about thirty hours to drive, so it's going to be an epic road trip. Hunter will meet you at the airport, though—domestic side." He smiled then, like something about that amused him.

I leaned against the dresser. "So how is Hunter going to help us go after the Arum? Didn't realize he's that important of a dude."

"Hunter's important but not that significant." Luc kicked his feet up so his legs were straight. I had no idea if the kid could ever sit still. "He's your ticket to the Arum playground. He knows where they're all cooling their feet. Getting Hunter to take you to his leader—master—whatever—isn't going to be the problem."

I arched a brow.

"It's going to be getting the Grand Poo-Bah to go along with it. The Arum are kind of like you guys. All they need is a leader, and then they'll follow him right off a cliff." He paused, scrunching his nose. "Never met the guy. Have heard some stuff about him."

"What stuff?" Kat asked.

He shrugged a shoulder. "Doesn't matter."

Kat's brows knit when she frowned.

"Anyway, I'm going to have to stay behind. Pretty sure my presence is needed to keep Nancy from doing something that will upset the balance of the universe. Archer will go with you guys. Both of you, right?" Luc glanced between us. "I seriously doubt either of you will stay behind."

"Not likely." I scrubbed my hand down my jaw. Thirty hours in a car with Kat could get interesting, real fun, but with Archer? I thought I might hurt myself.

"Speaking of Nancy . . ." Kat looked at the closed door before she continued. "You can't let those kids go back to her, no matter what you promised."

The corners of his mouth rose in a wide smile that was a tad bit on the creepy side. "Don't worry. She's not a problem. The whole thing with her will most definitely work itself out in the end."

The following morning, I sat at a white rectangular table that reminded me of a school cafeteria. I wasn't sure what to think about that. Did I miss school? Not really. Did I miss life before this crap, when it was just me, my trusty pen, and Kat sitting in front of me?

Yeah. Sometimes.

But it wasn't like anyone could go back in time.

Dawson sat across from me, scooping scrambled eggs from his plate onto Beth's. The chick was definitely eating for two, considering the amount of food she just put down, and she was still going strong.

Pregnancy was weird.

Kat sneaked a slice of bacon off my place.

She had no reason to eat that much other than loving food . . . and bacon. She grinned at me as she snapped it in two, dropping half of it back on my plate.

"I really think you need to stay here," I said, turning my attention back to my brother as I picked up the slice of my measly share of bacon.

Dawson frowned as he toyed with the bottle of chocolate milk. I knew what he was thinking. I could read him like an open book with big words and pictures.

"Look, you need to be here." My gaze flickered over to Beth, who had a huge forkful of eggs. "This is where you need to be. It's too dangerous out there for you or for Beth."

Beth glanced up. "Isn't it dangerous for you and Kat?"

"It is." Kat glanced at me, chewing on her lower lip. We hadn't told Dawson or Beth yet what Nancy told us about not being connected in the way they were. Kat took a deep breath, opened her mouth, and then Archer seemed to pop out of thin air.

He dropped down on the other side of Kat. "These two," he said, gesturing at us with a flick of his hand, "aren't connected—not like you and Beth."

Dawson frowned as he glanced between Kat and me. "What do you mean? He healed her. She's a hybrid—just like Beth."

"Yes, but apparently Daedalus gave Beth one serum and tested out the new one, the Prometheus serum, on Kat," Archer explained. "Which means they aren't connected like you and Beth."

As expected, Dawson argued that was impossible, but after I explained what Nancy had told us, my brother sat back, absolutely stunned.

"So, you see? You have too much to risk," I told him. "You have Beth and you have this baby to worry about."

Dawson cursed under his breath as he leaned back, rubbing his hands along the back of his neck. "You guys are really going to go after the Arum?"

"Yep." Sounded crazy, but it was better than doing nothing.

He shook his head. "Never thought the day would come that we'd go to the Arum for help."

I snickered. "No doubt."

"Luc is going to stay behind," Kat said, pushing what was left of her eggs around her plate. "To make sure Nancy behaves herself. We'll be leaving in a few hours. Then once we get the . . . when we get the Arum to help, we'll notify General Eaton. I guess at that point we'll start to head back here."

"But you have to leave so soon?" Beth shot a nervous glance at Dawson.

"We don't have a lot of time to get this done," I said. "But you two will be safe here."

"I'm not worried about us," Dawson said, and I wanted to smack him upside the head because he needed to be worried about them. "Letting you guys go off, meeting up with some damn Arum, and trying to convince them to help us out? That's crazy dangerous."

It was.

There was no denying that, and I'd never been a liar before, so I wasn't going to start now.

Archer leaned forward, resting his weight on his arms. His eyes met my brother's. "I understand you and I don't really know each other, and you have no reason to believe anything I say, but I promise you I will make sure Daemon and Katy come back *with* Dee. You can take that to the bank."

Sitting back, I stared at the Origin.

I'd never admit it, not in a million freaking years, but Archer . . . yeah, sometimes he was pretty cool in my book, and I did like the way he sounded. Hell-bent on fulfilling that promise and bringing back not only us, but Dee. He just didn't need to know I felt that way.

We finished up breakfast like it was any normal day, trying to forget that no matter what promises Luc and Archer made, it could be the very last time we saw each other. Kat and I packed up the changes of clothes Archer had found for us.

My heart kicked around my chest as I watched her shove the final sweater into a duffel bag we'd found in the closet. Once we left, things were going to happen fast, and I had no idea what we'd face on the road or when we met up with Hunter.

This literally could be the last time Kat and I were alone.

I wasn't being a pessimist. The truth was we'd be stuck with Archer. The three of us were glued together for the foreseeable future, and if things went south, well, this would truly be the last time we had a handful of minutes together.

Kat zipped up the bag and turned around. Her hair was

down, and I always liked it that way. There was a slight pink flush to her cheeks and her dove-gray eyes seemed to take up her whole face.

Her lips tipped up at the corners, and it said something powerful that she could still smile, like, really smile, when all this crap was going down around us. "What?" she asked.

"Nothing." I took a step forward and then another, until I was standing right in front of her and she had to tip her head back.

I slowly moved my gaze over her face as I cupped her cheeks, memorizing the high sweep of her cheekbones, the heavier fringe of the lashes at the outer corners of her eyes, down to the slight upturn in her nose and the fuller bottom lip.

Damn, I didn't want to waste these minutes. I wanted to spend them worshipping her. Most of all, I wished our paths had been different. Not that we wouldn't be together or some crap like that, but for the first time, I wished I were human and that my kind was hers and there was no invading race of aliens. That we'd graduated high school like normal teenagers, gone away to college together, and, instead of packing up to go knee-deep into the lair of sociopaths, we were planning a weekend at a beach or whatever the hell normal humans did when their planet wasn't at war. But spending time wishing for things that could never happen really was for losers. And I was wasting very limited time.

I lowered my mouth to hers, kissing her softly at first, and when her hands landed on my shoulders, slipping back around my neck, I deepened the kiss. God, I could live on the taste of her.

Taking my time—time we really didn't have—I traced the pattern of her lips, committing the feel of them to memory. A tiny, breathy moan came from Kat as she leaned into me, her fingers finding their way through the hair at my nape. Need slammed into me, invading every cell.

My hands slid down her sides, lingering around her waist for a moment, and then I smoothed my palm over her hips that rounded out sweetly. I wanted to be closer, all up in her. I was a needy bastard like that, but she liked it.

"Two minutes?" she asked.

I grinned against her mouth, and then forged a path of kisses to her ear. "Mmm, I like the way you think."

"I'm not surprised."

"You know me well."

Kat drew back, slipping out of my grasp. Meeting my eyes and wearing a mischievous grin, she reached down and pulled her sweater off over her head.

Hells yeah.

Then all rational thought fled when the pants came next, along with everything else she'd been wearing. The prettiest pink swept over her body, but she didn't duck her chin or hide from me.

Man, Kat fascinated me, every aspect of her. She was beautiful, but it went so beyond that. She was so incredibly strong, and she bore the scars of her strength like a prizefighter. She was smart and stubborn, but most of all, she was kind, and she'd given me the ultimate gift when she loved me in return.

That was the most important thing I'd always take from this.

Love was a gift.

Joining her in the buff, I wrapped my arms around her. I didn't need to tell her that I loved her. The words were meaningless because they were spoken so much. Actions were always louder, always more potent.

I showed her.

On my knees, and then on the narrow bed, with her breasts flush against my chest, and then I moved lower again. I wanted to do more, a whole lot more, but I hadn't had the forethought to bring any protection from the mayor's mansion with me, and the last thing either of us needed to worry about was a little Kat or Daemon on the way.

But like before, there were other . . . things we could do. And we did them until my senses were completely short-circuited, and I fell for her over and over again. We were greedy, pushing it until we were almost foolish in the way we felt for each other, pulling back at the last moment, and then falling over the edge together with our hands on each other and our mouths fused together.

It was perfect.

She was perfect.

And I was the luckiest guy.

When we finally left to meet up with Archer, Dawson was waiting at the exit doors, one arm over Beth's shoulders. I really didn't know what to say to him. Good-bye was wrong, too unforgiving. So I stopped and just stared at the two, hoping that even if we failed in the worst kind of way, my brother and his girl would go on. They'd be safe. They'd be okay.

Kat approached them first. She gave Dawson a hug and then Beth. The girl said something to her and Kat smiled in return.

I had to take a deep breath when I walked over to Dawson and clapped my hand down on his shoulder. "You're going to be okay here."

He leaned in until his forehead pressed against mine. "So are you."

"You know it."

Dawson grinned, and then he hugged me. We both knew the risks and how this could all play out. But we didn't voice it to each other as we said good-bye. Walking away from Dawson, leaving him in the same building with the woman who'd messed up his life so badly, went against everything I knew.

But I had to do it.

I had to let Dawson take care of himself, Beth, and his child. That was his job now.

My skin itched with the need to go back when I walked out those damn doors, but I ignored it and focused ahead. General Eaton was waiting for us beside a black Explorer, the kind of car Daedalus used to roll around in.

I sort of wanted to blow that bitch up, but that wouldn't go over well. Impulse control. I was proud of myself.

"We'll be waiting to hear from you," he said, meeting our gazes. "I don't think I need to remind you guys of how important this is and what is riding on you, but if you manage to pull this off, you'll spend the rest of your lives not worrying about any of us. I will make sure that no matter what precautions are taken in the future, you will have immunity to all laws and sanctions. You'll be free from all of this."

It took me a moment to process what he was saying as I met Kat's surprised stare. Once my brain kicked back into gear, I knew what she was thinking. "Not just for us."

The general eyed me.

"I want my family and friends to fall under that," I told him, glancing at Archer. I didn't know what he had planned when this was all said and done, but I didn't care. "And I also want Kat's family—her mom—safe from ever having to deal with any of this crap because of what we are."

Kat's lips trembled as she pressed them together. A fine mist covered her eyes.

"You get what I'm saying?" I asked.

"I do." He gave me a curt nod. "I can do that for you."

"I'll hold you to that."

There was another quick nod, and then there was no more time to hang out. I walked around the general and opened the passenger door for Kat. Whether or not Archer liked it, he was gonna be a backseat rider.

"What did Beth say to you?" I asked as I gripped the car door.

Kat smiled slightly as her gaze met mine. "She said the same thing I want to say to you."

"That I'm awesome?"

She laughed, and that sound brought a smile to my face. "No. She said thank you."

15

{ Katy }

"**D**id you know . . ." started Archer, and I closed my eyes, biting back a sigh. Here they go. Ten hours into the drive, my butt was starting to hurt and they bickered like an old married couple. "That typically there's a speed limit on these roads?" he finished.

"Yep," came Daemon's reply.

"I'm just curious." Archer was currently sitting behind us, but he might as well be in our laps. He'd positioned himself so he was right between our seats, his arms hanging off the back of them. "Because I'm pretty sure that sign over there reads fifty-five. Not eighty-five."

"You can read?" Daemon looked into the rearview mirror. "Holy shit. I'm so surprised."

Archer sighed. "Well, that was clever." There was a pause. "I just don't want to end up crashing into a fiery ball."

"You're an Origin. You'll be fine."

"I don't want to be a skid-mark Origin or a crispy Origin."

"Mmm," Daemon murmured. "Crispy Origin reminds me of fried chicken. I could go for some of that right now."

"KFC?" Archer asked, and I was surprised that he even knew what KFC chicken tasted like. "Or Popeye's?"

Huh. He also knew Popeye's.

Daemon's lip curled. "No. I'm talking homemade fried chicken. Dipped in egg and flour, fried up in a skillet. Dee can fry some bomb chicken."

"I've never had homemade fried chicken before."

His eyes rolled. "God, you're such a freak."

"I wonder if I can get Dee to make me some," Archer replied casually, ignoring Daemon. "You know, when she's not on Team Kill Everyone."

"She won't make you any chicken," Daemon retorted.

"Oh, she'll make me fried chicken." Archer laughed deeply. "She'll make me all the chicken I want."

A low sound of warning rumbled from Daemon, and I couldn't believe they were now arguing over the hypothetical situation of Dee making fried chicken or not. But I shouldn't be surprised. An hour or so ago, they were in a heated discussion over whether or not Shane would've been a better father than Rick on *The Walking Dead*. Somehow that had digressed into Daemon arguing that the governor, sociopathic tendencies aside, was a better father figure. The fact that Archer had never eaten at Olive Garden but knew about *The Walking Dead* absolutely befuddled me.

Archer sighed like a petulant teenager stuck in a car for too long. There was a beat of silence. "Are we there yet?"

Daemon groaned. "I'm going to sew your damn lips together."

I covered my smile with my hand as I stared out the

window. That smile faded, though, as I took in the scenery. I had no idea what state we were in. Everything from about a hundred miles outside of Billings had all looked the same.

Wastelands.

Absolute destruction.

For the last two hours, we hadn't seen another car on the major highway. Not a single moving car. There were a lot along the road. Some were abandoned with their backseats piled with personal items, as if the owners pulled over on the side of the road, got out, and left everything behind for the great unknown.

The others . . . the others were scary.

Burned-out shells of cars. A sad and twisted graveyard of wrecked and charred metal. I'd never seen anything like this. Read about it in books, seen it in movies, but viewing mile after mile of it in real life was something else.

"What do you think happened to them?" I asked when there was a lull in the arguing.

Archer pushed back from the seats, bending over so he could see out his own window. "Looks like some of them met up with unfriendly aliens. Others ran."

We passed an SUV with its back open. Clothing was strewn about it. A small brown teddy bear lay forgotten on the road behind it. I thought about that little girl in the grocery store, and I wanted to ask if they thought those who'd run for it made it to safety, but I didn't, because I was sure I already knew the answer.

Humans couldn't outrun Luxen.

"While you guys were doing things I don't want to know about in your room, some things were happening out here."

Daemon didn't look fazed by that statement, but my face turned into a ripe tomato. "Do tell."

"You know how they were saying there were cities completely lost, under the Luxen control? Well, those cities are functioning—TV is up, internet is blasting, and phone lines are working. It's like nothing happened there, except that more than half the population is made of human-hating aliens," Archer said, returning to his perch between our seats. "But there are a lot of cities that just . . . have been destroyed."

"Why would they do that?" I leaned back, shifting in the seat. "Wouldn't they want the cities virtually untouched so they were livable?"

"They do." Daemon glanced in the rearview mirror. "But if the humans found a way to fight back, even if the fighting back was pointless, then . . ."

"The cities get taken out in the process," Archer finished. "Things are going to be rough afterward, even if we stop them. A lot of rebuilding. There's going to be a lot of changes."

"Not *a lot*," I said as we coasted past a burned-out school bus that was more black than orange. I didn't want to even think about if the bus had been full or not, but the backs of my eyes still burned. "*Everything* will change."

We took the long way around Kansas City, since we didn't want to get within a billion miles of the Luxen-controlled city, and we ended up stopping outside of a small, unknown town in Missouri for Daemon and Archer to switch off driving.

Sleep was fitful over the next couple of hours, and it wasn't just the uncomfortable seating or Archer's questionable taste in music. My body was a bundle of nerves stretched too thin. We were about to literally drive into an Arum stronghold, and while Luc swore up and down that Hunter was cool, I hadn't met an Arum yet I didn't want to run from. But it was more than that.

I missed my mom. I missed Dee and Lesa. I missed my books and my blog, and in the hours when I couldn't sleep and Daemon had passed out in the backseat, I stared out the window and I couldn't imagine what tomorrow would be like or what a month from now would look like.

"You okay?" Archer asked quietly.

I hadn't realized that I'd been shifting restlessly. "Yeah."

"Can't sleep?"

"Nope."

"He doesn't seem to be having any problems."

Glancing behind me, I smiled. Daemon was stretched out on his back, one arm tossed over his face. His chest rose and fell in deep, steady breaths. I flipped around. "He needs it."

"So do you."

I shrugged. "What about you?"

He passed me a knowing look. "I didn't spend all my free time making out like the world was ending the next day."

My cheeks flamed. "You really don't need to keep reminding me that there's no such thing as privacy around you."

A quick grin flashed across his face as he focused on the dark road, but it disappeared as quickly as the star I'd been tracking in the sky earlier. I studied him out of the corner of my eye, the strong jaw and profile.

"Stop staring at me," he huffed.

"Sorry." But I looked at him fully, and I thought of—

"Yes."

I frowned.

"Like I told you before, I worry about her and I think about her. A lot." His fingers tapped the steering wheel. "I like her. The girl is . . . well, she's special."

Probably a good thing Daemon was passed out while we were having this conversation. "She likes you, too."

"I know." He chuckled under his breath. "Dee's not really good at hiding her thoughts. Actually, I don't even think she tries. That's one of the things I like about her."

"And she's absolutely stunning." I grinned.

"Yeah, that has something to do with it." His hands tightened around the wheel.

I folded my arms and returned to staring straight ahead, remembering the garden Dee and I had created around the front porch of my house. A sad feeling pierced my chest.

"We'll get her back," he said in a way that brokered no room for anything other than that.

Neither of us spoke for a long while after that, and I must've dozed off a little, because when I opened my eyes, Daemon was awake and dawn had broken.

"Where are we?" I asked, voice scratchy, so I reached for a bottle of water.

"Just crossed into Kentucky." Daemon's fingers found their way between the headrest and seat. He squeezed my shoulders as I looked out the window.

The highway was chock-full of discarded cars, slowing us to a near crawl as Archer carefully navigated the road. I was clenching the seat-belt strap each time we neared another cluster of deserted vehicles. The farther we went, the worse it got. The cars weren't just left there. Many were destroyed.

Daemon suddenly gripped my shoulders from behind. "Don't look, Kitten."

But it was too late. As we eased around a burned-out minivan, I had to, because there was something so innate, so human, that demanded you watch when everything inside of you was screaming no.

The van had been torched, most likely with the Source, but

unlike the other ones I'd seen or could see, the van wasn't empty. Oh God, no, it wasn't empty at all.

There were four forms in the van. Two up front and two in the back. One was twisted over the steering wheel, the other pressed against the passenger door as if it had desperately tried to get out but had run out of time. The bodies in the back . . . oh God, they were small, so tiny.

All of them were burned beyond recognition.

And it wasn't the only car like that. One after another, the vehicles were torched, and there were bodies inside.

Horrified, I pressed my hand against my throat like I was trying to stop the bile from rising. Out of everything I'd seen, this was the worst. This was horrific. Emotion swamped me, tightening my chest.

"Kitten," Daemon said softly, tugging on my shoulders. "Kat. Stop."

I forced myself to avert my gaze, and I saw a muscle pounding along Archer's jaw. Daemon had his hand on my cheek as he passed Archer a dark glare. "Can we get around these cars a little faster?"

"I'm going as fast as I can," he replied. "Unless you want to take this Explorer off road, and I'm not sure how smart of an—"

"*Crap.*" Daemon suddenly withdrew his hand as he narrowed his gaze on the congested road ahead.

Archer cursed.

I stiffened. "What?" When no one answered, I about bounced in my seat. "What?"

"I feel it," Archer said.

The only thing I felt was rising confusion and irritation. "I swear to God if you guys don't share, I'm going to punch both of you."

A wry smile twisted Daemon's lips. "There are Luxen nearby."

Oh no.

I leaned forward, planting my hands against the dashboard. Up ahead, there was an empty lane in the four-lane highway as far as I could see. "I don't see anything."

"You're looking in the wrong direction, Kitten."

My heart turned over heavily as I twisted around in my seat, peering out the back window. "Oh, holy alien butt crack."

A huge-ass Hummer was speeding down the hill we'd just traveled, plowing through the wreckage of the discarded cars.

"I'm going to take a wild guess and say they're not friend-lies." My stomach tumbled over itself.

"What gave that away?" Archer asked, winging the Explorer around a truck.

Daemon cursed again. "Definitely not. I can feel them pecking away at my head. They're calling out to me and I'm not answering."

"Which is making them mad?" asked Archer, frowning as he slammed on the gas, causing the tires to squeal.

"Yep."

"This whole Luxen two-way-radio thing is really weird," I said, because someone needed to say it.

"You have no idea." Daemon popped forward, stretching between the two front seats. Archer shouted and scowled at him, but he was a man on a mission. With his hands grasping my cheeks, he kissed me.

The contact was so sudden and unexpected that I sort of just sat there as he got all kinds of friendly with my mouth.

"Seriously? Kissing her right now is what we need to be doing when we have pissed-off aliens on us?"

"Kissing her is always the right thing to do." He pulled

back and gripped the seats. "We need to stop and take care of them. It's not like we can outrun them, and we don't need them following us right to the Arum."

Archer sighed. "This isn't going to be fun."

I was still sitting there, lips tingling, like a dork.

"Oh, this is going to be tons of fun." Daemon glanced at me. "You ready to play, Kitten?"

"Yeah," I mumbled. "Sure. Okay."

Daemon chuckled. "Let's do this."

Archer jerked the steering wheel to the right, bringing it to an abrupt stop along the side of the highway. Car doors opened, and as much as it sucked, I was the last one to get my damn seat belt unbuckled and to scramble out of the SUV.

"Keep low," Daemon ordered.

Huh? When he saw the look on my face, he motioned for me to crouch. I shot him a dirty look. "What? I'm not a freaking ninja."

"I've seen you fight." Archer strolled around the front of the Explorer like we were walking into a gas station or something. "You could be part ninja."

I gave him a quick smile. "Thank you."

"You'd be a hot ninja," Daemon said, winking when I looked at him. "I need you two to stay back for a moment."

Yeah. I so wasn't going to listen to that, but before I could prance into the street, Archer grabbed my arm. "For real," he said, holding me in place. "Stay here."

I started to pull free, but the Hummer crashed through a vehicle and the deafening thunder of clanging metal forced me to stand still.

The Hummer was barreling down on us as Daemon walked right out to the middle of the road, head bowed as he stretched out his arm. Concentration marked his expression.

He made a striking image as he stood there, legs spread wide and shoulders squared. Like a god about to meet a Titan head-on.

A shimmer of white enveloped him, and from where I stood, I could see his veins light from within, a bright white that followed a network of lines across his cheeks and down his throat, disappearing under the collar of his shirt, and then reappearing along his arm.

I'd seen him like this before, not all out, but when he'd stopped the truck that almost turned me into roadkill.

Daemon was freezing time.

The Hummer halted suddenly, pitching the occupants forward as the air around the car hummed with power. He'd stopped the car—but he couldn't freeze the Luxen inside. It didn't matter how many times I'd seen him do that, I was awed by the ability. A lot of energy had to be sucked up to freeze time, and I'd only done it once by accident.

Daemon jerked his hand back, and it was like the Hummer was attached to an invisible string. He'd unfrozen time, and the force of the vehicle snapped back, but it was a little too much for a thing called gravity.

The Hummer went up on the front two wheels in a perfect handstand and hovered there for a second, and then tipped over with the force of an elephant. Metal crunched as the roof caved.

"Boo-yah," Archer murmured.

The Luxen didn't stay down long. The doors groaned, and then flew off in a burst of whitish-red light. They came out—five of them—rushing toward us in their human forms.

"I got this," Daemon said as he crouched down, preparing for the massive impact of the five Luxen.

"What the hell?" I looked at Archer.

He nodded. "Yeah, we aren't just standing here while he has all the fun."

Archer let go, and I darted away from the SUV, toward the fray, just as a hood was ripped off a nearby sedan and shot across the wall like a giant knife. It hit one of the Luxen, cleaved him right in two, and there was no coming back from that, alien or not.

Damn.

I skidded to a stop when I saw Archer's downright evil grin. "Score."

"That was pretty cool," Daemon said, catching one of the Luxen by the waist. Lifting him up, he literally power-bombed the sucker in the road. Asphalt cracked. Shimmery blue liquid splattered across the road.

Yuck.

One Luxen veered off, charging me. Summoning the Source, I lifted my arm and concentrated on what I wanted to happen. Back in the day, when I was first getting used to the Source, it involved a whole lot of stuff smacking me in the face or crashing to the floor.

Now?

Not so much.

When the Luxen was less than a few feet from me, I flung her against the side of a semi-truck. There was a sickening crunch that I wanted to forget, but I had to hold on to it. Lunging forward, before the tool got back on her feet, I let the Source whip through me. It slammed into her chest, above the heart, like a lightning bolt. The Luxen lit up like a firework that fizzled out quickly.

Daemon had the one he'd power-bombed by the shoulders. He brought his knee up, making contact in the chest. Bones snapped and the Luxen howled. I turned as Daemon's arm cocked back, and the Source whipped down his arm.

I came face-to-face with Archer and the Glock he held in his hand. Our gazes collided, and fear exploded in my chest like buckshot. My breath caught in my throat as I froze. All I could see was the barrel of the gun, and then the spark as the trigger was pulled. I braced myself for the pain of metal ripping through my skin and bones.

Except it never came.

A body thunked on the ground behind me, and I spun around, gasping as I saw a Luxen facedown in the road in a pool of shimmery liquid.

"Bullet to the head," Archer said. "Even they don't get up from that."

"That's cheating," Daemon said as he whirled around, taking out the last Luxen with a blast from the Source, pinning him against a nearby truck.

"Whatever." Archer shoved the gun behind his back. "I'm all about conserving energy where I can."

Pushing the hair out of my face, I surveyed the grim scene. "That's all of them?"

Archer looked around. "I'm thinking it is for now."

For now? I wasn't sure I could go another round as I turned to where Daemon stood. My heart spasmed in my chest. Bluish-red liquid seeped out of the corner of his mouth. I jerked toward him, rocked. I hadn't even seen him injured. "You're hurt!"

"I'm fine," he assured me, but the sight of him—of Daemon bleeding—rattled me to the core. "Took a hit, but it's cool. In a couple of minutes it will be like nothing happened."

That did very little to ease the panic building.

"He's truly okay," Archer threw in. "He'll heal fast, especially since it's daytime."

I didn't quite get what he was saying at first, but then I remembered Daemon explaining all that time ago how the sun did wonders for the Luxen, while copious amounts of sugar worked for hybrids.

"We've got to hurry." Daemon grabbed my hand, tugging me back toward the Explorer. "More will feel us traveling, and it's only a matter of time before they figure out what we're doing."

And that would be bad—really bad.

16

{ Katy }

I'd gone through three chocolate candy bars by the time we neared Atlanta and was experiencing a major sugar rush. With Daemon behind the wheel and, as he had said, completely fine and dandy after taking the hit, we made up the time spent dealing with the Luxen on the road in Kentucky and might have shaved a few years off my life and Archer's.

We hadn't seen any more Luxen, and we didn't know exactly where they'd sensed us or if they'd communicated to others that we were on the move, or if they even knew who we were, but to be safe instead of sorry, we assumed eventually more would be coming.

As we crossed into Georgia, I saw something that looked like it was straight out of a movie. The trees on either side of the highway had been snapped in two, charred and broken. Wreckage from a plane crash could be seen through the thick stand of vegetation. A tail. A middle section with the tiny windows blown out.

I looked away, heartbroken by all the needless violence and destruction. The more I saw, the harder I believed it would be for us—for the world—to move on no matter what happened with the invading Luxen. Now that humans knew they were around us, how could they go on? How could they ever trust a Luxen after this?

I couldn't let myself dwell on those worries, kind of like not crossing that screwed-up bridge with a bunch of holes until we got to it. I really couldn't fathom what life was going to be like for anyone.

Surprisingly, the roads had cleared for the most part. Any abandoned car had been pushed to the shoulders, and the city, from the outer loop of the major highway, looked okay, all things considered.

Probably had something to do with the heavy military presence and the National Guard, but they would only hold the Luxen off for so long. It was close to seven in the evening when we arrived at the sprawling airport, and it looked like a curfew had been put into place, because there was hardly anyone anywhere. Then again, no one was getting on a plane right now.

"There we go." Archer pointed at a sleek foreign car with all the windows tinted out. "That's what he said he'd be driving. Nice car."

"I know asking you to stay in the car is too much, but please stay close to me." Daemon slowed down as he crossed the parking lot, heading toward the fancy black car. "Luc might trust the douche, but I don't."

I resisted the urge to roll my eyes. "It's not like I'm going to run up and hug him."

His expression turned bland. "I'd sure hope not. I might get jealous."

"You'd get jealous if she hugged a tree," Archer tossed out.

"Maybe." Daemon coasted to a stop in a parking space behind the car. "I'm needy like that."

I lost my urge not to roll my eyes as I opened the passenger door. "You both are ridiculous."

As we climbed out of the SUV, three doors on the flashy car popped open. Curiosity pecked at me. I'd never really seen an Arum who wasn't going to try to snack on my energy. So there was a certain level of novelty in really getting the chance to see and interact with one who hopefully wasn't going to turn into yet another thing that would try to kill us. I focused on the tall form unfolding from the driver's side.

Holy Arum . . .

The dark-haired man was as tall as Daemon but broader. The black shirt he wore stretched across the sort of shoulders and chest that reminded me of a boxer's build. Just from that alone, he looked like he could do some damage. From what I could see of the sculpted jawline and profile, his skin was pale, like all Arum, but not a ghastly color. More like alabaster or porcelain. His eyes were hidden behind black shades. Wearing dark denim, he looked more like one of those guys in *GQ* magazine than a soulless alien version of the goat-sucking chupacabra.

An identical replica of him stepped out of the backseat of the car. Except he wore trousers and a button-down shirt he appeared to have grown tired of buttoning up. Hard, pale flesh peeked through.

Arum came in fours—three males and one female. I expected to see another brother or a sister, but what was standing next to the passenger door was neither.

It was a human woman.

I gaped at the motley crew. What the hell was a human woman doing with them? She turned to where we stood, and I got a good look at the blonde. She was pretty—really pretty— and I couldn't figure out why she was here.

Then Daemon spoke. "What up, asshole?"

My jaw hit the ground.

"You really know how to greet people," Archer muttered.

The Arum who had been behind the wheel inclined his head with a sigh. "You again."

"You sound just as happy as I am to see you." Daemon's lips twisted into a mockery of a smile as he folded his arms. "Let's just get one thing straight before we go any further. If you plan on screwing us over in any way, it will be the last thing you plan to do."

Hunter smirked as he turned his head toward his brother. "Told you he's a cuddly one."

The other Arum leaned his arms on the roof of the car and a brow rose over the dark sunglasses he also wore. "Cuddly as a damn porcupine."

Daemon raised a middle finger.

This was going well.

Even though Hunter was wearing sunglasses, I could feel his gaze suddenly shift onto me. "So I see you got your girl out of Daedalus."

What the what?

"And I see that you still somehow have a human woman with you," Daemon replied. "I feel like I need to ask her if she's here against her own will."

Hunter barked out a syllable of a laugh. "Are you, Serena?"

The blonde rolled her eyes as she shook her head. "No."

"There's your answer," Hunter added.

"As amazingly well as this meet-and-greet is going, I think we should get to the point," Archer suggested. "We were told you'd be willing to take us to wherever the Arum are."

"I am." Hunter folded his arms, mimicking Daemon. There was a beat of silence, and I swore I felt his gaze on me again. "Are you guys sure you want to do this?"

Oh, that didn't sound good. I shifted my weight. "We have to do this."

The sun finally disappeared behind thick clouds, and dusk rapidly spread over the parking lot. Hunter reached up, removing his sunglasses. The pale hue of his ice-blue eyes was unnerving as hell. "Have any of you ever heard of Lotho?"

"Other than he's kind of like your little leader or something?" Daemon said. "No."

"Little leader?" The other Arum ducked his chin and laughed. "More like a little crazy."

"Or a lot crazy, Lore."

"Lore?" I said, feeling stupid. "Wait. That's your name? Lore."

He flashed straight white teeth. "Wait until you meet our other brother, Sin."

Sin? Lore? Wow, Hunter's name really sort of stood out. I shook my head, because seriously, none of that was important. "What do you mean, Lotho is a little crazy?"

"Well. He's a lot crazy," Hunter said, leaning against the car as Serena came to stand beside him. "Personally, I think he's a lunatic and a psychopath by human standards. I won't let him anywhere near Serena. Hell, I wouldn't let him anywhere near a pet cockroach if I had one."

Oh. Wow.

Daemon frowned. "This sounds really fun."

"And he's also very powerful," Hunter continued. "He feeds on Luxen like there's a shortage of them, and he's all decked out in opal. As in, it's sewn into his skin."

My eyes widened. "Ouch."

"He hates humans," Lore interjected. "But he hates Luxen more. And he's not a big fan of Origins or hybrids, either."

This whole thing was really beginning to suck.

"Sounds like this is going to be a great time," Daemon said drily.

Hunter laughed, but it was a chilling sound. "The Arum are loyal to him. They'll do whatever he wants, even if it means their deaths."

"And you're not?" Daemon asked.

"Hell to the no," Hunter replied as he draped an awfully protective-looking arm over Serena's shoulders and tugged her close. "Believe it or not, kid, I had no desire to make war with the Luxen before this whole crap went down. Now it seems like a necessity, but when it's all said and done, I don't give two shits what you, or any of your kind, are doing." He paused, glancing down at the woman in his arms. "I got better things to focus on. So does Lore."

Shock splashed across Daemon's face, replicating what I felt inside. The way Hunter looked at Serena? Wow. He really was in love with a woman—a human woman.

Daemon stared at him a moment, and then he tipped his head back and laughed. "All right. I can respect that."

Hunter didn't respond for what felt like an eternity. "If you can get him to agree to help, then you'll have one hell of an army. I'm just not sure you're going to find Lotho to be very agreeable."

"Yeah, well, we'll worry about that." Daemon cocked his head to the side while I seriously began to worry about that. "How many Arum does he have?"

"Thousands," Hunter said, and it felt like the ground moved under my feet. "Ones who've stayed under the radar, and even those who'd been with Daedalus until the Luxen showed up."

"And every one of them is with him now?" Archer scrubbed a hand over his crew cut, which was starting to grow out.

"Yep." Lore drew out the word, grinning. "It'll be like entering a cult. Be prepared."

"It's really weird." Serena twisted her hair and tossed it over her shoulder as she spoke. "They all stare at you like they're planning to eat you for dinner. The whole Arum thing is kind of freaky, to be honest." She glanced at Hunter and then Lore. "No offense."

Lore lifted his arm off the roof of the car with an easy smile. "None taken."

"So, you guys ready to do this?" Hunter asked.

Not really, but I didn't scream no when Daemon nodded. All I did was watch Hunter turn to Serena and clasp her cheeks with huge hands. The hold was so incredibly gentle, I was surprised an Arum was capable of it.

He lowered his head, kissed her, and she leaned into him as if it were second nature. I felt like a total ogre for staring, but I couldn't look away. An Arum and a human. Wowee. It hit me then that they probably thought the same thing when they saw a Luxen and human together.

"I'll be back soon," he said when he lifted his head.

Serena frowned. "I can go with—"

"You know I don't want you around Lotho and Sin, and you know I'll be fine," he reassured her. "Lore has promised to keep you entertained."

Lore nodded as he pursed his lips.

Serena still didn't look happy, and if she was afraid for Hunter and what he was about to embark on, I thought we needed to seriously rethink this.

But we didn't have any other options.

She hugged him fiercely, clinging to him for a few moments, and then she let go. Stepping around him, she patted his behind. "I'll be waiting."

The look Hunter sent her caused my cheeks to flush, but then Serena stopped and faced us. "Look, I've had some real bad experiences with Luxen in the past—the kind of Luxen who knew the rest of them were coming."

Daemon and I exchanged looks. "Care to give a little more detail?" he asked.

She took a deep breath. "There was a senator who was a Luxen, and he had two sons. My best friend . . . she accidentally saw them do their glow thing, and they killed her to keep her silent. They tried to kill me."

"Oh God," I whispered.

"Hunter was brought in by the government to keep me safe. Not because they really cared about me, but they didn't like how the Luxen thought they could kill whenever they wanted to—not following the rules." A sad look filled her eyes. "But it was more than that. My friend overheard the brothers talking about this—about Project Eagle. Something that had to do with Pennsylvania and some kids."

"Anything else?" Archer asked, gaze sharpening shrewdly.

She glanced at Hunter before nodding. "Project Eagle was in response to Daedalus—it was about contacting the other Luxen who were out there, wherever *there* is. It was about world domination. They've been planning this, and they were using the Origins to do it. We thought they were talking about kids—like little people right now."

"But they weren't," Hunter said, frowning. "We did a little digging. They were talking about Origins like him."

A muscle flexed along Archer's jaw. "As in, Origins fully grown?"

He nodded. "Yep."

Holy crap, we were totally right.

"We knew something like this was going to happen, or at least that they were going to try, but we couldn't do anything," she said.

"We have prices on our heads," Hunter explained. "Let's just say I pissed off the Luxen, some of the Arum, and Daedalus. We were between a rock and a really screwed-up hard place."

"We wanted to do something but couldn't, so helping you guys out . . . well, that's better than doing nothing again." And suddenly, I knew that Serena was probably the driving force behind Hunter fulfilling the favor he owed Luc. Her gaze drifted over to Daemon. "I know you don't trust Hunter, but we don't trust you, either. So if you do anything that puts him in danger, I know how to take a Luxen out, and I'm not afraid to."

Daemon's chest rose with a deep breath. "I got you."

"Good," she replied.

I liked her.

Hunter grinned. "Come on, guys. We don't have far to go."

The three of us followed Hunter over to a lamppost, which was like thirty feet from the car, and then he stopped. "We're here."

My brows rose as I looked around, seeing nothing. "Is this like some kind of magical Harry Potter door? Or something?"

He stared at me.

"What?" I asked sheepishly. "You know, like the Room of Requirement? The door kind of just appears . . . Oh, never mind."

"Okay." He gestured down by our feet. "We're going down."

All I saw was a manhole cover, and then he bent down, lifting the heavy steel, and my heart sank. We were literally going down.

"Here?" Archer asked.

He nodded with a tight smile. "Why else do you think I suggested the airport? It's not like I like to hang out here."

"How were we supposed to know?" Daemon responded, eyeing the manhole like it was the last thing he wanted to climb into. Ditto. "You're an Arum, so . . ."

"I really was hoping you'd drop that damn attitude by now."

Daemon smirked. "Kiss my ass."

"No, thank you," he replied, but neither of them had any real heat behind their words. Looking up, Hunter glanced at me, and then at Daemon. "I'm guessing you're going to want to get down there first before she does."

I resisted the urge to roll my eyes as I tugged my hair up into a quick ponytail. Archer crept over to the edge, saluted us, and then disappeared down the ladder. A few seconds later, his voice traveled from the great beyond. "It stinks. Really bad."

Great.

We quickly descended, and Archer hadn't been lying. The dimly lit tunnel smelled of mold and butt—moldy butt.

Hunter was the last one down. Not even taking the ladder, he landed in a nimble crouch beside us, since he was all kinds of special, apparently.

Straightening, he glanced over his shoulder as he strode forward. "We've got a ways to walk."

Turned out that "a ways to walk" equaled about a hundred miles to Hunter. In spite of my mutated genes, my legs ached as we walked for forever in the empty subway, which was silent with the exception of our footfalls. We traveled from one tunnel to the next, passing the underground commuter trains that had been abandoned and seemed to be the source of the nasty smell. I was eyeing the dirtied and broken windows on one of the trains when Hunter appeared right in front of me. Startled, I stumbled a step to the side.

Pale eyes met mine. "I wouldn't look too closely at those

trains. They're not empty. Some of the Luxen got hold of them. Lit up the insides. People were onboard and this is where the trains stopped. You get what I'm saying?"

My stomach roiled as I nodded. So much unnecessary death—it was horrifying, and it took a long time for me to clear my head. We went deep in the maze of tunnels, going through a steel door that looked like it hadn't been opened in the last decade, and entered a wide tunnel brightly lit with torches shoved into the grooves of the wall. Hunter stopped in front of a door up ahead, a circular steel one.

I bit down on my lip, sensing something was off. Like the air had suddenly turned stale, and it was hard to catch my next breath. A nervous sensation crept into my core like a thousand little ants.

Daemon stopped in front of me, stretching out an arm as he cocked his head to the side. Muscles up and down his spine rolled with tension. "There're a lot of Arum beyond that door."

Hunter smirked as he faced us. "I've told you. There are *thousands* down here."

I couldn't believe it. "How can there be so many? These are just subways."

The Arum placed a large hand on the door. "They've created a world here, little one."

I got hung up on the odd endearment. "Little" was the last adjective I'd use to describe myself.

"Lotho has been down here for years with many of the Arum, carving out an underground city with the help of those who are loyal to them. They come and go as they please, but they always come back." He reached for a heavy lever. "The way they live is a bit archaic, so what you're about to see—"

"Will probably result in my needing therapy later?" I nodded with a sigh. "Got it."

One side of his lips kicked up, and then he looked at Daemon. "Ready?"

"Let's get this over with." Daemon reached for my hand, circling his around mine, and I didn't mind.

I knew that what we were about to see, what we were about to walk into, was beyond dangerous, and we were going to do this together.

Hunter hesitated for a moment, like he really didn't want to be doing what he was doing, and then his biceps flexed as he opened the door. There was another hall, but this was different. The walls were wooden beams filled in with drywall sheets. The torches were on poles, something like totems with weird loopy engravings that reminded me of Celtic knots. At the end of the wide hall was a wooden door that reminded me of something straight out of a Renaissance fair.

The moment we stepped into the hallway, and before Hunter reached the door, it flew open, clanging against the wall as another Hunter appeared.

Ah, there was the third triplet.

Even though he looked like another Hunter, with the exception of hair that was longer and pulled back at the nape of his neck, he reminded me of a pirate. And not the fun Disney version, either.

This brother bled animosity into the air and breathed hatred. He took one long look at his brother, and then his icy blue eyes drifted over us. I shivered as the temperature dropped. Goose bumps raced across my skin, and as I expelled my next breath, it formed a puffy, misty white cloud.

"You really shouldn't have brought them here," the brother said. Hearing his voice was like being pelted with freezing rain.

Hunter inclined his head. "And I really don't need your permission, Sin."

Sin stared at his brother for a moment and then chortled. "Whatever."

Daemon had tensed, as if preparing for a battle to get through that door, and he didn't relax when Sin pivoted on his heel and disappeared. Neither did I. The bad feeling I had from the moment Hunter started talking about Lotho had increased to epic levels.

Archer appeared at my other side, and the three of us followed Hunter through the door. Nothing could've prepared me for what I saw.

Underground city? No joke.

It was like stepping into a different world. There seemed to be no ceiling, even though I knew we were still deep underground. As far as the eye could see was scaffolding that climbed up, creating dozens and dozens of walkways circling the wide chamber. Doorways were visible on the lower levels, and thick, furry-looking material dangled from some of the railings. The whole setup kind of reminded me of a prison made out of wood.

God forbid anyone got clumsy with a match.

My eyes were wide as we made our way down the center of the room. There were handcrafted tables in amazingly rich detail and cribs scattered along the edges of the room, mixed among tall and wide cabinets. A few were open, revealing normal contents—canned food, paper towels, sodas.

"This is so weird," I whispered to Daemon.

He nodded. "I had no idea any of this existed."

"It must be kept that way," Hunter said over his shoulder. "As much as I'm not a fan of Lotho, he's built something here for our kind—a sanctuary of sorts. No matter what happens, you cannot share this with anyone."

"We won't," Archer swore. "We have no need to tell anyone about this."

"Okay." Hunter reached for the door. "Let me do the talking. That means don't open your mouth, Daemon. Seriously."

Daemon frowned. "That's not insulting." I raised my brows at him, and he sighed. "Fine. I'll stay quiet."

We left the room and entered yet another hall and went through another door, but we could hear talking and laughter mixed with shouts and what sounded like banging. I had no idea what we were going to see beyond the door, and I tried to prepare myself for anything as Hunter pushed it opened, revealing a massive chamber.

Holy Arum babies, there was a buttload of Arum in here. They were everywhere, seated at long wooden tables and standing among them. My steps ground to a halt, and Daemon's hand tightened on mine.

Every Arum in the room stopped talking and literally seemed to freeze. Some had been in the process of standing. Others had huge cups that looked like medieval goblets halfway to their mouths. There were even women holding swaddled babies. All of them were pale. Most had pitch-black hair, and paired with their pale blue eyes, it was a startling combination. A few had bleached their hair blond or even bright punk red.

They all stared at us.

Oh boy, the hair along the back of my neck rose as icy fingers trailed down my spine.

"What in the hell, Hunter?" boomed a deep voice from behind us.

I spun around and sucked in a deep breath as my eyes almost bugged out of my head. There was a large wooden dais that overlooked what was obviously a dinner hall. The steps leading up to it were few but steep, as in I'd probably break my neck coming down.

A man was seated up there, and even though he wasn't standing, I could see that he was Jolly Green Giant size. The Arum was massive, broad in the shoulders and chest and thick in the thighs. He sat lazily, like he was barely awake, but there was a keen sense of acute observation in his pale blue eyes.

He was . . . he was handsome in a cold, unreal way. His features were sharp as if they'd been carved out of marble, lips full and expressive, nose straight and cheekbones high. His hair was bleached white, but his brows were dark. Somehow the odd combination worked. He gazed at us as he held a glass goblet full of amber-colored liquid in his right hand.

So this was the Grand Poo-Bah, as Luc had called him? I was reluctantly impressed.

Hunter stepped forward while I got a good look at what Lotho was sitting on, which appeared to be a throne made out of . . .

Holy run for the freaking hills and don't look back, were they actual bones? They were strange, though definitely not human. They were thinner and seemed more flexible, as if the cartilage could be shaped and reshaped over and over again, and they had a faint, luminous blue sheen—

Oh God.

They were Luxen bones.

This was bad, real bad.

"You know what is going on up there," Hunter began, but he didn't get much further. "Luxen have—"

"I know what is going on up there," Lotho interrupted, sipping his drink when I expected him to down it. "Luxen have come. Killed a bunch of humans and blah, blah, and a ton of other crap I don't care about. But that doesn't explain why you'd bring them here."

Hunter opened his mouth.

"Unless you are bringing us dinner." Lotho smiled, flashing white and oddly sharp-looking teeth. "If that is the case, thank you and the horse you rode in on."

"We're not here for dinner," Daemon said, voice as cold as the room, and I winced. "Nor are we dessert. We've come here for your help to fight the invading Luxen."

Wow. I looked at Daemon, sort of proud of him that he even uttered those words without a hint of sarcasm.

But Lotho looked like he might choke on the drink he just took. "Help?"

There was a rumbling of laughter all around us that echoed off the walls and caused my heart to pump too fast.

"Yes." Daemon tipped his chin up as his smiled. "Help. It's a pretty easy word. I could give you the definition if you like."

Whelp, there went the sarcasm-free Daemon.

The glass shattered in Lotho's hand.

Daemon frowned as shards of glass tinkled to the floor. "And that is why we can't have nice things."

I choked on my snicker, because I was pretty sure if I did laugh, the Arum might decide to snack on us.

There was a long stretch of silence, and I could feel the Arum rising from their seats behind us and pressing in close. Chills radiated down my spine and that suffocating feeling was back, weighing on my chest.

Sin crossed into my line of vision and stopped at the bottom of the stairs. "What do you want done with them?" The eagerness in his voice as he glanced over at us creeped me out.

Lotho smirked. "Kill them all and let their God sort them out."

17

{ Daemon }

Well, shit balls for dinner on Sunday.

That was the worst-case-scenario response.

I moved forward, positioning Kat between Archer and me. If I had to light this room up to get her out of here, so be it. And then what? This mission would be an absolute failure, the government would start e-bombing the crap out of cities, the world would decline into a place I sure as hell didn't want to be in, and worse yet, I would lose my sister. Forever.

Perhaps I should've just kept my mouth shut?

Lotho stood to his full height, which had to be damn near seven feet tall, and he eyeballed me like he wanted to chew me up and spit me back out. "Did you actually expect a different response from me?" He tipped his head back and laughed. Several of the Arum snickered around us. "That any of us would help a Luxen? Or a hybrid or whatever the hell that thing is?" He gestured at Archer. "You're either incredibly arrogant or seriously stupid."

Irritation pricked at the back of my neck, causing my skin

to hum with electricity. I knew I needed to keep it cool, at least until they made a real move against us. As much as it sucked, we needed them.

"What?" Lotho came down a step, and I stiffened. "You don't have something smartass you want to add?"

My eyes narrowed. "Give me a second. I'll come up with something."

Hunter groaned.

Small hands pushed into my back in warning. "I didn't expect any of you to hold our hands and sing 'Kumbaya,'" I said, and Lotho arched a brow. "I didn't expect any of you to actually welcome us here, but I did expect you all not to be a bunch of idiots."

"Oh God," Kat murmured behind me as she dug her nails into my back.

"That's not going to win you any friends." Hunter looked at me as if I were a few brain cells short of a complete set.

His brother, Pinky or Binky—I had no clue because I'd forgotten both of their names—appeared as if he was ready to go find himself a bib.

I took a deep breath. "You guys do realize what's going to happen once the Luxen take over Earth, right?"

Lotho's expression said he couldn't give two craps. "Do you think we care about humans? They are . . . useless to us."

I seriously began to question his intelligence. "Once they take over and subjugate every human here, they're going to come after you guys. They may not be worried about you now, but they will. And the last time I checked, the Luxen *owned* the Arum."

Lotho snorted. "They did not own us."

"Is that so?" Archer chimed in. "Because you're here on Earth, underground, living in subway tunnels. Just thought I'd point that out."

"He kind of has a point there," I added, smirking. "By then, they'll have learned how to fight your kind," I continued, hoping at least one of the Arum down here could make sense of logic. "Right now, they have no clue. It will be like a damn buffet for you. But later? After they've dealt with an Arum here and there? History is going to repeat itself."

"History will not ever repeat itself," sneered a female Arum. "They will never have control of us again."

"Keep telling yourself that while you hide down here," I retorted.

Pinky—I think it was Pinky—started to shift. "We are not hiding."

"Totally looks like you guys are hiding." Kat peeked around my shoulder, and Lotho's gaze slammed into her in a way that made me want to pull out his larynx and shove it down his mouth. "I mean, from an outside observer, I'd say you guys were hiding."

Hunter squeezed his eyes shut like he suddenly had a headache.

A heavy footfall later, Lotho was within ass-kicking range. He wasn't looking at me. My hands curled into fists.

Cool it, Archer warned me.

"You're not just a casual observer," Lotho said to Kat, voice as thick as the shadows gathering around him. "You're a whore of the Luxen who hides behind them."

I stiffened. "What—"

"Hold up. Excuse me." Kat darted out from behind me and raised one hand. "First off, the last time I checked, I'm not a whore for *anyone*. Secondly, I didn't cower behind him. Unlike *some* people."

Lotho cocked his head to the side.

"And thirdly? Not one of you in this room—not a single

one of you—caused the destruction of your planets, right? Is anyone in here old enough that they had a hand in that war between your two kinds?" When no one answered, she shook her head. "You guys are ridiculous! All of you."

Cold blasts of air hit from several directions. Not good. "Uh, Kitten . . ."

"Shut up," she snapped, and my eyes widened. "You're just as bad as they are."

"What the what?" I said.

Hunter's clone raised his brows. "I kind of want to hear where this is going."

More snickers from the peanut gallery.

"You two hate each other just because of what you are," Kat all but shouted.

"Well, they were kind of created to destroy us, so. . . ." I trailed off.

"And they committed genocide on our kind and *ensssslaved* our people," Lotho said, his voice becoming snakelike.

"Waah, waah, waah. Whine. That's all I hear." Kat threw her hands up. "Let me give you a brief history of mankind. We have constantly, systematically screwed one another over religion and race, doing far worse than what your two kinds have done to each other, more often than a history teacher has time to cover in class. Since the beginning, we have hurt one another over the stupidest things."

"Well, that's a glowing endorsement of humans," Hunter's brother said drily.

"You don't get it." For a second, I really thought she was going to stomp her foot. "Even though so many races on this planet have so much bad blood between them, when the shit hits the fan, we always come together. *Always*. Why? Because we know there are some moments when we have to fight together, and so we do. Then, when it's all over, we go back to hating on each other. And everything is right in the world."

Lotho's form solidified as he stared at her.

"God!" Kat did stomp her foot then. "Why can't you all act like humans just once?"

Silence, and then Lotho asked, "You're wanting us to forget everything that they have done to us and continue to do?"

"No. I want you to remember," she said. "I want you to remember everything that was done to you because these Luxen—the ones who just got here—they are the kind that totally screwed you over. Not Daemon. Not me. Not most of the Luxen who have been living here. The invaders are your enemies. I want you to remember that."

His lip curled. "As if there is a difference between them."

Kat shook her head in disbelief. "Things aren't always black and white. And if you really think that going after the invading Luxen isn't in your best interest, then . . . well, good luck with that."

Lotho looked away, his gaze traveling over the mass of his minions. He was as still as the air around us for a moment. Tiny hairs along my arms rose, and then he shot forward, going straight for Kat.

I whirled around, shifting into my true form as Lotho grabbed hold of Kat. He slammed her into the nearby wall with his hand around her neck.

Red-hot rage exploded inside of me. The sound that rose from my throat was raw and animalistic. I shot forward, shouting out in fury as Hunter's brother and another Arum clutched my arms. A heartbeat later, an additional Arum was at my back, pushing me down onto the slimy, cold floor. I didn't need to look to know that Archer was also surrounded.

I struggled, drawing in the Source, but these three Arum

were big guys—definitely not young—and they were strong, as if they'd recently fed on a few Luxen. Light pulsed and flared, snapping into the air. I lifted my head, seeing the world in white and red.

"What do you think is stopping me from ending your life right now?" Lotho snarled, inches from her face.

"Nothing," she gasped out. "But what does . . . killing me solve?"

"It'll amuse me." Lotho leaned into her, like all up in her personal space. He tilted his head to the side, and even from where I was, I could see his gaze move down the length of her. "And I'm pretty sure I'll enjoy it."

I lost my shit.

Pure energy rippled through me, expanding into a burst of light. The Arum at my back was flung like a beanbag. I rose, dragging Hunter's brother and his sidekick along with me. Power rolled from me in a tumultuous wave as I slammed my arms inward, knocking the two Arum's heads together.

Down they went.

I started forward, stopping long enough to drop-kick a rapidly shifting Arum into next week, and then another I caught under the chin, knocking him into the crowd of Arum.

"Let her go," I said, shifting into my human form as the Source crackled and roared down my arm. My heart pounded as the floor under my feet began to shake. "Or I will bring this whole damn place down on all of us."

Lotho glanced over his shoulder at me. "Look at you and your big, bad self. Rawr."

"You haven't see anything yet," I growled. "I'm giving you five seconds to back the hell off her. One. Four. Fi—"

He dropped her and faced me fully. "I don't think you know how to count."

"And I don't think you want to live."

Lotho stared at me a moment and then threw his head back, letting out a loud laugh as Hunter's brother picked himself up.

"Uh . . ." Hunter frowned, glancing at his brother as he staggered to the side. "Not expecting that."

Neither was I, but I didn't take my eyes off Lotho as I stalked forward, hitting his shoulder with mine when I reached Kat's side. "Are you okay?"

"Yeah," she said, swallowing hard as she watched Lotho. "He's laughing . . . ?"

I started toward Lotho, my vision still tinted in whitish-red. I was going to put my hand through his chest, but Kat clutched my arm, forcing me to stop.

"I kind of like them," Lotho said to Hunter, who appeared just as confused as the rest of us. "Which is great news for you, since I won't kill you for bringing them here."

Hunter scowled deeply as he folded his arms across his chest. "Good to know."

"Back up off of the freak," he ordered those surrounding Archer. He strode up the steps to the makeshift throne and then dropped down in an arrogant sprawl, thighs spread wide. "Okay, then. You want an army. I'll give you an army."

The mass of Arum around us shifted as some, but not nearly all, of the tension seeped out of my shoulders. I felt like I should say thank you, but those words wouldn't even form on my tongue.

"I give you my word, but there is one condition," he said, raising his chin.

"Of course," I muttered.

Lotho eyed me like I was some kind of insect under a microscope. "It's just one little thing that I demand."

Archer nodded, but out of the corner of my eye, I saw Hunter's shoulders square up as he squeezed his eyes shut. He muttered a curse under his breath.

"You let me feed off her."

I started. "I know I heard you wrong."

"No. You didn't," Lotho replied coolly. "You let me feed off *her*." He nodded at Kat. The blood drained from her face, but it rushed to every part of my body like a fiery flood. "I won't kill her. Just a taste. Or two. Maybe three."

A long moment passed as I stared at the soon-to-be-dead son of a bitch. Part of my head couldn't register that he'd dared to even make that request. Fury simmered in my gut, spreading into an inferno. My vision blurred as the world shifted colors.

Hunter shook his head as he rubbed the back of his neck. "That's so messed up, man."

"Yeah. I'm completely screwed up like that." Lotho smiled, and my rage knew no limit at that point. "That's my condition. Take it or get the hell out."

18

{ Katy }

I was going to hurl all over my sneakers.

This . . . this thing wanted to feed off me? *That* was his condition? Panic rose swiftly, sinking its poisonous venom into my bloodstream.

Daemon exploded. He shot forward, reaching the first step before Hunter and Archer got hold of him. The words that streamed out of his mouth were a steady onslaught of various F-bomb combinations I didn't even know were possible.

"You're out of your fucking mind," Daemon shouted. His eyes were all white, bright as diamonds, as he strained against the two guys. "You sick son of a bitch!"

Lotho arched a brow.

The edges of Daemon's body thrummed, casting frantic slivers of light into the gloom of this underworld. "Forget it. That's never going to happen, and you're never going to fucking walk again when I'm done with you."

One broad shoulder rose as Lotho stared down at him dispassionately. "Like I said, take it—"

Another ripe F-bomb was tossed in his direction. "If you think you're going to get anywhere near her, you're insane."

My stomach tumbled as Lotho continued to smirk. "Hey, if you don't want to play along, don't let the door hit ya where the good Lord split ya."

Daemon lurched forward, nearly dragging Archer and Hunter to the ground. Another explosive tirade ripped from him as my heart pounded like thunder in my chest.

"That's really your condition?" My voice was hoarse. "You're not going to help without that condition being met?"

He nodded. His lifeless eyes landed on me, and I knew he wasn't going to cave. We would leave with no Arum support. The military would drop their e-bombs all across the United States. Innocent humans and Luxen would die, along with hybrids and Origins. Dee would be lost, most likely killed. The world would rapidly rewind to the past, losing hundreds of years of technology and advancement.

We couldn't let that happen.

My stomach turned as reality slammed into me with the force of a freight truck packed full of dynamite. I was . . . I was going to have to let him do this. That was it. We had no other choice.

Archer and Hunter had managed to drag Daemon back a few steps, but the expression on his face was downright murderous as he glared at the Arum leader. I knew if he got free, he was going to go at him with everything he had. Maybe that was what Lotho really wanted.

Or maybe Lotho was seriously just a sick bastard.

I didn't know, and it really didn't matter.

My hands shook as I smoothed them down my sides. "Daemon."

It was like he didn't hear me; he was so focused on the Arum. Violence poured into the air around him. His chest heaved with every deep, ragged breath he took. He was a bottle with the lid about to be completely screwed off.

"Can you give us a few moments?" I asked.

Lotho gave a noncommittal wave of his hand. "I have all the time in the world. You all? Not so much."

Daemon started to shift. "You have less time than you think, you stupid freak of a mother—"

"Daemon!" I placed my hand on his arm, and his head whipped toward me, eyes blazing. "We need—"

"We don't need jack," he growled. "But I need to end his life right—"

"Stop," I said, staring into his burning eyes. "We need to talk about this."

"There's nothing to talk about." His gaze swung back to Lotho. "Unless you want to hear in detail what I plan to do to the bastard. Then we can talk all you want."

Archer's eyes met mine from the other side of Daemon. *It's our only choice.*

I know, I sent back.

Then you need to get him on board.

What the hell did Archer think I was doing? "Can you guys help me get him outside of this room?" Talking in here would just decline into him cussing out Lotho again.

Hunter nodded. "Come on, big boy. Let's take a walk and let you cool down."

It took a god-awful amount of time to get Daemon out into the tunnel leading into the main room. Both of the guys hesitated leaving him alone with me, as if they thought he'd bum-rush Lotho in the main room.

The way he was staring at the closed metal door, there was a good chance he might blast a hole right through it and go all Rambo on steroids on Lotho.

I watched him stand a few feet from me, his chest rising and falling deeply. The edges of his body were still blurred, and I could practically feel the bitter metallic taste of his anger.

"I can't believe he'd even suggest that," he said, his voice as razor sharp as broken glass.

"I can't either, but . . ." I took a deep breath when his luminous gaze found mine. "But that's his condition."

Daemon opened his mouth, closed it, and then opened it again. "I don't care if he could twitch his fucking nose and make the Luxen disappear; he's not going to feed off you."

"If he doesn't, then he's not going to help us," I reasoned carefully. "None of the Arum are going to help us."

"I. Don't. Care."

"Yes, you do. I know you care. There's too much at stake for you to not care."

He laughed harshly as he faced me. "You know me better than that."

"Exactly! I know you, and I know you're angry right now—"

"'Angry' isn't a strong enough word for what I'm feeling right now," he shot back.

"Okay." I raised my hands. "But we have to get him to help us."

"Not if it means you have to go through with that." He started to pace. "I can't allow it. There's no way I can let you go through being fed on. Nothing in this world is worth that. You have no idea—"

"I know what it's like to be fed on," I reminded him, and he flinched. I swore it was the first time I'd ever seen him do that. "When I got caught in Mount Weather, I was fed on. I know it's not fun and it won't be pretty and it's going to hurt, but—"

"No!" he shouted, hands curling into fists. He cursed again, thrusting his fingers through his hair as he twisted his upper body toward me. "It kills me that you even know what it feels like, that you had to experience it and I couldn't protect you."

"Daemon—"

"I'm not going to allow that to happen to you again. No way, so don't even think you can convince me."

"Then what do we do? Just say screw it?"

"Sounds like a plan to me."

I stared at him.

"What? We can go live in a damn cave," he said, pacing once more. "Look, I'm a selfish person. You know that. And I don't want you to go through that, so I'm willing to say screw it and we cut our losses."

"Really? What kind of life would that give us?"

"Don't bring logic into this conversation."

Frustration whirled inside me as I stepped in front of him, clasping his cheeks. The stubble grazed my palms. "Daemon, there is no life for any of us if we don't get them to help us."

"We can make it work. I know we can."

"Daemon . . ."

He broke away. "I can't even believe we're having this conversation."

"I know the idea is upsetting."

"Do you? Sounds like you don't."

My eyes narrowed and I planted my hands on my hips. "Come on, you know I don't want to do this. The very idea of—of feeling something like that again terrifies me and makes me sick, but if that's what it takes to get them to help us, then that's what I need to do. That's what we need to do."

"You do not need to," he snapped.

I dragged in several deep breaths. "We need to. For your sister."

"You're going to make me choose between you and her?" he shouted, eyes a vehement white.

"I'm not making you choose." I followed him around the tight circle he paced. "You are making that choice. By trying to protect me, you're letting her go."

He stopped and stared at me. I thought he'd lash out again, but he closed his eyes, his striking face taut and his body rigid.

I knew in that moment I had him thinking instead of feeling. I latched onto it. "Are you ready to do that? Because she'll probably die. I hate saying so, even thinking about it, but it's the truth."

Mashing his lips together, he turned away from me, his head bowed. Several moments passed. "He'll be touching you. He'll be—"

"It's not like Lotho wants to have sex with me."

He faced me, nostrils flared. "God, I'm going to kill him. Just even hearing his name and the word 'sex' in the same sentence—"

"Daemon."

"What?" He turned, thrusting both of his hands through his hair. "How can you ask me to be okay with this?"

"I'm not! I'm not asking you to be okay with it, but I'm asking you to understand why we have to do it, to acknowledge how much is at stake and *who* is at stake. I'm asking you to not think about me or think about yourself in this. I'm asking—"

"You're asking for the impossible."

Daemon lunged forward, and a second later, my back was flush against the wall and his mouth was on mine. The kiss . . . holy alien babies, the kiss was a raw combination of lust and possession. There was a taste of desperation and anger as our teeth clanged, but the hand against my cheek was so gentle, barely there, and all those emotions were in the kiss, but the love was far stronger than anything else.

As his mouth moved over mine and the deep sound from the back of his throat reverberated through my skull, I didn't feel the cold press of the damp wall or the bitter edge of panic that had started clawing at my insides the moment Lotho stated his condition.

Daemon kissed like he was staking a claim, but he already had me—all of me. My heart. My soul. My whole being.

When he lifted his head, his breath was warm against my lips. "I can't promise you that I'm going to let this happen. I also can't promise that I'm not going to walk back in that room and try to kill him. But you're right. We need them." Those three words sounded painful for him to say. "All I can promise is that I will try."

I closed my eyes, resting my forehead against his. What we were about to do—because it wasn't just going to be about what I was feeling or thinking, but both of us—wasn't going to be easy. Out of everything that we'd been through, I knew it was the hardest, and possibly the truest, test either of us had ever faced.

Nerves were going to get the best of me. Between the upcoming feeding—God, I didn't want to even think about it—and the way Daemon prowled the length of a large chamber we'd been led to after we'd agreed to Lotho's condition, I felt like I was seconds from freaking out.

But Daemon had one of his own conditions—he demanded to be with us. Lotho had smiled a bit too widely and too brightly at that. Instead of refusing him, he practically rolled out the red carpet.

Archer was outside, still in the main chamber, and while I knew he could handle himself, a lot of the Arum had been checking him out like he was an appetizer.

Daemon stopped in the middle of the room, glaring furiously straight ahead. Heart sinking, I followed his gaze to the massive bed covered with what looked like pelts of animal fur.

"His bedroom," he said, shoulders rising. "The son of a bitch just had to do this in his bedroom."

Yep. He had to.

I was beginning to think this whole thing was just to mess with our heads. There were plenty of places Lotho could do his thing. I shuddered, now unsure if I was going to be able to go through with it.

But I had to.

We both had to go through with it.

Bile was sitting at the base of my throat, ready to come up at any given second. Shaking my arms out, I closed my eyes and tried to release some of the tension building in my muscles.

I can do this. I can do this. I can do this.

"What are you doing?"

I stopped what had become an impromptu dance. "Sorry. Nervous."

"Don't apologize." He arched a brow. "It was interesting. Kind of reminded me of a flailing Muppet Baby."

A wry laugh escaped me. "Really?"

Daemon nodded. "Yep." He glanced at the bed again and swore. "Kat, this . . . this is screwed up."

My throat tightened as I whispered, "I know."

His brilliant emerald gaze centered on me. "Did you ever think this is where you'd end up when you knocked on my door asking for directions?"

I shook my head as I walked over to where he stood. "No.

Not even in a million years. I couldn't imagine any of this when I knocked on your door." I paused and forced a smile as I gazed up at him. "All I was really thinking about that day was your abs."

Daemon barked out a laugh.

"And that you were a flaming asshole," I added.

A cynical smile formed on his lips. "Sometimes I wonder if you ever regret it."

"Regret what?" My worried smile faded from my lips.

"This—all of this," he said, voice low. "Us."

"What?" I pressed my open hands against his chest. "No. Not once."

"Really?" Derision dripped from his voice. "I'm pretty sure there had to be moments where you've regretted stepping foot in West Virginia."

"There have been times that have sucked—sucked donkey balls—and I never want to relive them, but I don't regret us." My fingers curled around his shirt. "I couldn't, because I love you. I really love you, and love . . . it comes with the bad and the good. Right? I mean, I know my mom never wanted to experience everything that she went through with Dad and then losing him, but she doesn't regret loving him. Not even with all that pain and heartbreak, and I can't—"

Daemon kissed me, capturing my words with the soft and tender pressure of his lips. "I know there were many times when I didn't deserve you, especially with the way I treated you in the beginning, but I plan on using every second to make up for that."

"You already have." I kissed him back. "Many times."

As we drew apart, the heavy door to the chamber swung open, clanging off the blocks of the wall. I turned in Daemon's arms and got an unwelcome eyeful.

Lotho strode in, the leather pants hanging low—way low—on his narrow hips. There was a whole lot of pale skin on display. Stomach. Chest. But that wasn't the only thing. As he strode past us, I saw what Hunter and Lore had been talking about before we came down here.

Opal.

The gemstones glistened from where they were embedded in his back, following the straight line of his spine. Seeing them seriously sewn into his skin . . . that was crazy.

I squeezed my eyes shut. "Oh jeez."

"Did your shirt fall off?" Daemon asked, his arms tightening around me.

Lotho laughed. "No."

"So why do you need your shirt off to feed?" Even though Daemon sounded perfectly calm, I knew he was seconds from turning into the alien Terminator on bath salts.

"Feeding can get messy," he replied nonchalantly. "Don't want to ruin my favorite shirt."

Heat blew off from Daemon like nuclear fallout. Wrenching my eyes open, I watched Lotho make his way across the room and then throw himself onto the bed. He lay down in the middle, on his side.

Lotho winked as he patted the spot before him. "Let's do this."

My feet were attached to the floor. "I . . ."

Daemon's arms were like steel bands around mine. "No. Not like this."

"But I want it like this," Lotho purred as he rested his head on his closed fist. "After all, it will be really comfy."

I was going to puke.

"You're taking this too far," Daemon warned.

"I haven't even begun to take it too far." Lotho's pale eyes flashed. "It's not about me, now, is it? It's about how far you're willing to go to get my help."

A low, inhuman sound rumbled from deep within Daemon as I tried to drag in air, but the oxygen didn't make it past my throat.

"Need I remind you of the fact that I don't need shit from any of you?" he said with a slight, almost playful smile. "I'm not the one asking for a favor. You don't want to do this my way, fine. But there's no other way. So you can get the fu—"

"No." The word burst from me. "We can do this."

"We cannot," Daemon said.

Lotho arched his brows. "I'm confused."

I turned in his arms until I faced Daemon. "You promised to try."

"I did." He was staring over me, pupils white once more. "I tried. He's being a—"

"Nothing has even happened," I cut in, trying to reason with him. "So we haven't tried. Not yet." I really wished Lotho wasn't lying on the bed behind us, smirking, because that was so not helping anything.

"Please." I clasped Daemon's cheeks, forcing him to look at me. My words carried the weight of everything riding on this. "We have to do this."

Daemon closed his eyes, and several long moments passed before he spoke in a voice that ripped up my insides. He only said one word. "Go."

I let out the breath I didn't realize I was holding and then took another I didn't need. I tried to step back, but his grip was fierce. I gently grasped his arms, and it took everything in me to force him to let go.

He did, and by the way the heat flared off him, it looked like it killed him. And hell, it tore me up. Eyes burning with tears I couldn't let fall, I turned around and stepped toward Lotho.

I had to do this.

There would be pain—lots of it. There would be revulsion—a ton of that. As I forced my feet toward the edge of the bed, a bright white light reflected off the walls. Daemon had shifted into his true form.

Kitten . . .

Sucking in a shaky breath, I sat on the bed, my hands trembling so badly I couldn't feel the tips of my fingers. This was wrong, so wrong.

Lotho reached out, and I had to force myself to sit still as he placed his hand on my cheek. His fingers were so bitterly cold, and I flinched as he sat up, pressing his other hand into the bed next to my hip. He leaned in, and his hand slipped down my throat, sending waves of revulsion and fear rippling through me. Lotho wasn't even watching me. His gaze was fixed on where Daemon stood, his lips spread into a taunting grin.

I'm sorry. Those two words blazed through my consciousness. *I can't allow this.*

My body locked up as I prepared for a whole lot of bad to go down, and then it did. Daemon was a blur of light as he lunged toward us.

Everything happened so fast.

I was pulled off the bed, thrown away from the bone-chilling cold, and Daemon was leaning over Lotho. Horror set in as I realized it was Lotho holding him there without even touching him. Wind roared from behind me, blowing my hair across my face. It was like the Arum was a vacuum, sucking everything toward him.

Suddenly, Daemon was tossed back against the wall, and

he was held there, several feet off the floor, as Lotho stood at the foot of the bed.

I couldn't let this happen to Daemon, but we couldn't walk out of here without Lotho's help.

"Stop!" I shouted, rushing forward without really thinking that one through.

"Please! Just do it now."

Lotho glanced at me, a quizzical expression on his face, and then a toothy grin appeared. I squared my shoulders.

But he didn't. Lotho . . . he flopped onto his back and let out a loud cackle of laughter as he pulled his knees up and planted his booted feet on the bed. The force pinning Daemon against the wall eased off and he landed on the floor.

Uh.

I twisted around to where Daemon stood in his true form a mere foot or two from the bed. Was he seeing this, too?

Lotho continued to laugh, deep belly laughs that echoed off the cement walls. Backing away from the bed, I walked to Daemon as he shifted into his human form once more. I didn't get it. Nope. Did not compute.

Finally, after what felt like an eternity of him laughing himself to death, Lotho quieted down and sat up in one fluid motion. "Ah God, you guys are great." He smacked his hands down on his thick thighs. "Man, really."

"Yeah." Daemon drew out the word. "I'm not following this. At all."

A wide smile broke across Lotho's face and he almost looked . . . normal. Still a wee bit scary, but kind of normal. "You two were really going to go through with this, weren't you?"

I blinked.

"Holy shit, you really were going to let me go all yum-yum on you." He popped onto his feet, raising his arms above his head, stretching. His back bowed as he sneered. "Do you really think I'd feed off a hybrid? Sure, you guys might be snack-a-licious, but I only eat Grade-A Luxen. And a certain type. Unwilling usually does it for me."

I blinked again.

"What the fuck?" Daemon exploded like cannon.

Lotho threw his head back and laughed again, and we waited . . . again. "I seriously just wanted to see how far you guys were willing to go."

I blinked at him a third time. "Wait a minute. You never planned on feeding off me?"

"Don't take this the wrong way, hon. You're cute, but you're not my type."

Should I feel offended? "And if we didn't agree, you would've still let us leave without helping us."

"Yeah." He shrugged as he walked over to a high table and grabbed a bottle of Jack off it. Taking a swig, he faced us.

Oh my God, we'd just been dragged through an emotional wringer, and for what? Just so he could mess with our heads? Suddenly exhausted, all I wanted to do was shove my head under one of those animal pelts.

"I want to punch you," Daemon said. "In the face. And in other places."

Lotho shrugged again. "Most people do. Good news is that I know you two really are willing to do anything. I can respect that. So, you have your Arum army."

I really didn't know what to say. Shoulders slumped, I felt so many emotions all at once that I had moved beyond words.

Lotho swiped two glasses off the table, filled them, and then handed them over. I took one in a virtual state of shock.

"Let's toast," he said, eyes as cold as a January morning. "To a very unlikely, and very temporary, partnership."

19

{ Daemon }

It was taking everything in my power not to introduce my boot to Lotho's face. The Arum was crazy. Absolutely off his rocker and should be locked in a padded room. Better yet, he should be locked in a room full of metal spikes and then bounced around.

I wanted to punch him.

But I also wasn't stupid. Hunter and his brother hadn't been joking when they said Lotho was powerful. The little bit he'd displayed in that room told me he was capable of much more, and if we seriously had to get down to business, it would be ugly and really messy.

We were now seated in a small room that looked like someone had dug it out of rock and earth. The scent was musty and the torches shoved into the wall didn't cast much light.

I had Kat where I wanted her, in my lap with my fingers working the tense muscles in her shoulders and neck. She'd been quiet since we left Lotho's room, and I could tell she just wanted to get the hell out of here.

So did I.

"It'll take me a day or so to get them all rounded up." Lotho had progressed to vodka, and since we'd moved to this room, which had been maybe thirty minutes ago, he'd downed half the bottle. I was curious to see if Arum could get alcohol poisoning. "Some of my boys are out scouting."

Hunter stood near the door, leaning against the wall. He looked completely at ease, but the sharpness in his eyes said he was ready to spring into action. "How much time are they giving you guys?"

We'd explained the government plans to get overexcited with e-bombs. "We have time," Archer answered from where he was perched on a stool beside us. "About four or so days, but the sooner we can move against them, the better."

"Yeah . . ." Lotho took another healthy swig. "Worried about them getting trigger-happy, eh?"

Archer nodded as he eyed the Arum leader.

"Like I said, I need just a day or two. Tell your human masters we'll be there."

Human masters? I rolled my eyes as I dropped my arms to circle Kat's waist.

Lotho frowned as he glanced down at his now-empty bottle of vodka. "Where are we going again?"

Kat sighed.

"Right now, they want you at Mount Weather in Virginia," Archer explained. Again. "If that changes—"

"You'll call." Lotho tapped the back pocket of his leather pants. Asshole still hadn't found his shirt. "Got it." He paused as he tossed the bottle to the floor somewhere to his left. Glass shattered. He smiled. "You have my word that we will be there. That is something I don't mess around with."

My gaze flickered to Hunter, and he nodded.

"It's not like my kind or I will miss an opportunity to serve a little payback and get fed at the same time." Lotho gestured at the closed door. "It's been real nice chatting with you guys and we'll be seeing each other again, but y'all got to go. None of you is welcome here, including you," he said to Hunter.

He looked real torn up about that. Pushing off the wall, he didn't even bother to hide his grin. "We'll be in contact."

Kat stood and I followed, more than ready to get the hell out of Dodge, but as we walked past Lotho, he suddenly stepped in front of Kat. I started to pull her back from him, but he was fast.

"You have balls bigger than the males in this room," Lotho said, his face inches from her. "I like you. And I'd keep you if it weren't for the fact that you're part Luxen. So that's probably good news for you. Boo for me."

And then he kissed her. Full-on, mother-freaking kissed her.

Before either of us could react and I could unleash my fury, Lotho shifted into something that was nothing more than smoke and shadow, and was gone.

"I'm going to kill him," I swore, feeling the Source crackling along my skin.

Kat jerked out of my grip, her face pale and lips tinged in blue, like she'd been making out with a Popsicle, and she swung on Hunter and Archer. "I want to leave right now."

Hunter glanced at Archer. "Yeah, I think that's a good idea, before this whole trip goes to waste."

An hour later, we were finally topside. It was dawn the following morning, and I was still so angry that the metallic bitter taste filled my mouth with every breath I took.

"You guys are more than welcome to come back to Lore's

place if you want to chill out for a few hours before you hit the road again," Hunter offered. "Get some rest. Grab something to eat. Whatever."

As Kat climbed into the backseat of the Explorer, I glanced at Archer. We really could use the time to rest before we got back on the road. Kat had barely spoken the whole time it took to get out of the damn maze of underground tunnels, and I knew she was exhausted. Probably disturbed, too.

What do you think? I directed the question at Archer.

He opened the driver's door. *I think we could use the R&R and I think Lore and Hunter are good, um, people, but heads up, Kat doesn't want to go back to the base.*

My brows rose as I glanced into the interior of the backseat. She was fumbling with the seat belt. Smiling a little, I leaned in, brushed her fingers out of the way, and buckled her in. *Do tell?*

She wants to go home. She wants to see her mom. It's all she's really been thinking about for the last hour or so.

I sighed. I didn't have the heart to even broach that subject with Kat. Visiting her mom would be risky—too risky.

"Thanks for the offer," Archer said, turning to the Arum. "We'll take you up on it."

Hunter quickly gave him the directions before doing that shadow thing and taking the extraordinarily fast method of traveling. As Archer climbed into the driver's seat and I got in the back instead of the front passenger seat, he pulled his phone out of the compartment in the center console and tapped the screen. He frowned.

"What's up?" I asked.

He shook his head. "There's a missed call from Luc. Let me check this out, but he's probably just impatient, wanting to know how everything went with the Arum." Getting situated in his seat, he retrieved the voicemail. The minute his gaze flickered up and met mine, I knew whatever he was listening to wasn't good. When he lowered the phone, lines formed around his mouth. "Luc said . . . he said Nancy is missing."

"What?" Kat asked, her chin jerking up.

"I don't know. I need to call him," Archer replied. A nugget of unease sprouted in my gut and grew as I listened to the one-sided conversation. While Archer quickly explained what had gone down with Lotho and that the Arum was on board, the worry over what the hell Nancy was up to didn't lessen.

Archer hung up, dropping the phone in his lap as he twisted around to face us. "All right, so it looks like Nancy has gone MIA. Sometime after we left was the last time anyone at the base had seen her. Luc and General Eaton have no idea where she is."

Kat glanced at me. "But what does that mean?"

"I don't know," he admitted. "Luc seems to think she's probably heading to wherever those kids are stashed and he's got some people on the lookout for her, but with Nancy . . . man, you never know with her."

True. I didn't know what to think about that. If everything worked out with the Arum and we successfully took down the Luxen invaders, yet Nancy disappeared off the face of the Earth, it wasn't a good thing. No way was I living the rest of my life wondering where in the hell she was and if she was going to pop up again one day, when we least expected it.

"It's not the biggest of our problems right now." Archer's eyes met mine, and for a brief second, they flickered over to Kat. "Nowhere near it."

That was also true. "Luc will find her," I said, and I had to trust in that. But as I got all up and close with Kat, maneuvering her surprisingly pliable body around so she was stretched out across the seat and her head was in my lap, I couldn't stop thinking about Nancy Husher. Did she really go for those kids? Or was there something else? If I'd learned anything by being around her, it was that there was nothing the woman could do that would surprise me.

I leaned down, brushing my lips across Kat's cheek. "Get some rest, okay?"

She smiled a little. "That sounds bossy."

"Okay." I tried again as Archer fired up the Explorer. "Take a nap."

One brow rose. "That's still bossy."

I chuckled and brushed the hair off her cheek, sweeping it behind her ear. "Go to sleep."

"You really suck at understanding what bossy means." But she closed her eyes, and I'd swear by the time Archer figured out how to get out of the damn airport, she'd drifted off.

Lore lived on the outskirts of Atlanta, and even with the low-level traffic in and around the city, it took a while to get there. I tipped my head back against the seat and closed my eyes as Archer kept it quiet and my hand got all playful in Kat's hair.

Nancy was out running around, doing God knows what, and Kat . . . she wanted to go home and see her mom.

Hell.

I got why she did, and the last thing I wanted to do was break her heart by telling her there was no way we could risk doing that right now. The smart thing for us to do would be to get our butts back to the base and let the Arum do their thing, especially since Nancy was MIA.

That didn't sit well, though, settling like expired milk in my gut. Heading back to the base took the control right out of my hands, and it also meant I was leaving Dee to . . . well, to whatever fate was heading her way, which very well could be in the form of a thousand hungry Arum.

God, I didn't know if I could do that.

But how could I search her down? Doing so would mean heading straight into the heart of the danger zone, and that was more than just a risk. That was a straight-up death wish. And hell, how could I even suggest doing that when I didn't want Kat going back to Petersburg?

Hell in a handbasket.

I stirred as the Explorer slowed, turning down a narrow entryway that was nearly invisible from the road. I took notice as we eased up a long driveway and a sprawling house came into view.

Hunter's Porsche was parked out in front of the garage. There was a huge front porch covered with potted plants and hanging flowers.

Huh.

The house was a monstrosity in terms of size but surprisingly welcoming. I had been expecting something cold, run-down—in other words, a shitty place. This was far from that.

Kat sat up, pushing her hair back as Archer killed the engine. Her mouth dropped when she peered out the window. Obviously she hadn't been expecting something as nice as this, either.

I dropped my arm over her shoulders as we climbed the porch stairs. The whole place smelled like one giant flower. Color me shocked some more.

The door opened before we reached it, revealing Lore. He squinted, and I realized it was from the faint rays of sun streaking across the porch. "Come on in."

There was hesitation, as I was about to experience another first to add to going deep into the Arum's lair, teaming up with them, and now staying at an Arum's house that looked like it belonged on the front of *Better Homes and Gardens*.

I'd given up trying to figure anything out at this point.

Archer stepped in first, and then I ushered Kat inside. Lore closed the door behind us and padded down the foyer in his bare feet, into a living room with the blinds drawn.

Serena was standing in the middle of the room, staring at a piece of paper. "Is this all we need to get?"

Lore scanned the paper and nodded. "Looks good to me."

"We'll run out to get some food," Serena announced, smiling. "Lore is in the mood to cook, and trust me, you want to eat what he makes."

I arched a brow. "He . . . cooks?"

He strolled past us, tossing the keys to Hunter, who had appeared out of freaking nowhere, it seemed. "I also bake. I'm like a culinary master chef—you know, when I'm not out there killing innocent Luxen babies."

I had no idea what to say in response to all that sarcasm.

Serena inched closer, and I was aware of Hunter also drifting toward us, as if he didn't trust *us* near his woman. The role reversal was . . . odd. "There're two bathrooms on the second level that no one uses. I laid out some shampoo, soap, and fresh towels in them."

"Thank you," Kat said, smiling. She glanced at Lore and then Hunter. "Thank you for letting us come here, and for everything else."

Lore shrugged.

Hunter shrugged.

Everyone was shrugging.

Serena smiled brightly. "It's okay. I'm just glad we could help in some way. And it's about time all of us started working together."

Hunter stared at the ceiling.

Lore started messing with a giant potted palm tree–looking thing.

"Well, all righty then." Serena clapped her hands as the silence grew to an awkward level. "We'll head out."

"It should take us no longer than an hour," Lore said, and for some reason that came across as a warning. Like what would we do? Run around and rearrange the numerous plants and flowers he seemed to have growing out of the walls?

They skipped on out the doors, leaving the three of us in the house. Archer was the first to say what we probably all were thinking.

"I can't believe they left us here," he said, brows raised.

I grinned. "I feel like we should start rearranging rooms or something." I cast a long look over the skillfully decorated living room and adjoining den. "I think Lore would really appreciate that."

"Don't," Kat said, narrowing her eyes at me. "I know Arum and Luxen are BEFs, but seriously, they are being super cool by letting us stay here."

"BEFs?" I frowned.

"Best Enemies Forever," she replied, shrugging one shoulder. "Anyway, let's all play nice with one another. It would be a good change of pace."

"Yeah, especially if one of them doesn't end up kissing you," Archer said.

Pulling her hair back from her face in a low ponytail, she swung an arch look at him as heat blew off me. "Did you really need to remind me of that?"

He flashed a quick grin, and I wanted to punch off his face. The reminder got me all primed to do violence, and the damn Origin appeared completely shameless.

"I'm going to go get our bags," he offered.

I glared at him. "Yeah, you do that."

As he turned and left the room, Kat walked over to me.

Without saying a word, she placed her hands on my chest, stretched up, and kissed me softly. That flipped my raging aggression into something a lot more fun.

I swept an arm around her, fitting our bodies as close as we could get while standing. My other hand delved deep in her hair, and I took the kiss to a whole different level. The taste of her never failed to blow my mind, and so did the soft sound she made as I nipped at her lower lip.

Archer cleared his throat. "Seriously guys?"

Slowly, I lifted my mouth from Kat's and narrowed my eyes as she pressed her face against my chest. "Can't you go somewhere?"

"Oh, I don't know. What about you all? How about one of those bedrooms upstairs that have doors and stuff? Hey! That would be a good—"

I felt it the same moment Archer had. My senses sharpened as awareness settled over me like a too-warm cloak. I eased Kat back, swearing under my breath.

"What?" she demanded.

Archer turned toward the doorway he'd just come through, dropping our bags. "There are Luxen here."

"No," she said, dragging in a deep breath. "Do you think they'll be friendly, not wanting to—?"

The large picture window in the living room exploded. Pieces of plastic and glass turned into nasty little projectiles. Kat ducked down, throwing her arms up to shield her face as I stepped forward, summoning the Source and using it to push back the explosion of sharp and painful things.

They fell to the floor inches from where the three of us stood.

"I think that's your answer, Kitten."

She rose, hands balling into fists. "Dammit. All I want to do is shower and take a nap and eat some bacon!"

Archer slid a look at her. "Well, I think that will—"

A Luxen came through the window, a blur of bright light, and I shot forward, colliding with it as I shifted. We hit some antique-looking chair. The legs gave under our sudden weight. We tore right through the back. Stuffing flew into the air. The palm tree ended up as a drive-by casualty.

Landing hard on the floor, I reared back and slammed my hand down on the Luxen's chest, letting go of the Source and sending a steady shot right into the heart of the bastard, frying him from the inside out.

The light dulled as I pushed myself up, whirling around. *How many?*

I don't know. Kat was heading for the archway that led to the foyer.

Switching back into my human form, I joined her and Archer at the archway a second before the front door literally blew off its hinges and winged across the entryway, embedding deep into the opposite wall.

I knew before I even looked.

I felt it in my bones; in every cell that was me, I knew before I looked.

My sister stood in the doorway in her human form, and as her gaze swept over us, she smiled in a way that was so wrong for her.

"Gotcha," she said.

{ Katy }

Dee looked like a goddess of vengeance straight out of one of the books I'd read and cherished. She stood with her slender legs wide and shoulders back. With the sun behind her, forming a halo over her body, and her eyes glowing white, she looked fierce and really scary.

Fine. I might have read too many books, because this was real and she looked like she wanted to kill us. Like kill us dead.

Archer started forward. "Dee—"

She raised her hand, and he should've been able to move in time, but he was like Daemon, rooted to the spot he stood in. A bolt of the Source caught Archer in the shoulder, spinning him back.

Oh, she was so not messing around.

Dee turned to where we stood and then casually, like nothing was up, stepped into the house. Behind her, I saw more Luxen.

This was about to get bad.

"Shacking up with Arum?" Dee tsked as she spared a quick glance at Archer while he picked himself up. "How far you've fallen, brother."

Daemon stepped forward. "Dee—"

She lunged at him, flying the several feet between them as my heart lodged in my throat. All Daemon did was grip her by the shoulders. He made no move to do anything else, and she took complete advantage of that.

Dee shoved her hand at his chest. He only moved at the last second to avoid a direct hit to the heart, but he took an up-close-and-personal blast anyway. I cried out as he went down, his sister right on top of him.

I knew in that instant that she would either really hurt him or kill him unless he treated her like the Luxen he'd just taken out.

Archer had the other Luxen engaged as I shot forward, making up my mind.

Daemon might hate me if I ended up having to kill his

sister, but I'd rather he despise me than hate himself for hurting her worse.

I grabbed handfuls of her long hair and yanked her off Daemon. She hit the floor, arms and legs sprawled like a crab. She looked up, eyes glowing like diamonds.

"You don't want to do this," I said. "You—"

Dee popped up. Like didn't even bend her knees, just shot right up and was in my face. "Oh, you have no idea how badly I want to do this."

Then she drew her arm back and cold-cocked me right in the face.

The impact knocked me away, and I landed on my butt as pain lanced through my jaw and down my neck. Blinking fresh tears out of my eyes, I stared up at her.

"That felt so good," she said, cocking her head to the side. "I think I need to do it again."

Oh, it was on like Donkey Kong.

I lumbered to my feet, nowhere near as gracefully as Dee. Behind her, a Luxen zipped into the room just as Daemon rose. They two of them collided at the same moment I slammed my fist into Dee's jaw.

Her head snapped back, black tresses flying out around her in a way that made her hair look like Medusa's snakes. Dull pain flared along my knuckles, but there was no time to really pay attention to that.

Dee launched herself at me, grabbing my ponytail and jerking on my neck. A fiery sensation coursed down my spine, and I reached up, digging my fingers into her arms. She didn't let go, and there was a good chance she was going to rip my head off.

Time to get dirty.

Twisting in her grasp, I gripped her arms as I brought my knee up, shoving it right in her lady parts.

Dee shouted hoarsely and let go, bending over as I straightened. I clutched her hair and brought my knee up once more, connecting with her face. She went down on one knee as I stumbled back, breathing heavily.

"Please," I gasped out. "This isn't you, Dee. Whatever this is, it isn't you—"

She was up and her hand was bonding with my cheek in an epic smack, spinning me around in a little circle. Holy crap, that stung.

Dee slammed her hands into my back, knocking me onto my knees as she wrapped a slender arm around my neck and squeezed.

I gasped, fighting for air.

The little training Daedalus had taught me kicked in, and I grabbed her hand and then threw my weight forward. She went right over my shoulder, landing hard on her back.

She shouted something too furiously for me to understand, and I struggled not to find something sharp and plunge it into her eyeball. "We're best friends," I told her, pushing to my feet as she rose. "Don't you remember? We're best friends, Dee."

"You're just a stupid human." Bluish-red blood trickled from her lip. "Because that's all you are, underneath it, just a fragile, useless human who bleeds easily."

"Jesus. It's like I'm a muggle to your pure-blood or something."

She just glared at me.

I backed up, keeping an eye on her. This so wasn't the time for Harry Potter references. "We planted flowers together and you borrowed a lot of my books and never gave them back. You made Daemon talk to me and be nice—you hid his keys. And you—"

She tackled me to the floor, clawing and pulling my hair.

We were in full girl-fight mode.

Both of us had a hold of each other's hair as we rolled across the floor. I gained the upper hand for a second. "We hung out together on Halloween and watched stupid movies. And we fought Baruck together—"

Dee flipped me, her nails tearing the collar of my sweater. "None of that means anything." She grabbed my shoulders and slammed me back down with enough force that I was stunned for a second.

For long enough.

Hauling me up, she screamed as she spun around—*spun me*—and the next second I was flying through the air. I hit the wall. Plaster cracked and gave way. For a second, I could see clouds of white dust fly everywhere and then I was in the den, toppling over the back of a couch, hitting the floor.

That—that bitch! She'd thrown me through a wall!

I lay on the floor, unable to move as I stared up at the ceiling, blinking out the tiny stars clouding my vision. There was a ringing in my ears as I forced my body to shift onto its side.

Dee climbed through the Katy-size hole in the wall, which was pretty big. Good Lord, she wasn't going to give up.

Hands shaking, I pushed myself to my feet, breathing through the unholy burn surrounding my ribs and back. There was probably a lot of stuff broken, important stuff.

She landed on the couch and then dived at me with murder in her expression. I darted out of the way at the last second, and she hit the coffee table behind me. Glass shattered.

Now she looked stunned as she stared at the ceiling, her chest heaving. I didn't give her a chance to recover.

I landed on her, my knees digging into the broken glass, and slammed my hands onto her shoulders. "We're best friends," I tried again, not knowing what else to do. "You picked out my fake name—from one of my favorite books. You gave Daemon his new name." I shook her, rattling her head back and forth. "You were picturing Archer naked not that long ago and you wanted one perfect night with him." Her hand connected with my face again, wringing a pain-filled grunt from me. "We've been through some harsh stuff, but we've always made it out together, even after what happened to Adam."

She went wild, like some kind of demon straight out of a nightmare, smacking and bucking, kicking and scratching.

"You and Adam tried to help me," I shouted at her as I pinned her with all my weight, straining to avoid her swinging hands that hit my face and chest. "Do you even remember Adam?"

"Yes!" she shrieked. "I remember him! And I remember—"

"Me being the reason for him dying?" Every part of my body ached, and I could feel blood in a lot of places, some really uncomfortable places, but I had to get through to her. I had to. "It was my fault. I know that! And I'll never fully forgive myself for what it did to you and to our friendship. But we got past that, because you're like a sister to me."

Dee froze with her fingers curled along the torn hem of my shirt, like she was about to rip it straight off me, and at that point I honestly wouldn't have been surprised if she had.

"Do you think he'd be like this now? Adam loved everyone, and he would've hated this war—hated what his kind was doing to innocent people." I watched the white light fade from her green eyes. "He would've hated what has become of you. Can't you see that? You're better than this. You're—"

Dee threw her head back and she screamed—screamed like I was trying to murder her, and I eased off, raising my hands. The horrible, wretched sound was like a wounded animal, something dying. She shuddered under me and squeezed her eyes shut. Both of us were still for a handful of seconds, and then she screamed again, until the sound was raw and pained, until I thought there was a good chance she might be dying.

"I'm sorry," Dee whispered as another great tremble rocked her lithe frame. As I stared down at her, trying to catch my breath, trying to process the two words, her beautiful face crumpled and big, fat tears streamed down her cheeks. "I'm so sorry."

20

{ Daemon }

As the last Luxen dropped to the floor in a messy pile, I whipped around to where I'd last seen Kat and Dee. There was a massive hole in the plaster, exposing the wooden frame inside the wall, and that had also taken a hell of a beating.

They'd gone through the wall.

"Good God." My stomach dropped as I stepped over the dead Luxen and darted toward the open doorway that led into the other room.

I kept telling myself they had to be alive—both of them—because I would've felt it if either of them suffered a mortal wound. It did nothing to slow my racing heart or to ease the sick feeling curdling in my stomach.

Archer was standing just outside the den, his shoulders rising and falling in deep breaths. He didn't say anything as I pushed past him, stumbling to an abrupt stop. The room was absolutely destroyed—the couch broken, TV smashed, and vases shattered on the floor. Piles of dirt and shredded petals were embedded in the carpet.

My desperate gaze zeroed in on the middle of the room, and damn if my knees didn't almost give out on me.

They were on a smashed coffee table, Kat on top of my sister. They weren't fighting, but both seemed frozen. I was frozen. Then I heard it. The deep, destroyed sounds of a person breaking wide open.

Kat, her hair half in the ponytail and half out, lifted her head and shuddered, then rolled off my sister and slowly rose to her feet. She backed away, running shaky hands over her messy hair. She looked over at me with wide eyes. Blood trickled from her nose and mouth, and each breath she expelled seemed to wheeze out of her.

I started toward her, but stopped. My gaze swung back to my sister. When Kat had climbed off her, she'd rolled onto her side, curled up into a tiny ball. The sounds—the sounds were coming from her.

"Dee?" My voice cracked.

"I'm sorry," she said, her arms folded over her head. "I'm so sorry. I'm so sorry." And that was all she kept saying, over and over again between the sobs.

Glass crunched under my feet as I walked to where she lay, and when I reached her side, my knees did give out. I landed next to her and gently placed a hand on her shaking shoulder. "Is it really you, Dee?"

Her sobs grew more ragged, and there was a stream of words from her bouncing around in my skull. Most of it incoherent, one giant run-on thought, but there was no mistaking what it meant.

Somehow the connection to the rest of the Luxen had been broken. I didn't know how, but it didn't matter.

I gathered her off the ruined table and glass and sat back, pulling her against me, and she scrambled closer, like she used to do when she was small and was afraid of everything. As I held her close, I carefully picked out the pieces of glass stuck in her hair, in her clothes.

"God, Dee . . ." I tucked her against my shoulder. "You about killed me, you know?"

She was shaking as her fingers gripped my arms. "I don't know what happened. They came, and what they wanted was all I could think about."

"I know." I closed my eyes, smoothing my hand up her back. "It's okay now. Everything is okay now."

Dee didn't seem to hear me. "You don't know the things I did or what I was thinking, what I was okay with them doing to people."

But I did. At least some of it from the short period of time I'd been around her while she'd been connected to them. The things I'd seen and heard her do were things I forced myself not to acknowledge, because they hadn't been her fault.

And so I told her, over and over, that none of it mattered and none of it was her fault. She started spouting crazy shit, like her being evil, and the crap broke my heart. Tore me right up.

"What you did was their fault. Not yours. If you ever believe anything I've told you, you believe that." I folded my hand over the back of her head, willing her to accept my words. "You don't have an evil bone in your body. Never have, Dee. Never."

The trembling eased a little as I held her, and I don't know how long we sat in the wreckage, but when I opened my eyes finally, the room was a little blurry.

"It was Kat," she said, her breath coming not as fast as it had been before. "She did it. I wanted to kill her. Oh God, Daemon, I really wanted to kill her, but . . ."

"But what?"

"As we were fighting, she kept talking to me, forcing me to remember what it was like . . . before they came." Dee pulled back, her lashes thick with tears. "And it was about Adam." Her breath caught on his name. "She was talking about him, and I remembered more than just the pain and the anger. I don't know, but it just snapped, and suddenly I was looking at her and I wasn't hearing any of them anymore. My thoughts . . . they were my own."

I closed my eyes again briefly, promising myself that I'd repay Kat a millionfold as soon as I had the chance.

Once Dee settled down enough that I knew she was okay and wasn't seriously injured, I looked around the room. I hadn't realized that Archer and Kat had left. Concern for Kat worried away at me now that I knew Dee was going to be all right.

I helped her stand. "How are you doing?"

Dee wiped the tears and blood—bright red blood that couldn't belong to her—from her cheeks with the sleeves of her dark sweater. My heart thundered in my chest as she took a deep breath. "I'm okay, but Kat . . . It got pretty rough between us. Oh God, she probably hates me now. Like really—"

"No. She doesn't hate you. If she did, she wouldn't have tried to bring you back. Kat loves you like a sister, Dee. In fact, she's kind of like your sister now."

That statement pulled Dee out of her troubled thoughts. Her nose wrinkled. "What do you mean? Because that sounds a little . . . weird considering what you and her do and all that."

I laughed, and damn, it felt good to be standing in front of my sister again and laughing. "Kat and I are married."

Dee stared at me and then blinked wide eyes. "What?"

"Well, we're not really, really married, because we did it with our fake IDs when we were in Vegas— Ow!" I stepped back, rubbing my arm right in the spot where Dee had punched me. "What was that for?"

"You two got married and neither of you told me?" She stomped her foot, shimmering eyes on fire. "That's so wrong! I should've been a part of it." She spun around. "Where is she? I'm seriously going to hit her again."

"Whoa." I chuckled as I grabbed her arm. "Can you wait to hit her again until we make sure she's okay?"

"Oh yeah, probably a good idea." Then she whirled around and threw herself at me, circling her long arms around my neck, and I stumbled back a step. "You two really did it?"

Dee's lips trembled into a small smile and not the kind I'd seen on her lately. Not cold. Totally her. "That's amazing," she whispered as she pulled free. "I'm happy for you—for her. But I'm still going to punch her. After we make sure she's okay. Oh God." Her face fell. "What if she—?"

"It'll be okay." I placed a hand on her back, steering her out of the living room.

First person I saw was Archer. Of course. And he wasn't looking at me at all. Oh no. His face was pale, his eyes wide and pupils dilated. Shaken up. I'd never seen him look quite like that before, and I sure as hell didn't want to acknowledge why.

"She's outside," he murmured, staring at Dee, who was also staring at him, and they were like two people who had never seen another person before. Damn. "She's okay."

Dee was staring at Archer, and I bit back a curse. Her voice was low in her throat. "Go."

At least she'd forgotten about hitting Kat. I resisted the urge to warn Archer to do . . . well, to not do anything, but as I walked toward the doorway to the foyer and stopped to look back at them over my shoulder, what I saw should've had me going off like a rocket.

I hadn't heard either of them move, but they were standing toe to toe, and Archer was touching her cheeks with only the tips of his fingers as he gazed into her eyes. There was something sort of poignant about the moment. Yeah, I sounded like I'd be writing love sonnets by the end of the year, but in a moment of empathy and maturity I really hadn't realized I was capable of, I didn't lose my cool.

She needed this—she needed Archer, and who in the hell was I to begrudge her the solace when I had my Kat?

Blowing out a breath, I headed toward the front of the house and cringed when I saw the front door across the room. Oh, Lore and Hunter were gonna be pissed.

Kat was sitting at the top of the steps, curved slightly inward. As I walked around her and down the steps so I was in front of her, she slowly raised her head and her gray eyes met mine, reached right inside me, and squeezed my heart.

"She's okay." It wasn't a question but a statement.

I nodded as I knelt in front of her. "Because of you."

She shook her head.

"Yes. She told me what you did. She could've killed you, Kat."

"I know, but . . . I didn't want you to have to fight your sister, to have to hurt her. I didn't want you to have to ever make that choice and live with what happened."

It made me love her more than I thought possible. I placed my hands on her knees and leaned in, pressing my lips against her forehead. "Thank you. That's not enough, but thank you is the best I got."

"You don't even need to say that." Kat rested her forehead against mine and whispered, "I love you."

I moved up to sit beside her, wanting to pull her into my arms, but I resisted because I could tell she was hurting. "Where?"

She knew what I was asking. "I'm really okay."

"You look like you're in pain. Come on. You know I'm going to heal you. Don't fight me on this."

For a moment, she stared at me, and then she stuck out her tongue, which caused me to grin. "Pretty much everywhere, especially my ribs. She threw me through a wall."

I breathed around the flash of anger, telling myself Dee hadn't known better so I didn't get all "rage face," as Kat would say. Carefully, I touched her sides and let the healing begin. "Well, I need you back to perfection, because Dee's probably going to hit you again."

Kat winced. "Do I even want to know why?"

"Sit still," I said. "I told her we got married. She's happy, but she wants to punch you because she didn't get to be a part of it."

"Oh." She laughed and then cringed. "Was she happy about it? I mean, was she okay?"

"Of course." As the heat of my ability started making its way through Kat, her eyes drifted shut and her cheek ended up on my shoulder. I liked it. Kind of made me feel warm and fuzzy with her all cuddled up against me. "She's thrilled, actually. Just wait until I tell her we plan on doing the big, real ceremony. She might not hit you then."

When she laughed softly, this time it didn't end with her wincing in pain. Moving my hand to cup her cheek, I took care of the bruises there. "She's in there with Archer now," I said.

Kat sighed. "He's not a bad guy."

"He's an Origin."

She rolled her eyes. "Archer may be an Origin, but he's still a good guy, and he cares about her, Daemon. He really does, and he's been worried about her this entire time."

Ugh.

"You know he can protect her. And he'll be good for her, so—"

"I'm letting them be. I know she needs him, especially right now when she's . . . Well, she's got a lot going on in her head that she's dealing with."

Kat's eyes searched mine, and then she smiled broadly. The blood on her chin didn't deter from the beauty of it, but I smoothed my thumb over the red, wiping it away. "Wow. I'm sort of proud of you, Daemon."

"Don't be too proud, because I still don't like him."

"You know what I think?" She lowered her voice as if she were sharing a secret. "I think you do like Archer, and you just don't want to admit that you're in the beginning stages of a bromance to end all bromances."

I snorted. "Whatever."

Kat laughed again, and silence stretched out between us as my gaze drifted over her face. I started to lean in, but the sound of a car rolling up the long driveway forced us apart. It was Lore's car.

"Uh-oh," I murmured.

Kat cringed. "We've destroyed his house."

"It was an accident," I said, standing and moving down a step just in case Lore got rightfully upset. "He'll understand."

In other words, I'd make him understand.

Lore rolled to a stop next to the Explorer, and Hunter and Serena were the first out of the car, carrying a couple of bags. They rounded the porch and came to a complete stop as they saw the doorway . . . missing the door.

Hunter glanced at me. "Do I even want to know?"

"Well . . ." I started slowly.

Sighing, Hunter turned around and caught his brother by the arm. Lore had gotten a good look at the front of his house—the missing door, busted-out windows—and he was just standing there.

"We had a little problem," Kat began.

"What did you do to my house?" Lore asked. "We left you alone for an hour tops. Just an hour. Seriously."

If he thought this was bad, wait until he saw the inside. But then he was storming up the steps, and I figured he'd be finding out real soon as he entered the house. I placed my hand on the small of Kat's back as we followed him in.

"Holy . . ." Lore's voice faded off into stunned silence.

Hunter gave a low whistle as he took it in. "Damn, guys, this is kind of impressive."

My lips twitched, but I was smart enough to wipe the smile from my face when Lore spun on us. "Someone is going to clean this up, and it's not going to be me."

He was handling this surprisingly well, but I figured being an Arum and all, this wasn't the first time his house looked like a wrecking ball had gone into it.

I leaned around Hunter, scanning the last room I'd left Dee in, but when I didn't see her or Archer in there, I glanced at the spiral staircase.

My eyes narrowed. I was trying to be open and understanding and not a dick about them, but their asses better not be upstairs. My sudden change of heart was new to me and only went so far.

Hunter placed the bags on the floor, careful of the shattered glass as he eyed one of the bodies. "This is going to be messy."

Serena pressed close to him as she surveyed the damage.

"The fact that I'm not all that disturbed by this *actually* disturbs me more."

A slow grin spread across Kat's face as she turned to the woman. "I know the feeling."

Before the bonding moment could go any further, Dee and Archer came from the general direction of the kitchen. My relief that they weren't upstairs making it like bunnies was short-lived.

My sister's face was pale, and she opened her mouth, but then she saw Hunter and Lore. Her eyes widened.

Archer wrapped a hand around her shoulder. "I told you the Arum were helping us."

"I know, but it's one thing hearing it versus seeing it with my own eyes," she replied.

Lore frowned as he folded his arms. "You destroyed my house."

Dee flushed. "I'm sorry. Really, I am! It's a lovely house and I love all the plants and—"

"He gets that," I interrupted before this broke down into one of Dee's long-winded rambles. "What did you need to talk about?"

She glanced back at Archer, and then it all spilled out of her. Everything in one giant breath. "It's Ethan—he's an Origin and the whole colony knew it. He was working with a senator and a group of Luxen in Pennsylvania. He thinks if they can get the capital under control, they'll have everything. He wants you and Dawson either brought in or taken out."

Ethan Smith.

Elder extraordinaire.

The memory of the first time he'd met Kat rippled through my thoughts—the way he'd looked at her with barely contained distaste. He'd never been a big fan of humans, limiting interactions with them, and while I suspected Ethan was an Origin, it still rocked me. The Luxen we grew up with had been working to take out mankind for how long? Right under our noses from the beginning?

"I bet we know who that senator is," Serena said, visibly pale.

"That doesn't matter." Hunter's voice was hard. "Because that senator is no longer an issue, courtesy of me."

"Why?" Kat asked. "Do you know why Ethan has done this?"

Hunter snorted. "World domination? After all, it's in a Luxen's blood to rule and dominate."

I shot him a look.

"I don't know," Dee responded, twisting a large section of her hair between her hands. "But I got the feeling it was more than just that."

"Well, hell . . ." I dropped my hand and glanced up at the ceiling.

"Archer told me about the Arum." Excitement hummed in her voice. "You were right, Daemon. None of the invading Luxen has fought the Arum. They'll be able to take those bastards out like nothing."

Archer's brow rose at her curse word.

"But Ethan has, right?" Kat stared down at her sneakers, expression tense. "And the colony back home and the one in Pennsylvania will know how to fight the Arum—they will sense them coming, and they will—"

"They will run," Lore finished for her.

She closed her eyes, shoulders sinking in realization. "They will hide."

In other words, our brilliant plan of using the Arum wasn't so brilliant anymore. It had a big old hole in it a mile wide.

Hunter looked around the group. "If you asked me for my opinion—which you didn't, but I'm going to give it to you anyway—I'd say don't wait on Lotho to get up there. Take out this guy before they see you coming. Because if this Ethan is as smooth and smart as you all are saying, he's going to run when the shit hits the fan. Then what? Lotho and crew might take out most of the Luxen, but if he's still alive, that's a huge problem."

Archer nodded in agreement. "It would be like slapping a Band-Aid on a gunshot wound and hoping for the best."

He was right—both of them were. I looked over at Kat, and our gazes collided. "Going after Ethan isn't a part of the deal," I said to her, and I really didn't care what the rest of the group thought. I cared about what *she* thought. "We were to secure the Arum and then we can go back—hell, we could go any-where. You know what Eaton promised us. We don't have to do this."

Her lips parted. "I know."

"But . . ."

Kat drew in a deep breath and squared her shoulders. "We *don't* have to do this. But if Ethan hits the road before anyone gets there or if he escapes, then what? We're done. So you know what? Let's finish this."

21

{ Katy }

Freshly showered and rested enough that the aches from my battle royale with Dee had faded, I joined everyone in the living room. Before I'd left to scrape the blood and gross off me and take a nap, we'd put the living room and den back together.

Minus the missing door, busted-out windows, smashed furniture, and shattered potted plants—oh, and of course the hole in the wall.

I really felt bad about all of this. Lore was nice. His house *had been* nice. Actually, he was *really* nice, considering he didn't yell at us or try to eat us after discovering what happened to his house.

I was beginning to like the Arum.

Well, at least these two Arum. The rest of them, especially Lotho, still freaked me out.

Dee had already apologized a million times, from the second we were done talking about Ethan up to the moment I'd left to shower and take a power nap. So I wasn't surprised when she immediately turned those big green eyes on me when I entered the living room.

"Katy," she began, starting to rise, and I knew what was going to happen next. She was going to start crying, and then she would start apologizing.

I walked over to where she sat on the only piece of furniture not destroyed—an ottoman—and hugged her. "It's all right," I whispered into her ear. "Everything is okay between us."

And I meant it.

Life was really too short and twisted to hold grudges, especially over something she truly had no control over.

She squeezed my arm and whispered back, "Thank you. Now I won't hit you for not telling me you married my brother." Dee's smile spread, transforming her beauty into something that was truly out of this world, and God, how I'd missed that warm smile.

"We were just talking about our plan." Daemon sauntered up to me and nuzzled my cheek a second before lifting his head. "We're going to head back, which puts us less than a day, if that, ahead of when Lotho said he'd have his Arum army."

I glanced around the room, expecting more of a plan. "Okay?"

"But that's not all." Archer crossed his arms.

"It's simple," Daemon responded, his hand sliding off my shoulder and tangling in my damp hair. "We go home . . . and they will come to us."

I arched a brow. "That's a little too simple."

"He's being lazy in his descriptions," Hunter replied.

"Or totally distracted," commented Lore.

I flushed again, because when his fingers found their way out of my hair and then tiptoed down my spine, I seriously believed that he was.

"We're going to have to pretend that we're one of them." Dee twisted toward where we stood. "I know that probably sucks to hear, but we can do this. We can make them believe."

Oh, I really didn't like the sound of this, and I was trying not to pay attention to the hand on my back.

Dee wet her lips. "They don't know that I've gone AWOL or that the others . . . well, that they're not around anymore."

"How?"

"Dee was told not to check in until she took care of the problem with Daemon—either taking him out or bringing him into the fold," Archer explained, and the way Dee had busted up into the house, I didn't think she'd been interested in bringing him into anything except the afterlife. "They will be expecting to hear from her soon, but there's a damn good chance they don't know what's happened yet."

"A good chance?" I repeated dumbly.

Daemon's hand was south of the band on the back of my jeans. "The best chance we got, baby."

"So we're just going to go home, pretend that you all are evil, and then hope for the best?"

"We'll get to Ethan using Dee and Daemon. Get to him before the military or the Arum roll in," Archer said, amethyst eyes sharp. "Before he can run."

I got that part, but this . . . this was a risky and unreliable plan—one held together by duct tape, a lick, and a whole lot of wishing for good luck. The only good part about it was the fact that we were going home and I'd get to see my mom. If she was even there.

"But what about Nancy?" Daemon asked.

Dee glanced around the room. "What about her?"

"She ran off." I filled in his sister. "No one knows where she's at, but I doubt she'd head to where all the action is going down. That doesn't make any sense, so I think that's the last place she'd go."

Daemon tugged on the band of my jeans but didn't respond.

"She's right. They're looking for her now, but the likelihood of her heading to Petersburg is slim. I'm going to get in touch with Luc, let him know what's up and that the Luxen behind this are holed up in Petersburg, along with Ethan," Archer continued. "And then we'll get in touch with Lotho, let him know where we need them first."

That made sense. If the intel Dee had was correct, we needed to get them and the colony taken out, but we still had however many Origin to deal with afterward.

I winced.

Taken out. Deal with. I was starting to sound like a mobster. Or Luc.

"Well then," I said finally. "It's a plan."

Daemon patted my behind.

"You guys are going to need some stuff," Hunter said, and then he glanced down at Serena's blond head. "This is the end of the road for us."

I nodded. We could use their help, all the help we could get, actually, but rolling into town with two Arum would probably give away the card up our sleeve.

"Don't get us wrong," Serena said, her eyes searching out ours. "We want to do more, but—"

"But like I said before, I have a lot of enemies in the government. While Daedalus might be defunct, I don't trust anyone associated with it." Hunter's arm around Serena tightened. "And I'm not putting her in their crosshairs again."

"Totally understandable," Daemon announced, surprising me, since he didn't follow it up with a smartass response.

Lore straightened and walked over to the closet that still

had a door on it. When he opened it, I got a peek of a mini-arsenal. Glocks were attached to hooks on the interior walls. Rifles were propped against the wall from tallest to shortest. There were other guns I didn't recognize secured to the wall, guns that looked like Glocks . . . but weren't.

"Wow," I murmured.

"Probably should've told you guys this was here," he said, reaching inside. "I've collected quite a stash over the years." He pulled out a gun, handing it over to Archer. "The thing that everyone seems to forget is that Luxen, and even we, are susceptible to certain wounds."

"Bullet to the head or to the heart is catastrophic no matter the species." Hunter grinned, and it was kind of creepy. "Problem is, both of our kinds are a bit fast, so hitting them in the head or heart is kind of hard." "Not now." Lore was also grinning in the same creepy way.

"Holy crap," murmured Archer as he handled the odd-looking gun. "How did you get one of these?"

Lore smirked. "I have my ways."

Archer shook his head. "Hell, these things were never approved for widespread use. Daedalus had them, but I never thought I'd see one on the outside."

Daemon's hand slipped off me. "What's so special about the gun?"

"It's specially designed for Luxen. It's not a PEP weapon, not really." Archer was also now smiling in the über-creepy way. "The gun is rigged to handle bullets juiced with a charge of the same matter behind the PEP. It's not a DRT weapon."

"DRT?" asked Dee.

"Dead Right There," he explained. "But you shoot Luxen, hybrids, or Origins anywhere with one of these, they are going down. It's mostly fatal, especially if the bullet doesn't exit the body or they can't get it out quickly. It kills more slowly, which was why the guns were never approved."

"Because that would be like torturing someone." I felt sick.

"Yeah, but you don't have to really have good aim with this. Still need to be fast, but instead of sucking up energy and calling the Source, this will come in handy." Archer looked like a kid who'd just been handed a birthday cake in his favorite flavor. "Really handy."

"Each of you gets one," Lore said. "So never say I didn't give you anything. And I do expect a Christmas card this year."

Smiling slightly, I took my gun—my more-dangerous-than-normal gun—and tried to get used to the weight and feel of the cool plastic and metal.

I was holding a gun in my hand. Again.

And I really did feel like a mobster.

We were back out on the porch, positions slightly changed. Daemon was sitting on the top step and his legs were spread wide. I was between them, turned slightly so I could see his face in the waning sunlight.

At first, we really didn't say much. He was playing with my hair, twisting the length around his fingers and brushing the ends against my cheek. I had no idea what it was with Daemon and using things—my hair, pens, pencils, whatever—to touch me, but I didn't mind. There was something relaxing about it now, when it used to be ridiculously annoying. I was leaning back against his left leg, letting him do whatever he was doing. We'd have to leave soon so that we'd arrive sometime in the morning.

Archer had clued Luc in to the change of plans, and he

was going to relay the info to the powers that be. There were branches of the military close to Petersburg, mostly around Northern Virginia, but from what we could gather from Archer's conversation, we wouldn't be able to rely on them because they couldn't afford to leave D.C. We'd have to wait on other branches spaced throughout the United States, most holed up in Montana—a good thirty-hour drive or so, putting them in Petersburg around the same time the Arum *should* be arriving. Archer would be contacting Lotho—that is, if Lotho wasn't screwing with us and actually showed.

So basically if things went south, we were screwed up and down and from both sides. But I'd be home in Petersburg, where my mom should be—

I pulled the brakes on that collision course of thought. Mom would be okay. She had to be there waiting for me, because she would've never given up on me, no matter how long I'd been gone or what was going on in the world.

But I couldn't let myself think about Mom right now. I had to focus on what we were about to do.

"Thoughts?"

"This is a really bad plan," I admitted after a few seconds, glancing up at him.

"It is."

I stared into his eyes. "That's not reassuring."

One side of his lips kicked up. "You got a better idea?"

I thought about that for a couple of moments and then sighed. "No, not really. As long as they don't know Dee and the crew have gone off the rails, then they'll be expecting her to be all kill-everyone happy."

He dipped his head, brushing his lips over mine. "You're worried."

"Uh, duh."

"You know I'm going to take care of you."

"That's not what I'm worried about."

"It's not?" Before I could answer, he kissed me softly, causing my breath to catch. "Then what are you worried about?" he asked.

"You. Dee. Archer. Dawson and Beth, even though they're safe for now. I'm even worried about Luc." I paused, frowning. "Though Luc is probably the last person I should worry about because he's *Luc*, but I'm scared for him and even Hunter and Lore and Serena. I'm worried that—"

Daemon kissed me deeply, cutting off my words, and he took that kiss to a whole new stratosphere. "You've got a big heart, Kitten." His lips cruised over mine as he spoke. "That's what I love about you most. Well, that and I am a really big fan of your sweet body, but your heart? Yeah, that completes the package of you, wraps it up with a nice little bow. It makes you perfect to me."

"Sometimes . . ." I stared at him, blinking back wetness. "Sometimes you say the most amazing things."

"And I do love the sight of my hands on your ass, too."

A laugh burst out of me. "Oh my God, and then you say things like that."

"Got to be myself." He kissed me again. "Kitten, it's okay to be worried about everyone, but all of us can take care of ourselves." He rested his forehead against mine. "And I also know that no matter how bad this idea is, how dangerous it is, we're going to come out of this together. All of us. I'll make sure of it."

"Promise?" I whispered.

"Promise." He tipped up his chin and kissed the bridge of my nose. "And I've never broken a promise to you, have I?"

"No. You haven't."

22

{ Katy }

The ride to Petersburg was a lot more uneventful than the trip to Atlanta, with the exception of the bickering between Daemon and Archer and the state of some of the highways we traveled on.

I knew better than to look inside the cars this time, but Dee apparently didn't. Every so often, I'd catch sight of her in the front seat, staring out the window at the destruction, and she'd make a soft sound, like a swallowed cry. Had she had a hand in this? Maybe not physically, but had anything she'd done had a domino effect that ended with many, many lives lost?

I felt for her, and I was happy when I saw Archer's hand gravitate toward her whenever she appeared to get lost staring out that window. But the closer we got to West Virginia, the closer to home, I could no longer think about Dee.

My heart started pounding in my chest like it wanted to jump out and do a little dance the minute we entered Petersburg from the highway. Everything looked normal, like this little patch of the world, a few-stoplight town, had somehow been left out of the events the rest of the world faced. Except as we cruised through the main drag of downtown, no one was out on the streets. Not a single soul walked on the sidewalks. There were a few cars, but it felt like everyone was holed up inside their homes. And that wasn't the only thing.

"God," breathed Archer, his knuckles bleaching around the steering wheel as he quickly turned onto the nearest road that got us to where we needed to go. "They're everywhere."

I didn't need an explanation. He was talking about the Luxen.

Daemon leaned between the two front seats and placed a hand on his sister's shoulder. He didn't speak out loud, but when I saw Dee turn toward him, her lips were pressed together tightly and her face was pale.

My stomach got in the game with my heart, tumbling as it raced.

Dee nodded and then said out loud, "I can hear him, but I'm fine. I'm with you guys." She glanced at Archer in a way that almost made me swoon and forget what was going on. "I'm going to be okay."

I just hoped that was the case. We were obviously deep in enemy territory, and it would be no amount of time before they knew we were here. They might already know we were here.

And backup in the form of the Arum and the military was still many hours away. This could all go very badly, and very quickly, because we were intentionally walking into a trap. Dee and Daemon were really going to have to be convincing when it came to playing along with the enemy to get close to Ethan.

So convincing I really hoped they didn't switch sides.

Might be a needless fear, because I seriously believed what Daemon felt for me was strong enough to beat that, but the concern was still there. It was like a shadow in my blood, a constant thought in the back of my head, a tiny stone in my stomach that didn't go away.

This could really blow up in our faces.

As we neared the turnoff I hadn't seen in so long, I leaned forward and grasped the back of Dee's seat. My breath caught in my throat as the Explorer eased up the driveway. The grass looked overgrown, crowding the road with tall reeds; it was clear no one was concerned with landscaping, but I figured that was okay, with the world facing an alien apocalypse and all. Any other option was unacceptable for me to consider. Mom had to be fine, had to be waiting for me.

She was home, because her Prius was parked in the driveway, in front of the porch where the wooden swing still swayed back and forth in the breeze.

Archer turned the key in the ignition, cutting the engine as I stared at the flower box surrounding the porch. It was more weeds than flowers, but that was okay, too, because Mom had a daughter missing and an alien apocalypse to deal with. Plus, she wasn't really good with flowers and all that jazz.

My fingers were shaking as I unlatched my seat belt.

Mom had to be inside the house. Had she seen us pull up yet? Would the door open at any given moment and she'd be walking out? A prettier, classier, smarter, and nicer version of me—a version I hoped to be when I got older.

I could barely drag in enough air to get my lungs working. From our plans, I knew Daemon would be leading the show here, and the last thing any of us needed was for me to go running to my mom. But I wanted to see her. I needed to, because I missed her desperately and I had to make sure she was okay.

I was all she had left, and she needed to know that I was still here.

Daemon caught my arm, keeping me in the backseat while Dee and Archer hopped out and stared at her house with wary expressions.

"There are Luxen nearby," he said, smoothing his thumb along the edge of my sleeve, across my wrist. "I don't know if they're in any of the houses."

"Why would they be in our houses?" The moment the question left my mouth, I knew how stupid it sounded, because there could be any number of reasons why they'd be in my house or Daemon's.

He smiled tightly, but the worry in his eyes caused the little knots in my stomach to expand. "I know you want to check on your mom. I get that, but I need you to not run off. We're going to head over there, but if anything is off and I tell you to get out of there—"

"Why would things be off?"

Daemon cocked his head to the side. "Kat . . ."

"I know," I whispered. Stupid just kept spewing out of my mouth.

"Don't forget the gun." It was tucked in the back of my jeans, like a gangsta. His eyes searched mine and then he nodded. "I'm going to climb out after you, and Kat . . ." His stare turned intense, deep, and thorough. "If I have to talk to you a certain way or act like I did back in Idaho, I'm sorry."

"I get why. I can deal."

Daemon held my gaze a moment longer and then nodded. Drawing in a shallow breath, I turned and opened the car door. He slid out behind me and immediately curved a hand around the base of my neck. I imagined that the gesture looked like one of control and dominance, but there was something soothing in the weight of his hand. I knew he was there.

His sister had a hold of Archer's arm as she led him toward

the steps on the front porch leading to their house. Dee paused only to cast a look back at Daemon, and I had no idea if they were communicating or not, since there was a chance another Luxen could pick it up.

Daemon steered me around the front of the SUV, and as we walked closer to my house, I noted the weeds once again. Vines had formed, and they were so thick and numerous that they had started to climb up the sides of the porch, wrapping around the railings.

My gaze flickered toward the door.

It was open, with just the glass storm door closed. My heart was really going at it in my chest and I had to force myself to walk slowly, like Daemon was leading me instead of me leading him.

The steps groaned under our feet and the familiar creak from a loose board on the porch caused me to jerk a little.

"There are definitely Luxen nearby," he said under his breath.

Meaning they could be anywhere, in the surrounding woods or inside the house. With their presence so strong and thick, they could be sitting in the living room for all we knew. Shivers ran up and down my body as he reached around me with his free hand and opened the door. Our footsteps quiet, we stepped inside and were welcomed by the slightly warmer air of the interior and the scent I'd missed—fresh linen.

Tears pricked at my eyes as my gaze swung around the foyer. Things looked the same. Oh God, there were Amazon boxes by the door, along with media mail envelopes, and I knew they were full of books that had probably kept coming until publicists realized I hadn't updated my blog in many, many months.

My book bag was next to the lovely pile of unopened mail,

along with my sandals. Mom had left them there, like she knew I was coming back. That she wanted them there for me. My lower lip started to tremble, and I blinked furiously to keep the tears at bay.

We walked farther into the house, making no sound as we passed the doorway to the empty living room. I looked up the stairwell and then down the hall, toward the laundry room. The memory of dancing in my socks and falling on my butt when Daemon had let himself in, surprising me, rushed over me. The breath I took was too shaky. So many memories. They hurt in a good and bad way, wholly bittersweet. Daemon gently squeezed the back of my neck, and then we entered the dining room. From where we stood, I could see the kitchen.

My heart stopped in my chest and then sped up.

Daemon's hand tightened.

I saw her—I saw Mom.

She was standing at the sink, her back to us, and oh my God, it was her—shiny blond hair pulled up in a neat bun at the back of her head. She wasn't wearing scrubs, but dark jeans and a light sweater. Tears spilled out of my eyes. I couldn't stop them.

"Mom?" My voice cracked.

Her spine stiffened for a second and I started forward, done with the pretenses. Daemon grabbed at me, but I was fast when I needed to be, and I broke free.

Mom turned.

She was *here*. She was *okay*. She was *alive*.

"Kat!" Daemon shouted.

In a blur of tears I couldn't even see through, I was an emotional melting pot as I raced across the kitchen, around the table, reaching her in seconds, and I got all grabby, wrapping my arms around her. "Mom!"

I held her tight, inhaling the scent of her perfume and letting it wash over me, easing some of the knots in my—

Suddenly, arms were around my waist and I was hauled back against a hard chest and stomach. My brain raced. I didn't understand what was happening. Then my feet were skidding across the floor as I was shoved behind Daemon. He kept his arm out, backing me up.

"Daemon, stop." I struggled to get around him, knowing I was supposed to play it cool, but this was different. No one was in here but us. We were okay and I wanted my mom.

"Katy." Daemon spoke my name, and the hoarseness of it, the way it seemed to punch out of him, caused me to go very still.

I lifted my head, breathing heavily as I peered around Daemon and . . . and I got a look at Mom, a real good look.

My whole world imploded—shattered into broken little pieces that were jagged and cut deep, slicing my insides into shreds and ripping me apart.

Her eyes—they were a bright, unnatural blue.

So blue that they looked like two polished sapphires, and Mom's eyes . . . they should've been hazel, more green than brown, depending on her mood.

"No," I whispered, shaking my head. "No. No."

Mom tilted her head to the side as she looked from me to Daemon, and then she moved her lips into a smile that lacked any warmth. "We've been waiting for you."

No. No. No.

I wrenched free of Daemon, backing up as I stared at Mom—*no*, not Mom. This wasn't Mom. It wasn't *her*. The cold blue eyes followed my movements and her lips continued to curl up as she watched me with such apathy I could taste it.

"No." My voice was a broken record. It was all I could say as my chest split right open when the horror of the reality set in.

Mom wasn't here.

She would never be here. Never again.

Because she had been assimilated. Mom was gone. Forever.

{ Daemon }

I should've known.

In the back of my head, that was all I could think. I should've known that this was possible. That the invading Luxen would get to Kat's mom and do something so horrific in hopes that Kat or I or someone would come back here. Or maybe they hadn't really been waiting for us but had done this just to be cruel, because Ethan would've known Kat's mom, would've foreseen what it would've done.

The moment Kat's heart broke open, I felt it in my chest like it had been my own, and I'd experienced that kind of raw pain before when I was told that Dawson had died. I'd never wanted her to go through what she was feeling, but there was no stopping it.

Her eyes were wide as she stumbled back, bouncing into the wall like she didn't even know it was there, and she kept saying the same word over and over again.

No.

Tears streamed down her face as she raised her hands, like she wanted to fend off reality, hold it back. Then she doubled over, folding her arms around her midsection.

My gaze swung on the Luxen standing at the sink, smiling coldly as she watched Kat lose it. The bastards did this to her.

Rage lit me up from the inside, infusing every cell in my body. I didn't use the gun—the shot, the sound of it was too wrong to use in this situation, because even though this wasn't her mom, she looked like her. The female in front of me recognized what was about to happen a second too late. She started to shift as I let the fury go and a blast of the Source smacked into her chest, spinning her against the counter. She gripped the sink, staggered, but I let go another bolt and it hit the back of her head.

The Luxen's light flared a bright white once, and then twice, before dulling like a lightbulb going out. She fell over a bag of potatoes, smacking on the floor with a heavy *thud*. In her true form, the last of the light faded out of the network of veins, leaving behind a shell of a humanoid form.

Kat dropped to her knees, crying out as she dipped her chin against her chest.

I whipped toward her. "Katy . . . baby, I'm . . ." There really were no words except: "I'm so . . . so sorry."

She moved suddenly, planting her hands against the kitchen floor. Throwing back her head, she screamed, and that sound was full of sorrow and heartbreak.

It started as a low tremble under my feet and then increased, shaking the kitchen table and rattling the plates and cups in the cabinets. Then it was a rumble, causing the house to groan and small clouds of dust to drop from the ceiling. The table scuttled over the floor. A chair toppled over and then another. Somewhere in the living room, a window shattered.

Kat was going to bring the house down.

"Shit."

I dropped to her side, folding my arms around her and gathering her close. Her entire body shook as I sat back, landing on my ass. I pulled her into my lap, thrusting a hand into her hair, pressing her face against my chest. It did nothing to muffle the powerful sobs racking her entire body.

God, I didn't know what to do. I didn't know how to ease this, which was the only thing I cared about at the moment.

"Baby, it's going to be okay," I said into the top of her head. "I'm here, Kitten. I got you. I'm here."

There was no sign that she heard me as she burrowed into me, her chest rising and falling sharply, her pulse pounding way too fast. She curled into herself, her cries ragged and broken-sounding, tearing me up.

I should've known.

But there had been no way to decipher the presence of a Luxen in here or outside. Others would be coming, but all I could do was hold her, getting her as close as possible as I glanced at the ceiling. A crack had opened, cutting across the middle of the ceiling, but the house had settled, aside from a slight shiver of the foundation every few seconds.

I smoothed my hand up and down her back and pressed a kiss to the top of her head despite the feeling of another Luxen drawing close. When the front door slammed, I heard Dee calling out my name.

"In here."

Kat was still shaking in my arms, and while her sobs had quieted down, the burst of raw emotion was nowhere near over.

"What's going on . . . ?" Dee skidded to a halt outside of the kitchen, in the hall. Her gaze darted from the dead Luxen to where we sat on the floor. "Kat?"

Archer was behind her, curling a hand over her shoulder. He picked up on what had gone down here as I returned my attention to Kat. Curving my one hand along the back of her head, I lowered mine to rest on top of hers and just held on.

I knew the moment Archer told Dee what happened, because she cried out and then she was behind Kat, placing her hands on her, trying to wiggle her way in, but I couldn't let Kat go.

"We felt the house shaking," Dee said as her eyes met mine over Kat's head. "I know I shouldn't have come over here. That wasn't the plan, but I was worried."

The plan was out the window. There was no way I could continue to go through with any of this after what had just happened. I couldn't treat her like I would need to. I had to get her out of here.

"Screw this," Archer said in a gruff voice, echoing my thoughts. "We need to get out of here, get someplace safe and regroup. We can't . . ."

We couldn't put Kat through this, however it would turn out. I was ready to get in the Explorer and get her the hell away from here. Screw not only the plan but everything with it. We'd done our part. The Arum were coming, and all we had succeeded in doing now—all I had done—was exposing Kat to one of the worst pains there was, that of losing a loved one, of seeing it firsthand.

As Dee slowly backed away, I slid my hands to Kat's arms. "We have to go," I told her as I gradually stood, pulling her up.

Her legs didn't seem to be working once I got her standing, and her face was red from crying, lips trembling as she lifted her head. Those beautiful eyes were glassed over.

"Leaving?" Her voice cracked.

I started to nod, but Kat jerked free suddenly. She wheeled around, and when I grabbed for her, she turned and socked me right in the stomach. I barely felt it. "Kat . . ."

"No," she said, striking out again. Her hand connected with my arm. "No!" She swung again, her palm glancing off my cheek.

Eyes wide, Dee started toward her, but I held up my hand, warding her off. She shook her head as another one of Kat's mostly ineffective punches connected with another part of my body.

"It's all right," I told them. "I'll meet you outside."

Dee's brows pinched. "But—"

"Go!"

Dee hesitated, but Archer stepped forward and took her hand. They started for the door as I focused on Kat. I wasn't even sure she saw me. The pupils of her eyes glowed white. She moved to hit me again and I let her have it.

"Do what you need to do," I said, meaning it.

Kat's fists pounded my chest, first with some oomph behind them, but I stood there, and I let her work it out until her punches slowed and her shoulders shook. There was no amount of pain she could inflict on me that would equal what she was feeling.

"Oh God," she whispered, dropping her forehead to my chest. "Oh God, she's dead, she's really dead." Her arms fell to her sides. "They did . . . this to her. Why?"

I circled my arms around her. "I don't know, baby, but I'm sorry—I'm so sorry."

She shuddered as she stood there, and I hated that I couldn't give her time to adjust, to mourn. "We've got to—"

The shiver of awareness skated over my skin, and there it was, the ever-present hum increasing in my skull. Shit. I whipped around, shielding Kat's body with mine as the front door slammed again.

Heavy footsteps made their way through the hall, into the dining room. I tensed, knowing it wasn't Dee or Archer. The plan of going home and them coming to us had worked too well.

Ethan Smith walked into the kitchen.

23

{ Daemon }

The bastard strolled on in like he owned the place, completely at ease and with absolutely no fear. His damn black trousers and white shirt even looked pressed.

Shoved in the back of my jeans, the rigged gun burned my skin, but before I could go for it, he spoke.

"Don't even think about doing anything. I know neither you nor your sister is falling into line. I knew *you'd* be tough, but your sister surprised me. The game's over." He barely passed us a glance as he walked over to the table, straightened a chair, and sat down. "Your sister and the one with her will be slaughtered before you can blink an eye if you displease me. Keep that in mind."

A deep growl rolled up my throat.

He glanced at the dead Luxen and then his violet eyes slid back to us. He tsked under his breath. "Daemon Black, I had so much hope for you."

It took everything not to blast his ass into outer space.

"Funny. You sound so much like someone I know already. Disappointed her, too."

One dark eyebrow rose. "Hmm. Let me guess. Nancy Husher?"

I ground down on my molars. "You are on speaking terms with her?"

Ethan idly brushed the backs of his fingers along his pants, and then he hooked one knee over the other. "Not quite, Daemon. Please." He extended a hand, and two of the chairs flipped upright. "Have a seat."

"No thank you," I said as Kat shifted closer to me. I had no idea what kind of frame of mind she was in right now.

Ethan smiled tightly. "I really wasn't giving either of you an option. Sit or I'll send the message to the others outside to kill your sister. Slowly."

Anger was like a bitter acid in my blood as I stared down the Elder or whatever the hell he really was to our kind.

It was Kat who spoke, her voice surprisingly level considering what she'd just been through. "We'll sit."

Looking over at her, I saw that her face was pale and eyes slightly swollen, but her gray gaze was sharp. I took her hand.

Ethan chortled as he watched us. "Tell me, Daemon, what made you fall in love with a human?"

How in the hell was I supposed to answer that? I sat in the chair nearest to Ethan, which forced Kat farther away. "Why do you even want to know?"

"I'm curious." He cocked his head to the side. "Answer me."

My teeth were going to crack. "What's there about her not to love?"

"Well, she's a human." His gaze flickered over her, his upper lip curling. "She's mutated, but ultimately, she's a human underneath it all."

"So?" challenged Kat.

He ignored her. "She's human, Daemon."

"That doesn't matter to me."

"Really? Because I remember the Daemon who hated humans, hated what they'd done to his brother and brought onto his family," Ethan replied. "I remember the Daemon I had such great hope in."

"I was wrong to hate humans for what happened to Dawson. It wasn't Beth's fault or the fact that he fell in love with her. It was Daedalus."

"An organization run completely by humans."

I narrowed my eyes. All I could do was keep him talking, keep my brain blank from anything we planned. "Yeah, thanks for the clarification on that."

He looked unmoved. "You can't tell me that if your brother had never met that human girl, things would've been different. Same with you. Maybe even the whole world would've been different. After all, your actions in Vegas gave us the perfect opportunity."

A muscle along my jaw started to pop. *That human girl.* I remembered him calling Kat that twice and I hadn't really sensed the pure hatred then, just distaste, but I got it now. Oh yeah, I was really picking up on it now. "And guess what, Ethan?" I could feel Kat's eyes on me. "I wouldn't change a damn thing. Neither would Dawson. So chew on that."

A flare of white light behind his purple eyes came and went. "What if I told you that your parents were alive when they arrived here?"

For a moment I didn't think—couldn't think. His words did not make sense.

"What?" Kat demanded.

Ethan didn't even look her way. He was locked onto me like he was going to take me out to dinner later. "Your parents, Daemon. What if they came to Earth, but humans killed them? How would you feel about your precious human then? Or any human?"

Unable to stop myself from reacting to what he was saying, I sat back and stared at him. Again, I could feel Kat's eyes on me, and I didn't need to look deep to find the answer. "Yes. I would feel the same way."

He stared at me curiously.

"Were . . . were they alive?" Kat asked.

"That doesn't matter," I snapped. And it was true. None of that mattered now. "This is bullshit. All of it." My hands curled into fists atop the kitchen table. "What do you want, Ethan? Why this? You want to take over the world or something?"

"World domination?" Ethan chuckled. "That's so cliché. So damn silly. I don't give a damn about ruling this planet or any planet."

I raised my brows.

"My parents were killed, Daemon. But you probably already realize that, since you know exactly what I am and I'm sure Nancy told you . . . Well, told you half of the truth." Ethan folded his hands in his lap. "I was a part of the first group of Origins, before Nancy stepped in at a young and tender age to spearhead Daedalus."

One of the first groups? Yeah, if what Nancy had said about them was true, the first group really didn't have a great go at things.

"When they realized that my father had mutated my mother, they captured them. Started doing experiments. Whatever love those two might have had for each other was destroyed by the things they did to them and made them do, including my creation," he explained without a drop of emotion. "I was a part of a limited group of Origins, and I grew up in a lab."

"That sucks."

That tight smile appeared. "You have no idea. I lived for years knowing that they could end my life if I did one thing wrong. Over and over, I watched other Origins, too young to really understand what they were, get taken away and never seen again. They were killed. And then I watched them murder my parents for an infraction that I committed."

My hands, hell, my whole being itched to end this. "Like I said, that sucks, but I really don't get why you're telling me."

"You don't?" Ethan laughed, and for the first time, real emotion spread across his face. "I lived in Daedalus's lab until I was old enough to be placed outside, into a controlled position. Not like some who were placed as senators or doctors. No. I was placed within the Luxen community, ordered to keep an eye on them." He chuckled. "As if I would help them with anything. Or any Origin of my class would."

"Class?"

"Yes. There've been roughly five classes. I was a part of the first. Your friend outside was in the second batch, and there have been three more."

I was guessing that the last two were the ones including Luc and those freaking kids. "Are all the Origins from your group like you?"

"Like me," he huffed, shaking his head. "You mean do they want what I want or are they no longer under the control of Daedalus? The answer is twofold. No Origin can truly be controlled by anyone. We are practically the closest things to gods."

Wow, mouthed Kat.

"And those who are left of our class, which are few, want just what I do."

Kat sat forward, sliding her hands off the table. "Few? There aren't many left of your . . . uh, class?"

His gaze slid her way, and I didn't like it. Not one freaking bit. "When you two escaped from Daedalus and Vegas happened, Daedalus began cleaning up—eradicating the Origins."

Her brows pinched. "They said they started that when the Luxen arrived."

"And you believe anything a human says? Of course you do, because that is what you are." He sneered, his disgust evident, and he was *really* starting to piss me off. "They started cleaning house when you all decided to take down Vegas. All across the country, we dropped like flies, and it simply became time to end this."

"End this." I was so beginning to see where this was heading. "You found a way to communicate with the Luxen who hadn't been here."

"We'd been working on a way, and let's just say we opened the doors for them. It was perfect timing." He spread his hands wide. "And here we are. Most of the Luxen, both here and those who've arrived recently, answer to me." His smile went up a notch. "I can be very convincing."

Kat stared at him. A second ticked by. "You hate humans."

"Loathe them," he confirmed. "They disgust me. They are weak and fragile. They are fickle and dangerous. They deserve everything that is coming to them. The Luxen want to rule them, and they will. They already are, and that's fine by me. I don't care what they do, as long as humans suffer and experience everything that I have."

"All of this . . . all of this is because of what happened to you?" she asked, shaking her head slowly. Disbelief colored her tone. I didn't blame her. I was also shocked.

Taking over the world was at least something to aspire to. This? This was just nasty hatred and revenge and . . . yeah, crazy. How he managed to get so many Luxen behind him was beyond my understanding. How could they not have seen through what he was? Though hell, *I* had never seen him for what he was.

"You're doing this just because of what was done to you," Kat repeated.

"And what they did to others of my kind." His eyes flashed again. "And what they would've continued to do, even after dismantling Daedalus and their projects."

"But there are people who would've never done anything like that. Who would've welcomed the Luxen," she argued. "You can't judge an entire race of beings on what a small percentage of people have done."

"Already have," he replied.

Jesus. There were no words for this.

"That's insane!" Kat's cheeks flushed with anger, and damn, she was right. "That's worse than how the Luxen feel about the Arum and vice versa. That's absolutely—"

Ethan moved faster than even I could track for a moment. One second he was sitting, and the next second he was right beside Kat, his fingers curled around her throat.

I shot up from my chair, knocking it over. My form began to shift. *Let her go.*

His grip tightened on her neck. "Take one step toward me. Shift or summon the Source, and I will snap her neck. Let's see if you can heal her from that."

My heart—dammit—my heart stopped in my chest as I stared at them. He had *me* by the throat because he had my whole world in his hands. I forced the shift to back off and said one word I thought I'd never utter to the bastard.

"Please." I swallowed hard, but the words came out easier than I could've ever imagined. "Please don't hurt her."

Ethan sneered into her face. "You beg for a human who wouldn't do the same for you?"

"I'd do anything for her."

"And I would do . . . the same for him," Kat gasped out, her hands curling inward in her lap. "And I would . . . never be as batshit crazy as you."

"Kat," I warned.

Ethan's fingers tightened, and she jerked. "Excuse me?"

"You are worse . . . than the Luxen. You've judged billions of people for something they didn't do." Her voice cracked. "You hurt my mother. She never did anything to you, and you probably don't even know her name."

"That bitch?" Ethan spat back. "She isn't even worth knowing her name."

Several things happened at once. Blue light flared from the outside, a halo that lit up all the windows and danced over the walls. The sound of giant wings beat at the roof. There were shouts from almost every direction.

Ethan lifted his head, brows furrowing in a look of confusion.

Kat kicked her chair back, swinging one leg up. Her foot connected with Ethan's midsection. She wrenched back and he stumbled against the table. I shot toward her, grasping her by the shoulders before she could fall. I hauled her up and away from Ethan as I shifted.

The windows facing the front yard, over the sink, exploded. I spun Kat behind me, blocking her from the shards of flying glass.

Men in black with face shields landed in the kitchen like something straight out of an action flick, their boots crunching on the broken glass. Well, I assumed the military had arrived or a SWAT team had just busted up in the wrong house. The massive weapons they hoisted—PEP guns—told me my first assumption was correct.

I backed Kat up, not wanting her to get caught in the whole lot of bad that was about to go down, but I wasn't the only one worried about getting out of the middle of this.

Ethan spun, and the bastard ran.

{ Katy }

Too much emotion was swirling inside me. I was like a tornado, about to wipe out everything in my path. My senses were on overload and I was overwhelmed by everything that had happened—was happening.

Men had just rapelled into the house, through the windows.

Mom was dead.

The whole world had been upheaved on its axle. All because of revenge. That was all. Nothing important. Just crazy revenge, and it had changed the entire world—my world. There was no point behind this. No real reason.

When Ethan turned to run, I didn't stop to think about it. I didn't hesitate as I reached behind me, yanked on the butt of the Glock—the modified gun. It happened so quickly. I took aim as the men shouted at Ethan.

He was already at the sink, about to Houdini himself out the window, and I knew if he got outside we'd never find him. We'd have to start all over and he'd never pay for everything he had done.

I took aim at his head and pulled the trigger.

All of this happened within one or maybe two seconds, and the months and years leading up to it were over in a heartbeat.

Ethan toppled over face-first onto the kitchen floor.

Done.

Dead.

It was over for him in the span of time it took to move a finger. What had happened to my mom would've taken longer, would've been more painful. *Ethan is lucky*, I thought numbly. He was there one second and then gone in the blink of an eye.

My hand shook as I lowered the gun, and I was vaguely aware of Daemon staring at me and the strange men turned in my direction, their faces hidden behind shields, but I could feel their stares.

Ethan was dead.

It wasn't the same with the Luxen. There was no light show before he died. Ironically, he left this earth like the humans he hated—like the humans he was actually a part of, and how messed up was that? His mother had been a hybrid—part human. Did he hate himself, too? Why was I even thinking about this? Because it didn't matter.

I tried to take a breath, but it got stuck, and I felt cold and then hot, too hot.

One of the men turned, a gloved hand rising to the side of his helmet. There was a burst of static and he said, "They're here."

At first I thought he meant the Arum, but the pulses of light that suddenly lit up the outside told me that wasn't the Arum.

"Go! Go!" ordered one of the SWAT-looking guys.

The men—five of them—went out the same way they'd come in, through the windows. Dumbly, I wanted to point out the door a mere few feet from them, but then Daemon was reaching for me, going for the gun I was still holding.

I jerked back from him, tightening my grip on the gun.

"Kat . . ."

My gaze swung over Ethan to the dead Luxen who had assimilated my mom, and as I stood there, shouts rose from the outside. Although it was daytime, it looked like lightning striking horizontally. Daemon cursed, his attention divided between me and where his sister was, and I made the decision for him.

"This is *not* over," I told him in a voice that was pitched too high.

He took a measured step toward me, and his chin dipped as his gaze collided with mine. "It is for us, Kat. It is."

"No." It wasn't over. There was too much building in me, a reckless amount of energy and anger and a thousand other emotions. "No."

"Kat—"

I spun around and raced out of the kitchen, toward the front door. Daemon was right on my heels as I threw open the door.

Chaos.

A dozen or so Luxen had streamed out from the thick cluster of trees surrounding our homes, and with them were at least three Origins. I couldn't see Dee or Archer, but there were bodies littering the ground, both human and Luxen. Blasts from PEP weapons and from the Source zinged back and forth across the yard. There were more Luxen than humans standing, and in their true forms, their light was as bright as the sun breaking through the clouds overhead.

It was an all-out war scene, very much like what had gone down in Vegas. The trees closer to the yard were singed, and a few of the bare branches were burning, billowing black smoke into the air. A distinctive burned smell lingered in the air, curdling my stomach.

The Luxen were lobbing bolts at the men in black like they were throwing baseballs, one after another. One struck a man in the chest, spinning him back and onto the ground near the porch. The PEP weapon hit the ground and fired, sending a deadly blast in our direction.

Daemon shoved me to the side as the blast from the weapon cracked into the storm door behind us, shattering the glass.

Out of the corner of my vision, I saw Archer dart across the driveway, firing off rounds from the gun he held in his hand—the same kind I'd used on Ethan. He hit the Luxen, taking shots like a total badass. One went down . . . and then another and another. Their forms flickered in and out while one hit the ground, light fading into the shell of something sort of human.

Then I saw Dee behind Mom's car. Every couple of seconds, she stood and sent out a blast of the Source in the direction of the Luxen.

Daemon moved around me as an Origin raced toward the porch, rearing back as white light wrapped down his arm at an alarming rate. Daemon vaulted the railing, tackling the Origin before he could do a thing.

Damn, he was like a ninja, totally badass, too.

Unable to stand there and do nothing, I took aim with the gun and continued firing in the direction of the Luxen until I pulled the trigger and nothing came out of the barrel. I'd hit two, maybe three. They weren't kill shots, but Archer was on them, finishing them off with the Source.

I hurried down the steps, tossing the gun aside as another Origin headed toward where Daemon and the other were fighting hand to hand. Daemon was on top, straddling the douche, arm cocked back before he delivered a blow.

My heart lodged in my throat as a flash of whitish-red light came from a different direction, over by Daemon's house. I shouted his name, but it was too late. The energy smacked into his shoulder, knocking him off and onto his back. His face contorted with pain as he gripped his arm, his lips forming a string of curses.

Then he shifted into his true form and shot to his feet, his light white with vibrant red streaks through it. He was about to unleash a whole different level of badassery, but something deep and vicious was still building inside me.

My gaze centered on the Origin in the next yard. Static crackled down my skin. Fury fused my cells, mixing with the rage and pain already there. It burst from me like a shock wave, rolling out in a surge of power.

Mom's car rattled, forcing Dee to jump back. Her wide eyes swung toward me as her black curls blew around her head. Her mouth opened, but her words were tossed back in her face.

The force of power was like hurricane winds. It slammed into the Explorer, lifted it up on two tires, and then flipped it over. The vehicle rolled toward the Origin, who spun and ran.

Ran.

My brain had clicked off and my boots dug into the ground as I pushed and took off, giving chase. I heard my name shouted, but I couldn't stop and I couldn't listen. My feet picked up speed, and the burst of power and energy rolled through me.

I hit the edge of the forest as I heard my name yelled through my thoughts, but I didn't stop. I kept going, picking up more and more speed. My heart pounded like a jackhammer hitting cement, and my pulse was as frantic as the beating wings of a trapped bird.

Heat swept over my skin as my hair streamed out behind me. Branches snagged at me, catching pieces of my clothing, whipping back at my cheeks and arms like thin lashes. They didn't stop me. I leaped over rocks and fallen tree trunks, my muscles screaming as I pushed harder and harder.

I chased the Origin, who stayed a yard or two ahead of me through the forest, darting around trees and large rocks. In the back of my mind, I wondered about the violent energy bouncing inside and if I'd been tested enough to ensure I wouldn't self-destruct like some hybrids, like Carissa. What if they hadn't, and this—this was what self-destruction felt like?

I was burning up inside, full of murderous rage and frustration and sorrow that cut so deep it was like an endless well of hurting. And I couldn't believe that my heart could beat this fast and still keep going.

Kat!

I heard his voice again, but I was focused on the Origin, on the need to take him out, to end this with none of them getting away.

I had no idea how far I'd run, but the trees started to thin when the Origin glanced over his shoulder. Something about the look on his face caused my feet to stumble just the slightest.

But it was too late.

Up ahead, I could see the base of Seneca Rocks, their quartzite flecks glittering in the sunlight, rising as tall as I could see, their peaks like jagged fingers reaching into the sky, and I realized I'd run for *miles*.

The Origin broke free of the trees, and I was only a few seconds behind him, clearing the forest, when I stopped, or tried to. Sliding across the ground, I kicked up grass and loose soil as I stared at the rooftops of houses that sat at the base of the rocks, and then my gaze dipped, frantically traveling over the mass of people in front of me.

Hundreds, if not thousands, and they weren't really people. Nope. They were Luxen. Maybe even a few Origins. It didn't matter. My heart nearly came out of my chest as the horrifying realization kicked in.

"Oh shit," I gasped out.

One of the Luxen, a female, smiled while I started to back up, swallowing the rising panic. *Stupid. Stupid. Stupid.* I was so incredibly stupid and reckless and more stupid.

I'd run straight *into* the colony of Luxen.

There wasn't even a second to get the hell out of there. A blast of whitish-red light blinded me for a second, and then fiery pain lit up my shoulder. The power of the hit knocked me backward. My feet came off the ground and I saw the blue sky above me.

Oh God.

But I never hit the ground.

Heat enveloped me. Strong arms surrounded me. I was suspended for a moment, not touching the ground, and then I was pressed against Daemon, who stood before the colony in his true form.

He shielded me from his own kind.

They began to shift, one after another, like Christmas lights blinking on in succession. There were so many of them, too many. We would not be able to fight them all. We would not be able to escape. And this was my fault.

I'm sorry, I said to Daemon. The only thing I could think was that maybe one of us could get away if the other caused the distraction. He didn't deserve this. Shoulder aching and possibly smoking, I started to pull away from him. *I'm sorry.*

Daemon's arm tightened around me, and I didn't make it far at all. *No.* His voice wrapped around me. *Don't even hink it. If this is it, then we face it together.* His light receded, revealing the form I'd fallen in love with first. The unruly dark waves, broad cheekbones, and bright emerald-colored eyes. "Together," he repeated out loud.

My breath caught, and static built in the air around us. My body was trembling from the unspent energy and the knowledge that there was no escape.

"Together," I whispered.

Daemon bowed his head, lowering his mouth to mine, as a sudden rush of noise caused the blood to freeze in my veins. I feared that this was it—the end.

The great massive oaks and pines around us shook, branches rattled, and birds—thousands of them—took flight, their wings beating into the air as they circled high above the colony of homes, veering sharply to head in the direction of where we'd come from.

What the . . . ?

The strangest thing happened. Clouds, thick and so dark they were almost black, dropped from the sky above Seneca Rocks, and they continued to fall to the ground at a rapid pace.

Except they weren't clouds.

"Oh my God," I whispered.

Daemon hauled us back, farther away from the line of Luxen, as they started to shift in and out of their forms.

Someone—had to be a Luxen who'd been on Earth or an Origin—shouted. "Arum!"

24

{ Katy }

The mass of Arum hit the ground, their forms solidifying as they rose over the homes like oily shadows, and then they blanketed everything like black snow. A blast of arctic air hit us from behind.

We turned, and there were more, swooping down among the trees, rushing forward, barely missing us as they swarmed the ground like an army of ants.

"They're here," Daemon said. "He's here."

Oh, boy, were they ever. The Arum were everywhere.

It was like watching a hundred bowling balls knock down a thousands pins. The Arum on the ground slammed into the first line, appearing to swallow them whole as they converged on the Luxen.

Dropping from the sky above, they snatched up Luxen, tossing them into the air, where they were caught midflight by another Arum as some shifted into something that was both solid and yet not.

I stumbled back as a Luxen flew past me, slamming into

a tree. Before it could fall, an Arum sped forward, a blur of midnight, catching the Luxen and tossing it against the tree with enough power that it shattered the bark. Tiny bits flew into the air.

The Arum solidified into a tall woman with jet-black hair. She reared an arm back and then thrust her hand deep into the chest of the Luxen. The scream pierced the roar in my ears as she shifted back into oily smoke.

An Origin hit the ground from—I didn't even know where. The impact shook the branches above, and a shower of leaves floated down as the Origin slid across the ground, kicking up loose soil and rocks. The male struggled to his feet, letting loose a bolt of the Source that flew off-target as a thick shadow brought it back down to the ground. The blast of white light hit a tree, cracking the thick elm in half. It came down on the mass of Arum and Luxen. Some scattered out to the sides, and the brilliant lights of the Luxen were snuffed out as another wave of Arum descended into the fight.

"Holy . . ." I breathed, hands shaking.

Twisting around, I saw another Luxen snatched out of the air. The feedings had begun in full force, and I . . . I'd never seen anything like this. It was a mess of brutality, and yet, it was disturbingly awe-inspiring—the flashes of light and thick shadows. Such contrast.

One of the forms broke free and solidified in front of us, a tall creature with skin like polished obsidian, and then it took form. Sharp cheekbones. Lips. Straight nose. A bare chest and leather pants. Bleached blond hair.

Lotho stood in front of us, head thrown back. Shimmery blue liquid was splattered across his alabaster chest. He grinned madly. "Dinnertime."

Before either of us could respond, he headed back into

the . . . God, I didn't know what to call it. I imagined it was like when the Native Americans had decided they'd had enough of the Pilgrims and picked them off with skill and ease. A straight massacre—a well-deserved massacre, but still.

Shimmery blood tinted blue sprayed in every direction, coating the grass and paved sidewalks of the small village. Lights were going out like smashed lightning bugs. The fight moved farther away, toward the cluster of homes that had once been protected by the beta quartz embedded in the mountains.

Roofs of houses caved as Luxen and Arum crashed into them. Sparks flew as power lines fell to the ground. Flames erupted from inside the homes. A building exploded off in the distance, causing me to flinch as a wave of heat rolled through the clearing, but the red-hot blast quickly chilled.

Another house exploded—boards winging into the air and glass shattering. I jumped, thinking I heard Daemon call my name, but I couldn't turn away from the destruction. Fire speared the sky. The screams . . . they were coming from everywhere, all around us, ringing in my head and dragging over my too-tight skin.

My stomach roiled.

Which was stupid and weak, because I'd killed before.

That thought was like a second blast of frigid air dumped on my head. The scenery in front of me blurred. How many times had I killed? God, I think I'd lost count.

"Kat, your heart . . ." Daemon said, one hand moving to cup my cheek. His grip on my waist loosened, and as our gazes met and held, I couldn't believe there could be such beauty among such carnage. "Calm down, Katy. It's over."

Was it really? The energy spiked in me as I gazed back at the . . . the horror taking place, and then I pulled free.

Suddenly, I needed . . . I didn't know what I needed. My skin was still too tight and it tingled. The heat was back, burning from the inside. I had to get away from here, away from Daemon, away from everything.

My head was a mess as I turned, and I started running again, but this time I wasn't chasing anything. Or maybe I was chasing myself. I didn't know or understand. I just ran, and it wasn't until I'd cleared the colony and started up a rough incline, a path dug deep into soil and rock, that I realized I was running toward Seneca Rocks and up them.

The climb was hard, rough, and my feet slipped many times. Pressure slammed down on my chest the higher I went, until it was difficult to draw in a breath or to really think about what the hell I was doing. And I really didn't want to think about that, because this was crazy.

I knew I wasn't self-destructing. I think I knew that, because as I scrambled up the ragged path, stumbling over small bushes and sliding over pebbles, I remembered how it had been for Carissa. She had been like something shoved in a microwave that shouldn't have been placed in there.

My legs almost gave out when I reached the first of the peaks, a part that was nothing more than a ledge above a steep drop-off. I stopped—stopped walking, stopped thinking and climbing.

Dragging in deep breaths, I lifted my chin and looked up, and I swore I saw ghosts from the past. I thought I saw Dawson and Bethany looking down on me. My gaze traveled down the other peak to where I stood.

I didn't see ghosts.

It was a memory, a conversation about what had happened to them. It all had started here. Dawson had healed Beth after she'd fallen from the rocks, which had caused her uncle to contact

Daedalus, and then everything from that moment had led to this.

Everything had started with Dawson and Beth.

"Kat?"

My breath caught as I heard his voice. My chin dipped to my chest as I slowly wheeled around.

And everything ended with Daemon and me.

He stared at me from the path, his eyes brilliant as he watched me. His chest rose and fell as fast as mine. "Kat," he said again.

My head still didn't feel screwed on right as he took a step onto the ledge. I backed across the smooth rock, breathing heavily. I closed my eyes and I saw Mom—I saw her without blue eyes, but with beautiful hazel ones, and when I took a breath, it got stuck around a sob in my throat. I saw Ethan sitting in my kitchen and then standing on Daemon's porch, the first time I'd seen him. I saw Blake, that carefree, charming smile that had hidden so many secrets. I saw Carissa, who we would never get answers about, and then I saw countless faces with unknown names.

"Kitten," Daemon tried again, and I opened my eyes. I saw him. "What are we doing?"

We. Not you. *We.*

"I don't know," I admitted in a hoarse whisper. "I thought . . . I just needed to get away from it."

"That's understandable."

It was, wasn't it? I took another step back, my gaze never leaving his. It was obvious. I wasn't self-destructing. I sat down. Or plopped down. I wasn't sure which. Several moments passed and I remembered the strangest thing. "This . . . this is like Snowbird."

He stared at me like he was worried I had truly lost my mind. Maybe I had. "What?"

"The legend you told me about." I turned, looking over the ridge. Every muscle in my body ached. There was a good chance there was a hole in my shoulder, and I was so very, very tired. "This is like Princess Snowbird."

Daemon didn't respond.

"She climbed up these rocks and only one brave warrior kept pace with her until the end." I wet my dry lips, forcing my lungs open with another deep breath. "You told me all about it when we took that walk, before we saw the bear." My gaze shifted over to him, and his expression had softened. "You told me . . . told me about the most stunning people and what was inside them." I paused, frowning. "The way you said it sounded so very beautiful."

He came closer, stopping in front of me. He knelt down, his eyes shining. "I remember. I said, 'The most beautiful people, ones whose beauty is only rivaled by what is inside of them, are the ones who are quietly unaware of it.' Or something like that."

"That was it." I nodded.

He tilted his head to the side. "I was talking about you then. Those words were meant for you."

My eyes met his again and I swallowed. Hard.

"You had no idea how beautiful you were. I don't even think you do now, but it's what's inside of you." Carefully, he reached out and placed his hand between my breasts. "That's the most beautiful thing in the world. What's *in* you."

Tears rose, and I let out a shaky breath. Those words . . . well, they did something in me. I wasn't a murderer. I wasn't crazy. I was tired and I was a million other things, and to Daemon, I was also beautiful on the outside and inside.

"Thank you."

He made a sound in the back of his throat as he moved

toward me and circled his arms around my shoulders. "You never need to thank me for the truth."

I clutched at his shirt. "At least I didn't laugh at you this time."

"There's always that." There was a smile in his voice. "Oh, Kitten . . ."

From where we were, it looked like thick, dark clouds passing, snuffing out tiny stars, except the mass wasn't clouds and the lights flickering out weren't stars. Daemon rested his chin atop my head as he smoothed his hand up my back, and I felt the familiar warmth of his touch. "It's over."

Finally, I relaxed against him and closed my eyes. It was over.

{ Daemon }

I wasn't sure I closed my eyes at all during the night. Maybe I had slept a bit, but I couldn't confirm that. Watching Kat was the last thing and the first thing I remembered.

She was curled against me, her cheek resting on my now-numb arm. We were in my house and before she'd crashed last night, she had changed into one of my shirts that had been left untouched in my closet. It was way too big for her, sliding down her shoulder, exposing a tantalizing amount of skin.

I was pretty fascinated by that skin. With my not-dead arm, I trailed my fingers across her shoulder, following her collarbone. I'd been doing that for half the night. Every so often, she'd manage to snuggle closer, tossing a leg over mine or pressing her body against mine.

I worried about her.

Really freaking worried about her.

Even after discovering what had happened to her mother, she'd held it together yesterday, taken out Ethan, and witnessed the Arum swarming in. Yeah, she'd freaked and bolted. But hell, she had it controlled when the Arum had blown through the colony later, having suffered only minor losses before they headed toward Northern Virginia to finish it.

When word came late in the evening that the invading Luxen had turned into one giant buffet for the Arum, she'd smiled as those around us celebrated the victory, the end of this madness. But there hadn't been a lot of time to comfort her or to really talk about it. All I'd been able to do was hold her while she fell asleep. Didn't seem like enough.

There really wasn't ever enough.

My chest was heavy with the loss, with the pain I knew she'd suffer for a long time to come from a death that was so needless and cruel. Her family had been stripped away from her. Her father lost to cancer and her mother to one of my own kind.

Still, like some kind of miracle, her last words to me before she'd fallen asleep had been *I love you*. The fact that she still could feel something like that blew me away.

I would've done anything to save her from this pain, but like so many other things I wanted to go back and erase, this was one of them we would have to learn to accept, that we would have to face together.

Kat stirred against me, stretching out in a way that reminded me so much of the nickname I'd given her. A smile pulled at the corners of my lips as her lashes fluttered open.

Sleep clouded her pretty eyes as they met mine. "Hey."

"Hey yourself."

Her hand flattened out against my bare chest as her gaze swept across my face. "Have you been up long?"

"I'm not even sure I slept."

"So you've been watching me sleep?"

One side of my lips kicked up. "Maybe."

"Well, look who's being the creeper this time around."

"Call me what you want, I don't care." I moved my thumb along her lower lip. "I spent hours staring at the best damn scenery."

Her cheeks flushed. "Flattery will get you everything."

"I already have everything."

"That was sweet of you." She patted my chest like I was a good boy, and I ignored the parts of me that got all happy about that. Her gaze drifted away and circled the room before coming back to me. "It's really over, isn't it?"

I curled my arm around her, overlooking the rush of pins and needles. "I think so. I mean, for the most part. Things are going to be different. Life will be different, but it's over."

Kat's lashes lowered as she bit down on her lower lip in a way that got those parts of me paying close attention. "What are we going to do now?" she whispered.

"Whatever we want to do."

She rolled onto her back but didn't get very far. "That sounds really nice."

The sudden clanging of pots from the kitchen down below brought a winsome smile to her face. "I'm assuming Dee and Archer are up?"

"Yeah. I think I heard them moving around not too long ago. They're probably making good use of the fact that whoever was staying here kept the kitchen stocked." My brows knitted. "Archer supposedly slept in Dawson's room last night, but I heard a bedroom—"

"Daemon." She laughed.

I sighed. "I know. Turning over a new leaf and blah, blah." I started to get up. "I better go and see—"

Her arm had snaked up, looping around my neck, and she tugged me down. Yeah, I didn't resist. There was no such thing as willpower when it came to her, especially not when she lifted her head and kissed me.

Kat was all warm and soft under me, and that kiss quickly spun into something else. Her leg curled around my calf and her hands slid down my back, reaching the band on the pajama bottoms I'd found, and then slipped under.

Hot damn.

I forgot about sneaking around in bedrooms, about who was downstairs, and about almost everything else as she made this breathy sound that caused my skin to tighten. Her nails scraped along my skin as I got my hands under that borrowed shirt, over the length of her smooth skin. She arched into me, and I wanted her. I *always* wanted her. Hell, I'd spend eternity needing her, but we had time. Later today. Tonight. Tomorrow. We had a week, a month, and a year from now. We finally had a future and many more moments like this.

But right now, she needed me.

Her hands made their way to my front, and a ragged sound caught in my throat. Okay. Clarification. She needed more than *this*.

Finding the willpower I'd thought I didn't have earlier but discovered I could exercise when it really mattered, I pulled away from her, just a little, and got her hands back to where I could see them.

Her brows pinched as she stared up at me, eyes a deep, smoky gray. I kissed her softly, lingering longer than I should. "How are you doing?" I asked, my voice rough in my own ears.

"Um, well, I *was*—"

"Not that." I sat up, putting a little space between us so I wouldn't change my mind and do all kinds of things to her. "How are you feeling after . . . after yesterday?"

She stilled for a moment, and then her chest rose sharply as she squeezed her eyes shut. "I don't want to think about that right now."

"Kat—"

"I don't." She tucked her legs under her as she rose. Clasping my cheeks, she leaned in until we were eye to eye. When she spoke, I swore my heart cracked in my chest. The pain of her words was so very real. "I know what you're doing, and God, I love you for it, but I'm not ready, Daemon. I'm not, because I can't even think about it without wanting to bring down this house or go curl in a ball. I don't want to feel any of those things. When I lost my dad, it hurt—hurt so badly, and I don't want to experience that hurt. The only thing I want to feel is you right now. The only thing I want to think about is how you make me *feel*. That's what I need from you."

I was still for maybe five seconds, and then I sprang from the bed, found my thankfully still private stash, grabbed the small package, and was back on the bed in front of her in a heartbeat. "I can do that for you."

We stared at each other for another second, and then she straightened slightly, reaching down and lifting the shirt over her head.

I forgot how to breathe.

With just the tips of my fingers, I followed the map of her curves. "You're so beautiful." I kissed the tiny hollow between her collarbones. "You're stronger than you realize." Another kiss to the spot behind her ear. "You're perfect for me."

I put everything I felt into the gesture I'd never take for granted when it came to her.

Pressing her down onto her back and settling between her legs, I helped her hold the darkness back so that the only thing she felt was my hands, my skin, and everything I felt for her.

Showered and changed, we headed downstairs just in time to eat leftover bacon and eggs. The food was cold and Archer and my sister were staring at us like they knew exactly why it took us so long to come downstairs, but I didn't care. There was an edge of sadness to the soft smile Kat wore as she watched them, but she *was* smiling, and I had given her what she wanted when she needed it.

After she finished eating, she excused herself and stood. From behind my chair, she leaned over and kissed my cheek. "I'm going to step outside for a few. Okay?"

I started to follow her but realized that she probably wanted a few minutes alone and told myself to keep my ass in my chair. As she turned, though, I caught her arm and tugged her down until I could capture her mouth in a deep, scorching kiss that probably sent her mind back to what went down between us in the bedroom.

Archer coughed. "We're not standing here or anything."

"Whatever," I murmured as I let Kat go, and she surveyed the room with a red face. Giving an awkward wave, she turned and hurried out of the kitchen. I leaned back in my chair, shooting Archer a look that said, *Shut up.*

He raised his hands as he backed away from the table and then grabbed the trash, going right to where the can was under the sink, in the cabinet. I frowned. "You're awful familiar with my kitchen."

Archer snorted.

"How is she?" Dee asked as she sat beside me.

I sighed. "As can be expected."

Sympathy poured into her eyes. "I didn't know Ethan had her mom killed. I swear. I would've said something if I did."

"I know." I patted her arm. "Kat knows that, too."

"Totally sucks," Archer said, closing the cabinet door and straightening. "Probably good to get away from here."

"Yeah," I murmured, hoping she'd open up soon about what she was feeling. I knew from personal experience how that kind of pain and hurt could tear someone up. "I'll see—"

Archer's cell phone went off in his pocket. Frowning, he pulled it out and quickly answered. "What's up, Luc?" he asked as he turned back to the sink and grabbed a dish towel.

Who knew Archer was so domesticated? I looked at my sister, and she was grinning at him like he was the second coming of something great.

"What?" Archer turned to us slowly, frowning. "No. Not at all."

I sat up straight, on alert.

His eyes met mine. "Yeah, I know what you planned to do. It'll still happen." There was a pause, and sudden unease formed in my gut. "I'll call you if anything comes up here."

I was standing, and so was Dee by the time he disconnected the call. "What's going on?"'

He slipped his phone into his pocket. "Nancy was sighted."

"What?" The question boomed out of me. "A little more detail."

Archer walked over to the table and gripped the back of a chair. "Luc doesn't know the exact time frame. Sometime yesterday evening. With everything going on, word just got back to him. It was near Georgia. Maybe she was looking for us."

"Shit," I said, not liking the sound of that and knowing that this . . . this shit really wasn't over. Not with her. . . .

"He's ticked off. He planned on killing her."

"What?"

"You heard me correctly. Once this was all over, he wanted to take her out himself. He never had any intentions of releasing the Origins back to her."

There wasn't a single part of me that was unhappy to hear about those plans, and I didn't care how bad that made me look.

Archer scrubbed his jaw. "God, that woman could literally be anywhere and I'll tell you what, she's a loose cannon—" He cut himself off as he whirled around and looked at the clock on the wall. "Georgia . . . it didn't take us that long to make the trip— Oh, *shit*." He whipped around.

I was already racing toward the front door. There had been more than enough time for Nancy to make her way here, but I couldn't imagine that woman would be stupid enough to try to seek vengeance on us. I threw the door open and rushed out onto the front porch, scanning the yard. A burst of air left me as I spotted Kat in front of her house. She was on her knees, her hair up in a knot, pulling the weeds out of the flower box. Frankly, she was *ripping* them out.

She looked up as I jogged over to where she was. Without saying a word, I reached down and hauled her up, pulling her into my arms and squeezing the ever-loving daylights out of her.

"Hey." Her voice was muffled. "Is everything okay?"

Holding on to her, I lifted her up off her feet. "Yeah," I said against the top of her head. "I just missed you."

"I've only been gone a few minutes."

I lowered her to her feet, not sure how to tell her about Nancy or even if I should bring it up. That might be wrong as hell, but God, I didn't want to mention that piece of bad news.

Not with everything she'd just gone through and the fact that I knew she was trying to focus on a future she hadn't believed possible days before.

"You are so weird sometimes," she said, grinning as she looked up at me. "But I still love—" Whatever she was saying ended in a shout of warning.

Time slowed as I whirled around, and sure as hell, there was Nancy looking like a mess, dark hair standing out in every direction, that god-awful suit wrinkled. There was a gun in her hand, but it didn't look like a normal pistol. Instead it looked like a Glock that had been manipulated into something else.

Something really deadly.

There was a moment when my brain registered what was happening, what was about to go down, and that moment felt like an eternity as my gaze met Nancy's and the hatred in her eyes told me everything I needed to know. She wasn't going to kill me.

No.

She wanted me—one of her ultimate prizes—to suffer.

The gun wasn't pointed at me.

Nancy smiled. "You ruined everything."

The time it would take to summon the Source, a handful of seconds, wasn't a risk I was willing to take. Before that thought was even finished, I was moving. My hands circled Kat's arms as she raised a hand, preparing to tap into her ability. I took her down as a spark of blue light flared, followed by a low popping sound.

My eyes met Kat's.

Shouts exploded from my nearby house and I heard Dee scream—a mixture of horror and the kind of fury that ended lives. There was a blast of the Source, a short howl of pain, and the sound of Nancy hitting the ground—dead.

And then there was silence.

I looked down, between our bodies. The front of her cream-colored sweater looked wrong, like it had been splattered with a paintbrush dipped in red and . . .

"Kitten?" I gasped out.

It wasn't her blood.

Thank God, it wasn't *her* blood.

But I didn't understand what had happened. I hadn't even felt it. How strange was that? I'd never been shot before, but I figured it would have to hurt the moment the bullet ripped through me, but it didn't.

Now my back and chest were on fire.

"Daemon?" she whispered.

Oh shit.

My lungs tried to expand but seemed to get stuck. I didn't look away from her eyes as I lifted myself off her, tried to stand, but realized that my brain wasn't connecting to my legs. I went down on one hand, feeling the warm wetness traveling down my stomach. My arm gave out and I landed on my side.

Kat was suddenly above me, and I was on my back and all I could see were her beautiful gray eyes—eyes that had become my whole life, probably before I even realized they had.

But those eyes were wide with fear and shining in a way that made me want to touch her, to make sure she was okay. I managed to lift my arm and trail the tips of my fingers across her cheek, but I couldn't hold it up. It was like dead meat.

"Daemon!"

I tried to respond, but all I could do was focus on those eyes. As she leaned over me, her sweet lips so close to mine, my name on her tongue, I thought that if I had to die, if this would be the end, then at least I was seeing her and nothing else.

25

"Daemon?" My heart was pounding against my ribs, but it felt wrong—it felt worn out and sluggish. Fire traveled up and down my back, but I knew I wasn't hurt. It was Daemon.

Oh God, it was *him*.

I slid my hand over his chest, crying out as my hand came back soaked with the reddish-blue blood. "Oh. No . . ."

My name was called out. So was Daemon's, but I didn't look to see what was happening. My eyes were locked with Daemon's. His lips, leached of all color, moved, but there were no words.

This wasn't happening!

This could not be happening!

We hadn't survived everything that we'd faced, on top of an alien invasion, for Daemon to die like this.

"No! No. No!" I searched for the source of the wound, but he'd taken the shot in the back.

It hadn't been a normal gun.

Daemon's form started to flicker, and horror kicked me in the chest. I grabbed his cheeks as my lungs desperately tried to force air in. His eyes were closed. "Open your eyes! Dammit, open your eyes!"

My legs started to shake with the effort to hold myself up in a kneeling position, and then Archer and Dee were there, and I couldn't help but think of that horrible time in my house, when the situation had been flipped and it had been me lying on the floor. Then we thought we were purely connected, and if one died, so did the other, but now we knew the truth.

I ignored the pain roaring through my body and the weakness creeping into my muscles, invading my very being, followed by coldness, a chill of death. My overworked heart turned over.

"No!" Dee cried out, dropping down by Daemon's head. Her hands landed on her brother's shoulders and she immediately shifted into her true form. Her light was brilliant, much like an angel's halo.

"Fix him, please." My vision blurred as I started to tilt toward the ground. "Please, please fix him."

Archer caught me, but I shrugged him off, clinging to Daemon as tears streamed down my face. "What . . . do we do?" I couldn't look away as Daemon continued to flicker in and out, his beautifully strong light dulling, and the coldness spread like a disease inside me. "It wasn't a . . . normal gun. It was one of those . . . weapons we were given. Please . . . do something . . ."

"It's the modified PEP weapon." Archer placed his hands above mine, his face twisting in concentration. "Dammit. We need to make sure the bullet is out. If it's not, then . . ."

The words sank in as I slid down to my side, unable to hold myself up. One of my hands slipped off his cheek. I could no longer get my tongue to work, and I labored for breath. I threw everything in me into reaching Daemon. *Don't . . . leave me. Oh God . . . please don't . . . leave me. I love you. Daemon, I love you. Please don't let go. Please!*

Archer cursed under his breath as his gaze bounced between Dee and me. "Kat, I . . ."

I didn't feel myself falling, but I was suddenly flat on my back and staring up at the cloudless blue sky. Such a beautiful sky, but my heart hurt. My chest seized, and my entire body went rigid.

No. No. No.

We were supposed to have tonight and tomorrow, and many weeks and months, but we didn't have even another minute. My face was wet, soaked, and my heart was slowing. The world started to slip away.

I love you. I love you. I love you.

Then Daemon and I . . . we had nothing and there was nothing.

My body came back online slowly, tingling and aching as if I'd run a zombie marathon and gotten chewed on in the process. There was an odd beeping sound. It annoyed me, because all I wanted to do was slip back into the oblivion where there was nothing. I didn't want to remember exactly why I didn't want to open my eyes.

Reality existed on the fringes of my consciousness, a reality that would be cold and shattering and heartbreaking, and I didn't want to go there. I wanted to stay where there was nothing.

The beeping wouldn't let me slip away, though. It was faint, and every beep was accompanied by another beep, as if it were chasing mine or I was chasing the other beep, so I listened as my fingers twitched. A tremor coursed up my arm and then made its way through my body.

"Katy?"

I recognized the voice and the voice hurt, because it reminded me of. . . .

No.

I couldn't go there. I didn't want to.

A warm hand folded over mine and squeezed gently. "Katy?"

The beeping picked up speed and so did the other.

The other.

Something flared in my chest, like a tiny flame sparking to life. My senses were whirling to the forefront. I could feel something cool against my chest—stuck there. The beeping was starting to go crazy. And then I knew what it was.

A heart monitor.

And there were two separate beeps, one virtually on top of the other. Two. That had to mean . . . Surrounded by a familiar earthy scent, I willed my eyes to open and dragged in a deep breath.

Dee was hovering over me, her green eyes bright with relief. "There you are. I was beginning to wonder if you were going to wake up."

My mouth was dry from panic as I stared at her. She looked okay—maybe a little stressed. Her hair was a bit crazy-looking, her face a little pale, but she was smiling. Her hand squeezed mine again.

I took another breath and slowly turned my head to the left. My heart exploded in my chest as I gasped.

He lay there, *his* normal, deeply tanned skin a shade or two paler. I could only see half of his face, but it was a strong, beautiful profile—the cut jaw and straight nose.

I glanced back at Dee in confusion and then quickly looked back at the bed near mine, afraid to blink in fear he'd disappear. I was shaking as I pushed myself up. "I'm . . . I'm awake?"

"Yes."

My breath caught, but not in that painful way. "I don't understand."

She eased away from the bed, giving me room to swing my legs off the side. "You should probably take it easy."

I ignored her, pulling the sticky things off my chest as I placed my bare feet on the cold floor. It was then I realized I was in a hospital gown and we were in a hospital room. "I don't understand," I repeated.

Dee moved to the foot of *his* bed and smiled tiredly. "The bullet was normal, but it had this electric current in it, sort of like an encasing. If it had stayed in him longer, it would've killed him . . ." She trailed off, shaking her head. "It *should've* killed him, but he hung on."

He hung on.

My legs were wobbly as I stumbled toward the bed, staring at the steady rise and fall of his chest. *He* was alive. *He* was breathing. My heart was pounding out of my chest.

I was beyond words as I reached out and placed my fingers on his arm. The skin was warm and dry. My breath caught once more.

"Archer called the general and told him what happened. There were still a lot of military nearby, and he sent a helicopter to pick you guys up."

My hand trembled as I slid it up his arm.

"They flew him and you out. We're at a military base in Maryland. They had doctors here," she explained. "They were able to get the bullet out. They say . . . he'll be okay, Katy."

I lowered my head to his chest and I heard it—Daemon's

heartbeat moving as fast as mine. "Oh my God . . ." I sat on the edge of his bed, keeping my ear plastered to his chest. "Please . . . tell me this is real," I whispered, eyes filling up with tears. "That I won't wake up again and find this is a cruel dream. *Please*."

"It isn't a dream. I promise you." She moved to where I sat and leaned down, hugging me gently. "This is real. He's going to be okay, Katy."

"Thank you," I said, voice thick with emotion. "Tell Archer I said thank you."

Dee responded, but I was focused on the sound of Daemon's heart. I was only vaguely aware that after some time, Dee left the room. I stayed where I was and there was no stopping the tears. They kept coming, streaming down my face, dampening the thin blue blanket that was tucked under his arms.

Minutes passed. Maybe hours. I didn't move—wasn't capable of it and didn't want to. My heart finally slowed. So did his, and then it thumped when a heavy arm settled over my waist. Startled and full of hope, I lifted my head.

My eyes locked with a pair of brilliant emerald ones.

"Daemon," I breathed. The waterworks really picked up then, and his beautiful face blurred.

His lips slowly parted. "Don't cry, Kitten." As if it took great effort, he lifted his other arm, brushing the tears off my cheeks with the back of his hand. "Come on."

My chest twisted. "I never thought . . . I'd hear you say that again. I thought you were gone and . . ." My throat closed off as I placed my hand over his, pulling it to my mouth. I kissed his knuckles.

He made a sound in the back of his throat. "Did you think I'd leave you?"

I shuddered.

"I heard you," he said, and then he tried to sit up.

"Don't," I said, my eyes going wide.

He made that sound again, this time more frustrated. "I heard you out in the yard. I wouldn't leave you, Kat. I'd never do that. Now . . . get down here and kiss me."

"But you . . . you took a bullet for me, Daemon." My breath hitched in my throat again. "She was going to shoot me and you . . . you could've died. I thought you *had* died."

A moment passed as he stared at me like I'd grown two heads. "What else would I've done?"

Now I gaped at him through fresh tears.

"I love you," he said, his eyes incredibly bright as he spoke those words. "If your life is in danger, I'm going to do everything I can to make sure you're safe. That's what love makes you do. Right?"

"Right," I whispered, still stunned somewhat. He spoke as if it wasn't a big deal.

"I'd do it again."

Oh God. "Daemon, I . . . thank you."

He frowned. "You don't need to thank me."

"I do."

The corner of his lips tipped up. "Okay. Thank me by getting down here and kissing me."

I did just that. I lowered my mouth to his and kissed him softly, reveling in his taste and the warmth of his lips. "I love you so very much, and I'm going to spend every waking moment proving it to you."

"I like the sound of that." He tugged on my hair as I lifted my head. "Where . . . are we?"

I gave him the quick version of what Dee had told me. "They're not sure how you survived." I sniffled, using my shoulder to wipe the tears off my cheek. "But you're so stubborn."

Daemon coughed out a dry laugh and the grip on my hand tightened. "You know how I love a challenge."

My heart lurched as I remembered those words from the day we'd learned we were connected, and I'd shot him down when he suggested we should get together. I leaned over him, brushing my lips across his forehead. I closed my eyes, sent up as many thank-yous as I could to every God and deity and prophet I knew. "So do I, Daemon. So do I."

EPILOGUE

Eleven months later . . .

(Katy)

Bright sunlight streamed in through the bedroom window of the townhome at the foothills of the Flatirons. An early bout of October snow had capped the tips of the mountains, turning them white.

It really was beautiful here in Colorado—the air fresh and trees everywhere. It reminded me of home, my old home, but with easy access to a lot more cool stuff.

Like Starbucks.

Which had reopened two months earlier, just in time for the return of the pumpkin spice latte, a sure sign mankind would trek on. Humans were probably the most resilient and stubborn creatures in all the universes.

Something the invading Luxen, those who'd managed to escape the Arum, had learned quickly. Days after the battle, while our little group had holed up in Northern Virginia trying to decide how and where to move on, the remaining invading Luxen left.

It had been like a reverse D-Day.

Lights had flashed upward in steady streams, all across the

world, for several hours. It had been a sight to see, just like it had been when they'd come. Something I would never forget.

But we all knew that there still could be some here, and there was no stopping them from coming back. Maybe one day they would, but if I'd learned anything in the last two years, it was that I could not look toward the future if I lived in the past.

It was hard.

Not a day went by that I didn't think of my mom. Like with my dad, it got a little easier, but there were days when something would happen or I'd just get bored or want to talk to her, and I'd reach for my phone, seconds away from calling her when I'd realize she wasn't there, that she'd never be there.

Those days were rough, full of tears and anger. I wanted to resurrect Ethan just so I could kick him in his junk and kill him all over again. The fury and helplessness and, oh God, the hurt could be so raw some days. If it weren't for Daemon and my friends—my new family—it would be unbearable.

I glanced over my shoulder.

Daemon rested against the headboard of the king-size bed—a bed big enough for half of my economics class. His arms were folded behind his head, one leg bent at the knee. No shirt. Just faded denim jeans, and I knew for a fact that that seriously was all. The corded biceps drew my gaze and I soaked in the naturally tan expanse of his chest and the tightly rolled muscles of his stomach. To this day, I had no idea how he got that dip on either side of his hips. Like what kind of sit-ups does one do for that? The only time I sat up from lying down was to get out of bed.

Or get some chocolate.

Or a book.

But yeah, Daemon Black . . . well, he totally made it bearable.

He winked one green eye, and somehow, when most guys would look all kinds of douchey, he made it look sexy. "Like what you see?"

I didn't even dignify that with a response. Instead I faced my computer, my fingers hovering over the keys—the enter button to be exact. My heart was racing like it had been when Daemon and I had submitted our applications, the day the University of Colorado had finally opened their enrollment and resumed classes.

That had been major.

Still felt epic.

We both were doing something I thought we'd never be able to do. Going to college had seemed like a fantasy, but it had come true.

We were college students—Daemon and me.

Neither of us had declared a major yet. We had no idea what we wanted to do, but that was okay. We'd figure it out eventually.

"Just do it," Daemon said, his voice closer than I expected, causing me to jump. His chuckle stirred loose strands of hair around my temple. He tugged my ponytail, tipping my head back. He kissed me softly, almost making me forget what I was doing, and when he lifted his head, he grinned down at me from behind. "You've been obsessing over it for weeks. Do it."

I bit my lip, still tasting him.

"Come on." He picked up a pen off my desk and tapped the tip of my nose with it. I swatted at his hand, and he laughed. "Your inner book nerd will have a book nerd orgasm."

My brows knitted. "That just . . . sounds weird and kind of gross."

He snickered as he let go of my ponytail. His gaze landed on the screen of my brand-spanking-new MacBook that I'd protect with my last dying breath. I'd even named her Brittany, because she had to be a girl, and she was shiny and red and perfect and she might not have ten toes and ten fingers, but she was my baby.

And I loved her.

Taking a deep breath, I flexed my fingers. Daemon dropped his hands onto the arms of my chair and leaned over me. The warmth that rolled off him and trailed down my back turned the corners of my mouth up.

I hit publish and then sucked in a sharp breath as everything on the screen refreshed into a brand-spanking-new blog.

"Katy's Krazy Book Obsession is alive once more." He kissed my cheek. "You nerd."

I laughed as some kind of weight drifted off my shoulders. "I think the pink and brown go well together."

He grunted some sort of reply as my smile grew into creepy proportions. I *almost* clapped. And I almost got up, knocked Daemon over, and raced into our extra bedroom, where all my books—all my pretties—were.

After everything had gone down, Daemon and I had traveled back to my house. Archer had shown up with Dee, and the four of us had packed up all of the stuff. We'd managed to get my books shipped to Colorado once we decided that was where we were going to try to put down some roots.

The blog was a big deal to me. It wasn't just pretending everything was fine or grasping at normalcy, but grabbing it by the ears and making it my bitch. Blogging about books was something I'd loved to do and missed fiercely. Books were a part of me that I was going to get back, starting now.

"Hey." Daemon pointed at the screen. "You already have a follower." A dark eyebrow cocked up. "*The YA Sisterhood*? Hmm. That kind of sounds like fun."

I rolled my eyes so far it actually hurt. "You're so perverted."

He nipped my ear, causing me to wiggle in my chair. Leaning forward, I closed my laptop so I didn't obsessively start following every blogger out there. I'd leave that for another day when I had more time.

As Daemon backed off and I pushed out of the chair, my gaze danced over the stack of magazines piled on the corner of the desk, wedding gown after wedding gown staring back at me, stealing my breath a little.

My gaze dropped to my left hand.

The shimmery diamond on my ring finger drew some major attention. Some days when the light hit it the right way, it would literally dazzle me into staring at it for several minutes.

We were going to get married, the whole deal—white gown, ceremony, bridesmaids and groomsmen, reception, DJ, and most importantly, the wedding cake. For real this time, under our legit names. The fake IDs were left behind, though I kind of missed them a little.

Kaidan Rowe was a Hottie McHotters.

But General Eaton had kept his promise. The ARP—Alien Registration Program—did not affect us, and as of today, no one had recognized either of us from the brief time the Vegas videos had been up on the internet.

The ARP was General Eaton's and the government's answer to weeding out any Luxen and Origins who may be flying the unfriendly skies. All Luxen, hybrids, Origins, and Arum were required to register—all except us. Some days I wondered if that would change, and it always caused knots of unease to form in my belly.

Now that the alien was really out of the bag, and with all the terrible things the invading Luxen had done, aliens weren't all that . . . accepted in communities. Every day, there was something in the news about an attack on a suspected Luxen or colony. Many innocent Luxen had been injured in the past months and some . . . they'd been killed just because of what they were.

That was scary, knowing that someone you saw every day, who thought you were a nice and normal human, could turn on you so quickly once he or she realized that wasn't what you were. And God forbid if the general populace learned how onyx and diamond, or even a low-dose Taser, could affect us.

Things weren't easy or perfect, and the future seemed shaky at times, but life wasn't wrapped up in neat little bows.

I ran my fingers over the multicolored tabs poking out of the tops of the magazines that marked pages with the gowns, decorations, and cakes I liked.

Daemon wasn't much of a planner when it came to the whole wedding thing, even though it had been his idea, but whenever I dragged out one of those thick magazines, he didn't moan and complain as I thumbed through it.

Although he seemed disturbingly fascinated with the selection of garter belts.

When I lifted my gaze, he watched me intently, in that all-consuming way that always made me feel like I was stripped bare for him.

A rush of warmth flowed through my veins. I bit down on my lip as I glanced at the clock on the wall.

"We have time," Daemon said, voice rough as sandpaper.

I arched my brow even as my heart skipped a beat. "Time for what?"

"Uh-huh. Don't play coy with me." He walked around my abandoned chair, causing my stomach to dip in the most pleasant way as he stalked toward me. "I know what you're thinking."

"Do not." I took a step back, my toes digging into the carpet.

"Do too," he murmured, one side of his lips kicking up.

"That's just your overactive ego and your wishful thinking talking."

Dark eyebrows rose. "Is that so, Kitten?"

Fighting a grin, I nodded as I glanced at the clock again. We so had time. I shrugged.

Challenge flared, deepening the hue of his eyes to a forest green, and a burst of excitement went off inside me like a firecracker. "I think I can prove that's not the case."

"Whatever."

In the blink of an eye, Daemon was in front of me. I started to yell at him, because I still hated that, but he captured my mouth in a searing kiss that went straight to my knees.

"All I need is ten minutes," he said, voice gruff.

"What happened to only needing two minutes?"

Daemon chuckled as he reached down, caught the hem of my shirt, and tugged it over my head. "Well, what I plan to do is going to take a little longer than that."

He was remarkably skilled at taking my clothes off in record time. Before I knew it, I was standing there, feeling a wee bit exposed.

Daemon stepped back, as if he was admiring his handiwork. "If I haven't told you this before . . ." He dragged his gaze up, lingering on my chest until it felt like a physical touch. "I want you. I'll always want you."

"Always?" I whispered.

He stepped forward again, his hands closing around my arms as he lowered his head, brushing his lips along the curve of my cheek. "Always."

My chest rose, grazing his. The sensation rocked me. He made a deep sound in the back of his throat that twisted up my insides. He kissed me again as his hands skimmed down my arms to settle around my waist. I shivered, and at this rate, I didn't think he'd even need two minutes.

Daemon lifted me up, and I wrapped my legs around his waist. Not once did he break the kiss, and by the time my back hit the mattress, I was breathless with a thousand different kinds of wants.

"How many minutes do we have left?" he asked as he shucked off his jeans.

I smiled as he climbed over the top of me, and as he leaned down, the edges of his hair tickled my cheek. "I've totally forgotten about the minute thing."

"Wow. Already?" he murmured against my lips and curled an arm around my waist, lifting me up so our bodies were pressed together at all the amazing points. "I'm a little amazed by my own skill."

A laugh burst out of me, and he caught the sound with a grin and kiss, and then there really wasn't room for laughing. He trailed a path of hot, tiny kisses across my forehead and then down, way down, where he lingered until he completely erased the whole idea of time and the fact we had things to do.

When he rose again, my body was shaking as our hips met. "Kat, God . . . I love you."

There would never come a time when I'd grow tired of hearing those words or experiencing just how much he truly did love me. I wrapped my arms around his shoulders, raining kisses across his cheek, his lips, and when his control shattered, I went along with it.

I don't know how long he moved while I was awash in a riot of sensations, but when I opened my eyes and his face was pressed against my neck, his brilliant light flickered over the ceiling.

A lazy, contented smile pulled at my lips as he lifted his

head and placed a kiss to my damp temple, and I fell in love all over again. When he rolled onto his side, he tugged me right along with him, and I rested my head on his chest, listening to the rapid thrum of his heart matching the pace in my chest.

At some point, Daemon looked over his shoulder and cursed under his breath. "We have ten minutes before they show up."

"Holy crap!" I shot up, smacking his chest.

He laughed as I scrambled off the bed. "Where are you going?"

"I need to shower." I tugged my hair out of the ponytail and then twisted it high up. Hurrying around the bed, I shot him a look.

His gaze was trained way below my face. "You don't need to shower."

"Yes I do!" I threw open the bathroom door. "I smell like—like you!"

Daemon's deep laugh followed me into the quickest shower I'd ever taken, which was surprising, because he hopped in and bathed like a total dude. Some soap here. Some soap there. That was all.

I hated boys.

There was enough time for me to grab the gift bag from my makeshift library of awesome books and run down the stairs before the front door rang.

Daemon slid past me, reaching the door as I placed the pink gift bag on the couch. He shot me a look. "You still smell like me."

My mouth dropped open.

He threw open the door before I could shriek and run back upstairs. And I was sure I looked really weird, because our guests stood at the door, wearing identical WTF expressions.

Or else freaking Archer was peeping in my head.

His amethyst-colored eyes glimmered with amusement. "Maybe." He drew the word out, and my eyes narrowed.

"You really need to stop doing that." Dee brushed past him, her thick, curly hair trailing out behind her like a glossy high-def cape. "You know what he did yesterday?"

"Do I even want to know?" Daemon muttered.

Archer stepped in. "No."

"Great."

"We were at Olive Garden, and by the way, thank you for talking up the endless breadsticks crap, because I think we've eaten there like ten times this month, and I'm going to start smelling like garlic," Dee went on, plopping in the recliner and tapping her ballet flats on the floor.

"I like their soup and salad," he said, shrugging as he walked over to the armchair and sat down.

Daemon's forehead wrinkled.

"Anyway," Dee said. "I thought our waitress was checking him out. Like nonstop. Like I wasn't even there."

That was hard to imagine, treating Dee like she wasn't there.

"So I was, you know, doing something normal," she said.

"Normal?" Archer barked out a short laugh. "She was fantasizing running the poor waitress over with the car. Like in complete gory detail."

One slender shoulder rose as she shrugged. "Like I said, you shouldn't look into people's thoughts and then complain about what you see."

"I wasn't necessarily complaining," he said, leaning down so his mouth brushed the curve of her ear. "If I remember correctly, I'd told you that it was kind of hot and that it made me want—"

"All right," Daemon shouted. "That is stuff I just don't even want to think about."

Dee frowned at her brother. "What? You think we don't have wild—"

"Stop," he warned, waving his hand. "Seriously. I barely like him as it is, so please don't make me want to hurt him."

"But I like you," Archer replied.

Daemon shot him a look that would send most running in the opposite direction. "I really regret suggesting that Dee get a place here. I wouldn't have done it if I knew that was an invite when it came to you."

"Where I go," Dee chirped, "he goes. We're like a two-for-one special. Deal with it or get over it."

My smile grew when Dee's eyes, so much like her brothers', met mine. It was another thing I thought about a lot. The "what ifs" of everything, like what if Dee hadn't broken the hold the Luxen held over her. Would she have died in the fight or would she have survived, only to leave Earth or be hunted down?

Losing Dee, on top of what happened to my mother, was something I don't think I ever would've gotten over. And Daemon? I didn't want to even think about how he would've been affected. It would've broken him, almost had when Dee stood against us.

She glanced at the small pink bag as she tucked her hair back. "What's in there?"

"Oh!" I snatched up the bag. "Something I had ordered."

Daemon shrugged when Archer glanced at him. "I don't know what it is. She hasn't told me."

Excited about my find, I reached inside the bag and held up the one-piece sleeper for their inspection. "What do you think?"

Daemon's brows rose as he read the words in black block lettering. "Boyfriends Are Better in Books?"

Giggling, I placed it on the arm of the chair. "I think Dawson and Beth will appreciate it."

Archer looked confused. "I don't get it."

"I'm not surprised," Dee responded drily. "I think it's adorable."

"Me, too." I folded it up and tucked it back into the bag. "I'm going to get her addicted to book boyfriends at a young age."

"*Her.*" Archer shook his head as he blew out a breath. "I don't know how long it's going to take for me to get used to hearing that."

"You need to, because I doubt that's going to change any time soon," Daemon responded.

"How do you know?" Archer shrugged. "She's one of the first female Origins ever. Who knows what that kid will be capable of."

"Well, I seriously doubt changing genders is one of them." Dee wrinkled her nose. "At least I hope not, because that would be weird."

Dawson and Beth had brought the surprise to end all surprises into the world when Beth gave birth to a baby girl, so much so that the first thing I thought of was *Nessie*, and then I couldn't stop cackling for like fifteen minutes.

"You guys ready?" Archer asked. He was already at the door, holding it open. "Guess who I heard from this morning?" He paused as Daemon strutted past him. "No, jackass, it wasn't Justin Bieber and I'm not in love with him. What the hell?"

Daemon chuckled.

"Who?" I asked before the whole conversation derailed.

He smiled at me as the door shut, locking behind me. Dee was already calling shotgun on the Jeep Archer was driving. "Hunter checked in. He was wondering how everyone was doing."

I exchanged a look with Daemon as he took my hand. We'd heard from him and Serena a few months ago. They'd been planning on moving out of his brother's house, heading west. "Did he move?"

"Yeah, he's actually not that far from here. I think he settled in Boulder or somewhere close, since Serena's from around here." Archer fished out his car keys and we picked up the conversation once Daemon and I had piled into the back. "I imagine you might be getting a visit from them, sooner or later."

"Great," Daemon muttered.

Every Saturday we made the drive to their house. Even though the baby was old enough to go out and about, it wouldn't be . . . um, the brightest idea. The baby had an odd habit of moving things without touching them, doing the eye-glowy thing, and last week, she'd levitated.

Right off the floor.

The house was on an acre of land, and thick trees gave the front of the house much-needed privacy. Dawson answered the door, smiling as he let us in. I frowned, because he looked different.

Dee stretched up, rubbing his head. "Is this a dad haircut?"

Ah. That. His hair was shorter now, cut close along the sides and a little longer on the top. It looked good on him. Then again, the brothers could go bald and they'd still look great.

"I like it," Archer said, grinning because it was nearly identical to his haircut.

Beth appeared in the doorway leading to the living room.

Propped against her hip was a smiling baby with a head full of dark curls. "I ordered Chinese," she said, wincing. "I was going to make lasagna, but . . ."

"Oh! Chinese is fine with us." Dee sent me a look as she hurried down the hall, immediately going for the baby's cheeks.

We all had learned quickly that Beth couldn't boil water. Ordering out was the much better option.

We were herded into the living room, and I couldn't help but be amazed by how different Beth looked. Her hair was pulled up in a high ponytail, her face fresh and glowing. She still had moments of . . . darkness and when she didn't seem to have a tight grasp on reality, but she was much, much better.

Daemon placed the gift bag on the end table where toys covered one corner of the living room. In the center of the stuffed animals and dolls were baby blocks spelling out a name.

Ashley.

It was beyond kind and perfect that Dawson and Beth had decided to name her after Ash. If it hadn't been for her sacrifice, the three of them wouldn't be here today.

"You see that?" Dawson's gaze followed mine, and his prideful grin was hard to miss. "She did that this morning."

My mouth dropped open. "She spelled her own name?"

"Yep." Beth glanced at Dawson. "Ash was on her mat, playing with her toys, and the next thing we know, she's spelled her name."

Dee sat on a love seat beside Archer, pouting. "I couldn't spell my name until I was, like, in the first grade, and that's really sad, because my name is, like, three letters."

I laughed.

"Want to hold her?" Beth asked.

It would be rude to say no, so I nodded and lifted my arms awkwardly. I wasn't good with the whole holding-babies thing, even after they weren't newborns and could easily hold their heads up. I just never knew what to do with them once I had them in my hands. Like, should I rock them? Bounce them up and down? And dear God, what was I supposed to say to them?

A second later, the little bundle of Origin was in my hands, with big, purple-colored eyes fixed right on mine, and I seriously hoped the kid wasn't reading my thoughts and understanding any of what I was thinking.

Because I was a little concerned about accidentally dropping her.

As I lifted little Ashley closer to my chest, she was quick to grab hold of two of my fingers and squeeze. Hard. I laughed. "Wow. She's got a grip on her."

"She's pretty strong." Dawson smiled as Beth sat beside him on the couch. "Just the other day, she threw her teddy from the living room clear into the kitchen."

"Damn," Archer murmured.

"Maybe she can be a softball player," Dee suggested.

Beth's laugh was light and surprisingly carefree. "If she gets any stronger, I'm afraid she's going to throw something through a wall."

"Well, that would be awkward," I said to Ashley, who just giggled in response. Her gaze flickered over my shoulder, and I could feel Daemon drawing closer. Her stare was serious, curious as she studied him. "I'm not sure she likes you."

He laughed. "Everyone likes me."

Archer snorted.

Daemon brushed his lips over my cheek as he circled his arms around my waist, holding me as I held Dawson and Beth's child. Ashley reached out with one short arm, splaying her chubby fingers alongside his jaw.

Like always, she was absolutely fascinated with touching his face.

Maybe one day, I'd be holding our child. Who knew? But it would be a long, long time from now, like *decades* from now, and I wasn't sure that day might ever come. The idea of raising a child was still something foreign to the both of us, and we preferred it that way. As Daemon's arms tightened around my waist, I knew we'd be happy if it was just the two of us, or three of us. But I was really hoping that the third member of our family would turn out to be a puppy or a kitten. Babies seemed like a lot of work.

Ashley's gaze trailed back to mine, and as I cooed and smiled at her, her little bow-shaped lips parted in a big grin and the dark pupils in the center of her eyes suddenly lightened, turning a brilliant shade of white.

"She's special," Daemon murmured.

That she was.

"You're still more special," he whispered into my ear, and I laughed as I leaned back into his embrace.

I looked up, my gaze traveling over the faces of those sitting in the room. Dee. Archer. Dawson. Beth. And then I found myself staring into Ashley's glowing eyes. She'd finally stopped feeling up Daemon's face and rested her head under my chin, making little murmuring noises as she appeared to soak everything in like a sponge.

Dee and Beth started talking about the wedding—my wedding—and what colors they hoped I decided on. I think Dee was praying for pink. Archer and Dawson sat between them, looking thoroughly confused by the whole conversation. My smile felt permanently plastered across my face.

No matter how rough the future got, this was my family,

and I would do anything to keep them safe, even if one of them was currently drooling all over my shirt.

A knock on the door pulled me out of my thoughts, and when my gaze swept across the room, it landed on Archer. He was grinning like a fool.

"Who could that be?" Daemon asked. "We're all here."

Dawson stood. "I have no idea. Let me check."

I kept staring at Archer and my stomach tumbled. *Is it?*

Archer's grin spread.

Turning toward the entryway, my breath held in my throat, and then Dawson was strolling back into the room. Behind him was someone we hadn't seen since we'd left Montana.

Luc strolled into the room, his long-legged pace easy and fluid, and holy crap, he'd grown even taller since the last time I'd seen him. "How dare you guys have a get-together and not invite me."

My lips broke into a wide grin, and I almost—almost—ran over and hugged him, because of so many reasons. But I didn't, because I knew Luc wasn't the hugging type.

Dee, however, didn't get that.

She jumped up from where she sat like there was a spring beneath her and got to Luc before he could react, enfolding him in one of her epic hugs. His slightly wide eyes met mine over Dee's shoulder.

It was hard calling Luc a friend, but I liked to think he was one, and my heart ached for him. As far as we knew, the serum—the Prometheus serum—hadn't done what he'd hoped for Nadia. That was the sucky thing about Daedalus. In some ways, they'd had good intentions, and maybe if they'd had more time, they'd have been able to craft a medicine that would eradicate most human diseases.

But not everyone got their happy ending.

When he finally got free of Dee, he ended up in front of

Daemon and me. He wasn't really looking at us, but studying Ashley like I was holding a new species in my arm.

Which I totally was.

In a low voice, I asked, "How are you doing?"

Luc shrugged. "You know, I'm doing my thing like a chicken wing."

My brow arched.

Daemon sounded like he choked. "Did you seriously just say that?"

"I did and I'm cool like that."

I smiled as I watched him tilt his head to the side. "Are you still with the Origins?"

He nodded as he squinted at Ashley. "For the time being. I think it's good for them, because like I said, I'm pretty damn cool and they're learning from the best."

No one in the room responded to that, because well, Luc was . . . Luc. Yeah, the Origin kids were better off now that Nancy wasn't around and neither was Daedalus, but what in the world could Luc be teaching them?

I was pretty sure I didn't want to know. And I also didn't want to know who was watching over them while he was here.

"Can I?" Luc asked, extending his arms.

My gaze found Beth's and she nodded. "Sure."

Luc took Ashley from my hands like he had a lot of experience holding really small people. He hoisted her up, and Ashley seemed to look back at him like *she* was studying *him*.

"Hey there," Luc said.

Ashley responded by smacking a baby palm against his cheek with one hand and then grasping his hair with the other.

"That means she likes you," Dawson said, hovering between Beth and Luc.

"Interesting," he murmured.

Ashley hooted or did some kind of weird baby laugh, and Luc cracked a grin. "You're something special," he said, echoing what Daemon had said earlier.

Watching Luc turn with Ashley, facing Dawson and Beth, I was only vaguely listening to the conversation they started. Something to do with potato chips, mayo, and awkward locations, and that was all I wanted to hear about that.

"Kitten?" murmured Daemon.

I turned my head slightly and, like always, I was simply struck by him, had been from the first time I'd knocked on his door and wanted to punch him in the face. He was mine, all of him—the prickly side and the warm, playful, and loving side.

"What?"

His lips brushed my ear as he whispered a string of words that widened my eyes and scalded my cheeks. And I recognized the words.

They were what he'd written on the note he'd passed to me in class so long ago.

"You game for that?" he asked, eyes burning a luminous green. "I'm really hoping so. Been thinking about it for, like, two years. Don't let me down, Kitten."

My heart thumped like thunder in my chest as I said the truest words ever. "I'm game for anything with you, Daemon Black."

ACKNOWLEDGMENTS

Closing out a series is never an easy thing to do. It's an awesome moment, but it's also hugely bittersweet. And it also would've never been possible without a whole buttload of people working behind the scenes to bring Katy and Daemon to you.

First and foremost, none of this would've been possible without Liz Pelletier. Like seriously. It was she who asked me on the day I turned in another book if I had ever considered writing about aliens in high school. I had laughed and said no, because for real, aliens in high school? But then I thought about it, came up with Katy and then Daemon, and then the rest was Luxen history. So thank you.

I also wanted to thank the team at Entangled Teen and Macmillan—editors, publicists, assistants, and everyone who had a hand in the series over the years. Thank you to my agent of awesome, Kevan Lyon, and to my foreign rights agents Rebecca Mancini and Taryn Fagerness, to my film agent Brandy Rivers, and to my publicists KP Simmon, Deb Shapiro, and Heather Riccio.

Another huge thank-you to Nancy Holder for providing a wonderful blurb for *Opal* and to Wendy Higgins for doing the same. To Laura Kaye, Molly McAdams, Sophie Jordan, thank you for helping me procrastinate for hours. The same thing goes for Tiffany Snow, Jen Fisher, Damaris Cardinali, Lesa Rodrigues, Dawn Ransom, and Tiffany King for answering the phone when I call, probably even when they don't want to. And I can't forget to thank Vi for allowing me to borrow her kid for events, and Jena Freeth for being willing to run around at events for me and buy books.

Stacey Morgan—you rock. You know this, even if you and technology will never get along.

There are so many more people I would like to thank—the bloggers/reviewers who supported the series from day one. You guys have a piece of my heart always. And every reader who picked up any of my books, thank you.

Thank you for taking this journey with me.

SHADOWS

A Lux Prequel Novella

from #1 *NYT* bestselling author

JENNIFER L. ARMENTROUT

Entangled Publishing, LLC
2614 South Timberline Road
Suite 109
Fort Collins, CO 80525
Visit our website at www.entangledpublishing.com.

Edited by Liz Pelletier
Cover design by Liz Pelletier
Text design by E. J. Strongin, Neuwirth & Associates, Inc.

Ebook ISBN 978-1-62061-008-4
Paperback ISBN 978-1-62061-115-9

Manufactured in the United States of America

First Edition February 2012

For all those who believe

PROLOGUE

A shadow glided over the frozen hills, moving too quickly to likely be cast by something of this Earth. Being that it really wasn't attached to anything was a sure sign of what it was and where it was heading. And that would be straight toward Dawson Black.

Oh, goodie gumdrops.

Arum.

Just thinking the name filled the back of his mouth with a metallic taste. The SOB had come like a druggie after his favorite fix. They always traveled in fours, and one of them had already been killed the night before, which left three more of the greasy bastards out there—and one was heading straight for him.

Dawson stood and stretched out his muscles, then brushed the clumps of snow off his jeans. The Arum had come way too close to their home this time. The rocks were supposed to protect them, to throw off the unique wavelengths that set them apart from the humans, but the Arum had found them. Close as the length of a football field from the one thing he'd give his life in a heartbeat to protect. Yeah, screw that. Something had to be done. And that something was taking two of the three, which meant the remaining one would be a tad peeved. They wanted to play? Whatever. Bring it.

Stalking out to the middle of the clearing, he welcomed the biting wind that brushed the hair off his forehead. It reminded him of being on the top of Seneca Rocks, staring out over the valley. It was always cold as crap up there.

Eyes narrowing, he started to count down from ten. At five, he closed his eyes and let his human skin slip away, replaced by pure power—a light that pulsed with that bright sheen of blue. Shedding his human form was like taking off too-tight clothes and running naked. Freedom—not real freedom, because God knew they weren't really free, but this was the closest thing to it.

By the time he reached one, the Arum had crested the hill, speeding toward him like a bullet heading straight for a brain. Waiting until the last second, he darted to the side and spun, pulling forth the power the enemy coveted. No wonder. The stuff was like a nuclear bomb in a bottle. Toss it and watch it go boom.

He launched a nice bolt of it at the Arum, hitting what appeared to be his shoulder. In his true form, the Arum was nothing more than thick shadows that seeped oily arms and legs, but the rush of power connected with something.

The impact spun the Arum around and as he came back, something pitch-black and slick shot toward Dawson. He dodged the missile. What they had wasn't nearly as powerful. More like napalm. Burned like a bitch, but it would take a lot more jabs to bring down a Luxen. Obviously, that wasn't how an Arum killed.

Give up, young one, the Arum taunted, rising in the dark sky. *You can't defeat me. I promissse to make it painlesss.*

Dawson gave a mental eye roll. Sure the Arum would. As painless as eating the last ice cream in the house and facing down his sister.

Darting across the clearing, he sent bolt after bolt of the good stuff at the Arum. Hitting and missing. The damn thing stayed up in the trees, the perfect camouflage.

Well, he had a plan for that.

Lifting arms encased in light, he smiled as the trees began to shake. A thundering groan echoed throughout the valley, and then the trees broke free from the ground. Shooting straight up into the sky, the trees had large clumps of dirt hanging from their chunky, snakelike roots. Spreading his arms wide, he threw the trees back, revealing the rat bastard.

Gotcha, he shot back.

He let loose another jolt of power and it raced across the space between them, hitting the Arum in the chest.

Falling out of the sky like a torpedo, the Arum spun toward the ground, flashing in and out of his true form. Dawson caught a glimpse of leather pants and laughed. This weak excuse for an enemy was decked out like one of the Village People.

He landed in a bumpy heap a few feet away, twitching for a couple of seconds and then going still. In his true form, the thing was huge. At least nine feet long and shaped like The Blob. And he . . . smelled like *metal*? Cold, sharp metal. Weird.

Dawson drifted over to check the Arum was really dead before he headed back home. It was late. School was early—

The Arum rose up. *Gotcha*.

And man, did he get owned.

A split second later, the Arum was on him like ugly on an ape. Christ. For a moment, Dawson lost his form and was back in his worn jeans and light sweater. Black strands of hair obscured his eyes as the shadow slipped over the ground at an alarming rate. Thick tentacles reached out, arching in the air like cobras, then struck, punching straight into Dawson's stomach.

He screamed for the first time in his life, really let loose like a pansy, but damn, the Arum *got* him.

Like a match thrown on a pool of gasoline, fire swept

through his body as the Arum drained him. His light—his very essence—flickered wildly, casting a whitish-blue halo onto the dark, bare branches overhead. He couldn't hold his form. Human. Luxen. Human. Luxen. The pain . . . it was everything, his whole being. The Arum was taking long drags, sucking Dawson's power right down to his core.

He was dying.

Dying on ground so frozen that life hadn't even begun to seep back through again. Dying before he'd ever really gotten to see this human world and experience it without all the rules handicapping him. Dying before he even knew what love really was. How it felt and tasted.

This was so freaking unfair.

Dammit, if he got out of here alive, he was going to really live. Screw this. He *would* live.

Another long, sucking drag and swallow by the Arum, and Dawson's back bowed off the ground. His wide eyes saw nothing . . . Then a faster, brighter light that burned a whitish-red lit up his entire world, shooting among the still-standing trees, coming at them faster than sound.

Brother.

Pulling back, the Arum tried to take his human form. Vulnerable as he was in his true form, he wouldn't stand a chance with *him*. None of the Arum did.

Dawson was betting that Arum even knew the name to the light, had whispered it in fear. A dry, rasping laugh caught in Dawson's throat. His brother would love that.

White light crashed into the shadowy form, throwing the Arum back several feet. Trees shook and the ground rolled, tossing him to and fro like he was nothing more than a pile of limp socks. And the light took up a fighter stance before him, protective and ready to give his life for his family.

A series of bolts of intense light shot over Dawson, smacking into the Arum. A keening, high-pitched wail pierced the sky. A dying sound. God, did he hate that sound. And probably should've waited to hear it before he'd approached the Arum earlier. Water under the bridge.

Since the draining had been cut off, feeling was returning to his limbs. Pins and needles spread up his legs, over his chest. Sitting up, he still flickered in and out. From the corner of his eye, he saw his brother back the Arum up and then take human form. Bold. Brazen. He'd kill the Arum by hand. Show-off.

And he did. Pulling out a knife made of obsidian, he launched himself at the Arum, said something in a menacing tone before shoving the blade deep into his stomach. A gurgle cut off another wail.

As the Arum splintered into smoky, shadowy pieces, Dawson concentrated on who he was—what he was. Closing lids that weren't really there in his true form, he pictured his human body. The form he came to favor over his Luxen one and connected to in a way that should've brought forth a wealth of shame but never really did.

"Dawson?" his brother called out, then spun around and rushed to his side. "Are you okay, man?"

"Freaking peachy."

"Christ. Don't ever scare me like that again. I thought—" Daemon cut off, dragging his fingers through his hair. "I mean it. Don't ever scare me like that again."

Dawson climbed to his feet without help, standing on shaky legs and swaying a little to the left. He looked into eyes that were identical to his own. No more words needed to be spoken. No thanks necessary.

Not when there were still more out there.

1

Students filed into class, yawning and still trying to rub the sleep out of their eyes. Melted snow dripped off their parkas and pooled on the scuffed floor. Dawson stretched out his long legs, propping them on the empty seat in front of him. Idly scratching his jaw, he watched the front of the room as Lesa strolled in, making a face at Kimmy, who looked horrified by what the snow had done to her hair.

"It's just snow," Lesa said, rolling her eyes. "It's not going to hurt you."

Kimmy smoothed her hands over her blond hair. "Sugar melts."

"Yeah, and shit floats." Lesa took her seat, yanking out last night's English homework.

A deep, low chuckle came from behind, and Dawson grinned. The girl cracked him up.

Kimmy flipped her off as she flounced to her seat, her eyes trained on him like she was planning her next meal. Dawson gave her a tight smile back, though he knew he should've just ignored her. To Kimmy, any attention appeared to be good attention, especially since she had broken up with Simon.

Or had Simon broken up with her?

Hell if he knew or really cared, but he didn't have it in him to completely ignore her. Placing a zebra-print bag on her desk, Kimmy continued to smile at him for another good ten seconds before looking away.

He shook out his shoulders, positive he'd just been visually molested—and so not in a good way.

The laugh came again, and then in a voice low enough only for him to hear, "Playa. Playa . . ."

Stretching his arms back, he smacked at his brother's face as he grinned. "Shut up, Daemon."

His brother knocked his hands out of his face. "Don't hate the game . . ."

Dawson shook his head, still half smiling. A lot of people, mostly humans, didn't get Daemon like he and his sister did. Very few made him laugh like Daemon did. And even fewer pissed him off as much. But if Dawson ever needed anything or if there was an Arum nearby, Daemon was the man.

Or Luxen. Whatever.

A portly older man strolled into class, clutching a stack of papers that signaled their quizzes had been graded. A chorus of groans traveled through the room, with the exception of Daemon and him. They knew they totally aced it without even trying.

Dawson picked up his pen, rolling it between long fingers and sighing. Tuesday was already shaping up to be another long day of boring classes. He'd rather be outside, hiking in the woods despite the snow and brutal cold. His aversion to school wasn't as bad as Daemon's, though. Some days were worse than others, but Dawson found his classmates made the experience more tolerable. He was like his sister in that way, a people person hidden in an alien body.

He smirked.

Seconds before the bell rang, a girl hurried into class, clutching a yellow slip of paper in her hand. Immediately, he knew the chick wasn't from around here. The fact she was in a sweater and not a heavy jacket when it was below thirty outside sort of gave it away. His gaze roamed down her legs—really nice, long, and curvy—to her thin flats.

Yep, she wasn't from around here.

Handing over the paper to the teacher, she lifted her slightly sharp chin and gazed across the room.

Dawson's feet hit the floor with an audible *thump.*

Holy crap, she was . . . she was beautiful.

And he *knew* beautiful. Their race had won the genetic roulette when they adopted human forms, but the way this girl's elfin features were pieced together was absolute perfection. Chocolate-colored hair slid over her shoulders as she kept scanning the room. Her skin held a healthy glow from being out in the sun a lot—recently, too, from the vibrancy of it. Finely groomed eyebrows set off tilted eyes framed with heavy lashes. Warm brown eyes connected with his, then his shoulder, and then she blinked several times as if trying to clear her vision.

That kind of look happened a lot when people saw Daemon and him together for the first time. They were identical, after all. Black wavy hair, same swimmer's build, both of them well over six feet. They shared the same features: broad cheekbones, full mouths, and extraordinarily bright green eyes. Other than their own kind, no one could tell them apart. Something both boys loved using to their advantage.

Dawson grinded his molars until his jaw ached.

For the first time, he wished there wasn't a carbon-copy image of him. That someone would look at him—really see *him* and not the mirror image right beside him. And that was a completely unexpected reaction.

But then her gaze found his again and she smiled.

The pen slipped from his suddenly limp fingers, rolled across the desk, and clattered onto the floor. Heat swept across his cheeks, but his own lips responded, and there was nothing fake or forced about his reaction.

Daemon snickered as he leaned over, smacking down on the pen with his sneaker. Embarrassed to the *n*th degree, Dawson swiped his pen from under his brother's shoe.

Mr. Patterson said something to her, drawing her attention, and she laughed. Feeling that husky sound all the way to his toes, he sat straighter in his seat. A prickly feeling spread over his skin.

As the tardy bell rang, she headed straight for the seat in front of him. Screw hiking in the snow. This was so not going to be another boring Tuesday.

She started digging around in her bag, searching for a pen, he guessed. Part of him knew it was a perfect excuse to break the ice. He could just offer her a pen, say hello, and go from there. But he was frozen in his seat, torn between wanting to lean forward to see what kind of perfume she was wearing and not wanting to look like a total creep.

He kept his ass planted firmly in the chair.

And . . . stared at the chocolate strands of her hair where they curled over the back of her seat.

Dawson scratched his neck, shoulders twitching. What was her name? And why in the hell did he care so much? This wasn't the first time he was attracted to a human girl. Hell, many of their kind hooked up with them, since males outnumbered their females two to one. He had. Even his usually superior-complex-ridden brother had when he wasn't with his on-and-off-again girlfriend, but still . . .

Glancing over her shoulder, the girl swept up her lashes, and she locked eyes with him.

Strangest thing happened then. Dawson felt the years peel away. Years of moving, of making and losing friends. Of seeing those of his kind he had grown to care for die at the hands of the Arum or the DOD. Years of trying to fit in with humans but never really becoming one of them. All of it just . . . slipped away.

Dazed by the sudden lifting of weight, all he could do was stare. Stare like a freaking idiot. But she stared right back.

The new girl shifted her gaze, but those warm, whiskey-colored eyes came right back to his. Her lips tipped up at the corners in a small smile, and then she faced the front of the class again.

Daemon cleared his throat and shifted his desk. His brother demanded in a low voice, "What are you thinking?"

Most of the time, Daemon knew what he was thinking. Same with Dee. They were triplets, closer than most of the Luxen. But right now, Dawson knew without a doubt that Daemon had no clue what he was thinking. 'Cuz if he did, he would've fallen out of his chair.

Dawson let out a breath. "Nothing—I'm not thinking anything."

"Yeah," his brother said, sitting back. "That's what I thought."

After the bell rang, Bethany Williams gathered up her bag and headed into the hallway without hanging around. Being the new kid sucked. There were no friends to chat with or walk to the next class with. Strangers surrounded her, which was just perfect considering she was living in a strange house and she was seeing a lot of her uncle, who was *also* a complete stranger to her.

And she needed to find her next class. Glancing down at her schedule, her eyes narrowed at the faded printout. Room 20 . . . 3? Or was it room 208? Great. West Virginia was where printers went to die.

Shouldering her bag, she dodged around a group of girls huddled across from her English class. No stretch of the imagination to think they were waiting on the incredibly hot duo in her class to come out. Good God, she'd lived in Nevada her whole life and never once saw anyone who looked like that, let alone *two* of them.

Who knew West Virginia was hiding such hotness?

And those eyes, they were . . . wow. A vibrant, untarnished green that reminded her of fresh spring grass. Those peepers were something else.

If she'd known this before, she would've begged her parents to move here a hell of a lot sooner just for the eye candy. Shame snapped on the heels of that thought. Her family was here because her uncle was sick, because it was the right thing to do, and not—

"Hey, hold up."

The unfamiliar, deep timbre of a boy's voice rolled down her spine, and she slowed, glancing over her shoulder. She came to an abrupt stop.

It was half of the incredibly hot duo. Calling to her, right? Because he was looking straight at her with those eyes, grinning with lips that were full on the bottom, almost too perfect.

She suddenly had a mad desire to start painting his face with the new oil colors her mom had bought her. Snapping out of it, she forced her mouth to work.

"Hi," she squeaked. *Hot, really hot . . .*

The boy grinned, and her chest did a little flutter. "I wanted to introduce myself," he said, catching up to her. "My name is Dawson Black. I'm the—"

"You were the twin sitting behind me in English."

Surprise flooded his face. "How'd you know? Most can't tell us apart."

"Your smile." Flushing, she wanted to hit herself. *Your smile?* Wow. She glanced down at her schedule quickly, realizing she had to go to the second floor. "I mean, the other one didn't smile at all, like, the entire class."

He chuckled at that. "Yeah, he's worried that smiling will give him premature wrinkles."

Bethany laughed. Funny and cute? *Me likey*. "And you're not worried?"

"Oh, no, I plan on aging gracefully. Looking forward to it." His grin was easy, lighting up eyes that couldn't be real. They had to be contacts. He continued. "*Cocoon* is my favorite movie, actually."

"*Cocoon?*" She busted out laughing, and his grin tipped higher. "I think that's my great-great-great grandmother's favorite movie."

"I think I might like your great-great-great grandmother. She's got good taste." Leaning around her, he opened one side of the heavy double doors. Students veered out of his way as if he were a self-contained wrecking ball. "You can't go wrong with it. Eternal youth. Aliens. Shiny things in the pool."

"Pod people?" she added, dipping under his outstretched arm—a nice, well-defined arm that stretched the material of his sweater. Cheeks flushing, she quickly averted her eyes and headed up the stairs. "So, you're big on the golden oldies?"

She felt him shrug beside her. In the wide stairwell that smelled faintly of mold and gym socks, he remained right by her side, leaving a small space for people to get around them.

Dawson looked over her shoulder as they rounded the landing. "What class do you have next?"

Holding up the schedule, she wrinkled her nose. "Uh . . . history in room . . ."

He grabbed the paper from her hand, quickly scanning it. "Room 208. And it's your lucky day."

Since a guy like him was chatting with her, she was going to have to agree. "Why is that?"

"Two things," he said, handing the schedule back to her. "We have art and then last period—gym—together. Or it could just be my lucky day."

Unbelievably hot. Funny. And knew all the right things to say? Score. He held the second door open for her, and she added "gentleman" to the list. Biting her lip, she searched for something to say.

Finally, she asked, "What class do you have next?"

"Science on the first floor."

Her brows shot up as she glanced around. As expected, people were definitely staring. Mostly girls. "Then why are you on the second floor?"

"Because I wanted to be." He said it so matter-of-factly that she had the impression he made a habit of doing whatever he wanted on a regular basis.

His eyes met hers and held them. Something in his stare made her feel hyperaware of herself—of everything around her. In a sudden moment of clarity, she knew her mom would take one look at a guy like Dawson and send her off to an all-girls' school. Boys like him usually left a trail of broken hearts as long as the Mississippi behind them. And she should be running into her class—which couldn't be too far away now—as fast as she could, because the last thing Bethany wanted was another broken heart.

But she was just standing there, not moving. Neither of them was. This . . . this was intense. More so than the first time she kissed a boy. The kicker was they weren't even touching. She didn't even *know* him.

Needing space, she stepped to the side and swallowed. Yep, space was a good idea. But his concentrated stare still reached her from behind thick lashes.

Without breaking eye contact, he motioned toward a door over his shoulder. "That's room 208."

Okay. Say something or nod, you idiot. Definitely not making a good impression here. What eventually came out of her mouth was sort of horrifying. "Are your eyes real?"

Aw, hell, awkward much?

Dawson blinked, as if the question surprised him. How could it? People had to ask him that all the time. She'd never seen eyes like the twins'. "Yeah," he drawled. "They're real."

"Oh . . . well, they're really pretty." Heat swept across her cheeks. "I mean, they're beautiful." *Beautiful?* She needed to stop talking now.

His grin went right back to full wattage. She liked it. "Thank you." He cocked his head to the side. "So . . . you're going to leave me hanging?"

Out of the corner of her eye, she noticed a tall blond boy who looked as if he'd stepped off the pages of a teen magazine. He caught sight of Dawson and stopped abruptly, causing another guy to barrel into his back. With a half grin, the tall boy apologized but never took his eyes off Dawson. And they were blue, like cornflower blue. None of her paints could even hope to capture the intensity of the color. Just like she was equally sure they would never be able to do justice to Dawson's eyes, either.

"Huh?" she said, focusing on Dawson.

"Your name? You never told me what your name is."

"Elizabeth, but everyone calls me Bethany."

"Elizabeth." He repeated her name as if he were tasting the sound. "Does Bethany come with a last name?"

Heat crept up her neck as she gripped the strap on her bag. "Williams—my last name is Williams."

"Well, Bethany *Williams*, this is where I have to leave you." Goodness, he sounded genuinely dismayed. "For now."

"Thank—"

"No need." As he backed away from her, his eyes glimmered under the light. Dazzling. "We'll see each other soon. I'm sure of it."

2

All the roads just outside of Petersburg looked the same to Bethany. Three times she missed the turnoff for her new home—an old farmhouse that had been converted into a livable space. The road was narrow, marked only by a minuscule white post, and surrounded by trees. Being used to suburban America, she was way out of her element. Even the GPS in her car had run screaming several miles back.

Ugh.

And thank God for snow chains. Her sedan would never make the trek up or down the gravel road to the old farmhouse otherwise. But the place was beautiful—the snow-capped mountains, thick elm trees, and rolling white hills. Her fingers itched to put it on canvas.

Just like her fingers were itching to do something else. Something she really shouldn't do. Painting a boy's face was obsessive on a stalkerish level, and good God, if her mom snuck through her paintings again? She'd have a stroke.

Freezing drizzle smacked Bethany's face when she hopped out of the car and nearly busted her ass on the slick driveway as she skirted around her uncle's Porsche. Doctors made good money. Childish giggles and the aroma of sugar cookies greeted Bethany as she dropped her messenger bag inside the door. She shook off the frozen rain and took one step forward.

"Bethany?" Her mom's voice rang out like an alarm—a damn carpet alarm. "Take off those shoes!"

Rolling her eyes, Bethany kicked off the shoes and placed the tips of her soaked flats on the edge of the carpet. *Ha. Take that, Mom.* Happy with her lame attempt at rebellion, she followed the sweet smell to a kitchen worthy of the Food Network.

Mom liked to cook. Clean. Cook some more, and keep a near-fanatical eye on Bethany. One look and everyone knew why her mom was determined to keep a hawkish eye on her daughter's virtue.

Jane Williams was *young*. As in, partied a little too hard one night and at age sixteen, got knocked up *young*. Bethany never met her biological dad and really didn't have the desire to search him out. Her real dad was the one who'd raised her—the only one who mattered.

Her mom was bound and determined to prevent Bethany from making the same mistake. In other words: she went private-eye on Beth's social life like nothing else. But since Bethany turned sixteen last month, she figured she'd loosen up eventually.

Hopefully.

Mom was at the kitchen table, mixing a bowl of dough while Beth's two-year-old half brother watched. There was more sugary dough on Phillip's face than in the bowl, but he seemed to be having a good time. He looked over at her, and the shock of his red hair and the splatter of freckles on his cheeks made him look so different from her. Brown eyes were the only thing they shared.

That and a love for raw cookie dough.

Darting around the table, Bethany scooped up a handful of dough. "Yum," she said, widening her eyes comically at him.

Phillip giggled, clasping a mound of the dough. Chunks fell to the floor. Oh, no. Code Red in the kitchen.

Strands of dark hair fell out of her mom's French twist as she sighed. "Look at what you've done, Elizabeth."

Popping the sugary goodness in her mouth, Bethany grabbed paper towels off the stainless steel countertop. "It's not going to rot the floor, Mom."

As Bethany cleaned up the mess, Phillip reached for her with chubby arms. She tossed the trash, then pulled him out of the high chair. Cradling the little guy against her hip, she glided around the kitchen like she was dancing.

Pressing her forehead against his flushed one, she grinned. "What's going on, little butt?"

He roared with laughter at that, but her mom sighed as she smacked a ball of dough on the cookie sheet. "I wish you wouldn't call him that."

"Why?" Bethany made faces as she twirled around the island. "Little butt likes being called little butt, because he has such a little butt."

A smile cracked her mom's face. "How was your first day?"

Bethany leaned back, avoiding a face full of dough that had probably been in Phillip's mouth. Yuck. "It was okay. A much smaller school, but it has a kick-butt art class."

"Language," her mom admonished. "Were the kids nice?"

Kick butt, she mouthed at Phillip.

"Butt," he repeated.

Bethany nodded as she dipped him over her arm. "Yeah, they seemed pretty cool." One in particular seemed really cool, but she wasn't going down that road. "Do you know what cool is, little butt?"

"Uh huh!" He nodded for extra effort.

Grinning, she stopped beside her mom and bumped her with her hip. A piece of dough hit the table. "Have you talked to Dad? Does he like the job in Fairfax?"

Her mom scooped at the piece of dough and placed it on the napkin. A clean house was a happy house—her mom's official motto. Bethany loved to turn on the TV show *Hoarders* whenever her mom was in the room. She went apoplectic.

"Your father would be happy anywhere, as long as there were ledgers and counting involved." Love filled her smile. "But he hates the drive. Nearly three hours. He might get an apartment halfway, just to cut back on the time."

Bethany frowned. "That blows."

Her mom nodded and finished off the last row. She stood, making her way to the double ovens. "It is what it is." Sliding the tray in, she closed the door and straightened. "Anyway, I'm glad your first day was good and you made friends."

Made friends? Ah, not really. Bethany placed Phillip back in the high chair and grimaced at the feeling of sugar coating her hands. Slobber-covered sugar . . . gross. She went to the sink and scrubbed her hands like a surgeon preparing for an operation.

The only person she'd really talked to was Dawson. Her cheeks flushed. He'd made the empty seat beside her in art his home and proceeded to drill her with questions about Nevada and her old school. Gym was boys vs. girls ping-pong, so no talking there. But there was a lot of smiling and that—

The slow, uneven footsteps cut off her internal swoon-fest. Looking over her shoulder, she turned off the water. Her slim, frail uncle appeared in the doorway of the kitchen. Skin grayish and pasty, he was bald, and the flannel robe hung off his shoulders.

He looked like death.

And she felt like a tool for even thinking that. Drying off her hands, she hoped her face didn't convey what she was thinking. But then he looked at her. Dark shadows surrounded bloodshot, pale eyes.

He knew. Sick people always knew.

Diverting her eyes, she went over to Phillip and pretended to be engrossed in whatever he was jabbering about. Honestly, she was still surprised her mom had packed up everything and moved out here. She'd never been close to her brother or her family, given that the whole teenage-pregnancy thing had been frowned upon. But that was her mom. Blood was thicker than water. Her brother—her perfect, MD-carrying brother was sick with some kind of blood disease, and she'd rushed to his side.

Her mother spun around and let out a startled gasp. Rushing over, she wrapped an arm around his shoulders and led him to the table. "Will, what are you doing out of bed? You know you're not supposed to be walking around after one of your treatments."

Uncle Will sat stiffly. "It's chemo, not a bone marrow transplant. Moving around is good. It's what I need to be doing instead of lying in a bed all day."

"I know." Her mom hovered over him. "But you look so . . . tired."

His hairless brows shot down. Wrong words. Bethany shook her head. "You look better," she said, and poked Phillip's belly, loving the sound of his giggle. "The treatment helped?"

A brittle smile appeared. "It's working like it should. I'm not terminal."

Being a doctor and getting sick must suck. You'd know all the statistics, the treatments, the side effects, and prognoses inside and out. No escaping the truth behind the disease or cushioning what was to come.

And Bethany hated being around it. Did that make her a terrible person? Uncle Will was family. But death had never really touched her life. Neither had sickness outside of a cold or flu.

Uncle Will was staying with them while he went through his treatments. Once he was feeling better, he'd move back into his own house, but they'd still stay here. The close call with death had her mom yearning to make what was left of her family close-knit.

Mom buzzed around Uncle Will some more, making him a cup of hot tea while he asked about school. Bethany excused herself as soon as she could. Giving Phillip one last tickle, she bolted from the kitchen and headed upstairs.

The top floor had once been nothing but a loft. Now it had three bedrooms and two baths. She went down the narrow hall and nudged open her bedroom door.

It was a sad bedroom.

No posters. No real personal effects except the canvas and a small table full of paints by the large picture window in the corner. A desk was beside it, holding a laptop she rarely used. Internet was spotty at best here, and she'd rather be spending her time painting than lurking on the net. A TV sat on the dresser. Another thing she rarely messed with.

The fact that she wasn't big on TV shows or movies usually made it hard for her to connect with other people her age. She couldn't tell anyone who the hottest new singer was or the name of the teen heartthrob sweating up the silver screen.

Bethany didn't really care.

Head in the clouds was what her mom always said.

Rolling her stool toward the easel, she tugged her hair up into a messy bun and sat down. An empty mind was always best to start with when she wanted to paint. Let whatever came to her flow to the paper. Except it wasn't happening today. When she closed her eyes, she kept seeing one thing. Well, one *person*.

Dawson.

Bethany wasn't boy crazy. Sure, she had her moments of wanting to skip around like a demented puppet when a cute guy showed interest, but guys didn't really affect her. Not to the point that a *name* brought a flush to her cheeks. Even Daniel—ex-boyfriend extraordinaire—hadn't made her feel this way, and they'd almost gone all the way.

Sorry, Mom.

But there was something about Dawson. More than just how good he looked. When he'd talked to her in art class, he seemed . . . in awe of her. Had to be her imagination, just like her reaction to him, because she didn't know him and an attraction of that magnitude just didn't happen. Not at first sight, and not in real life. Stress—it had to be stress.

Picking up a sharpened pencil, she shook out her shoulders. She wasn't going to let herself get obsessed with a boy.

Without giving much thought to what she was doing, she stared at a blank piece of canvas, and then started to sketch the outline of a face. A face she would eventually fill in later. Glancing at the table of paints, she frowned, knowing there was no way she'd get that hue of green right.

Yep, not obsessed at all.

3

He was obsessed.

Dawson stared up at his bedroom ceiling, flipping in and out of his true form like someone was throwing a switch. The room was dark . . . and then whitish-blue light bounced off the walls. On. Off. On. Off. Unable to keep form was a sure sign of agitation or a severe distraction.

And his distraction had a name.

Bethany Williams.

In his human form, he rubbed the heels of his palms down his face and groaned. There was no reason why he'd spent the last three hours thinking about her. Ha. Three hours? Try the last ten hours.

A blur shot through the room, and before Dawson could lower his hands, Dee flopped down on the bed beside him, her eyes wide.

Dee was probably the only real love of his and Daemon's lives. Both of them would rain down hell on anyone who messed with their sister. She was their treasure. At *home*, the females of their race had been cherished. Something the human males didn't seem to do.

Full of energy and a natural love of just being around others, Dee was like a cyclone that blew through people's lives. She was also his best friend. They had a bond, one that ran deeper than what they shared with Daemon. Dawson never knew why it was like that. There was this wall around his brother that even they couldn't really break through. Growing up, it had always been Dee and Dawson.

Dee's hand fluttered around her as she spoke. "I was outside, and it looked as if a light show was going on in your bedroom. Daemon said you were probably mas—"

And Dee also knew no boundaries. "Ah, no, please don't finish that sentence." He lowered his hands, eyes narrowing at his sister. "Don't ever finish that sentence."

She rolled her eyes as she tucked her legs under her. "So, what were you doing?"

"I was thinking."

Her delicate brows arched. "Thinking caused the light show? Wow. That's kind of sad, Dawson."

He grinned. "I know, right?"

She nudged his leg. "Yeah, and you're not telling me the truth."

"And yeah, it's late. Shouldn't you be asleep?"

Her evergreen eyes rolled. "When did you become Dad? It's bad enough that Daemon is all parental on us. Not you, too."

Daemon *was* parental. He was only a few minutes older than them, but he made sure those few minutes counted.

And the last thing Dawson wanted to do was talk about Bethany with Dee. Talking about Bethany with any of them would be an unnecessary complication at this point. Luxen weren't forbidden to date humans per se, but the DOD wasn't down for it and what was the point? Hooking up was one thing, but a relationship? It wasn't like Dawson could be upfront about what he was. If he did, the DOD would make sure the human disappeared, and who wanted that on his conscience? Then there was the big question. How could you be in a serious relationship with someone and hide who you were?

Not to mention the fact that no one knew if humans and Luxen could even . . . mate. Offspring were unheard of.

"Why were you outside?" he asked instead.

Her shoulders deflated immediately. "Ash was here."

Oh, no.

"So, she and Daemon aren't seeing each other. Again." Their relationship was like a soap opera for sixteen-year-olds. Granted, the Luxen matured a lot faster than humans, but Dawson couldn't figure the two out. "And she was outside, yelling at him. Can't believe you didn't hear." That's because he was so wrapped up in thinking about Bethany. "Why was she yelling?"

"I don't know. Daemon probably was looking at another girl or something." She sighed. "Or he didn't want to hang out. You never know with her. I sometimes wish they'd break up and stay apart."

"You just don't like Ash."

"It's not that I *dislike* her." Dee pushed off the bed and shot across the room, appearing beside his window. "I just think she's a bitch."

Dawson choked on his laugh. "Yeah, you don't dislike her at all."

She spun around, hands planted on her hips. "She's not right for Daemon. And he's not right for her."

Sitting up, Dawson swung his legs off the bed and stood. Close to midnight and he felt like he could go for a run. It was going to be a long night. "Who is right for Daemon?"

"Someone who's not needy, for starters," she said,

skipping over to the bed. "And someone who really cares about him. You know Ash chases after him because it's expected. Not because she really loves him."

Dawson's eyes narrowed into a shrewd stare. "Does this have more to do with you and Adam than Daemon and Ash?"

Her lips puckered. "Not at all."

"Uh-huh." Sympathy for his sister and brother unfurled, and he started pacing. The Elders didn't control who they were mated with, but they made suggestions, which were more like expectations. Their race was thinning out and needed repopulating. He got that. Didn't mean he had to agree with it.

But for right now, Dawson had lucked out. There weren't any other females in his age group here, but one day he knew another Luxen female would be brought in. Or he would be forced to go to her.

And leave his family behind.

He ran his hands through his hair, already knowing he was probably going to be an outcast one day. He'd deny the Elders' wishes, plain and simple. Just like he knew Daemon would eventually, because he would never end up with a Luxen like Ash.

But Dee? He glanced at her, feeling anger stir. Dee would be with Adam, whether she loved him or not, and that killed him. His sister deserved better.

All of them deserved better.

Dawson had barely slept, but he was up and jonesing to get to school, even though the March sun had broken through the heavy clouds, already melting the remnants of snow. It would be a great morning to cut class and go out on one of the many trails, but not today . . .

On his third bowl of Count Chocula, he leaned against the

counter and dug in. "Good morning, bro," he said, watching Daemon shuffle into the kitchen.

Daemon grumbled something as he ambled toward the pantry. Grabbing a Pop-Tart, he unwrapped and devoured the pastry without toasting it. His gaze flicked up, meeting Dawson's. "What?"

"Nothing," Dawson said, swallowing another mouthful. "Gonna be an awesome day."

Eyes narrowing, his brother asked pointedly, "Why are you so chirpy this morning?"

"I don't think it's possible for anyone to be chirpy."

Dee zipped into the kitchen, her light fading out and revealing a cascade of dark, wavy hair falling over her slender shoulders. She grabbed the jug of milk and went for the Froot Loops. All of them were eating the breakfast of champions.

"Good morning!" She whipped a bowl out of the cupboard.

Daemon arched a brow. "That's chirpy."

"And I sound nothing like that," Dawson replied. "Just saying."

A frown creased Dee's brow. "What am I missing?"

"Your brother is all excitable this morning," Daemon said. "For school. There's something inherently wrong with that."

Dawson smirked. "There's something inherently wrong with the fact that Dee and I have to stand here and talk to you while you're in your boxers."

"True that," Dee murmured, making a gagging motion with her finger.

"Whatever." Daemon stretched, flashing a lazy grin. "Don't be jealous that I'm the better-looking brother."

Rolling his eyes, Dawson didn't even bother pointing out the fact that there wasn't a single thing different about them. Well, other than the fact that Dawson had a way better attitude. Instead of dumping the bowl and spoon like he normally did, he washed and dried them, setting them aside. Pivoting around, he darted his eyes back and forth between his siblings.

They stared openmouthed at him.

"What?" he demanded.

"Did you just . . . clean a dish?" Dee backed away slowly, blinking. She glanced at Daemon. "The world is going to end. And I'm still a vir—"

"No!" both the brothers yelled in unison.

Daemon looked like he was actually going to vomit. "Jesus, don't ever finish that statement. Actually, don't ever change *that*. Thank you."

Her mouth dropped open. "You expect me to never have—"

"This isn't a conversation I want to start my morning with." Dawson grabbed his book bag off the kitchen table. "I'm so leaving for school before this gets more detailed."

"And why aren't you dressed yet?" Dee demanded, her full attention concentrated on Daemon. "You're going to be late."

"I'm always late."

"Punctuality makes perfect."

Daemon's sigh traveled through the whole downstairs. "It's practice makes perfect, sis."

"Same thing."

There was a pause. "You're right. Totally the same thing."

As Dawson reached the front door, he heard Dee say, "You know you're my favorite brother, right?"

Dawson smiled.

A deep chuckle came from the kitchen, and then, "I heard you telling Dawson that two days ago. I guess that means today you want to ride with me."

"Maybe." She drew out the word.

Closing the door behind him, Dawson stepped outside and headed toward his car. It didn't take long for Dawson to get to school. Quicker if he lost his human skin but also hard to explain. Since he was early, he listened to music in his Jetta. Then he filed into school, tapped his foot through homeroom, all but bum-rushed the English room, and took his seat, avoiding Kimmy's all-too-happy smiles.

Twenty seconds in, Dawson realized he wasn't breathing. Like, not breathing at all. Luxen didn't need oxygen, but they went through the mechanics to keep up appearances. Looking around frantically, he was relieved to see that no one seemed to notice.

Jesus. He could see the headlines now. *Aliens Among Us. Run!*

But when Bethany came into class, her dark hair pulled back into a low ponytail, showing off her graceful neck, he may have stopped breathing again. A thousand charming words strung together in his head in a nanosecond, but he averted his eyes to his empty notebook. Notes? Who really took notes in class? Dawson wanted to see if she would talk to him first.

God, he was like a teenage girl. He was so screwed.

Bethany slid around in her chair, pulling one leg up against her chest. She twirled a pen in her right hand. "Hey, Dawson."

She. Spoke. To. Him. First. It was like winning the lottery, getting laid, and climbing the highest cliff all rolled into one. But he needed to play it cool, because he was trending into lame-o land at a quick pace.

Lifting his chin, he smiled. "You decided to come back for day two. Brave girl."

"I'm adventurous. What can I say?"

How adventurous? "After I saw the way you handled the paddle yesterday in gym, I can imagine."

Her cheeks flushed, and it made her all the more

pretty. "I'm like a professional ping-pong player. I got skills."

Without realizing it, he was leaning forward. Only a few inches separated their faces. God, how he loved the fact she didn't pull away or act coy. She stared back, meeting him head-on.

Words came right out of his mouth. "What are you doing this weekend?"

The pen she held in her hand stopped moving. She blinked, as if surprised, and then her lashes swept back up. "Dad's been working all week, so we barely see him, and we have family time on Saturday with Uncle Will—" She cut herself off. "But I'm free on Sunday."

Sunday seemed way too far away, but he'd take it. "Would you like to get lunch?"

Her rosy lips formed an *O* and then slipped into a grin. "Are you asking me out, Dawson?"

Before he could answer, Daemon strolled down the aisle, his acute gaze drifting over Bethany's upturned face. He gave her a slight, tight-lipped smile. The smile he typically gave people before he ate them alive.

Bethany smiled back.

Dawson wanted to pummel his brother into the ground. The territorial reaction caused a gut check with reality that didn't go unnoticed with Daemon. His eyes narrowed. Using the path of communication their kind favored, he sent his brother a little message. *Knock it off, brother.*

There wasn't a flicker of emotion on Daemon's expression. *What am I doing?*

Dawson started to fire back but stopped. What the hell was he warning his brother about? Looking at Bethany wrong? Daemon didn't shy away from human females, but he also didn't make a habit of going after them.

Deciding to ignore him for right now, because he was sure he'd have to explain himself later, he refocused on what was important. Bethany. "Am I asking you out? That's what it sounds like."

Behind him, Daemon sounded like he was choking, and then in Dawson's head, *What the hell, brother?*

Dawson didn't respond, but there was no mistaking the tension rolling off Daemon, nor the conversation Dawson knew was coming, but oddly, he really didn't care.

He smiled at Bethany.

4

Bethany was sort of shocked. Yeah, she expected Dawson to chat with her, maybe even flirt a little, but ask her out? Just like that? Color her surprised . . . and impressed.

"Good." She glanced down at the pen in her fingers, wondering how she'd get out of the house with a boy. "Um, should I meet you somewhere . . . ?"

A flash of satisfaction deepened the hue of his green eyes. "I can pick you up."

Oh, no no no. She could see her mother's shrewd stare now as Bethany prepped for the inevitable interrogation. The embarrassment was already wiggling through her, causing her fingers to tighten around the pen. "Um, I'd rather meet you somewhere. Nothing personal, but my parents—"

"Are strict? Totally cool." He didn't miss a beat, and she appreciated that. "There's a diner in town. Nothing special, but the food is great. The Smoke Hole Diner—have you heard of it?"

She hadn't, and Dawson quickly gave her directions. Nothing was too hard to find in Petersburg, as long as it wasn't around a bunch of back roads that all looked the same to her.

While they talked, Bethany noticed several of the girls, namely a blonde in front of her, blatantly eavesdropping. The blonde had the perfect body and face—tiny, perky-looking. Being close to five eight, Bethany felt like Godzilla just sitting behind her. And then she noticed Dawson's twin.

He was also listening.

Over Dawson's shoulder, he watched them with narrowed eyes. Something in his hard expression said he wasn't too pleased with what he was hearing. The thumping muscle in his jaw kind of gave him away, too.

Whatever his deal was, Bethany didn't know, but she decided it would be best to steer clear of him . . . and of the Barbie.

Class started. *Pride and Prejudice* was on the reading list. Grumbles came from most of the guys in the room as Mr. Patterson handed out the novels. She'd already read the book—three times—so the essay on underlying social issues of the time wouldn't be killer.

Placing the novel on her desk, she willed herself to focus on the lecture, but her mind kept going to the boy behind her. His aftershave—or was it even aftershave?—was a woodsy, outdoorsy scent that reminded her of campfires.

A very nice smell.

Unique and nothing boyish about it. Hell, there wasn't *anything* boyish about Dawson. He was obviously her age, sixteen, but if she'd run into him outside of her school, she would've pegged him for a college guy. He had extraordinary confidence, something that most boys lacked at this age.

Maybe she was out of her league on this one. Guys like him tended to have a whole harem of girlfriends. Girlfriends like Barbie. Not girls who usually had paint under their fingernails.

Looking down at her hand, she cringed. Green paint was

under her pinkie from last night. Crimson stained her cheeks. Last night she'd painted Dawson's face, even though she'd told herself not to go there.

But she went there and then some.

Dammit. Obsessions always started with painting someone's face, didn't they?

Biting on the cap of her pen, she pretended to stretch her neck left, then right. Glancing over her shoulder, she saw Dawson watching her with those intense eyes.

Their gazes locked.

And the air went right out of her lungs. Again, the concentrated power in his stare sent a shiver dancing over her skin. Like in the hallway yesterday, she felt the urge to move back. Because whatever was in his eyes . . . wasn't normal; it was a real power that she couldn't capture in the painting. An almost luminous quality she couldn't get quite right.

He winked, and damn if it wasn't sexy. Not skeevy at all or stupid-looking. It was the kind of wink that movie stars did on the screen. Something no one in real life could pull off.

Yep, out of her league. Excitement hummed through her.

Grinning around her pen, she faced the front of the class before the teacher noticed her.

Dear God, she was seconds from melting into a useless pool of girlie girl.

When the bell rang, Dawson was already on his feet, standing beside her desk. His brother stopped behind him and remained there as Bethany shoved her books into her bag and stood. It seemed like something unspoken passed between the twins, because Dawson smirked at his brother.

The twin finally edged around Dawson, glancing over his shoulder with a lopsided grin. "Behave," was all he said. Out loud, at least.

Bethany's brows rose. "Uh . . ."

"Ignore Daemon. That's what I do most of the time." Dawson extended his arm, and she slid in front of him. "He has poor social skills."

Unsure if he was joking, she decided to skip right over that one. "It must be cool having a twin, though."

"Ah, not sure if *cool* is the right word." He flashed a grin. "But we're not twins."

Out in the crowded hallway, Bethany frowned. "You're not? Could've fooled me and the world."

His laugh was husky, deep, and really nice to hear. "We're triplets."

Her eyes popped wide. "Holy crap, there're three of you?"

"We have a sister." He walked close to her, so their shoulders bumped every few steps. She found that deliciously distracting. "She's fraternal and a lot prettier than us."

There were three of them but one was a girl. Triplets. Craziness. "Are you guys close?"

He nodded, following her up the stairs like yesterday. Apparently being on time to class wasn't a big deal for him. "Yeah, we're pretty close. Especially Dee, my sister, and me. She's a doll." He paused, angling his body around a flock of students. "Daemon isn't too bad, either. The boy would give his left arm for the two of us. Do you have any siblings?"

"A brother—half brother," she said, smiling. When he spoke of his sister and brother, there was real love in his voice. So rare nowadays. Most of her old friends back in Nevada did nothing but bitch about their brothers and sisters. "He's only two."

"Ah, a little butt . . ."

Bethany stopped right in the middle of the hall. "What did you say?"

Dawson's brows lowered. "Uh, I said little butt. I hope that wasn't, uh, offensive?"

"No." She stared up at him, which alone was a feat. "It's just what I call Phillip—little butt. That's his nickname."

Dawson's expression relaxed into a grin. "Really? That's so funny. Daemon and I call Dee that all the time. She hates it."

Folding her arms, she met his stare. "Do you watch a lot of TV?"

"Only when Daemon forces me to."

Holy moley . . . "What about movies?"

The grin reached his eyes. "Not that big of a fan. I'm an outdoors kind of guy. I'd rather be hiking than sitting around."

She thought of painting and how she'd rather be doing that than anything else. There was just one more thing. "Do you love sugar? Like, always have to eat a lot of sugar?"

He laughed. "Yeah, any more questions? The bell's about to ring."

Love of sugar had to mean true love. It just had to. A smile spread across her face, so big that she should've been embarrassed. "No. That's all."

"Good." He reached out, tucking a strand of hair that had escaped her ponytail back behind her ear. The brush of his knuckles across her skin went through her system like a bolt of lightning. "What are you doing after school? Want to grab something to eat?"

"I thought we were doing that on Sunday?"

"Yeah, we are, but I just wanted to make plans for this weekend. That has nothing to do with today."

Her mouth opened and a laugh snuck out. God, he was just . . . there were no words. Mom would be expecting her home right after school, and that's what she should do. Plans had been set for Sunday, but that seemed so far away. Days away . . .

The warning bell shrieked, causing her to jump.

"Bethany Williams." He said her name teasingly.

Her lashes lifted and she started to shake her head no. "Yes."

Bethany should've known that Dawson Black was trouble with a capital *T*, all rounded up in six feet and then some of lean muscle and disarming smile, from the moment she'd spotted him.

Boys were so complicated.

And boys like Dawson? Ah, so much more complicated. Most guys didn't have an ounce of the charisma he exuded. No wonder she liked him and was already planning to tell her mom that she was staying after school to do some art stuff. An easy, believable lie, since she'd done plenty of extracurricular work like that several times a week in Nevada. That she was already so willing to lie about him only further cemented in her mind the fact that she liked him way too much. And they had only spoken a few times. Bethany wasn't sure if that was a good or bad thing yet.

She hadn't expected how quickly he got under her skin. And she really wasn't prepared for the slightly empty feeling in the pit of her stomach as she watched him jog around the corner to his science class. God . . . she actually missed him.

She definitely wasn't looking over her shoulder in the hallway for him when she stopped at her locker before lunch. Nope. Not at all. Her mind wasn't wrapped up in a boy she'd just met. And she definitely didn't keep comparing every color of green to eyes that shone like polished emeralds.

Bethany drifted through the rest of her classes, nervous and excited and wound up like the tight ball of rubber bands that Simon Cutters always held in his hand throughout chemistry. After he'd tossed it in the air for about the fiftieth time, she wanted to grab it and throw it through the fogged-over windows in their classroom.

In gym, she kept staring at Dawson, who was at another ping-pong table playing against Carissa, a quiet girl with the coolest horn-rimmed glasses Bethany had ever seen. Her gaze went right back to him.

Damn, he made plain white T-shirts a thing to worship.

With every sweep of the paddle, the shirt stretched over taut muscles. Did he run? Work out a lot? Teenage boys usually didn't sport that kind of a hard body.

Dawson smacked the ball toward Carissa again. She missed it, and in that tiny space of time while she hunted it down, he glanced over at Bethany and smiled.

Her heart skipped right out of her chest. Bad, oh so bad.

A plastic yellow ball zinged past her face, almost kissing her cheek.

Kimmy, her partner, popped her hands on her hips. "You're not even paying attention."

She winced, because she wasn't paying attention at all. "Sorry," she mumbled, turning around and searching the floor for the damn ball. It was all the way over by the bleachers. "I'll get it."

Kimmy sighed, studying her manicured nails. "Yeah, not like I was planning to in the first place."

Ignoring her, Bethany stalked over to the ball. The whole gawking thing was already getting out of hand, and she had a feeling it was going to get worse. Even now she was fighting the mad urge to look over her shoulder to see if he was watching her. It felt like he was. *Do not do it*. The muscles in her neck cramped. *Absolutely not.* Her fingers twitched around the paddle. She bent and—

A golden hand reached the ball before she could. Startled, she took a step back as her gaze drifted up . . . and up. Where in the hell had *he* come from? It was the blond from the hallway yesterday—the model-perfect boy with wavy hair that kept falling into crystalline blue eyes. If she remembered correctly, he had been at least four tables over, and there was a good five feet in between each one. She hadn't even seen him move, and it wasn't like you could miss something that gorgeous walking around.

Or maybe she just had a bad case of Dawson on the brain.

"Um, thanks for getting . . ." Her words trailed off as her eyes met his. The coldness in his stare chilled her. He did nothing to hide his dislike. It practically rolled off him and crawled over her skin like a dozen spiders.

"What's your name?" he demanded.

Bethany blinked. The sound of his voice matched his eyes. Frigid. Hard. Full of snobbish loathing. Back in her old school, she'd been on the receiving end of that kind of a stare more than a few times, especially after she and Daniel had broken up. He'd been the popular one . . .

The boy smirked. "You have a name, right? Or can you not understand English?"

A hot flush shot over her cheeks, turning them cherry red, she was sure. Her mouth opened but nothing came out. Confrontation wasn't her thing and this was a confrontation. Okay, so she had no problem getting into it with her mom over things, but with other people? Yeah, she stared at him like she was a mute.

He stepped closer to her, and even though it made her feel

crazy for thinking it, she could have sworn that waves of heat blew off of him like he was some kind of electric radiator. Sweat dotted her brow. "I said, what is your name?" the boy asked again.

"Her name isn't any of your business," a smooth, deep voice cut in.

Dawson stood beside her, but he was glowering at the other boy. He cocked his head to the side. "Give her back the ball, Andrew."

The temperature in the gym skyrocketed. Kids were starting to stare.

Andrew's lips curved into a half grin.

"Or do *you* have a problem understanding English?" Dawson asked. There was a smile on his face, but the way his muscles were tensing up, he was a second away from taking the ball from the other kid.

All of this over a ping-pong ball? How completely bizarre. She cleared her throat and extended her hand. "My name is Bethany. Now can I please have my ball back?"

"That wasn't so hard, was it?" Andrew's eyes never left Dawson's. "We're going to have to talk soon."

"Or not," Dawson replied.

Andrew dropped the ball in her outstretched hand with an arched brow. Then he pivoted around, stalking off toward his table.

"Wow," she mumbled, unsure of what to make of all of this.

Dawson cleared his throat. "He's a bit . . . ah, yeah, Andrew's just an ass of the highest order. Don't pay attention to him."

Bethany nodded and glanced down at her palm, sucking in a sharp breath. Holy smokes . . .

The ping-pong ball had been melted into an irregular circle.

5

Weirded out to the max by Andrew's hostility toward her and the microwaved ping-pong ball, Bethany took her time cleaning up and changing after gym. Something was going down between the two guys, like they were communicating through epic death glares. It reminded her of the way Dawson and his twin had acted that morning. Like their epic death stares were something else entirely.

Shaking her head, she pulled the band out of her hair and ran her brush through it, then she tossed the brush in her bag and turned around, letting out a little yelp.

Kimmy stood behind her, slender arms crossed over her chest. Lips so glossed they looked like an oil slick.

"God, you scared me." Bethany picked up her bag, slipping it over her shoulder, and waited for Kimmy to say something. Anything. And she waited some more. Silence. Oookay. "Did you need something? 'Cuz I'm running late."

"Late to what?" she asked.

Bethany glared at her. As if her comings and goings were any of Barbie's business. *Don't think so.* She stepped around her. "See you later."

"Wait." Kimmy darted in front of her, blocking both doors. "Is it true Dawson asked you out?" She didn't wait for an answer. "Because I heard him ask you during class earlier and my friend Kelly said he asked you to do something today, too."

If she'd heard him in class, why was she asking now?

"Look, let me give you a piece of advice." Kimmy smiled, a poor attempt at being gracious, as if she were talking to a dear friend. It was so, so fake. "Dawson is a total player. Been through the entire school and then some. So has his brother, and they like to mess with people. Pretending to be each other, if you get my drift."

Disappointment spiked. Memories of her relationship with Daniel surfaced and flickered through her mind. Old wounds were lanced open, and she blurted out, "Why are you telling me this?"

Kimmy gave her an *are you for real* look. "You're the new girl. Why else do you think he's so interested in you?" Her gaze traveled over Bethany's jeans and sweater like she seriously couldn't figure it out. "I'm just trying to do my good deed of the day and warn you. That boy . . . well, he's been around."

With that, Kimmy turned on her heel and strutted off.

"What the hell?" Bethany said out loud, her voice echoing in the empty room. Was everyone in the school always this friendly? Geez.

Taking a deep breath, she left the locker room, telling herself not to read too much into what Kimmy had said. It could be jealousy. It could be pure girl bitchiness.

Or it could be true, whispered an evil, nasty voice. Why would she be surprised if it was? She wouldn't. Both of the brothers were hotness incarnate. She'd be stupid to believe that Dawson didn't have an acre of ex-girlfriends. Pushing open the door with more of a punch than anything necessary, she wondered if she should cancel on him. The last thing she needed was to be a notch on his belt, no matter how fine that belt was. And the fact that she was already pissy about the idea spoke volumes.

She was way into him.

And he was waiting for her in the hall, leaning against a trophy case, hands shoved into the pockets of his jeans. He must've showered, because locks of dark hair curled over his forehead. The V-neck sweater clung to his shoulders.

Her heart did a pitter-patter in her chest at the sight of him. She stopped short, clutching the strap on her bag. "Hey."

He didn't smile or grin, only watched her with intense eyes. "I wanted to apologize for my friend."

That douche was his friend? "It's not your fault, but maybe—"

"Yeah, it kind of is." Pushing off the locker, he ran his hand through his hair. "I know that doesn't make sense, but I'm just sorry he was such a tool to you. And I hope you didn't change your mind about grabbing something to eat. Not that I'd blame you if you did."

Now she was confused. Yes, she was changing her mind, but not because of Andrew. And she honestly couldn't figure out why his friend's behavior was his problem. But the sincerity in Dawson's voice and eyes got to her. Player or not, he felt bad when he had no reason to.

Dawson nodded slowly, as if her lack of answer had been one. "All right, I guess it is what it is."

Her mouth snapped open but nothing came out. Why did this keep happening around the boys in West Virginia?

Standing there before him, she stared, wanting to tell him that it was okay and that she still, against all common sense, wanted to grab something to eat with him. Wanted to hang out and be friends . . . maybe even more than friends.

But she didn't say anything.

Giving her a faint smile, he stepped forward. "Do you have a piece of paper and a pen?"

"Uh, sure." She dug the items out of her bag and handed them over. He immediately started to scribble something. "Dawson, I really—"

"It's okay. Here," he said, handing her the paper and pen back. "That's my number. Call me anytime, if you want. And again, I'm sorry."

She glanced at the piece of notebook paper, surprised to see that his handwriting was as fluid and graceful as his movements. When she looked up, Dawson was already gone.

Dawson was pissed. He wanted to go over to the asshat's house and drive his car through it. The fact he liked his Jetta was the only thing that stopped him from giving them a new doorway. Well, and Adam, the good twin, as he'd come to refer to him, was a pretty cool guy. So was Ash, when she wasn't with Daemon.

Andrew had a problem with Bethany only because he'd seen Dawson checking her out in gym, and of course, he was one nosy son of a brat. Out of all the Luxen who lived outside of the community, Andrew was the only one who seemed better suited for living among their kind.

Halfway to his house, Dawson's phone beeped. Hoping it was Bethany and feeling like a fool for doing so, he leaned back and pulled out the slim iPhone from his front pocket.

And of course it was from his darling brother. Message was short and to the point.

Come home now.

Part of him wanted to say screw it and go anywhere but home, but he'd have to go there sometime. However, he did slow down to a near crawl, ticking off the row of trucks with bumper stickers like *Real Women Love Ford* and *Trucks Do It Better.*

The road winding up to his house was silent and empty, like every house that shared the same street. But his driveway was packed. Great. Climbing out of the car, he slammed the door shut.

A crew of Luxen was waiting for him inside. His brother and sister, Adam, Andrew, and Ash, and even Matthew, their unofficial guardian, was there.

Dawson leaned against the door, folding his arms. "Is this an intervention? I can't wait to hear your letters."

Daemon's eyes flashed white light. "Tell me it's not true."

"Not sure what 'it' is."

Sprawled on the couch beside Ash, Andrew arched a brow. "You wanted to go all glow bright on me and beat me down in gym class over a girl. A. Human. Girl."

Dawson smirked. "I want to beat you down every day, Andrew. Today was no exception."

Andrew flipped him off. "Hardy har har, shit—"

"Don't," Daemon snapped, turning on Andrew so quickly that the blond had to see his life flash before his eyes. "Don't even think about calling my brother a name."

Holding up his hands, Andrew said, "Whatever, man. All I'm saying is that your bro wanted to go Chuck Norris on my ass over a human girl today."

Dawson sort of wished he had. "Need I remind you that you *melted* a ping-pong ball with your hand?"

Reason stepped forward in the form of Matthew. "Is that true, Andrew?"

Andrew rolled his eyes. "It was just a ping-pong ball."

A frown creased Matthew's face. "Wait. This is all over a *ping-pong ball*?"

"No," Andrew said at the same time Dawson replied with a, "Yes."

"I'm getting a headache." Adam sighed. "Already."

So was Dawson. And it had a name. He glared at Andrew. "This isn't about anything. I don't know why we had to call a Captain Planet meeting for this."

His brother folded his arms, mirroring his stance. "Is this about Bethany?"

"Yes!" exclaimed Andrew.

"Who's Bethany?" Ash asked, sounding bored, but her voice was shrewd. No doubt she was worried about competition for Daemon.

"She's a girl—"

"A girl?" Dee pulled her nose out of a magazine. "What about a girl? Is she nice? Do I know her?"

Oh, for the love of all things holy. Dawson groaned. "Bethany is a girl from school. And I don't see what the big deal is. We've just talked."

Dee looked crestfallen. "So I don't know her?"

"No." His patience was running thin. "I don't think you have any classes with her."

"But she's human?" Dee glanced around the room, brows arching. "So, I'm with Dawson on this one. What's the big deal? It's not like we're not allowed to . . ." Her cheeks suddenly matched the color of a tomato. "I don't get it," she finished.

"It's true there are no rules stopping any of us from having . . . relations, but it is not wise." Matthew looked like he did when he'd tried to explain the mechanics of sex several years ago. It had been horrifying for all of them. "The DOD does frown upon it, and there really isn't much of a point."

"Too dangerous for the humans," Daemon said, unfolding his arms. He sat on the arm of the recliner where Dee was sitting. "If the DOD even suspected that we let the alien out of the bag, the human goes bye-bye. Not to mention the risk of lighting her up."

Dawson rolled his eyes. "Yeah, because I plan on turning every human I meet into a disco ball just for the fun of it."

His brother's brows lowered in a clear warning.

He sighed. "Anyway, it's not a big deal."

"Did you threaten Andrew over her?" Matthew asked, looking like he seriously hoped Dawson didn't. Well, then, he'd keep his mouth shut, because he wasn't going to like the answer. "Dawson?"

"Possibly . . ."

Andrew shot him a bland look. "I would go with yes."

Man, he wanted to beat Andrew down.

"What did you say?" Daemon asked him, and Dee watched on in interest.

"Fine," Dawson grumbled. "I told him that if he talked to Bethany again, I was going to shove a certain body part into his mouth."

Daemon strung together an atrocity of F-bombs. Quite imaginative, too, and even Matthew looked impressed. When he was finished, he said, "You threatened one of your own over a human girl?"

Dawson shrugged.

There went the F-bombs again. "Add that to the way you've been staring at her, and we've got a problem."

"How has he been staring at her?" Dee asked, sounding ridiculously innocent. All the guys groaned. "What?" she demanded.

"He stares at her like she's . . ." There was an odd pause, almost like Daemon really didn't know how to phrase it, as if he'd never stared at a girl that way before—and he hadn't. "Like she's the finest cut of steak and he's starving."

Dawson's brows shot up. Was that how he stared at Beth? Like she was steak?

"You never look at me like that." Ash pouted.

Daemon stared at her. Definitely not like *that*.

"Whatever," Dawson said. "Other than the fact that I will now think of steak every time I see Bethany, there isn't anything going on. I like her. She's cool. So what? You guys have nothing to worry about."

His brother frowned as he glanced at Andrew. "What did you say to the girl?"

Andrew said nothing.

"He kept demanding her name like a freak." Dawson sighed, so over this conversation.

"Well, to me, it sounds like normal human hating." Adam glared at his twin. "You got everyone riled up for no reason . . . as always. It isn't a big deal."

It wasn't a big deal to them, but to him? Dawson wished it wasn't. His shoulders slumped as he started toward the stairs, done with this conversation. Whatever had been between him and Bethany was finished before it even got started. Looking over his shoulder, he tried to ignore the crushing weight settling on his chest. "There's nothing to worry about. Thanks to Andrew, she doesn't want anything to do with me."

Andrew looked proud.

"So, yeah, there's nothing to worry about."

6

Bethany stared at the crumpled piece of paper that held Dawson's number. Past ten, it was late, probably too late to be calling his house if his parents were anything like hers. And she really shouldn't be calling him, especially if what Kimmy said were true.

But when did she start taking the word of a complete stranger?

When she should've listened to the girl who'd told her Daniel was cheating on her, that's when. Bethany hadn't listened and ended up finding him in the library of all places with another girl, his hands where they shouldn't have been, and making like he was tying a cherry stem with his tongue.

On the Friday before Homecoming.

Jerk-face.

She glanced at the piece of paper for the zillionth time and then at her phone. *Should I? Could I? Would I?* Her gaze darted to her easel.

Even in the dark, Dawson stared back at her. The curve of his strong jaw, the broad cheekbones, the nose and lips that were slightly tilted, were all him. But the eyes were all wrong.

No amount of mixing paints had captured the right color of green.

Her gaze swung back to the piece of paper.

She decided she'd just enter the number into her phone and that was all. What her finger did next, by pushing send on her cell, was completely out of her control.

As her heart did jumping jacks in her chest, she listened to the phone ring once . . . then twice.

"Hello?" A deep voice came through the line.

Crap. Bethany hadn't meant to call him. Really, she hadn't. She took no ownership for her finger. And she also found herself mute. Again.

A door shut on the other end of the phone. "Bethany?"

She blinked. "How . . . how did you know it was me? I didn't give you my number."

The relieved-sounding laugh had her smiling. "I don't give my number out a lot. So you're the only unknown number who should have it."

Surprise caused her to jerk straight up in bed, her legs tangling with the comforter. "You don't?"

"I don't what?"

"Give your phone number out a lot?" And boy was that a nice way to start off the conversation. Yeesh.

"Ah, no, I don't." Bedsprings groaned, and her entire body went haywire at the sudden vision of him in bed. She so needed to get off the phone, but he continued. "Actually, I can't remember the last time I gave a girl my digits."

Part of her wanted to believe him, but she wasn't that stupid. "Um, I'm going to be honest here."

"Good. I want you to be honest."

She closed her eyes. "I have a hard time believing you don't give your number to girls."

"I don't." More creaking, like he was settling down. "But that doesn't mean I haven't gotten *their* numbers."

Something like a red-hot poker went through her eyes. It. Could. Not. Be. Jealousy. "Is there a difference?"

"Most def," he said. "Giving someone my number means she can get in touch with me whenever she wants. For the most part, I'm not down with that. Having someone else's number is totally different. Get what I'm saying?"

A second passed. Yep, she did. Meaning he only gave his number to people he really wanted to call him. Not just anyone. And somehow she'd fallen into this privileged group. "Oh, okay. Um, thanks?"

Dawson laughed. "Anyway, I'm really glad you called. I wasn't expecting this."

Neither was she.

"I thought after everything with Andrew . . ."

"Your friend's weirdness has nothing to do with you." Deciding to be honest, she took a deep breath. "Actually, I still wanted to go grab something to eat with you after school today." *Because I'm an idiot.* "And I was sort of disappointed when you walked off." *Because I'm really an idiot.* "So, yep, that's all I have to say."

Silence stretched out between them, and Bethany was immediately regretting opening her big mouth. "Okay. Maybe I misread—"

"No. No!" he said quickly. "I'm just surprised. I thought . . . It doesn't matter. You still want to grab something to eat Sunday?"

"Yes." Her voice came out a breathless whisper, as if she'd just run up a flight of stairs . . . or worked as a sex phone operator. How embarrassing.

"What about tomorrow?"

Bethany laughed. "You . . . you can't wait until Sunday?"

"Hell no. It's hard to get to know you when we only have a few minutes before class to talk." He stopped and man, oh man, his voice dropped low enough to send a shiver through her. "And I really want to get to know you."

The back of her head hit the heavy down pillows at the top of her bed. She had a decision to make. Operate off what Kimmy said and her own old fears, or go with the flow, wherever it may take her.

Eyes on the ceiling, she fought a big, goofy smile. "We can get to know each other now, right?"

Another deep laugh had her feeling fuzzy. "I'm liking where this is heading."

So was she.

Daemon stalked the woods surrounding his family's home. Brutal winds whipped down from the looming mountains and rolled right into him. Dammit, it was cold outside. Cold enough he wished he'd picked up a jacket for once in his life.

Shoving his hands in the pockets of his jeans, he stared over the frozen lake he visited more times than he could count. Moonlight reflected off the ice, casting a silvery light that reminded him of a well-polished blade.

Being that he was out on patrol, the last thing he should be doing was standing here, thinking about his brother's love life like a freaking nosy girl. There was another Arum close by. He hadn't seen one since he yanked the other off his brother and disposed of him, but he knew it in his bones. Well, in his human bones. Whatever.

But instead of focusing on combing the county like he should, he was *worrying* . . . while his brother rested up in his toasty bedroom. Up there having no idea that Daemon knew what he was doing.

Talking on the phone with that human girl Bethany.

It wasn't like chatting it up with a human girl was a code red. But when you combined the way Dawson had been staring at her, how he'd ordered Daemon to back down in class, and then how he'd threatened Andrew? Yeah, there was a problem.

A big problem.

Withdrawing his hand from his pocket, he tugged it through his wind-whipped hair. His brother had always been one to do whatever he wanted. Not because he didn't give a flying monkey about anyone, but because Dawson was just that strong. If any of them was willing to risk being cast out by the Elders and forced to live the rest of his life in exile, it was his brother.

Daemon pivoted around and waited for his head to explode or something. Needing some sort of action, he shook off his human skin before he took a step. In his natural form, he was nothing but light and quicker than air.

Zipping across the lake, he headed for the Rocks. Once he got there, he'd have to tone down the shine. But it was the best place to keep an eye on the shadows and how they moved.

On the way up, he ran through his options.

Lock Dawson in his room and keep him from school, therefore away from the girl.

Scare the crap out of the girl so she stayed away from Dawson.

Throw all the phones away and slash Dawson's tires.

Yeah, his plans weren't so good. First off, he wasn't into imprisonment. Spending those years under the DOD's thumb in New Mexico was enough of that for all of them. Secondly,

he had a mean streak the size of the Grand Canyon, but he wasn't about threatening girls. And finally, Dawson had just gotten that phone after Dee accidentally zapped the other one, and he'd cry if anything happened to his Jetta.

Maybe there was nothing to be done. Maybe they all had overreacted. This wasn't the first time Dawson went out with a human girl. Hell, even Daemon had swung that way a few times. Anything to take a break from Ash sometimes.

It wasn't like Dawson was in love with the girl, thank God.

Feeling better, he shot up the side of the mountain like lightning. It was just infatuation, and it would fade.

Dawson and the girl had only known each other a few days. It wasn't like it was too late or anything.

Was it?

When the phone beeped in her ear, Bethany pulled it back and frowned. "Wait. The battery is dying. Don't go anywhere."

There was a deep chuckle. "Don't plan on it."

Stretching down, she plugged the cord into the wall outlet, and then settled back against the pillows. "Okay. So you've lived in Colorado, New Mexico, and South Dakota?"

"Yep. And New York."

"Wow. Do your parents travel for work or something?"

Silence and then, "Yeah, you could say that."

She frowned as she plucked at the comforter. That wasn't much of an answer. He had a habit of doing that whenever the questions got too personal. "Okay, so where were you born?"

Bedsprings groaned before he answered. "My family was born on a small island off of Greece. Not sure it even has a name."

"Wow." She rolled onto her side, now smiling. "Well, that explains it."

"Explains what?" Curiosity marked his tone.

"You guys don't even look . . . real." At his laugh, she blushed. "I mean, you look foreign. Like you come from some-place else."

Another laugh and he said, "Yeah, we do come from some-place else."

"It must be neat, though. Greece? Always wanted to visit there."

"I don't remember much about it, but I'd love to go back. Enough about me. I saw your drawing in the art room earlier."

She twisted her fingers around the phone cord. "The flow-ers in the vase?"

"Yeah," he said. "Man, you've got amazing skills. It looked just like the example Mrs. Pan had on the board. Mine looked like an elephant trunk eating weeds."

Bethany giggled. "It wasn't that bad."

"That's sweet, but I know you're lying. Do you draw a lot?"

"No." Her gaze went to the painting in the corner. "I paint, actually."

"Now that is cool—a real talent. I would love to see them one day, your paintings."

She'd die a thousand deaths before she let him see the last one she'd done. "Ah, I'm not that good."

"Whatever," he replied.

"How would you know? You can't judge by flowers."

"Ah, I just know. That's my talent, if you're wondering. I just know things."

She rolled her eyes, but she was grinning. "What a unique talent."

"I know. I amaze myself." There was a soft intake of breath.

"I bet you're the type of guy not afraid of anything, huh?"

"Oh, no, there are things that terrify me."

"Like what?"

"Muppets," came his solemn reply.

"What?" She laughed. "Muppets?"

"Yes. Those things are terrifying. And you're laughing at me."

She smiled. "Sorry. You're right. Muppets can be scary." Closing her eyes, she smothered a yawn. "We should get off the phone."

Dawson's sigh was audible. "I know."

"Okay, well, I guess I'll see you . . ." She glanced at the clock and laughed. "In about five hours, then?"

"Yeah, I'll be waiting for you."

God, she liked the sound of that. *Him* waiting for *her*. "Okay. Good—"

"Wait." His voice sounded urgent. "I don't want to hang up."

Her breath caught. "I second that."

His laugh warmed her. "Good. Tell me about some of the favorite things you like to paint."

And she did. They talked until they both fell asleep, their phones cradled between their shoulders and cheeks.

7

Unable to remember the last time he had been this close to hyperventilating, which was amazing, since he didn't really need to breathe, he glanced down at his phone. Again.

The text message from Bethany hadn't changed in the thirty seconds since he'd last looked. According to the words on his phone, Bethany couldn't wait for their late lunch date at two. He knew she wasn't going to bail, especially since they'd talked on the phone every night since Wednesday.

But he was as nervous as a long-tailed cat in a room full of rocking chairs.

His gaze flickered to the dashboard. Thirty minutes early. Should he go ahead and go in? Get one of those booths near the cranking fireplace? Bethany would like that, he thought, and so he did.

As he waited for her to show, he played a round of *FreeCell* on his phone. Lost. Played another, and because he kept glancing up every time the chimes above the door rang, he lost another two rounds.

Good God, it was like he'd never been on a date before. If

he kept this up, he'd start flickering like the Northern lights. Not good.

When the tinkling sound came again and he looked up, every nerve in his body fired at once.

It was Bethany.

Her warm brown eyes scanned the rock formations in the center of the diner, over the tables, and finally to the booth he'd found by the fireplace. When her gaze met his, she smiled and therefore sucked the marrow right out of his bones . . . in a totally good way.

Heading straight for their booth, she only had eyes for him. Meaning she didn't see the college-age guy's stare follow her. Dawson so didn't like how the human was staring at Bethany. Like he'd never seen a female before, and Dawson was more than ready to introduce himself. Every territorial instinct in him went off. It took everything for him not to get up and pummel the dude into the old wooden floors.

"Hey," Bethany said, shrugging off her chunky cardigan. Underneath she wore a black turtleneck that fit her curves. "You haven't been waiting long, have you?"

Forcing his eyes north, he smiled. "No, I just got here."

She slid into the booth, tucking her hair behind her ears. He loved that her hair was down, spilling over her shoulders. Looking around the diner, she bit her lower lip. "It's really cozy in here. I like it. Sort of homey."

"It's really nice. Great food." He cleared his throat, wanting to kick himself. "I'm glad you came."

Her eyes darted back to his. "Me, too."

The waitress appeared, saving them from the awkward silence while they placed their drink orders. "Do you come here often?" she asked once the waitress left.

Dawson nodded. "We come about twice a week."

"Your brother and sister?"

"Yeah, Dee and I come every Thursday, and the three of us come every Wednesday." He laughed. "It's kind of bad how often we eat here, actually."

"Do your parents not cook a lot?"

Ah, a bomb of a question, considering their parents passed away before any of them knew what they looked like. "No, they don't cook."

The waitress was back, sliding their glasses across the table. An oven-baked pizza, extra green peppers, light on sauce, was ordered, along with breadsticks.

Bethany fiddled with the straw, folding it into little squares so that it looked like an accordion when she was done. "I swear, my mom lives to bake. Every day I come home, there're cookies, fresh bread, or some kind of cake."

An unfamiliar, deep sense of yearning built in his chest. What would it be like to have a mom and dad to go home to? All they had was Matthew, not that he was chopped liver or anything, but he didn't even live with them. At least not since they were thirteen and deemed mature enough to get by on their own. Matthew probably would have kept them with him forever, but Daemon had needed space of his own.

"That . . . has to be nice," he said.

"It is." She twirled the straw around, knocking the ice cubes against the glass. "She cooks more now, since Dad is gone most of the week and her brother is staying with us. Food is her coping mechanism."

Remembering what she'd said about the man, he felt for her. Luxen didn't get sick. Like, ever. "How is he doing?"

"Better. He just looks . . . worse than how he feels, I think." A half smile appeared as she watched the ice cubes dance.

"I feel bad, because I don't know what to say to him. Like I barely know him and he's going through this . . . life-altering event, and whatever I say just sounds lame."

"I'm sure he appreciates you just being there."

"You think?" Hope sparkled in her tone.

"Yeah, I do." Wanting to reassure her, he reached across the table and placed his hand over her free one.

A shock passed through their hands, and Bethany let out a startled gasp. Looking up, she jerked her other hand holding the straw as their eyes met. The glass tipped toward her, the contents ready to make a run for it.

Letting go of her hand, he caught the glass just as it started to fall. A bit of liquid sloshed over the rim as he settled the glass. "Careful," he murmured.

Bethany stared at him, mouth open.

"What?"

She blinked. "I . . . I just didn't see your arm move. One second you were holding my hand and the next you caught my glass."

Oh. Shit. Sometimes, Dawson just didn't stop to think. A human probably couldn't have stopped the glass from kamikaze-ing into her lap. Forcing a grin, he played it off. "I have hella quick reflexes."

"I can see that," she murmured, grabbing a napkin and swiping up the mess. "You should play sports . . . or something."

Ha. Yeah, that wouldn't happen. He'd demolish the humans even if he held back. Luckily for him, Bethany seemed to accept his answer and their conversation slipped into the easy chatter that kept them going for hours on the phone. When the pizza arrived, they both dug in. He laughed as she dipped her breadstick in the pizza sauce. It was something both he and Dee did.

And thinking his sister's name must've spooked her up, because the chimes went off and he felt a familiar presence. Eyes glued to the front of the diner, he almost toppled out of the booth when his suspicions were confirmed.

Dee was here. And she wasn't alone. Adam was with her.

Beth's brows puckered as she saw his expression. Glancing over her shoulder, she pursed her lips. "That has to be your sister . . . with your, uh, nice friend."

Please don't come back here. Please don't come back here. "That's Dee, but that's not Andrew. That's his brother, Adam."

Her head whipped back toward him. "Twins?"

"Triplets like us." His gaze bounced back to the front of the diner. Aaaaaand his prayers went unanswered. Dee's gaze locked with his and her eyes went so wide you'd think she was staring at the president of the United States. She made a beeline straight for them, Adam in tow. The string of curses he had going inside his head would've made Daemon proud. "I am so sorry. I swear I didn't invite them."

Beth's head cocked to the side. "It's okay. Don't worry."

He wasn't so much worried about how Dee and Adam would behave. They were totally Team Human, but his sister . . . God love her, but she was a bit much to take in sometimes.

Dee stopped in front of the table, her forest-green eyes bouncing from Dawson to Bethany. "What a complete surprise to find you here. I had no idea you were coming. If you'd said something, you know, like a decent brother would have, Adam and I could've come with. Except now we're like total stalkers, because you were here first."

Dee took a deep breath. "And you have company. So we're

totally busting up in your . . . date? Is it a date or just like two friends hanging out?"

Dawson's mouth worked but nothing came out as he glanced at Bethany, who kept looking between the two of them, her lips twitching as if she were trying not to smile.

"Ah, lack of answer totally means a date." Dee grinned as she tossed her hair over her shoulder. Then she swung on Bethany and did another verbal aerobic feat. "So you're the girl who Dawson stays up talking to half the night? He thinks I don't know, but I do. Anyway, your name must be Bethany Williams? We haven't met yet." She shoved her slender hand out. "I'm Dee."

Bethany shook her hand. "Nice to meet you . . . and yeah, I guess I am that girl."

His sister shook Beth's hand, which actually shook her *entire* body, good God. "You're really pretty. And I can already tell you're nice, which is good, because Dawson is my favorite brother, and if—"

"Whoa there, girl, slow it down." Adam placed his hand on Dee's shoulder. His sympathetic gaze met Dawson's. "We were just picking up some food."

Dawson let out a breath of relief.

"Oh, that's too bad." Bethany actually sounded sincere. Wow. Most people would've collapsed from exhaustion by now. "We could've shared a table."

Dee's smile was the size of a Volkswagen bus. "I was right! You are nice." She turned to her brother, brows arching. "Actually, you're probably too nice for him."

"Dee," Adam muttered.

Dawson grinned. "I thought I was your favorite brother."

"You are. When I want you to be." She twirled back

to Bethany. "Well, we shall leave you guys to your . . . ?"

There was no way out of this one, and Dawson didn't want to hide what he was doing. Saying the word would start a bunch of crap, but considering how everyone already had their suspicions . . . oh, what the hell.

"It's a date," Dawson said. And then he wanted to scream it.

Bethany blushed.

Adam grabbed Dee's hand, pulling her back toward the counter. He glanced over his shoulder, mouthing, *Sorry*.

"Well . . ." Dawson let out a loud sigh, wondering who would stroll through the door next. Daemon? Dear God. "That would be my sister."

Bethany placed her cheek in her palm and grinned. Her eyes danced. "I like her."

"Her mouth . . . is bionic."

She giggled. "She seems really sweet."

"And hyper."

Smacking his arm lightly, she leaned back. "And Adam is way nicer than his brother."

"A rabid hyena is nicer than Andrew," he retorted. "When we were kids, he locked me in an old chest once. Left me there for hours."

"What? Geez, that's terrible." There was a pause. "So, back to the fact that there are two sets of triplets in a town the size of a gnat. Odd, right?"

She had no idea. There was a truckload of triplets around this town, but they stayed in the Luxen community deep inside the forest surrounding Seneca Rocks, rarely seen by the human populace. Only one or two of the siblings worked out in the human world. There was safety in numbers and the Elders liked to keep everyone under their thumbs. At least that's what Daemon believed.

"Our families have been friends for years. When we moved here, so did they." It was the closest thing to the truth.

Genuine interest flickered in her eyes. She asked about Daemon next. Describing his older brother to Bethany was about as easy as trying to avoid stepping on a landmine in the middle of a war. They were there for more than two hours, which gained them a lot of impatient stares from the staff, who probably wanted to free up the table.

When it finally came time to leave, Dawson realized, once again, that he felt reluctant at the thought of their parting. He hung by her car, twirling his keys around a finger. "I had a really good time."

"I did, too." Her cheeks were ruddy in the wind. Pretty. She met his eyes, and then her gaze jumped away. "We should do it again."

"I plan on it." Dawson wanted to kiss her. Right then. Right there. But instead, he held back and gave her a lame-ass hug like a good guy. "See you tomorrow?"

Dumb question, since they had school tomorrow.

Bethany nodded and then stretched up on the tips of her toes, placing her hand on his chest for support. Stepping into his body, she wrapped one arm around the small of his back. He didn't dare move. She pressed her lips against his cheek. "Talk to you tonight?"

He lowered his head, inhaling the clean scent of her hair. Being this close to her, he felt like he was in his true form, and he opened his eyes just to make sure he hadn't flipped his glow switch.

"Of course," he murmured, running his hand up her arm, fingers brushing the small hand pressed against his chest. A shiver rolled through her body and into his, causing him to tense up. "What are we doing tonight, again?"

She laughed, slipping free from his embrace. "You're calling me."

Dawson took a step toward her, chin lowering. The way her flush deepened had him wanting to touch her again. "Yeah, that's right."

"Good." She kept backing up, until she was on the other side of her car, opening the door. "Because I really don't think I can go to sleep without hearing your voice now."

Dawson's thoughts scattered. All he could do was stand there and watch her drive away. And only when he was sure she couldn't see him, he let his lips split into a smile so wide it'd put Dee's to shame.

Turning on his heel, he started toward his Jetta and then came to a sudden stop. The small hairs on the back of his neck rose, and it had nothing to do with the wind.

Someone was watching him.

Dawson scanned the parking lot in the waning light. The place was crowded, full of trucks and other obscenely large vehicles. One stood out.

A black Expedition with heavily tinted windows was parked toward the back, engine running.

Anger rose in him so quickly he almost lost his hold. And wouldn't his stalkers like that? A Luxen doing the Full Monty right in front of humans. Freaking DOD. Dawson was accustomed to them checking in, which really meant stalking them. Today was really no different. Except they had seen him with Bethany, and as he pivoted around and headed back to his car, it took everything in him not to walk over to that truck and light their asses up.

Three days later and Bethany was still floating from Sunday. Corny as hell, but she was floating like there were clouds on her feet. Arriving late to her locker before lunch, she stood in the empty hall, switching out books. The grin on her face was inked on, going nowhere. Her manic happiness had a name and—

"Hey there," Dawson said, his breath warming her ear.

Squeaking, she spun and dropped her book. Clasping a hand over her chest, she stared at Dawson, wide-eyed. "How . . . how in the world? I didn't even hear you."

He picked up the book and handed it over, then leaned against the locker beside her, giving a lopsided shrug. "I'm quiet."

Quiet didn't even cover it. A mouse sneezed in these halls and it echoed. She shoved the book in her bag. Then it hit her. "What are you doing in the hall?"

A lazy grin appeared. "Going to lunch."

"Wait. Don't you have class now?"

He leaned in, breathing the same air as her, causing her breath to catch. That damn half grin did funny things to her. They'd gone to the diner again on Tuesday, parting ways without a kiss—a real kiss. But when his forehead touched hers, she really believed he was going to kiss her, right in the hall.

Bethany was totally okay with that.

"I have study hall," he said, tilting his head just a little to the side, lining up their mouths. "And I charmed my way out of class. I wanted to see you."

"You charmed your way?" Her eyes drifted shut. "How'd you do that?"

"I'll never tell my secrets. You know better than that." Dawson pulled back, capturing her free hand. Feeling like what she wanted—*needed*—had just been taken from her, she glared at him. His grin spread. "I wanted to have lunch with you."

More than flattered, she let him pull her down the hall . . . away from the cafeteria, it appeared. "Hey, where are we going?"

"It's a surprise." He pulled her to his side, draping a heavy arm over her shoulders. The length of his body was fit against hers like it was made to be.

"Are we leaving campus?"

"Yep."

"Are we going to get in trouble?"

He stopped, turning her in his arms. They were *almost* chest to chest, his arm still around her shoulders. "Questions, questions, Bethany. Trust me. You won't get in trouble with me."

She arched a brow. "Because of your charmer skills, huh?"

"Exactly." He grinned.

Dawson continued on and she went with him, imagining what her mom would do if they got caught and the school called her. Mandatory pregnancy tests were in her future. She glanced at Dawson and decided it was worth it.

As they went out the back doors, she expected an alarm to sound and the rent-a-cop to come running at breakneck speed. When that didn't happen and their feet hit pavement, she started to relax.

Dawson let go of her hand, picking up the pace as he dug his keys out of his pocket. "Where I want to take you is two blocks down. We can drive if you want." He glanced over his shoulder, his eyes starting at the top of her head and drifting all the way to her toes.

Geez, when he looked at her like that, did he expect her to be able to communicate? She was mush now, useless mush.

His smile tipped higher, as if he knew what he was doing to her. "It's kind of too cold for you."

"What about you?" He faced the front, flipping those keys around. "I'm fine. This is your world, though."

She smiled at his back. "It is kind of co—" Her words ended in a startled shriek as her foot hit a thick patch of ice that hadn't thawed. Before she knew it, her arms were flailing as she sought to keep her balance.

Not going to happen.

In those teeny, tiny seconds, she'd resigned herself to cracking her skull wide open in front of Dawson. An ambulance would need to be called. Mom would find out. Dad would get summoned from work. She'd be grounded, with a concussion. Or worse.

Warm arms surrounded her, catching her a half second before she went *splat*. And there she remained, suspended in air, her hair brushing the slick asphalt. Dawson's face was inches from hers, eyes closed in concentration, face tight and grim.

Bethany couldn't even speak around her shock. Dawson had been several feet ahead. For him to get to her so quickly was mind-boggling.

Breathless, she stared up at him and swallowed hard. "Okay. You have the reflexes of a cat on steroids."

"Yeah," he said, sounding almost as out of breath as she was. "You okay?"

Wetting her lips, she nodded and then realized he couldn't see that. "Yes, I'm fine."

Slowly straightening, he had her back on her feet before he released her. His eyes opened, and Bethany couldn't believe what she was seeing. The irises were still a beautiful green, but the pupils . . . the pupils were *white*.

Without realizing it, she took a step forward. "Dawson . . ."

He blinked and his eyes were normal. "Yeah?"

Shaking her head, she didn't know if her mind was messing with her or what. Pupils couldn't be white. And he was fast—like Olympic gold medalist fast. And quiet, too. Quiet as a ghost on a weight loss program. And his friend could melt ping-pong balls . . .

8

Over the next month, Bethany saw more and more of Dawson. They hung out as much as they could at school. How he managed to finagle his way out of fourth period on a consistent basis amazed her. Charm? Hell, he needed to bottle that stuff.

On the days they shared lunch, he took her to the Mom and Pop diner down the street. There hadn't been any more near-death experiences in the parking lot and no more amazing feats of speed on Dawson's end.

And no more glowy pupils. It sounded crazy now and even she wanted to laugh, but every time they touched, there was an electric shock that passed between them. Lately, it was more than that. After the initial static charge faded, it felt like his skin . . . hummed or vibrated.

It was the strangest damn thing.

Pacing back and forth, she was wearing a path in the floor. Ordinarily, she was never this wrapped up in a boy. But there was something about him. He was a constant shadow in her thoughts.

They talked every day, in between classes, at lunch, on the

phone at night, and what not, and even though she knew a lot about him, there was still so much she *didn't* know. Like she didn't know anything about his parents, very little about his siblings, and she had a suspicion that he may be related to one of the teachers at school, because she always saw him with the guy.

She'd just been scratching the surface of Dawson. Knew his likes and dislikes and his love of hiking and being outside, discovered that stupid jokes made them both laugh and that he wasn't big on TV. But the real stuff? His past? Nope.

Glancing at her bed, she stared down at Phillip. He'd wanted to watch her paint after school and had fallen asleep on her bed. Now he was all curled up like a little lima bean, his thumb in his mouth and his cherub face peaceful.

A flash of white light shot across her laptop as the screensaver kicked on. It was a moving image of falling stars.

Sitting down beside her brother, she stared at the screen. The white was intense, consuming. Like Dawson's pupils had been. But she'd been seeing things, right? Stress-induced reaction caused by nearly sucking face with the icy pavement. There was no logical explanation for what she'd seen afterward. Not that it really mattered. He could be a llama in disguise and she'd still be . . . fascinated by him.

She was falling for Dawson in spite of the fact that she knew there were things he was hiding from her. Falling hard. But he wasn't the only one holding back. If Bethany was being honest with herself—which she was—she had to admit that she had been holding back, too.

Rolling onto her side, she grabbed her phone. A master plan formed in her mind as she sent Dawson a quick text, inviting him over to her house on Saturday.

His response was immediate. *What time?*

Now she just needed to break the news to her parents.

9

Dawson didn't need directions to Beth's house, but he went through the motions of asking for them anyway. It wasn't as totally stalkerish as it looked, though. Mainly it was due to the fact that it really wasn't that hard to find anything around Petersburg. Especially when you knew the layout of the area as well as he did.

Ever since the day outside of the school, when he pulled the Superman-speed crap, he felt like he was walking around on pins and needles. Bethany hadn't brought it up again, but he knew she was thinking about it. Every so often, he caught her looking at him as if she were trying to *really* see him. See behind the clothes and the skin, to what really existed underneath.

Part of him liked that. The other part was terrified. If she ever found out . . .

Easing the Jetta down the narrow road choked with elm trees, he took a deep breath. No doubt she wouldn't want anything to do with him if she knew that more than 90 percent of his DNA was from out of this solar system.

Was it wrong, lying to her? He wasn't sure. Honestly, he'd

never even asked himself that when he'd messed around with human girls before.

He had no clue what that really said about him.

The old farmhouse came into view, rising up against the gray skies of early April, and he saw three cars parked out front. One was a Porsche, which he knew belonged to her uncle.

Dawson had been surprised when she'd asked him last night if he wanted to come over. From what he'd gathered, her parents would flip if she brought a boy home. But here he was.

He parked the car and climbed out, smoothing his hands over his jeans. Probably should've worn something nicer. Not that he met a lot of human parents, since his interactions with human girls didn't get this far.

Stopping in front of the door, he let out a long breath. Sneaking out so that Dee didn't question where he was going had been the hard part. Parents would be a piece of cake.

Yeah, keep telling yourself that. Mom and Dad will be so proud that she brought home an alien.

Before he could knock on the door, it opened, revealing a tall, slender woman who looked waaay too young to be Bethany's mom. Eyes that matched Bethany's met his. The woman blinked and looked like she wanted to take a step back.

"You must be Dawson," she said, placing a hand against her chest.

Dawson smiled. "Yes, ma'am. I'm here to see Bethany."

Footsteps pounded down the stairs, cutting off Mrs. Williams's response. Bethany appeared behind her mom, eyes wide. She wiggled around her, grabbing Dawson's hand. She pulled him inside.

"Mom, meet Dawson. Dawson, meet Mom."

Her mom arched a brow. "That's not how you typically introduce people, Bethany."

"Works for me," she quipped, tugging him toward the stairs.

A man stepped out from what appeared to be a living room, a remote control in his hand and a confused expression on his face. "Uh . . ."

"And that's Dad. Little butt—er, Phillip is taking a nap."

Over her father's shoulder was a frail, thin wisp of a man. Dawson almost didn't recognize him from the few times he'd seen the doctor around town.

"And that's my uncle."

Dawson gave them a wave. "It's nice to meet—"

"We're going upstairs." She started for the steps, shooting him a look that had him grinning.

"Keep the door open," her mom called from the bottom.

"Mom," Bethany whined, cheeks flushed. "It's not like that."

Dammit. He wanted it to be *like that* and then some. Her mother repeated the order again, and Bethany pulled him down the hallway.

"I'm so sorry. My mom thinks whenever a boy is in my bedroom that must mean we're making out or something." She dropped his hand, opening her door. "It's so embarrassing."

Dawson stepped around her, scanning her bedroom. Music played on low from her laptop. There wasn't much going on, just the basics, with the exception of the easel sitting in front of the window. "Do you have boys in your bedroom a lot?"

She laughed as she skirted around him. "Oh, yeah, all the time. It's like a train station in here."

His brows shot up. He couldn't tell if she was joking or not. Seeing his expression, she laughed again. He loved that sound—loved that she laughed so much. "I'm joking," she said, sitting down on the bed. She patted the spot next to her. "Actually, you're the first boy to be in my bedroom."

A rush of possessiveness hit him hard. Ignoring it, he sat beside her and leaned back, watching her from behind hooded eyes. "Well, you *are* new still. Unless you work fast, I'd hope I'm the first guy."

She twisted around, sitting cross-legged. "I bet you've been in *many*, many girls' bedrooms."

He shrugged one shoulder.

Her eyes narrowed. "Come on, with someone who looks like you, there's probably a line of girls hoping to take you home."

"So?" He reached out, tugging on the hem of her jeans. "I'm here with you, aren't I?"

"Yeah, you are." She frowned. "Sometimes I wonder why."

Dawson stared at her a moment, then laughed. She couldn't be serious. There was no way she didn't know how pretty she was or how her laugh drew people to her.

Her frown deepened. "Are you laughing at me?"

"Yes," he replied. He shot forward, moving faster than he should have, and caught her hand. "You can't tell me you're surprised that I'm here. I've been your shadow since the first day you arrived."

Beth's eyes dropped to where his hand wrapped around hers. After a moment, she settled down. "I know I'm not ugly, but you're . . . you're . . ."

A grin pulled at his lips. "I'm what?"

Crimson stained her cheeks, and his grin spread into a smile. She pulled her hand free, but he didn't think she was mad. "You know what you are," she said, reaching over and picking up a large album. "Anyway, I found this old photo album. You want to look at it?"

He leaned back on his elbows. "We can do whatever you want."

Her lashes lifted, and he felt as if he'd been punched in the stomach when their eyes met. No. Not that. Like when he shed his human skin and took his real form. That rush of pure electricity and power when his being became light.

That was what he felt when Bethany looked at him.

More than anything, he wanted to know what was going on in that head of hers, what was making her eyes so dark that it was almost difficult to tell the difference between her pupils and irises. Did she feel it? God, he hoped he wasn't reading her wrong, because if so, this was all about to get really awkward.

But it wasn't like humans were all that different from Luxen, once you got past the whole alien thing.

She showed him pictures of her family from Nevada, flipping through the album with a soft smile on her face as she made a comment about this relative and that one. But man, did he ever have a hard time paying attention to them.

All he wanted to see was sitting right next to him—on a bed, no less.

He couldn't stop staring at her—at the finely arched eyebrows, her cheekbones, the way her lips curved, how she tilted her head—

Bethany laughed, lifting her chin. "You're not even looking at the pictures, Dawson."

He thought about lying but grinned instead. "Sorry. You're distracting."

"Whatever."

She had no idea that he could literally stare at her all day. It was like he was obsessed. *Whipped* was what Daemon would say, but his brother didn't understand. Hell, Dawson wasn't even sure *he* understood what he was doing here, with this girl—this beautiful human girl.

This was trouble.

And he really didn't care.

Over the low hum of music, he could hear her parents talking with the doctor. His eyes flicked to the bedroom door. Willing it closed the rest of the way with a soft *click*, he turned his attention back to Bethany, but she didn't appear to notice.

"I'm glad you invited me over," he said.

She turned slightly and surprise flickered across her face.

His gaze dropped to her parted lips. They were dangerously close to his, which meant he was on the verge of doing something he couldn't turn back from. "Bethany?"

"Yeah?" she murmured, lashes lowering.

"Nothing . . ." He leaned in just a fraction and inhaled deeply. Damn. She smelled wonderful. Like vanilla and roses. Every part of him liked that. Reaching up slowly, he placed his palm against her cheek.

Bethany didn't pull back.

Reassured by that, he spread his fingers out, cupping the delicate curves. Her lashes lowered completely, shielding lovely eyes. Warmth gathered inside him, like a tightly wound ball. Why, out of everyone, did he have to feel this way with her—a human?

Did it matter? Honestly? Dawson had never looked at humans the way Daemon and most of the other Luxen did. They weren't frail, helpless, or inferior creatures. So why would he be surprised at being attracted to one?

And then it hit him. Dawson just hadn't expected *her*.

Several heartbeats passed before Bethany swallowed. Inviting Dawson to her house was pretty much a bold move on her part. So she'd been a ball of nerves all day. When she'd broken the news to her parents, she'd had to give them Dawson's life story, which wasn't much. Then she'd been all jumpy with him in her bedroom, so close to the damn paintings she'd done of him now hidden away in her closet.

Somehow, with him sitting on her bed, it changed things.

The whole point of inviting him over was so that he'd return the invite—bring her to his house. Now she wasn't really thinking about that.

Dawson was inching closer, his breath moving over her lashes, the tip of her nose, her cheek . . . She felt like she'd lost her balance.

"Have I told you how beautiful you are?" he asked, voice deep and husky.

"No." But he really didn't have to. She could tell by the way he looked at her, and that was better than any pretty words.

His breath danced over her chin. "You're beautiful."

Okay, hearing the words really was super nice. "Thank you. You aren't too bad yourself."

As Dawson laughed, his nose brushed hers, and she sucked in air like she'd never breathed before. He was so damn close . . .

"I want to kiss you." There was a pause, and her heart soared, chest swelled. "Is that all right with you?" he asked.

Was it? Oh, wow, yes it was. But she couldn't find the words. So she nodded. Before she could close her eyes, Dawson breached the minuscule space separating them and brought his mouth flush against hers.

He brushed his lips over hers, and she felt the velvety-soft touch all the way to the tips of her curled toes. Then his mouth moved over hers again, as if testing what she thought, waiting for her response. With her heart in her throat, she placed her hands on his shoulders and leaned in.

A shudder rolled through Dawson, and he cupped her cheek. Her skin hummed as the kiss deepened. Somehow one of her hands ended up clutching the front of his sweater, pulling him closer, because there was still some space between them and that space was too much.

Dawson's hand slid to the nape of her neck, guiding her down so that she was under him and his arms were the perfect kind of cage. And he kept kissing her, changing the angle, causing her pulse to thrum through her body and along her nerve endings. Then he pressed down, fitted against her from knees to shoulders, and she was drifting in raw emotions and heat.

A very real, intense heat that beat at her, lapped at her in waves.

There was something magical in the way he kissed, because she swore she was seeing stars behind her lids. It was taking the air right out of her lungs. Slow, heady warmth stole through her veins. Something buzzed, like a timer in her ears, but boy oh boy, she didn't care. Not when Dawson was kissing her. Not when a hand fell to her shoulder, slid down her arm, over the curve of her waist, to her hip.

Not even when the white light behind her lids grew to be so intense she had to open her eyes.

10

The Arum was nearby. Every cell in Daemon's body was telling him so. Nasty SOB was bold, too, because the sun was way up in the sky for the Arum to be so close to what was his.

Oh, hell no, this wasn't going to fly.

Dee stopped twirling her straw in her soda as her features pinched. For a moment, all he heard was the crackling of the logs coming from the fireplace. Jocelyn, the manager of the Smoke Hole Diner, straightened as her fingers tightened around the poker.

"One of them is near?" Dee whispered.

Jocelyn came to their table, her pale hand fluttering over her rounded belly. "Do you feel that?" Her voice was low as her eyes searched the windows. "A darkness has come."

Daemon glanced down at his half-eaten meatloaf sandwich. More like a pain in his ass had come. Funny how seeing a culinary work of art go to waste made you mean as a snake.

The Arum was going to die.

Grabbing a napkin, he cleaned his hands off as he stood. He

only saw his sister. "Call Adam and Andrew, and do not leave this place until they come get you."

A flush covered her cheeks. "But I can help you," she said in a low voice. "I can fight."

"Over my dead body." He turned to Jocelyn. "If she tries to leave here with the Thompson brothers, I give you permission to tackle her."

Jocelyn glanced down at her belly as if she were trying to figure out how she was supposed to do that when Dee groaned. "Fine. Just come back alive, all right?"

"I always come back," he replied.

He started around the table but stopped and kissed Dee's cheek. "I love you."

Tears filled her eyes, and he knew part of the reason was because he wasn't letting her get involved. His siblings were the only things he had left, so she could cry him a river and that wasn't changing a damn thing. There was no way he was going to let Dee put herself in danger. It was bad enough Dawson patrolled. If Daemon had his way, neither of his siblings would be out there looking for Arum. Shouldering the responsibility of protecting them wasn't something he took lightly or regretted. In a way, it gave him back some kind of control when the DOD ran everything else.

Outside the diner, he casually strolled across the parking lot, nodding at an elderly couple who smiled. Look at him, being all civil and stuff. When his booted feet crunched over fallen branches, his hands flexed. He kept going, far enough that no one would see him pull his superhero stunt. Deep in the woods, he closed his eyes and let his senses spread out.

Squirrels or some other tiny woodland creatures skittered across the floor of the forest. Birds sang. Spring was on the way . . . and so was one big, pissed-off, evil alien.

Shedding his human form took a second. Power surged from deep inside him, and the uncanny sense to root out a nearby Arum took hold. They left a dark stain on the fringe of a Luxen's consciousness—an inkblot that was like a fingerprint.

It worked the same way for the Arum outside the range of the beta quartz that made up the Seneca Rocks. It was why living here was peaceful. Daemon's kind was protected, but every once in a while, an Arum stumbled too close. Contact was made, and then the Arum brought in his buddies.

Three of them had already been taken out. This should be the last one.

As Daemon zipped through the trees at a blinding speed, he wondered what the hell his brother was doing. On Saturdays, they usually spent the day watching all the *Ghost Investigator* episodes TiVoed that week.

But Dawson had bailed on him.

Oh, yeah, he had a clue where he was. Chilling with the human—

The blast of dark energy hit him square in the chest, sending him flying backward like a ball that had just been knocked out of the park. He smacked into a tree hard enough that it groaned and shook as he slid down to the mossy bed of the woods.

God. Dammit.

Sheer grit got him off the ground. Immeasurable stupidity had him bum-rushing the thick shadow coming at him like a souped-up bulldozer.

The Arum switched into his human form at the last moment, losing the vulnerability. All decked out in leather pants . . . and nothing else. Nice. Just what Daemon wanted to do—wrestle with a half-naked dude.

Okay, so the Arum wanted to play hard? Well, it was his lucky day. Taking on his human form, Daemon swung his arm forward, hitting the Arum with a damn good uppercut. The thing grunted and threw a meaty arm at Daemon's head.

He ducked under the arm, shooting up behind the Arum. Leaning back, Daemon planted his foot in the Arum's spine. Funny thing about taking human form was that skin bled and bones broke. Both of their kinds would have to flip back to their real form to heal, and then they'd be at their weakest. Hopefully this Arum would be stupid enough to fall for it. Daemon had a blade dying to make friends.

But the Arum wasn't.

The Arum whipped around, rearing back with one hand. Dark energy shot forth, narrowly missing Daemon as he darted to the side.

You're going to be tasssty, the Arum taunted.

"If I had a dollar every time I heard that." Daemon threw his hand out. A streak of light hit a thick branch, breaking it off. He raced forward, catching the massive limb and holding it like a bat. He smiled. "Batter up, mofo."

The Arum hissed—literally hissed at him. What. The. Hell.

He came at Daemon like a train, and Daemon swung. The *crack* shook his entire body, and the sickening *thud* pleased him in ways he should be worried about.

But the Arum didn't go down.

Pulling into himself like someone had shoved a vacuum into his back, the Arum retreated into a small black ball and shot off through the trees, running like a pansy.

Daemon started to give chase, but he knew from experience when an Arum ran, there was no capturing him. Tossing the splintered limb aside, he pivoted around, ignoring the raw pain shooting through his hip. Once he was at home, he would change and heal. Until then, he would deal with the bruises and aches.

But once he got back to his house and took care of that, all he was going to do was just chill. Like everyone else in this damn world did.

God, Dawson had never felt this way before. Every part of his body burned as he tasted her kiss and familiarized himself with the way she felt beneath him. Intense white light seared his eyes. The breathy, little feminine sounds she was making were music to his ears, a beautiful melody of sighs.

And then his song stopped.

Beth's hand jerked off his shoulder, and she gasped against his mouth. "Oh my God . . ."

He lifted his head and opened his eyes. Oh, hell . . . All he saw was white glow that bathed Beth's face, reflected off the walls, covered the entire bed . . .

Oh, holy shit.

Dawson sprang off the bed, but his feet never touched the floor beside it. He hovered, staring down at himself. He was glowing.

Like in full motherfreaking alien mode up in her house, in her bedroom.

Bethany skittered across the bed and pressed against the headboard. Her eyes were wide as she stared at him, her mouth working but no words coming out.

Shock suspended time. Everything seemed surreal to him. He wasn't in Bethany's bedroom. He hadn't exposed what he truly was. And this girl—this beautiful human he was falling for—wasn't staring at him like he was king freak.

Grasping the edge of her comforter, she shook her head

back and forth. Like she was having trouble processing what she was seeing, which was understandable.

Dawson was glowing like a star.

His heart was racing so fast he could feel it in his finger-tips. Partly due to the whole kissing thing and partly because he was still in his true form. And she was glowing faintly, like someone had dipped a paintbrush into white paint and shaded her edges. Of course, Bethany couldn't see it. No human could. The trace surrounding her was a reaction of the high EMF surrounding him when he was in his real skin.

Crap—she *was* glowing.

Bethany blinked slowly, her fingers easing off the blanket. "Dawson?"

Do something, he ordered himself. But his control had slipped, and he couldn't pull it back. Light radiated from him, filling every inch of the room.

She rose to her knees little by little. He was certain he could see her heart pounding through her sweater, could smell her fear. She was seconds from bolting from the room, screaming. Bethany inched across the bed, making her way toward him.

Dawson drifted back, wanting to say something, but in his true form, he didn't speak like a human. Luxen used . . . different paths.

At the edge of the bed, she peered up at him. In her brown eyes, he could see his reflection, and he hated what he saw.

"Dawson," she whispered, clasping her hands under her chin. "Is that you?"

Yes, he said. But she couldn't hear him.

When the silence stretched, became unbearable, she swung her legs off the bed and stood. Instead of running for the door like any sane person would, she reached out, bringing her fingers within inches of touching his light.

Dawson jerked back.

Bethany yanked her hand to her chest. "What . . . what are you?"

God, wasn't that a loaded question? The whole telling part seemed a moot point now, but how could he explain what happened? *Hey, honey, I'm an alien and apparently I just doused you with some radioactive loving! Wanna catch a movie?* Yeah, not cool.

So many things were rushing through his thoughts. He'd exposed his kind—his family, putting them in danger, risking Beth. There was no stopping her if she decided to scream *alien* or *giant light bug*.

But he needed to rein it in. Her parents were downstairs, and he had a feeling the longer he stayed in this form, the stronger her trace would be.

Moving to the far side of the room, away from Beth, he willed his out-of-control emotions to stabilize. It was hard as hell, but eventually he managed to take his human form, and the room was cast in shadows again.

Everything except Beth—there was a soft halo around her.

"I'm sorry," he croaked.

Bethany's legs seemed to collapse beneath her. She plopped down on the bed, shaking her head again. "What are you?"

Leaning against the wall, he closed his eyes. There was no point in lying now or keeping secrets. The damage was done. All he could hope was that he could convince her not to go public with this.

"I'm an alien." The words sounded thick and foreign to his ears, and he barked a laugh. "I'm a Luxen."

She pulled up her knees, tucking them against her chest. "An alien? Like in *Close Encounters of the Third Kind*?" She laughed then, and it carried a sort of hysterical edge to it.

When the sound trickled off, her head snapped toward him. "That's why you like that dumb movie *Cocoon* so much. This . . . this isn't real. It can't be. Oh my God, I'm crazy . . . Schizophrenia."

Dawson swallowed. "You're not crazy, Bethany. I'm sorry. You weren't supposed to know, and I don't even know how . . . how this happened."

"What? You don't normally light up when you kiss girls? Because that could get real awkward, right?" She clapped her hand over her mouth. "Sorry. Oh, God, I don't know . . . Alien?"

Hearing the confusion in her voice tore through him, and he wanted to somehow make it better, but how? At least he didn't sense any fear in her anymore. Amazing.

He took a tentative step forward, and when she didn't move, he was reassured. "Maybe it will help if I start over?"

She nodded slowly.

Taking a deep breath, he sat before her and tilted his head back, meeting her eyes. What he was about to do was unheard of. The rules he was about to break were astronomical. An image of his brother and sister formed in his head, and his chest squeezed. He knew if this went badly, it went badly for them, too.

And it would also go badly for Bethany.

11

All Bethany could do was stare at Dawson. That was pretty much all she was capable of. Alien? The logical part of her brain kept spewing things like, *This is just a hallucination or a dream.* Or, *This is the onset of a mental disease.* Maybe Dawson never existed, but then again, that didn't make sense. Pretty sure she'd seen other people interacting with him. Unless her hallucinations were on such an epic level she *believed* she'd seen people—

"Bethany." His quiet voice intruded.

Her heart turned over heavily. "This is real, right?"

His face contorted as if he were in pain. "Yes, it's real."

Crazy people probably did things like this all the time. Asked their imaginary alien friends if they were real, and of course, they'd say yes.

She placed her hands against her cheeks and then ran them through her tangled hair. Did crazy people also make out with their hallucinations? Because that was probably the only upside to all of this.

Dawson placed his hand on her knee. "I can't even begin to understand what you're going through. I really can't, but I promise you that this is real and you're not crazy." He squeezed her leg. "And I'm so sorry for making you feel this way and for you finding out like this."

"Don't apologize." Her voice sounded hoarse. "It's just . . . a lot to comprehend. I mean, I never really thought about aliens. Like, okay, maybe they do exist somewhere out there, but . . . yeah, I don't know if I really did believe. And you can't be an alien."

She laughed again and then winced. It sounded like a whole lot of crazy. "I just saw you . . . glow, but it was more than just glowing. You were light, right? A human form of light—arms and legs made out of *light*."

Dawson nodded. "We're called Luxen. In our true forms we are nothing more than light, but . . . it's not like you think. You can touch us—we have form and shape."

"Form and shape," she mumbled.

"Yes." He lowered his lashes, and in that instant, he seemed terribly young and vulnerable. "We're from a planet called Lux. Well, it was once called that. It doesn't exist anymore. Destroyed. But that's neither here nor there. We've been here for hundreds, if not thousands of years, on and off."

Her stomach did a twisty motion. "You're . . . *that* old?"

"No. No!" Dawson laughed, lifting his eyes. "I'm sixteen. We—my family—came here when we were children, very young, and we age the same way you do."

"On a spaceship?" She almost laughed again, but managed to keep it down. A spaceship—a freaking spaceship. Dear God, that was a word she thought she'd never utter. This was . . . Wow.

Dawson shifted, clasping his hands in his lap. "We don't have spaceships. We travel in our true form. Uh, we travel as light. And in that form, we don't breathe like you would. So different atmospheres, yeah . . ." He shrugged. "When we got here, we . . . picked our human forms, melding our DNA in a way, but we can look like anyone."

Bethany sat straighter. This had just gone from bizarro land into *Twilight Zone* territory. "You can look like anyone?"

He nodded. "We don't do it a lot; only when we need to."

Trying to wrap her brain around this, she tugged on her hair with both hands. "Okay, so what you look like now, that's not real?"

"No, this"—he tapped his chest—"this is real. Like I said, our DNA adapts quickly to our environment. And we are always born in threes—"

"Andrew and his siblings—they are Luxen, too?" When he nodded, she was almost relieved. "Andrew did melt the ping-pong ball!"

"Yeah, see, we control things related to light, which is heat and at times fire." He still hadn't looked at her, not directly. "I don't know why he did that. The general population can't know about us. So, it's important that we don't do anything stupid. And that was stupid. Hell, what I just did was colossally stupid."

She watched him. Now that the shock was ebbing away, her mind was starting to put things together. At least now she knew how such a small town could have six insanely gorgeous people. Go figure they weren't human in nature. Then it struck her—the whole episode in the icy parking lot. "What else can you do?"

His features pinched. "I really shouldn't—"

"But I already know, right?" She slid off the bed, sitting in front of him so her knees pressed into his. He jerked as if surprised by the contact but didn't move. "What harm can it cause now?"

His brows shot up. "It can cause a lot of problems."

Dread inched up her spine, sending shivers over her shoulders. "Like what?"

He opened his mouth but shook his head. "It's nothing. Uh,

you want to know what else we can do? We can move fast. That's how I caught you in the parking lot. We can also harness energy—our light. It's pretty strong. A human wouldn't survive a hit from us."

Her eyes widened. That wasn't good news, but she couldn't picture Dawson hurting anyone. Maybe that's why she wasn't afraid. Or she was just naive.

"What else?"

"That basically covers that side of things."

She knew there was more to it, and she wanted to push the topic, but there were just so many more questions. "How many are here?"

"A lot," he said, watching his hands. "Most of our kind live in colonies. The government is aware of us—the Department of Defense, that is. They monitor us."

Okay, now she was getting visions of *Men in Black*. Sitting back, she let it sink in. A whole other world had just opened up in front of her. One she suspected not a lot of people were aware of, even if the government had something to do with it. Crazy as it sounded, she felt . . . privileged somehow.

"Are you okay?" he asked.

"Yeah, I'm just soaking this up." She paused. "Why Earth?"

Dawson's smile was faint. "Our kind has been coming here since humans walked the Earth, or maybe longer than that. In a way, it's familiar to us, I guess."

"And your parents—"

"My parents are dead," he said in a monotone. "So are the Thompsons' parents."

Her chest squeezed. "Oh, I'm sorry. I didn't know." She wanted to reach out, comfort him, but right now, he acted as if he was afraid of her, which was odd, all things considered. "I really am sorry."

"It's okay." His chest rose unevenly. "They died when we were babies."

"How . . . how do you get by without parents, though? Wouldn't people suspect something?"

"That's when the changing shape is handy. One of us pretends to be the parent," he explained. "And the DOD keeps a roof over our heads and stuff."

Fascinated, she started spouting off more and more questions. Hours went by as she practically interrogated him in between her mom checking in on them. What about the colony? He wouldn't talk about it, so she moved on. Did any other humans around here know? The answer was no. How involved was the DOD? From what she could gather from Dawson, heavily involved. They monitored every aspect of the Luxen's lives, from where they chose to live, what colleges they went to, down to when they applied for a driver's license. Another fun fact was they didn't get sick. No flu. No common colds. No cancers or nerve diseases. There was no need for a doctor. If they were injured in their human form, they only needed to resort back to their true form to heal "most" injuries.

"Let me get this right," Bethany said, leaning toward him. "You can't be hurt, then? Not really?"

Dawson shook his head. "We can be hurt. The Arum are our greatest enemies."

"The who?"

He rubbed the heel of his hand against his temple. "They are like us, sort of. Instead of three born at the same time, there are four. They are from our sister planet. And they are mostly comprised of shadows, but their DNA adapted like ours. They look human most of the time."

"And they're dangerous?"

"They hunted us into near extinction, destroyed our planet. They followed us here."

Her throat felt dry. "Why do they hunt you?"

"For our abilities," he explained. "Without them, they are weak. The more Luxen they kill, the more abilities they absorb."

"That . . . that is messed up."

He looked up then, meeting her eyes. "They are only one of the reasons why we have to be careful around humans."

Knots formed in her stomach. She thought of the light—the intensity and heat. "Can you harm people in your true form?"

"No—I mean, we distort electromagnetic fields when we use our abilities. That increases them. Too much of it can make a human sick or nauseated and nervous, but nothing permanent. And sometimes we vibrate . . . or hum."

"I've felt that before." She smiled a little, remembering the way his hand had thrummed beneath hers.

Dawson's eyes glittered. "But whenever we use our abilities or go into our true form, we leave a trace behind on the human. Like right now, you have a faint glow around you."

"A trace?"

"Yes," he said. "We stay here and in places like Petersburg, because there is a large concentration of beta quartz in the rocks. It disrupts the fields around us, blocking our detection from the Arum, but it doesn't block traces."

Her breath caught, somehow knowing where this was leading. "So, these Arum can see the trace around me and . . . and find you through that trace?"

"Yes."

"Oh, God." She placed a hand over her heart.

"Your trace is very faint. I don't think it will be a problem." Relief flooded her, and he seemed to try to smile. "I feel stupid for even saying this, but you can't tell anyone about this, Bethany. No one must know."

She laughed then, knowing she surprised him. "Dawson, no one would *believe* me."

"It doesn't stop people, though. There have been some who have discovered the truth. Who have seen a Luxen in his or her true form and tried to tell other people." His eyes were doing that shiny thing again, like there was a white light behind the pupils. She guessed there was. "Those people disappeared."

Ice covered the knots in her stomach. "What do you mean?"

"The DOD takes care of them. How? I don't know. But their main job is to cloak us in secrecy and make sure no one threatens that objective."

Kind of scary to think of that, but she also understood why. Humans would freak if they knew aliens were running around. Aliens who could change identities, move as fast as light, and harness whatever energy.

And on the flip side, a human holding that kind of knowledge wielded a lot of power, didn't she? Money would probably be involved, if one went public with details.

Bethany shook her head. It wouldn't be right, though, for several reasons. "I won't say anything, Dawson. I know promising I won't doesn't mean much, but . . . I really don't want to disappear, and I don't want to get you in trouble."

He exhaled loudly. "I do believe you. Thank you."

Heartbeats passed in silence as she studied his downturned face. God, he was beautiful. His features perfectly pieced together. Should've known some kind of foreign DNA was somehow involved. Then she remembered their first phone call and how he'd said he was from far away. Funny thing was he hadn't lied to her then.

Bethany really didn't know what to say or think. Obviously

she wasn't crazy. Dawson was . . . an alien, but she had a hard time seeing it. Not that she didn't accept what he was, but as she stared at him, all she saw was *Dawson*.

Dawson who spoke to her the first day here, who followed her out into the hallway, and who skipped class to spend lunch with her. Dawson who devoted hours on the phone with her, talking until they both fell asleep like goobers.

All she really saw was Dawson—a boy she was falling for.

He'd stayed still while she'd been staring at him, but he looked away now, a muscle flexing in his jaw.

Bethany rose to her knees suddenly. "Can I touch you? When you're in your . . . true form?"

His eyes snapped to hers, the green churning with a mixture of hope and panic, relief and sorrow. There was also this oddly tender look on his face that pulled at her heart, made it *thump* harder. "Why would you want to?"

She bit her lip, wondering if she'd somehow insulted him. Was touching in their true form uncouth? He had jumped away from her awfully fast. "I don't know. I just do."

Shock splashed across his face. "You really want to?"

Holding her breath, she nodded.

Dawson shook his head but rose to his knees, too. He closed his eyes, and a second later he faded out. His clothes, the shape under them, everything just faded away but was quickly replaced by white light edged in blue.

He extended one arm and fingers formed. Five of them. Just like hers. Beth's gaze darted up and his head tilted to the side, waiting.

His light illuminated the entire room. Warmth radiated from him. As strange as it was seeing this, he was beautiful. So beautiful there were tears in her eyes, which had nothing to do with the intensity of the light.

With her heart in her throat, she reached out her hand. When her fingers brushed the light, a weak shock of electricity rolled up her arm, and then she felt the faint vibration. Her fingers clasped his—and it felt the same. Warm. Smooth. Strong. It was Dawson's hand.

It just looked different.

Bethany inched closer, careful not to freak him out. "Can I touch more of you?"

After a pause, he nodded.

Then it struck her. "You can't talk to me in this form, can you?"

Dawson shook his head.

"That's sad." But then she placed her hand where she assumed his chest was and his light pulsed. There was a distinct crackle in the room, like a socket blowing. The humming sensation rolled up her arm, reminding her of pushing a lawn mower.

Her hand slipped down, and the light grew even more powerful. She started to smile, but then she realized she was feeling him up, and, well, that was awkward. Pulling her hand back, she hoped he didn't notice her blush.

Dawson lowered his arm, and the light dimmed. Like before, he faded out and took the form she was familiar with, jeans and all.

"Hey," he said.

"Beautiful," she blurted out. "You're beautiful."

His eyes widened, and she felt sort of dumb. "I mean, what you are isn't something . . . bad."

"Thank you."

She nodded. "Your secret is safe with me. I promise you. You don't have anything to worry about."

"You're okay, then?"

"Everything is okay," she whispered, still awestruck by the beauty of his true form.

"Good." He smiled, but it rang false as he stood, running his hands down his thighs. "You can't imagine how thankful I am that you understand, and don't worry, I *also* understand."

She frowned. "Understand what?"

"That you don't want to see me . . . like this anymore." There was a pause as he flinched. "I know you probably hate me for pretending to be human and then for kissing you. It was wrong. And it probably disgusts you. After the trace fades, I'll leave you alone. I swear. But I need to stay close to you now, just to be careful. I don't want you to worry. The likelihood of an Arum finding you is slim."

"Whoa. Wait." Bethany stood, her heart thumping in her chest again. "Dawson, why would I be disgusted or hate you?"

He gave her a bland look.

"What?" She shook her head.

"I'm an alien." He said it slowly.

"But you're still Dawson, right? I mean, I get that you're what you are, but you're still Dawson." She paused, working up her courage to throw it all out there. "You're still the guy I like. And if—if you still like me, then I don't see what the big deal is."

He paused, and she was pretty sure he stopped breathing. And she tried not to notice or get freaked out by it, because it so wouldn't help anything right now.

Dawson just stared at her.

Ah, maybe she'd read this wrong? The kissing, too? "I mean, if you still like me? I don't know what kind of rules or—"

He'd crossed the distance between them so quickly she hadn't even seen him move. One second she was standing there, yapping away, and the next she was in his arms, his head buried in her hair. Strong arms trembled around her.

She wrapped her arms around his neck and held on. A lump formed in her throat. Tears burned her eyes. It dawned on her how incredibly lonely they had to be, living among the humans but never really being a part of them.

"Bethany," he murmured, inhaling deeply. "You have no idea what this . . . means to me."

Snuggling closer and breathing in his crisp scent, she held him tighter. There weren't really any words.

"I'm thinking," he said, voice rough.

"About . . . ?"

"You. Me. Together. Like going out together, being together." There was a pause, and then he laughed. "Wow. That was probably the lamest attempt ever at asking you to be my girlfriend."

Beth's heart sped up. Lame or not, she was seconds from swooning. "You want to be my boyfriend?" He nodded, and her breath came out in a little gasp. "Well, you kind of have to be with me now." Lifting her head, she grinned up at him. "I know your big, bad secret."

Dawson laughed, and his eyes lightened. "Oh, blackmail, huh?"

When she nodded, he bent down, pressing his head against her forehead. "Seriously though, I want this—I want you." The earlier awkwardness was gone from his voice. He was all intent and purpose now. "More than I've ever wanted any-thing. So, yeah, I want to be with you."

Nothing in this world could stop her smile. "I really, really like the sound of that."

Bethany knew the truth, knew how much he risked, but in her arms, he was and would always be Dawson.

12

The ride home was a blur to Dawson. He didn't even remember parking the car and heading upstairs. Lying in bed, he stared at the ceiling, his thoughts racing and spilling atop one another.

He'd flipped into his true form. Holy crap on a cracker. He actually changed in front of her. There were no words.

Never in his life had that happened.

But she hadn't freaked. God, no, she'd actually *accepted* him. Other than UFO fanatics, Dawson didn't expect that from any human.

Pulling his cell out of his pocket, he sent her a quick text, asking if she was okay. Her response came back immediately. Then his phone beeped again.

        See each other tmrw?

The grin that spread across his face probably made him look like a dumb SOB, but he didn't care. Responding back, he told her yes and then dropped the cell on his nightstand. Not a second later, his bedroom door opened, and Dee popped her head in.

"Hey," she said. "Can I come in?"

"Sure." Dawson sat up. "What's up?"

Dee sat in the chair by his desk, folding her slender arms. "Daemon went after the Arum today. He was close to the diner."

Dawson's chest clenched. *Bethany*. She may have accepted him, but damn, how could he forget about that trace? "Is Daemon okay?"

"A little banged up, but he'll be fine." There was a pause and then a sigh. "He'll always be okay. You know how he is."

Yeah, Daemon was a freaking machine. "Let me guess— he's out there hunting the Arum again right now."

She nodded. "Were you with Bethany?"

"I hung out at her house, met her parents."

"Sounds serious," she whispered.

Serious as an alien invasion, he thought. Crossing his ankles, he narrowed his eyes. "Are you okay?"

Dee blinked out of the chair and appeared on the foot of the bed, her knees tucked against her chest. "I'm fine. I just miss you. Daemon's a bore."

He chuckled. "Daemon is more exciting than I am."

She scrunched up her nose. "Whatever. So, Bethany—it is serious, right? Meeting parents? You've never done that before." They had a close relationship, he and Dee. Although a lot of the details about his hookups were absent, Dee knew everything about him. And he trusted her implicitly.

"I really do like her," he said finally, closing his eyes. "She's amazing."

Dee didn't respond immediately, and he knew what she was thinking. Bethany could be amazing, perfect even, and it wouldn't matter. Aliens and humans didn't mix. "Dawson—"

"She knows."

He'd said it quietly, but the two words were like a nuclear bomb.

"What?" Dee shrieked.

Dawson winced. When he opened his eyes, she was standing straight up on the bed, eyes wide and hands shaking. He sat up. "Dee, it's okay."

"How can it be okay? Humans can't know about us! And what about the DOD and—"

"Dee, sit and get a grip. Okay?" He waited until she settled back down. Her whole body was vibrating. It happened whenever she got excited or upset. "I didn't tell her on purpose."

Her head cocked to the side. "How did you *accidentally* let it slip? 'Oh, by the way, I'm an alien. Let's kiss'?"

Huh, she had it backward.

"What happened?" she demanded.

"I'm not sure you want to know the details."

"Did you guys have sex? Because that's pretty much the only thing you won't tell me, which I do appreciate, and on second thought, don't answer that question. It was gross."

"No. We didn't have sex." He choked on his laugh. "Geez, Dee . . ."

She rolled her eyes. "Then what happened?"

Rubbing his temples, he glanced at the door. "Bethany and I were making out and something happened that's never happened before."

Dee leaned back. A look of supreme disgust clouded her pretty face. "Uh, yuck if this is about any kind of premat—"

"Oh my God, shut up and listen, okay?" He dragged a hand through his hair. "We were making out, and I lost my hold on my human form. I lit up like a freaking Christmas tree."

His sister's mouth dropped open. "No shit . . ."

"Yeah, and she saw me. I had to tell her, because it's not like I could hide after that."

Dee blinked several times. "Wait. Rewind. You lost hold because you were kissing?"

"Yep."

"Wow." Another emotion washed away the disgust. Something he couldn't place and probably didn't want to. "You must really, really like her."

"I do." Dawson smiled then, unable to help himself. He was such a dork.

"I've never been kissed like that."

There went his smile. "You better not be kissed like that. And I don't want to hear about it if you do."

"Hey, it's caring and sharing time, right?"

"No."

She waved her hand, dismissing him. "What did she do?"

Dawson explained how well Bethany handled it once she got over her expected shock. Respect filled his sister's eyes. Any Luxen could appreciate a human's understanding of keeping this on the down low, and if he believed that Bethany would, Dee seemed to trust that.

"Wait. Is she glowing?" She whispered the last bit, as if saying it out loud was some sort of sin.

Dawson nodded. "A little bit."

"Oh, man. Daemon is going to kill you."

"Thanks. That helps, Dee."

"Sorry." She lifted her hands. "But once he sees her, yeah, not good."

Dawson leaned against the headboard, running his hands down his face. Dammit, it wasn't good. Not by a long shot. Who cared about Daemon killing him? Bethany was glowing. He'd left his proverbial mark on her.

And that would draw an Arum right to her doorstep.

Staring at a blank stretch of canvas on Sunday, Bethany held a paintbrush in one hand, and her other was busy feeling her lips—lips that had touched Dawson's. Gosh, he'd kissed her as if he'd been starving, leaving her dizzy and breathless.

He'd left a little while ago, just before supper. They hadn't kissed again. Explaining that he wanted to wait until the trace faded before he attempted it, their time together had been Disney Channel–approved. But they had cuddled a lot, and that had been just as good as kissing, in her book. Just being next to him, with his arms around her, made her heart race, her nerve endings firing left and right.

Amazingly, the entire time she'd been with him, she really hadn't thought about what he was. Sure, now that he was gone, she couldn't stop thinking about it.

Dawson was an alien.

The whole town was populated with them, apparently. It was all so . . . out of this world.

Bethany smirked.

She placed the brush back on the little table butted up against her dresser and stood. Moving to the window, she brushed the thick curtain aside. Dusk had turned the bare trees gray. Leaning her flushed forehead against the cool windowpane, she closed her eyes.

The room—everything—felt cold without him there. It had to be the heat he threw off. Or it was just him and how he made her feel. Girlie melodrama, but it was true.

Pushing away from the window, she resisted the urge to text or call him. But she was worried for him. Tonight he was telling Daemon that she knew. If he didn't, Daemon would apparently see this trace around her tomorrow. Better to have his brother freak out in the privacy of their home instead of in the middle of English class.

She seriously hoped Daemon didn't kill Dawson. She'd grown fond of the boy.

Trying not to obsess over it, she forced herself out of the room, away from the phone. Downstairs, her mom was in the kitchen. Big surprise there. Dad sat at the table, looking over documents while Phillip turned his mac 'n' cheese into finger food. She steered clear of him and went toward the living room.

Her dad highlighted a portion of the document. "Look who finally came out of her room to join the living."

Bethany made a face. "Ha. Ha."

At the stove, her mom turned around, a baking sheet full of cookies in hand. "Honey, can you check on your uncle and see if he wants something to eat or drink?"

"Sure." She kept walking into the living room.

Uncle Will was sitting on the couch stiffly, looking exhausted. The days leading up to his treatment were always the worst. From what Bethany gathered, the steroids given along with his medicine wore off fast.

"I heard your mother," he said before she could utter a word. His voice was weak and raspy. "If I'm thirsty, I know where the fridge is."

Bethany focused on the TV. One of the Godfather movies was on. "I can get you—"

"I'm fine." He waved his hand. It looked paper-thin and white. "Sit down. I never really get to talk to you."

Chatting with her uncle was the last thing she wanted to do, and she felt terrible for that. But she never knew what to say. Uncle Will liked to pretend he wasn't knocking on death's door, and Bethany sucked at making small talk. Avoiding his sickness was like ignoring a giant ape climbing the walls and throwing bananas.

She sat in the recliner, tucking her legs under her as she frantically searched for something to say. Luckily, Uncle Will started off the conversation.

"So, how long have you been seeing that boy?"

Her mouth dropped open. Okay, so maybe she wasn't that lucky. After Dawson had left, her parents had interrogated her about him. Again. "We're . . . just friends."

"Is that so? I haven't . . ." His words ended in a body-racking cough. Impossible as it seemed, he was even whiter. When the episode ended, he closed his eyes and cleared his throat. "I haven't really seen him with any other girls. His . . . his family sticks together."

Oh, boy, Uncle Will had *no* idea. "Yeah, they seem really close."

"Good kids, I guess. Never really get in trouble." He fiddled with the patchwork quilt draped over his legs. Their outline was thin. "Can't tell them apart, though. Which one was here?"

It was funny to her—how no one could tell Dawson and Daemon apart. "It was Dawson."

He nodded. "Ah, Dawson . . . good choice."

She frowned. "Do you know him?"

He shook his head. "Not really, but he seems the friendlier of the two . . . whenever I've seen them in town. Have you been to his house? Met his parents?"

Her frown deepened as she stared at the screen. Of course, her uncle was pulling the protective role, but it made her uncomfortable to be questioned about Dawson. An immediate, almost irrational urge to protect him and their secret rushed to the surface.

"They work a lot out of town, but I hear them on the phone sometimes."

"Hmm." Will picked up the remote, signaling the end of the conversation. Thank God.

Blessed silence ensued, and when she couldn't sit there any longer, she excused herself and went back upstairs.

And, of course, went straight to her phone.

She wasn't the praying type, and praying that one brother didn't murder the other seemed wrong on a lot of levels, but she may have said a teeny prayer.

Dawson felt like he was preparing to go in front of a firing squad. And he kind of was.

He backed away from the farmhouse, shoving his hands into his pockets. Unbeknownst to Bethany, he'd walked back after his conversation with Dee. A light flipped on in Bethany's bedroom. He wanted to wait to see if he caught a glimpse of her, but that turned him from just keeping an eye on her into a complete stalker.

Bethany was safe in her house right now. There were no Arum lurking in the shadows, and the glow was so faint that they may not even sense it. So there was no reason for him to camp outside her house.

And he needed to go home and talk to Daemon.

Turning around, he moved deeper into the forest, and when he was sure no one could see his light, he switched into his true form and took off, dreading what was about to go down.

Two minutes later, he was walking up to his driveway, letting his light fade until he looked like any other human. Dragging his feet, he opened the front door.

The foyer was dark, and as he stopped, he frowned. Music

thumped through the house. The lyrics *Whoomp, there it is!* blasted from the speakers. He knew before he entered the living room that Daemon was listening to one of those TV channels that played nothing but music.

Sprawled across the couch, with his arms behind his head, Daemon moved his bare feet in perfect sync with the song.

Dawson's brows arched up. "'Whoomp There It Is'?"

"What?" He tilted his head toward Dawson, grinning. "I like the song."

"You have such questionable musical taste."

"Don't hate." He sat up in one fluid motion, dropping his feet onto the floor. "Where have you been all day?"

"Where's Dee?" he asked instead of answering the question.

Daemon waved his hand, and the channels flipped rapidly. "In her bedroom."

"Oh." The likelihood of Daemon killing him with their sister home was slim. Good news.

"Yeah."

Sighing, he sat on the arm of the chair. "I need to tell you something, but you have to promise me that you won't flip out."

Daemon slowly turned his head to him, eyes narrowing. The TV stopped on a golden oldies station. "Chantilly Lace" started playing. "Whenever anyone starts a conversation off like that, I'm pretty sure I am going to flip out."

Ah, good point. "It has to do with Beth."

His brother's face went blank.

"I went to see her at her house," he continued. "And something happened."

There was still no response from his brother. A quiet

Daemon was a Daemon about to explode. "I don't know how it happened or why, but it did. We were kissing . . . and I lost hold on my human form."

Daemon sucked in a sharp breath and started to stand, but stopped. *"Jesus . . ."*

"It left a faint trace on her." And here came the bad part. "And she knows the truth."

Like a switch being thrown, Daemon was up and in his face in a split second. "Are you serious?"

Dawson met his brother's hard stare. "I don't think I'd joke about something like this."

"And I didn't think you'd be so damn careless, Dawson!" Daemon flickered out and reappeared on the other side of the room, his spine rigid and shoulders tense. "Dammit!"

"I didn't mean for it to happen." Dawson took total owner-ship for his mistake, but there was always something about Daemon that made him feel like a kid standing before an angry parent. "Lighting her up with a trace was the last thing I wanted to do, but it wasn't like I couldn't tell her afterward. She completely understands that no one can know. She won't say—"

"And you believe her?"

"Yes. I do."

Daemon's eyes flared. "And just because you believe her, the rest of us are supposed to be okay with this?"

"I know it's a lot to ask, but Bethany would never tell anyone."

Daemon barked out a cold laugh. "God, you're stupid, bro, really stupid."

A red-hot wave traveled up his spine. "I'm not stupid."

"I beg to differ," his brother growled.

Dawson's hands opened and closed at his sides. "I get

that you're disappointed with me marking Bethany, and her knowing the truth is a gross atrocity to you, but it wasn't like I meant to do this."

"I know you didn't mean to, but that doesn't change the fact that it did happen." Daemon leaned against the wall, tilting his chin up. Tension radiated from him, and Dawson knew that he was trying to come up with a way to fix this. That's what Daemon did. He fixed things.

Daemon made a low sound in the back of his throat. "So, you kissed her and this happened?"

"Yeah, awkward, I know."

One side of his lips twitched. "And the trace is faint?" When Dawson assured him, Daemon lowered his chin. "Okay. You need to stay away from her."

"What?"

"Maybe you didn't understand the English I was just speaking." Daemon's eyes flared with anger. "You need to stay away from her."

That was the smartest thing to do—what he *should* do. Leave Bethany alone. But a sour taste filled his mouth. Imagining himself never talking to her again or touching her made his skin feel like it was too tight.

"What if I can't?" he asked, looking away when Daemon scowled.

His brother swore. "Are you kidding me? It's not hard. You. Stay. Away. From. Her."

As if it were that easy. Daemon didn't get it. "But she's glowing right now. Nothing serious, but there's an Arum around, and she's not safe."

"You probably should have thought about that before you Lite-Brited her ass."

Dawson swung toward his brother, eyes narrowing. Anger

caused his body heat to rocket. "So? Is that it? You just don't care if she gets hurt?"

"I care if *you* get hurt." Daemon took a step forward, hands balling into fists. "I care if *Dee* get hurts. This girl, as ignorant as this sounds, means nothing to me."

Dawson looked his brother over, taking in the sharp eyes and features identical to his own. Funny how at times Daemon appeared like a perfect stranger to him. "You sound just as bad as Andrew."

"Whatever, man." Daemon stalked across the room, grabbing a throw pillow. "I'm not human-hating here. I'm stating a fact." He fluffed the pillow before tossing it against the back cushion. "Obviously, you got a thing for her. Something more than what you've felt before."

Well, no doubt. He'd never lost his form around a human girl before. And when he thought of Beth, yeah, he'd never felt this way.

"And because of that, you need to stay away from her," Daemon said, as if his word was law. He stopped in front of Dawson, folding his arms. "I'll go to Matthew and explain what's happened."

Dawson's back straightened. "No."

Daemon drew in a sharp breath. "Matthew needs to know what you've done."

"If you go to Matthew, he will go to the DOD, and they will take Bethany away." When Daemon opened his mouth, Dawson stepped forward. "And don't you dare say you don't care."

"You ask too much!" Daemon exploded. "I have to warn the others just in case your girlfriend decides to go *National Enquirer* on us."

"She won't." Dee's quiet voice intruded from the top of the

stairs. The brothers turned to her. "If Dawson believes that Bethany will remain quiet, then I believe him."

"You're not helping here," Daemon snapped.

She ignored him. "We still have to tell the others, Dawson, because they have a right to be prepared. They should know, especially when they see her trace, but Daemon can convince Matthew not to go to the DOD or the Elders."

"This isn't Daemon's problem," he argued. "It's mine. I should be—"

"If it involves you, it's my problem." Impatience etched into Daemon's features.

Shame rose inside Dawson, like an ugly wisp of smoke. "I am not a child, dammit. You are only older by a few minutes! That doesn't give you—"

"I know." Daemon rubbed his brow as if his head ached. "I don't mean to treat you like a kid, but dammit, Dawson, you know what you have to do here."

Dee appeared between them, her hands on her hips as she twisted toward Daemon. "You have to trust Dawson on this."

The look on Daemon's face said he'd rather stick his head in a meat grinder. "This is insane."

Daemon stepped back, putting the heels of his hands on his forehead. "Okay. I get your . . . need to make sure she is safe while she has the trace, and yeah, maybe she won't say crap, but afterward, you cannot run the risk of something like this happening again."

"I can control myself," Dawson said.

"Oh, what the fuc—"

"Don't ask me to give her up before I even really get to know her." Once the words left his mouth, his will was forged with cement and a bunker of nuclear bombs. "Because you're not going to like my response."

Daemon blinked as if he were stunned. And it struck Dawson then, that even though he did his own thing most of the time, he never really stood up to his brother. Even Dee looked surprised.

"You can't mean that," Daemon said, voice tight.

"I do."

"Oh, for the love of baby humans everywhere, you're an idiot." Daemon shot across the room, going toe-to-toe with him. "So, you 'get to know her' and you fall in *love*." He spat the last word out as if he'd swallowed nails. "Then what? You're going to try to stay with her? Get married? Have the little house with a white picket fence plus the two-point-five kids?"

God, he hadn't thought that far ahead. "Maybe. Maybe not."

"Yeah, let me know how that works out with the DOD."

There was a good chance that Dawson was going to crack the banister. "It's not impossible. Nothing is."

Again, shock shot across Daemon's face, and then his expression hardened. "You risk being an outcast! Worse yet, you risk your sister if this happens again."

"Daemon," Dee protested, eyes glittering with unshed tears. "Don't put that on him."

Anger turned Daemon's skin dark. His eyes started to glow. "No. He needs to understand what he's done. Bethany could lead an Arum right here. And God knows what the DOD will do if they find out she knows. So tell me, is Bethany worth that?"

Dawson hated what he was about to say next, and man, it made him a selfish piece of crap, but it was the truth. "Yes, she's worth it."

13

When Bethany entered English class on Monday, she was one step away from full-on girl freak-out mode, especially when her eyes went straight to the desk behind her and latched onto Dawson.

Last night, he'd called and told her he'd explained everything to Daemon. Though he'd claimed everything went fine, the strain in his voice said otherwise.

Taking her seat, she dropped her bag onto the floor and dared a look at him. "Hey."

He nodded in return, his gaze moving all around her. "Everything is going to be okay."

And that made her more nervous. As it turned out, she had good reason. When Daemon stalked into the classroom, the look on his face promised all kinds of bad things. Bethany shrank back as her eyes met Daemon's. It felt like being smacked by an icy wind.

Dawson leaned forward, wrapping his fingers around her arm. "Ignore him," he whispered. "He's fine."

If "fine" were sporting a serial-killer glare, then she'd hate to see what "not fine" was. She dared another quick look over Dawson's shoulder.

Daemon's lips slipped into a one-sided smile that lacked humor or affection.

Swallowing against the sudden tightening in her throat, she spoke lowly. "Okay. He's scaring me."

Dawson rubbed her arm. "All bark, no bite."

"That's your opinion," Daemon replied.

Bethany stiffened as her eyes widened. The bell rang and she swung toward the front of the class. Oh, this was going to be a long period. The back of her neck burned from the glare Dawson couldn't block.

She felt Dawson's fingers on her back, and she relaxed. Class discussion centered on the themes in *Pride and Prejudice*. Love was the main topic.

"What can you learn about love from *Pride and Prejudice*?" Mr. Patterson asked, sitting on the edge of the desk. "Lesa?"

"Besides the fact courtships took forever back in the day?" Tossing thick curls off her shoulders, she shrugged. "I guess love is only possible if it's not influenced by society."

"But Charlotte married for money," Kimmy reasoned, as if that were something to be proud of.

"Yeah, but Mr. Collins was an idiot," Lesa said.

"A *rich* idiot," someone else said.

Lesa rolled her eyes. "But that's not love—marrying someone for money."

"All good points," Mr. Patterson said, smiling. "Do you think Austen was being a realist or cynical in nature when it came to the theme of love?"

And then Daemon's deep, smooth voice said, "I think she

was pointing out that sometimes making decisions based on the heart is stupid."

Bethany closed her eyes.

"Or she is showing that making decisions based on anything else ends badly," Dawson replied, voice even. "That true love can conquer anything."

Her heart sped up as she glanced over her shoulder, meeting Dawson's gaze. He smiled, and she turned to mush.

"True love?" Daemon scoffed. "The entire concept of true love is stupid."

The class erupted in a debate that went way off topic, but Bethany and Dawson were still staring at each other. True love? Was that what this was? Before meeting Dawson, she would've been on board with Daemon's thinking. Now she believed in the gooey stuff.

Dawson's eyes deepened, turning a mosaic of greens.

Oh, yeah, bring on the gooey stuff.

When class ended, Dawson waited for her to gather up her stuff and then offered his hand. "Ready?"

Aware of all the eyes on them, she nodded.

Daemon stomped past them, bumping into his brother's shoulder. "You make my head hurt," he said, scowling.

"And you make me all warm and fuzzy inside," Dawson replied, threading his fingers through hers.

His twin glanced at Beth. "Be very careful, little girl." And then he was out the door.

Beth's mouth dropped open. "Whoa."

"Believe it or not, that's a toned-down version of Daemon." He led her through the door. Out in the hallway, he squeezed her hand as he whispered, "We have to tell the rest . . . the rest of us who live outside the, well, you know."

Fear tripped up her heart. "Are they going to be okay with it?"

"Daemon will make sure they are."

"Really?" she asked, shaking her head. "He didn't look very supportive."

He reassured her, but she wasn't buying it.

As they neared the stairwell, one of the blond twins came out of the double doors and looked at them. Evil alien twin or good twin? His golden-colored skin paled, and as he continued staring at them, he tripped over his own feet.

"Did he, uh, see my trace?" she whispered.

Dawson nodded. "You may get some . . . odd looks throughout the day. Just pretend like you have no clue why."

Get some odd looks? Dawson hadn't been kidding. A teacher in the hall during class change gaped at her. One of the administrative support ladies gasped. And during gym, the coach looked like he was a second away from a stroke.

She was surrounded by aliens.

Or she was becoming paranoid, because when Carissa waved at her with the paddle, she was half afraid the girl was going to chuck it at her head.

A ping-pong ball whizzed past her. Kimmy turned around. "I'm not getting it."

"Of course not," Bethany muttered.

While rooting around for her MIA ball, she heard the sounds of hushed whispering. Looking up, she squinted through the tiny cracks in the bleachers. She made out two forms—Dawson and the asshole Andrew.

"What the hell are you thinking?" Andrew demanded, leaning into Dawson's face.

"It's none of your business."

Andrew laughed harshly. "Oh, yeah, are you really going to go there? Explain to me how this doesn't have something to do with me or the rest of us."

"I don't owe you an explanation."

Andrew looked dumbfounded. "You need to stay away from that human. She's not good for you, for any of us."

Resisting the urge to bum-rush Andrew and defend herself, she backed away from the bleachers. Wait. Screw this. Obviously all the little Luxen running around knew about her. She wasn't going to let Dawson deal with this by himself.

A ping-pong ball smacked off the back of her head before she took another step forward. Whipping around, she rubbed her skull. "Ouch!"

Kimmy cocked her head to the side. "I've been calling your name for the last two minutes. God. Did you zone out or are you just that much of an idiot?"

A red-hot feeling slipped through her veins, a combination of the overheard conversation and Kimmy's pure bitchiness. She picked up the ball and launched it back. The little round piece of plastic was like a heat-seeking tomahawk, finding Kimmy's cheek. A very satisfying *thud* later, Bethany stalked past a twitching Kimmy.

"I can't believe you threw that at my—"

"My paddle is next," Bethany warned, flipping the paddle in her hand.

Carissa giggled from her partnerless table. "That was hilarious."

Kimmy turned on the girl, about to pull a Linda Blair, no doubt. "Are you laughing at me?"

"Um." Carissa pushed up her glasses. "I think so."

"Oh, you just—"

Coach Anderson decided to interrupt then. "All right, ladies, eyes on the table—on the game."

Beth squeezed the paddle and took a deep breath. Coach must've realized then that Carissa was all alone and headed toward her just as Dawson and Andrew reappeared, looking like they were two seconds from throwing down in the middle of the gym.

"Unless there's a table behind those bleachers, I'm curious as to what you two were doing back there," Coach said. "Get back to your assigned tables now."

Kimmy smirked.

Dawson went to his side of the table, picking up his paddle. "You ready?" he asked Carissa.

She nodded, reaching for the ball, but Andrew's hand swiped across the table, snatching it up. "Here," he said, smiling. "Let me give it to you."

Bethany had a real bad feeling about this.

A slow, cold smile crept across Dawson's face, and she suddenly saw his twin in that expression. It was eerie. "Yeah, you do that."

Andrew cocked back his arm so fast, it was a blur to Beth. He let loose, and that little ball had to have broken the sound barrier. Good God, it zinged across the table like a bullet.

Without taking his eyes off the blond, Dawson snapped up his hand and caught the ball. There was a loud *thud* that made Bethany wince, but he didn't flinch. "Thanks, buddy."

"Christ on a crutch," Carissa murmured.

Dawson grinned as he raised his arms and folded his hands behind his back. The shirt he wore rode up, exposing a flash of taut stomach muscles. Wow. No doubt he had a six-pack in kindergarten. He seemed oblivious to the fact that all three girls were staring at him.

To say the rest of the class was awkward was a massive understatement. After changing, she punched open the door and saw Dawson waiting for her.

His brows knitted. "You doing okay over there?"

"I think I should be asking you that question."

He took her hand, pulling her to him. Bethany pressed her cheek against his chest. "It hasn't been bad. I've gotten to see you."

She smiled and lifted her chin. Their gazes locked. Heat flooded through her. "You always say the right things. A really good skill to have."

His nose brushed along hers. "Only with you."

A knot formed in her throat at the same moment a whole truckload of butterflies took flight in her stomach. "See. There you go again."

"Hmm," he murmured, wrapping his arm around her waist. Never before had she been big on PDA in the halls. Usually she rolled her eyes and made some kind of internal snarky comment whenever she saw it, but she was discovering that she liked being that girl with Dawson.

"Can I come over after school?" he asked.

"I was hoping you'd want to."

"I'll stop by after supper, okay?" He kissed her cheek and pulled back. Taking her hand, he walked her out to the parking lot. At her car, he lifted her hand and pressed his lips against her palm. "I have a feeling there's going to be a meeting of the minds when I get home, so I might be a little late."

She winced. "I wish I could be there with you. It's not right that you have to defend yourself and me all alone."

Tenderness filled his brilliant green gaze. "I've got it covered."

"But—"

Dawson kissed her palm again, and the sweet gesture simply floored her. "Don't worry about them. I don't want you to worry at all." He let go of her hand and started backing up. "I'll be over as soon as I can."

"I'll be waiting."

14

Intervention Round Two went as expected.

In other words, it consisted of everyone taking turns bitching him out and sometimes more than one at a time. Dee and Adam were the only ones who didn't take part. Sitting side by side on the couch, they had identical somber expressions.

Matthew wanted to go to the DOD, like they were supposed to in cases of exposure, but Daemon and Dawson managed to convince him that the risk wasn't high. After an hour of straight arguing, he relented reluctantly.

"This is so risky," Matthew said, pacing the living room. "If she tells a single—"

"She won't tell anyone. I swear to you."

Ash shook her head. "How can you be so sure?"

"Look. This is a done deal," Daemon said, cutting her off. "We're not going to the DOD or to the Elders. It's over."

"This isn't moveon.org, Daemon," she snapped back. "This affects all of us. And with her glowing—"

"I will protect her. I will also make sure no Arum gets close enough to even see her." Dawson crossed his arms.

Ash gaped. "This is going to blow up in your face—in all of

our faces. There's a reason why humans don't know about us. They are fickle and insane!"

Even Dee's eyebrows rose on that. Ash was pretty damn nuts when she wanted to be.

Then Ash twisted toward Daemon, her cheeks flushed. "I can't believe you're allowing him to do this. Next thing we know, *you'll* be dating a human."

Daemon busted out laughing. "Yeah, not going to happen."

The bitchfest went on for another hour before the Thompsons left. On the way out, Adam pulled Dawson aside while his siblings stewed in the car.

"Look, I don't care if you're in love with the girl—"

"I'm not—"

"Don't even say you're not in love," Adam said, glancing at the empty house next door. "I don't care if you do or don't. It's really not the point, but you have got to be careful."

Dawson folded his arms. "I am being careful."

"Dude, this isn't careful. *Everyone* is pissed. This is going to affect Bethany." He took a breath. "I'll try talking some sense into those two, but your problems aren't just the Arum or the DOD, if you get my drift."

Aw man, the kind of rage that shot up his spine was enough to rain down some wrath. "If they do *anything*, I will—"

"I know, but you have to expect this. Even with Daemon and Matthew backing your...lifestyle, it's not going to be easy."

Now he was starting to lose his patience. His "lifestyle" was him wanting to be with the person he cared about. As if that was a bad choice or something. "Adam—"

"You're my friend." Adam clamped his hand on Dawson's shoulder, meeting his eyes. "I got your back, but you need to be real sure about the road you're traveling down."

Dawson exhaled roughly. "I . . . don't know— Shit. I don't know what you want me to say." Mainly because he didn't even know how to begin to put what he felt for Bethany into words. Maybe Adam had a point. Maybe it was the big *L*.

A keen sense of understanding marred with sadness crept across Adam's face. "Look, what kind of future do you have with her? Is she worth pissing off and alienating everyone?"

"I think the answer to that is pretty obvious."

"True," he said, dropping his hand. "But this is huge. Know of any Luxen and human who have made it work? Lived to talk about it?"

Yeah, now entering Downersville, population one.

Adam gave a little smile. "I don't envy you, because I really don't think we can help how we feel. God knows I'm well familiar with that." He winced, and Dawson wondered if he were talking about Dee. "I just worry, because I don't think Dee and Daemon could deal if something bad happened. And I don't think you could if something happened to Bethany."

Dawson watched his friend leave. Adam had given him a lot of food for thought. Bad, cheap, leftover yuck food for thought.

But mostly, he was consumed by how he felt for Bethany. Because he was risking everything and everyone, and that was selfish. God, there was only one thing that could cause anyone to be that self-centered.

It didn't take Bethany long to realize that there weren't many Team Dawson-and-Bethany fans. Over the next couple of days, Daemon spent the bulk of English class glaring at his brother and ignoring her, even when she tried to be civil.

It also became easy for her to tell Andrew and Adam apart.

The nice one was distant whenever they crossed paths or when he chatted with Dawson, but he smiled at her. The other, evil alien twin scared the living bejeebus out of her. Daemon's glares had nothing on Andrew's. He was someone she didn't want to cross paths with alone. Luckily, Dawson stuck close to her side and by Friday, good news. Her trace had faded. Six days was all it took.

She and Dawson spent the weekend together, holed up in her bedroom. Door kept open, of course. Mom popped her head in, but each time, she brought cookies. There was a good chance that Dawson was falling in love with her mom.

The boy could eat.

He explained once, after his third Big Mac, that it had to do with their metabolism and the amount of energy they used. Trying not to be jealous, Bethany had poked at her cheese-burger, which she knew would go straight to her butt.

The boy could also cuddle.

When they felt relatively sure that her mom wouldn't bust up in her bedroom or the living room, Dawson would hold her close, as if he needed to be touching some part of her. At times, his whole body vibrated.

She didn't get to see him in his true form again, because of the trace it would leave behind, but with each passing day, Dawson loosened up around her. His new favorite pastime seemed to be popping out and appearing right in front of her, giving her a minor stroke each time he did it. He also moved a lot of things without touching them. These little actions didn't throw off a lot of energy, but they were really neat to see.

Things were going well. And then she met Ash, formally, on Monday.

She'd seen the blonde in the halls every once in a while.

Hell, it wasn't like you could miss her. Like Dee, she was gorgeous, almost too beautiful to be walking the halls of high school. Ash seemed better fit for the catwalks of Milan.

Bethany was heading out of chem class, surprised when the lithe blonde spun around, bright sapphire eyes locking on hers. "Bethany?"

She nodded as she sidestepped a group of students.

Ash's gaze slipped from hers, drifting over her plain cardigan and worn jeans. Ash's finely groomed brows knitted as if she were looking for something Bethany clearly didn't have. "I must admit. I am a bit confused."

So was Bethany. "Care to explain?"

Ash's blue eyes snapped to hers. "I'm not sure what Dawson sees in you."

Whoa. Way to be blunt. Bethany had to force her jaw closed. "Excuse me?"

Ash smiled tightly and waited until another group of kids shuffled past them. "I don't get what he sees in you, but I think you heard and understood me the first time around." Then her voice lowered. "He can do better. And he will. Eventually he'll grow tired of the greener grass and move on."

Bethany was almost too stunned to respond. "Sorry you feel that way, but—"

"What do you have to offer him other than risks?" Ash stepped closer, and Bethany had to fight the urge to back up. "You guys aren't going to last. One way or another. So why don't you do both yourself and Dawson a favor, and leave him alone."

Bethany felt like a shaken soda can about to be popped open. Yeah, she knew she didn't hold a candle to a girl like Ash, but geez, she wasn't yesterday's leftover fast food, either. But before she could let loose a doozy of an *eff off*, the taller girl pivoted gracefully and stalked away, moving among the other students effortlessly.

Bethany stood there, mouth agape. That did not happen. She got the whole unhappy-about-her-knowing-their-truth part, but that had seemed personal. Was she an ex-girlfriend of Dawson's? God, wouldn't that be her luck? She was competing against the memory of an alien Victoria's Secret model.

Dawson was at the far end of the corridor. He turned, as if sensing her. "Hey . . ." The smile faded from his handsome face. "What's up?"

She stopped beside him, glancing around. "So I just had a tiny chitchat with Ash."

And there went the rest of the smile. "Oh, God, what did she say?"

"Did you guys date or something?" The minute those words left her mouth, she regretted them.

"What? Oh, hell no."

Bethany folded her arms. "Really?"

To her surprise, he laughed and cupped her elbow, guiding her toward the dirtied window overlooking the back parking lot. "She and my brother are dating—well, not right now, but on and off for as long as I can remember."

Annoyed by the fact that she was relieved to hear it, she frowned. "What? Since they were ten or something?"

Dawson shrugged. "What did she say to you?"

Bethany gave him the quick-and-dirty version. By the time she finished, Dawson looked like he wanted to punch something. "Do they really see me as that big of a threat?" she asked.

His jaw ticked. "Yeah, they do." He kept his voice low. "See, they don't know you. And they don't know any humans outside the DOD who are aware of them. This is new for them, but inexcusable."

Part of her was glad he was so pissed, but she didn't want to come between them any more than she already had. Forcing a smile, she stretched up on the tips of her toes and kissed the corner of his lip.

A shudder rolled through his entire body.

Bethany grinned, loving the effect she had on him. Sure, he was an alien with pretty much unlimited power, but she made him tremble. Score one for the pitiful human!

"You know, I have an idea," she said.

"You do?" He snaked an arm around her waist as his head dipped, running his jaw up the side of her neck. For a moment she totally forgot what she was saying. "Bethany?"

"Oh." She flushed, pulling back. Students were practically gawking at them. "I was thinking maybe things would be easier if we didn't act like it was a big deal. If we didn't try to . . . stay away from them. Maybe if they got to know me . . ."

Bethany trailed off because he was staring at her like she'd just kicked a baby into the street. "Okay. Never mind."

"No." He blinked and then grinned. "It's a great idea. I should've come up with that."

She beamed. "Yay me."

He dropped his arm over her shoulder. "Well, let's get this over with, then."

Wait—what? She slowed her footsteps. "Huh?"

"How about we make an appearance at lunch? Most of them share your period."

The great idea sounded good in theory, but now that they were putting it to the test, she sort of wished she'd kept her mouth shut. But she pulled her big-girl panties on and prepared for probably one of the most awkward lunch periods of her life.

PHS's cafeteria was like every high school cafeteria. White

square tables crammed into a room that smelled like Pine-Sol and burned food. The loud hum of conversation was actually kind of comforting to her. Normal. The line for food moved quickly. Dawson stacked his plate with what may've been meatloaf, and she grabbed a bottle of water. She always packed her lunch—peanut butter and jelly. Her day wouldn't be complete without it.

Bethany didn't need to know where his friends sat. She felt their stares and wondered if that was a super-alien power—drilling holes through bodies with just the power of their eyes.

Beside her, Dawson was a picture of ease. The easy half grin was plastered across his striking face, and he seemed oblivious to the stares he was getting as they headed down the middle of the cafeteria.

Dee and Daemon were at the table, sitting beside who she suspected was Andrew by the open-mouthed stare he was giving them. She assumed the rest of the students sitting at the table were human, because Dawson had said that most of the Luxen were younger or older.

"Hey, guys, mind if we join you today?" Dawson sat across from his brother before anyone could answer, tugging Bethany into the seat beside Dee. "Thanks."

Bethany put her paper bag on the table, holding her breath.

"Bold move," Daemon murmured, lips twisted into a smirk.

Dawson shrugged. "Nah, we just missed you guys."

Daemon picked up a fork, and Bethany seriously hoped it wasn't going to turn into a weapon. "I'm sure you did." His familiar-yet-foreign green eyes slid to her. "How are you doing, Bethany?"

"I'm doing well." She pulled out her sandwich, hating the fact that she could feel her cheeks blazing. "You?"

"Great." He stabbed the meatloaf. "Don't see you in here

often. Are you skipping along with my *responsible* brother?"

"I usually eat in the art room." She paused, pulling her sandwich into chunks. An odd habit of hers that Dawson made fun of.

"In the art room?" Dee questioned.

She nodded, lifting her gaze. There wasn't an outright look of scorn or anything on the beautiful girl's face. Mostly curiosity. "I paint. So I'll eat in there and work on projects."

"She's really good," Dawson threw in. His lunch was half devoured. "My girl has skills."

Andrew leaned forward and said in a low voice, "*Your* girl is going to turn into one huge, mother—"

"Finish that sentence and I will stab you in the eye with the spork Bethany's about to pull out of her bag for her apple sauce." He smiled gamely. "And she'd be very upset if I got her spork all messed up. She's rather fond of the thing."

Yeah, she would be upset over that . . . for many reasons.

Andrew sat back, his jaw tightening. On the other side, Daemon did the strangest thing. He laughed—really loudly. It was a nice sound, deeper than Dawson's.

"A spork," Dee said, grabbing her bag. "What is a spork?"

Bethany's mouth dropped open. "You've never seen one?"

"Dee doesn't get out much," Dawson replied, grinning.

"Shut up." Dee pulled out the fork-and-spoon-in-one and smiled. "I've never seen one of these! Ha. This is so handy." She looked over at Daemon, eyes dancing. "We could get rid of more than half of our silverware and get like ten of these and we'd be set for life."

Daemon shook his head, but the look on his face was one of utter fondness. And Bethany got it then. That no matter how much the three of them were pissed off with one another, there was a deep, loving bond among them. Seeing that caused her to relax. As much as Daemon was upset with Dawson or Dee was worried, they would always stick together. It made her want to run home, hug Phillip, and be a better sister.

Lunch wasn't that bad afterward. The only downside was Andrew, but he left after a while, and she was so grateful that Ash was a no-show. They left with a few minutes before class to spare.

Outside of the cafeteria, Bethany grinned up at Dawson, motivated by the experience. "That wasn't too bad, was it?"

The smile he wore warmed her. "Yeah, it was okay. I think we should do it again."

She laughed, and then he reached over and took her hand. He pulled her into an empty classroom full of computers. Without saying a word, he slipped the strap of her bag off her shoulder and placed it on the floor. Bethany shivered, unsure if it was because of the frigid air circulating or the determined look on his face.

She took a step back, wetting her lower lip nervously. His green eyes flared. "What . . . are you doing?"

"I'm going to kiss you again."

Anticipation rose quickly, leaving her dizzy. "Uh, do you think this is a great place to test that out again?"

"I don't know, but I can't wait any longer." He looked determined as he took a step toward her. So determined that she inched back and kept going until she was against the wall.

Reaching out slowly with both hands, he cupped her cheeks and tilted her chin up. On their own accord, her lashes fluttered closed. Like the first time they'd kissed, his lips were soft as a breath. There was a pause, as if he were waiting for something to happen, and then he kissed her more deeply.

Oh . . . oh, God, she melted into that kiss, into him, and her chest expanded, filled with air until she felt like she'd float right up to the ceiling. Sliding her arms around his neck, her fingers got tangled in the soft waves at the nape of his neck. His hands, well, they were on the move, too, slipping down her waist, over her hip to her thigh. Dawson made a sound in the back of his throat, a growl-like noise that sent her blood pressure into heart-attack territory. And there was this heat blowing off, strong enough to melt ice cream. It left her in a heady, pleasant fog as his hand moved back to gripping her hip.

Dawson pulled back slightly and his lips spread into a lazy grin against hers. "That . . . that was good. Great. Perfect."

"Yeah," she admitted, breathless. "All of those things and more."

His thumbs moved over her cheeks, his hands strong yet tender as he held her right there, dipping his head to hers again. He kissed her deeply, holding her against him. When they broke apart the second time, his eyes were luminous and full of an emotion that sent her heart thundering against her ribs. Because she was sure she saw in his eyes what she felt.

Love.

15

After school on Tuesday, Dawson headed home instead of going straight to Bethany's house, where he wanted to be. Bethany had promised to get the groceries after dinner as a part of her chores that week, so she'd be pretty busy that evening.

It was that time of the month.

Once a month, he had to check in with the DOD. Every Luxen was required, even more so since he lived outside the colony. And it could be worse. Being summoned by the Elders usually consisted of one, if not both, of the brothers getting their rears chewed out for some reason or another, made to feel guilty for "being like a human," and getting pestered about when they'd mate. In other words, would Daemon marry Ash at eighteen and would Dawson find another female Luxen of the same age?

The DOD would just ask the same old questions.

Yeah, fun would be had by all. He so didn't need to do this right now.

A black Ford Expedition was already parked in front of his house when he pulled into the driveway. Counting the ways this was going to suck, he climbed out of his Jetta and headed inside.

The suits—two of them—were in the living room, sitting on the couch. Both were middle-age males and bore the same empty expression. Their postures were stiff, though, probably because Daemon leaned against the wall, glaring at them as if he wished to do something terrible to their bodies.

Dawson recognized one of them—he'd been coming to them since they'd moved to West Virginia—but the other was new.

Dee looked up from where she was perched on the edge of her chair. Relief flickered in her shining eyes. Usually that meant things were not going well between Daemon and the DOD, and Dawson would play peacemaker.

Crossing his arms, Dawson said, "Well, this looks like a happy meeting of the minds."

Daemon's pointed gaze slid toward him. "Sounds about right."

Officer Lane cleared his throat. "How have you been, Dawson?" A wave of revulsion and distrust accompanied his greeting. Lane pretended—barely—to like the Luxen. All of them knew better.

"Good," Dawson said. "You?"

"Officer Vaughn and I are doing great." Lane clapped his hands together, while the other left his hanging by his hips, near the gun Dawson knew they carried. Funny. Like a bullet would be faster than them. "We've been talking to Daemon here, and he's been . . . very helpful." Dawson almost laughed. Not likely, and if Daemon's stance was anything to go by, whatever questions he'd been asked didn't sit well with him. Unease trickled through Dawson's veins. Had they found out about Bethany and her faint trace? That couldn't be the case. The DOD didn't know it could be left on humans, and no one, not even Andrew, would relay that kind of information.

Vaughn glanced at his partner before he spoke. "There has been some unusual activity over the last month or so—an increase in EM fields in this area. Your brother appears to have no knowledge of how this could be happening."

Since the government thought Arum were just psycho Luxen, it wasn't like they could tell them they'd been hunting or fighting. If the DOD ever discovered that the Arum hunted the Luxen for their abilities, then it was game over. Back to New Mexico, back to living in underground housing, treated like freaks and lab rats.

Dawson shrugged. "Well, we've been doing a lot of running in our true forms. Maybe that's it?"

Vaughn's lips twisted. "As far as our records indicate, being in your alien form would not cause such a disruption." The man said *alien* as if he'd swallowed something nasty. "We find that hard to believe, after looking over the last six months of field reports from around here."

The DOD needed a hobby, something other than monitoring them.

Dee crossed her legs. "Officers, my brothers do like their physical activity. Sometimes they get a little out of hand. See, they like to play a Luxen form of football."

"And what would that be?" Lane smiled, because everyone smiled at Dee.

She grinned. "Imagine the football being more of a ball of pure energy. They like to toss that at each other. Maybe that's what's registering."

"Really?" Lane shook his head, eyes widening. "That would be interesting to see."

"You're always welcome to join in," Daemon said with a smirk. "Although I doubt you'd enjoy it."

Vaughn's face flushed. "You have a smart mouth, Daemon."

"Better than a dumb one," Dawson replied. "At least, that's what I like to say."

Daemon chuckled softly. "Well, boys, this has been fun, but if there isn't anything else, you know where the door is."

Used to Daemon, Officer Lane stood, but Vaughn remained seated and said, "Why has your . . . *family* chosen to stay outside the colony?"

"We enjoy taking part in the human world," Dee said cheerfully, quick to answer. God only knew how Daemon would've responded. "You know, being contributing members of society and whatnot. It's the same reason why any Luxen chooses to branch out."

Dawson had trouble keeping his expression straight. For real. The truth was that living in the colony was no better than living in one of the DOD's facilities they used to "prepare" the Luxen for assimilation. If not worse, even.

Vaughn looked doubtful, but Officer Lane managed to get him up and toward the door. Before they left, though, they reminded the three of them they needed to check in by the end of April for mandatory registration. The DOD kept count religiously of how many lived inside and out of the colony.

Dee slumped in her chair as Dawson closed the door. "I hate when they come by," she said, scrunching up her face. "They act as if we've done something wrong."

"That new one really is a fan favorite, isn't he?" Dawson sat on the arm of his sister's chair. "God, what a dick."

"He hasn't been the worst," Daemon said. And God, wasn't that the truth. At least Vaughn tried to hide his animosity.

"Good save, Dee. Football?" He laughed. "Almost makes me want to try that out."

Dawson winced. "Yeah, you talk Andrew into doing that with you. I pass."

"Do you think they'll ever find out about the Arum?" Dee sat up, dropping her elbows on her knees. "Realize that we aren't the same?" Fear roughened her voice.

Dawson leaned down, wrapping his arm around his sister's slender shoulders, and winked. "Nah, they're not as bright as we are."

"It's not ignorance," Daemon said, eyes trained on the window. "They're too prideful to consider they don't know everything there is to know about us. As long as humans believe they're the most intelligent and strongest life-form on this planet, the better it is for us."

Bethany wanted to kick herself for agreeing to do the groceries as a part of her chores. Washing dishes by hand would've been better than searching down every last item on Mom's list, especially the ones she couldn't even pronounce from the organic section.

Pushing the overloaded cart to the mile-long checkout lanes, she wondered how Dawson's meeting went. A trickle of unease slithered through her veins. She hated the idea of the DOD checking in on them like that, the intrusive questions they had to be answering and the unfairness of how they were monitored.

To her, the Luxen weren't any different. And she seriously doubted most humans would be afraid of them. The Luxen were just like them.

Once done with checking out and *bugging* out at how

much the food cost, she wheeled her load to the parking lot.

When she'd first arrived, the lot had been crowded, so she'd gotten stuck in the nosebleed section at the back. Heavy, thick trees crowded over the parking lot, and she kept waiting for a deer to dart out and tackle her as she loaded the groceries.

"Bethany."

She whipped around, and her heart tumbled unsteadily. One of the Thompson twins stood behind her, so close she caught the scent of his citrus aftershave.

Taking a step back, she knocked into the bumper. "I . . . I didn't know you were there."

The twin's expression was blank as he cocked his head. "We can be very quiet when we want."

No shit. Reaching behind her, she pulled the trunk down, still unsure which one stood before her. Usually, she knew by the way they acted. But now . . . she had no idea.

"Are you shopping?" she asked, clenching her car keys. The sky was already darkening, and so close to the woods, very little light got through. She felt cut off.

"Ah, I'm not really shopping."

Her eyes darted around the parking lot. "I really—"

One second he was there, and then he was right in her face, towering over her. In an instant, she knew which one stood before her.

Andrew smiled coldly. "But I do have a list. And you're on it."

No joke, her heart was pounding. Fear coated her mouth, forming a knot in her throat, making it hard for her to breathe. But she refused to shrink away, to run or scream. Inherently, she knew that's what he wanted. To scare her.

His smile tipped higher. "You know, my sister and I

can't understand what Dawson sees in you. You're just a s illy little human." His arm shot out so fast it was a blur, picked up a strand of her hair. "And you're really not even that pretty."

Oh . . . oh, that stung more than it should have. Tears burned her eyes as she fought to keep her voice level. "I guess it's a good thing, then. A relationship between us would never work."

His eyes narrowed. "And why is that?"

"Because I'm allergic to assholes."

Andrew did a cough/laugh as he looked to the side. "You think you're funny. Want to know what's funny?"

"No. Not really." She started to turn, but his hands slammed into the trunk. Metal crunched and gave. She was trapped.

"It's funny that you think anything is going to work or last with you and Dawson." He laughed again, the sound cold and grating. "So what? You know our secret. Congrats. Here's a cookie. But you know what? All it takes is one *anonymous* call in to the DOD and then bye-bye Beth."

She gasped. "You wouldn't . . . ?"

He pushed off the car and stepped back. "Yeah, even I'm not that much of an ass. Dawson pisses me off, but I'd never do that to him. But if we know, then the rest will know eventually, Bethany. And they barely have any bonds with us." He rocked back on his heels. "You guys keep this up, one or both of you is going to end up hurt."

In a blink of an eye, he was gone. Bethany slowly turned around, seeing the empty parking lot. In a daze, she climbed into the car. Her cell phone went off, the screen flashing Dawson's name.

"Hey," she croaked.

"You okay?"

Her immediate instinct was to tell him what had happened, but God knew he'd flip out. So she forced herself to pretend she was calm. "How was the meeting?"

As Dawson gave her a brief rundown, she drove home, her hands shaking the entire way.

It was close to eight when Dawson got off the phone with Bethany. He roamed his bedroom, restless. Something had been off about her. He'd asked to the point of annoyance if she was okay. Each time she said yes, but he sensed something.

Half an hour later, his phone rang. Hoping it was Bethany, he snatched it off his bed, but frowned when he looked at the caller ID. "Adam?"

"Hey, got a sec?"

He sat. "Sure."

There was a pause. "Man, I hate to tell you this, but Andrew came home earlier, and I heard him talking to Ash."

Unease built inside Dawson. "About what?"

"Apparently, he ran into your girl. I think he may have said some crap to her," Adam said, sighing. "I just thought I'd let you know."

Dawson was on his feet without realizing, struggling not to slip into his true form and fry his phone. Again. So angry he could barely speak, he thanked Adam for the heads up and dialed Beth. It took a few tries to get her to 'fess up, and when he did, he saw red.

Andrew had basically threatened her.

Dawson reassured Bethany everything was cool, but when he hung up the phone, he didn't even bother grabbing his car keys.

He was about to go apeshit.

Flipping into his true form, he went out the front door and to the woods, taking the back way to the Thompsons' house. They lived on the other side of Petersburg, which was a whopping dozen or so miles that took him about thirty seconds to cross. He stopped at the paved driveway, an unheard-of luxury for homes this far off the beaten track.

Dawson had always hated the Thompson house. It was out in the middle of nowhere, as big as a goddamned mansion, and had the warmth of a mausoleum.

Adam answered the door, cringing when he saw Dawson's harsh expression. "Uh, this isn't going to be a happy visit, is it?"

"Are your nosy, pain-in-my-ass siblings still home?"

Adam nodded and stepped aside. "They're in the movie room."

Knowing the way, he slid past Adam and stalked through the massive foyer, the dining room no one in his or her right mind used, and into a den. Adam was right behind him, not saying a word.

Dawson waved his hand, opening the door to the theater. Light spilled into the dark room, casting yellowish light between the recliners. They were watching an old episode of *90210*. Lame didn't even do that justice. Andrew turned around, scowling when he saw Dawson. "Unless you've come to apologize for being such an ass to me, I don't want any of what you're selling."

His sister held a nail file over her fingers. "Somehow I doubt that's why he's here, Andy."

"Yeah, you'd be correct on that." Dawson's hands formed fists at his sides. "I want you two to listen, because I swear this will be the last time I say this. I want both of you to leave

Bethany alone. Don't talk to her. Don't approach her. Hell, don't even consider thinking about her."

Andrew raised himself fluidly, his blue eyes starting to glow like diamonds. "Or what?"

The back of Dawson's neck started to burn. Screw the whole telling-him part. He shed his human form in an instant and shot down the narrow aisle, slamming into a still-human Andrew. Over the roar in his ears, he heard Ash's surprised shriek. The force of his impact took them both all the way to the screen, and when they hit, it ripped right over the dickhead's face.

Wrapping his hand around Andrew's throat, he rose off the ground, dragging the struggling boy with him. Andrew had switched forms, but he couldn't break Dawson's hold. Dawson took him all the way to the vaulted ceiling, pinning him there.

Or what? Dawson spoke directly into Andrew's thoughts, driving the point home. *You threaten Bethany again, in any way, and I'll make sure you can't talk again. To anyone. Ever. Do you understand me?*

"Dawson!" Ash yelled from below. "What are you doing? Stop! Do something, Adam!"

Adam's laugh followed. "Someone needed to put Andrew in his place. I always figured it would be Daemon. Who knew."

Energy crackled up Dawson's arm. He was this close to letting it go and knocking Andrew into next week. The flare of his light caused Andrew to shrink away from him. *Do you understand me?*

Andrew hesitated, but then he nodded.

Good, because this isn't happening again. Then he dropped Andrew.

Andrew hit the floor of the theater, flipping into his human form. He lifted his head, shooting Dawson a murderous look, but amazingly, he kept his mouth shut.

Coming back down to the floor, he turned on Ash. *And that includes you. Stay away from her. Better yet, I'd love it if you stayed away from my brother.*

Her mouth dropped open. "Why?"

You wanna know why? He can do so much better than you. Still furious, he struggled to bring back his human form, and when he did, his voice was frigid. "If any of you want to treat humans like they're not good enough for us to be near, then go back to the damn colony. You'll fit in perfectly there." Turning from a stunned Ash to Adam, he took a deep breath. "Sorry, man. You're cool."

Adam shrugged. "Don't worry. We're totally cool."

Dawson nodded and headed toward the den. "I'll see my way out."

The thing was, every Luxen feared Daemon's notorious temper. His brother was like a lit fuse, ready to explode at any minute, but what they didn't know was that it was another thing Dawson shared with Daemon. When push came to shove, and it involved someone he cared about, he could be just as mean.

16

After that, Adam and Ash backed off, way off. And things . . . ah, they were great. School was almost out, and he and Bethany honestly couldn't get enough of each other. Daemon had said he was whipped a few days ago, but Dawson didn't care. Thinking about her brought a smile to his face. And being with her completed him in a way he'd never thought possible. With Bethany, he didn't think of himself as something separate from the thousands of people around him.

He just was . . . himself.

Dee even started hanging out with them the times he'd brought Bethany to their house. Daemon was never there when she was, and he really hadn't warmed up to her yet, but when they joined him for lunch, he kept it cool.

It killed him that Daemon still hadn't accepted their relationship. And he knew it bothered Bethany, too, because she didn't want to be the cause of any of their problems, but it wasn't like they weren't trying. It was on Daemon. He'd come around only when he wanted to.

And right now, he knew where Daemon was. With Ash. They were back together again. As much as that bothered him, he kept his mouth shut. The whole throwing-stones-in-glass-houses stuff sucked.

There was a knock on the front door. Smiling, Dawson swung his legs off the couch and went to answer.

Bethany stood there, hair pulled back in a high ponytail. His gaze drifted over her, and damn, he had more reasons to love warm weather. She was wearing shorts that showed off her legs and a hoodie over her tank top.

She stuck out one foot. "These are the only sneakers I have. You think they'll work?"

Without saying a word, he wrapped his arms around her waist, lifting her off her feet with ease. "You'll look cute up there."

She laughed. "Dawson—"

Lowering her slowly against his chest, he grinned as her cheeks flushed. Her whiskey-colored eyes heated seconds before he kissed her. When he settled her on her feet again, she swayed a little.

"That's the kind of greeting I like," she said, touching her lips.

His eyes followed her movements to those pink lips. There was green paint on her pinkie, and seeing that, his heart expanded. As he wrapped his hand around the one on her mouth, he realized he was absolutely crazy about her. Pulling her into the living room, he kept going until the backs of his legs hit the couch and he sat. Bethany climbed into his lap and wrapped her arms around his neck.

Dawson stopped breathing as he tilted his head back, and she lowered her mouth to his. The kiss was deep and scorching, endless. Not breaking contact, she unzipped her hoodie and he pushed it off her shoulders. Running his fingers up her bare arms, he grinned against her mouth when she shivered.

He could feel the cells in his body striving to change as he slipped his fingers under the hem of her shirt, going up and up until she was making soft little sounds. The rush of sensations firing through him drowned out everything else. When she started moving against him, his hands dropped to her hips, his fingers digging into the denim of her shorts.

Thank God no one was home, because they would've gotten an eyeful.

And that snapped him out of the haze. He clasped her cheeks, his thumb stroking along her jaw. "We . . . we have to stop . . . or I won't be able to."

For a second, it seemed like Bethany didn't get it, and then her face turned cherry red. "Oh."

"Yeah," he murmured, his eyes dropping to her swollen lips. God, she was beautiful to him—perfect.

Bethany shuddered. "We don't have to stop, you know? I'm . . . I'm ready."

He almost lost his hold then. The images her words brought forth tested what self-control he had. Wanting nothing more than to carry her upstairs and show her just how much she got to him, he wanted their first time to be special. Dinner, a movie, maybe some flowers and candles—not doing it on the couch or on his unmade bed in his messy bedroom that had socks and God knows what else strewn across the floor.

"Later," he promised, meaning it.

She snuggled in, resting her cheek on his shoulder. "Soon?"

"Very soon . . ."

Several minutes passed and then she said, ""So . . . back to the shoes. They'll work, right?"

"They're perfect for where I'm taking you." They were going hiking again. Two weekends ago, he'd taken her on the trails, but today, he wanted to show her one of his favorite lookout spots. They were supposed to go last weekend, but it had rained for days, saturating the ground.

Bethany climbed off him. It was time to get this show on the road, because if he didn't, his best intentions were going to fly right out the window. He grabbed two bottles of water from the fridge, and they headed to his car.

They drove about a mile down the road, turning onto a little-known access road to the Seneca Rocks. Park rangers steered clear of this part. Mainly because it led to the colony deep within the forests surrounding the Rocks. And tourists were forbidden. Signs warning against trespassing were everywhere.

Parking about two miles from the entrance, they hoofed it for about forty minutes. Bethany laughed and chattered the whole way. Several times they stopped so she could take pictures of the scenery she wanted to paint later.

When they reached the base of the mountains, Bethany swallowed hard. The slope running up the side to the little outcropping that gave a decent view was for beginners, no gear necessary, so Dawson wasn't worried.

"Are you sure I can climb this without killing myself?" she asked, shielding her eyes with her hand.

"You'll do fine." He bent down, kissing her cheek. "It really isn't that hard, and I won't let anything happen to you. I promise."

She smiled at that and spent the next ten minutes snapping pictures of the glittering rocks. Then they started up the rocky hill bathed in sunlight, moving slowly so that Bethany could get a feel for the terrain. Pebbles and loose dirt streamed down behind them as they made their way up.

"This really isn't bad," she said, stopping and glancing behind her. "Whoa. Okay. Remind me not to look back."

He turned around. Beth's spine was ramrod straight. "You okay?"

She nodded.

Backtracking to her, he slid a little as he placed a hand on her shoulder. Face pale, she gripped his arm. "Are you sure?" he asked, worried.

"Yeah, I just don't think I've ever been this high up before."

Dawson smiled. "We aren't that high up, Bethany."

Her throat worked. "It doesn't feel that way."

Was she afraid of heights? Oh crap, if that were the case, this was a bad idea. "You want to head back down? We can."

"No." She shook her head, giving him a wobbly smile as she pried her fingers off his arm. "I want to do this with you. Just . . . just go slowly, okay?"

Part of him wanted to pick her up and zip her back down to the meadow below, but she insisted and he trusted her to tell him when she'd had enough.

Twenty minutes later, he scrambled up the flat rock and reached down to her. "Give me your hand. I'll pull you up."

Eyes narrowed with determination, she placed her hand in his. Warmth cascaded through his chest in response to her trust. Tugging her up, he held her until she was ready to stand. And when she did, he noticed that her legs shook a little as she turned around.

Bethany clutched the camera hanging around her neck. "It's beautiful."

He rose to his feet, placing his hands on his hips as he took it all in. The sky was that rare, perfect kind of blue. Clouds were fluffy, looking like they were painted in. Tips of ancient elms rose up, concealing the ground below.

"Yeah," he said slowly. "It's amazing. A different world up here."

She glanced over her shoulder at him. "It would be so cool to be able to sit up here and paint."

"We could do that."

Bethany laughed. "I don't think I'd be able to get my stuff up here."

"Ye of little faith," he teased. "I can zip your stuff up here and have it ready in three seconds."

She grinned. "It's so strange. Sometimes I just forget . . . what you are."

Most people wouldn't know how to take that, but he recognized it for what it was. And that was why he . . . why he loved her.

Looking away, he clamped his mouth shut. The words had been in his chest for weeks, maybe months, demanding to be spoken, but any time he tried to force them out of his mouth, he locked up. Bethany hadn't said those words, either, and if she didn't feel the same, he was afraid he'd scare her off.

Out of the corner of his eye, he saw her inch cautiously toward the edge. "Be careful," he said.

"I'm always careful."

Dawson pivoted around and crossed to the other side of the rock. From where he stood, he was almost in perfect alignment with where the colony existed. He sighed, closing his eyes. Neither he nor Daemon had heard from them since the beginning of this year. Soon, he realized, soon he would have to face them, and they'd want to talk about mating. What would he say? There was no way he could even entertain the idea of being with someone else. But he couldn't tell them about Bethany. He wouldn't be able to tell them anything. And that would go over like a—

A wicked sense of dread shot through him, forcing his eyes open. He glanced down at the sandstone rocks below his feet. The crystals embedded deep into the sediment winked. The surface was shiny, still damp from the recent rain. Slick—

A gasp shattered his core, barely audible but as loud as thunder. The scream that came next chilled his entire body.

There hadn't even been a second—time seemed to have stopped, though. His heart pounded in his chest as he whipped around, catching the blurred outline of Beth's flailing arms.

Lead settled in his stomach, but he shot forward, slipping out of his form without thinking about it. He was fast, but all it took was a second—a second for gravity to do its thing. To reach up and suck Bethany down into nothing but space.

But it was worse than just empty air, because then he would've had time to catch her.

He went over the edge blindly, knowing that the side she'd slipped off of had several jagged outcroppings that were bone breaking.

And one, a spike about ten feet long and six feet wide, had stopped her fall about thirty feet down.

17

D awson wasn't thinking.

Two seconds had passed. Two fucking seconds for him to shed his human form and reach her body, which lay at an odd angle—one leg under the other, an arm hanging limply over the side.

Bethany wasn't moving.

Something red pooled under the left side of her head. Not blood—it couldn't be blood. Whatever it was—because it couldn't be what it was—leaked from her ears. The camera was gone, having fallen even farther.

He couldn't think.

A part of his brain, the human side, clicked off. Reaching for Beth, he cradled her against his chest, swallowing her in the whitish-blue light.

Bethany. Bethany. Bethany. Her name was on repeat. He rocked back against the smooth wall, and he screamed and screamed. His entire world shattered. *Open your eyes. Please open your eyes.*

She didn't move.

She wouldn't move. Some part of him recognized that a

human couldn't have survived that fall depending on how they landed, but Beth . . . not his Bethany.

This . . . this couldn't be happening.

His light flared around them, until he could no longer see her pale face but only an outline.

He'd promised he wouldn't let anything happen to her. A second—a goddamn second—he had turned away from her. This was his fault. He shouldn't have brought her up here after so much rain had soaked the ground, coating the bottom of her sneakers. He shouldn't have kept going up the hill when he'd seen how nervous she was, how shaky her legs were.

He should've been able to stop this—to save her. What the hell kind of power did he have if he couldn't have *saved* her?

Dawson screamed again, the sound in his ears that of sorrow and rage. But Bethany couldn't hear it. No one could hear it. Something wet was on his cheeks. Tears, maybe. He wasn't sure. He couldn't see past the pulsating light.

He rested his head against hers, his mouth inches away from her parted lips. His body shook. He inhaled and then exhaled . . . and the world seemed to stop again.

Wake up. Wake up. Please wake up.

An unknown instinct propelled him forward, a whispering of ages before him. An image filled his mind, of Bethany basked inside and outside in light—*his* light. It poured through her body, a part of him attaching to her skin, muscles, and bones. He invaded her blood, wrapped himself around her on a cellular level, mending and repairing, healing torn skin and muscle, stitching together shattered bones. It went on and on, seconds into minutes, minutes into hours. Or maybe it wasn't even a minute that had passed. Dawson didn't know. But he wasn't breathing; he wasn't losing the image or the pleading litany in his head.

Wake up. Wake up. Please wake up.

At first, he wasn't sure what was happening. He thought he felt her stir in his arms. Then he thought he heard a rough first breath—a weak gulp of air.

Wake up. Wake up. Please wake up.

He was shaking, his light pulsating erratically.

"Dawson?"

The sound of her voice—oh, her sweet voice—destroyed his world for the third time. His eyes flew open, but he still couldn't see her beyond his own light.

Bethany? Are you . . . ? He couldn't say the words, couldn't believe somehow she was alive in his arms. And how could she be? Along with losing her, he'd lost his mind. A wave of raw pain crashed through him. *Bethany, I love you. I'm sorry I never told you. I love you. I wish I had told you. I love you. And I can't—*

I love you, too.

Those whispered words weren't spoken out loud. They were inside him, reverberating through his body and the part of him that had developed something human—a soul.

He pulled his light back into himself. He couldn't believe what he saw.

Bethany stared up at him, her warm brown eyes shining with tears. Her face was still pale, but color infused her cheeks. There were smudges of blood around her ears and at the corner of her mouth, but she was looking at him.

"Bethany?" he croaked.

She nodded and whispered, "Yeah."

Hands shaking, he touched her face, and when she closed her eyes, he panicked. "Bethany!"

Her eyes flew open. "I'm here. I'm okay."

It couldn't be, but she was alive and breathing in his arms.

He ran his fingers down her cheeks, smoothing away the hair caked with blood. His chest was doing that crazy swelling thing again. "Oh, God, I thought . . . I thought I lost you."

"I think you might have." She gave a shaky laugh. "I'm so, so sorry. I should've been paying—"

"No. Don't apologize. This wasn't your fault." He kissed her forehead, then her cheek and the tip of her nose. "How are you feeling?"

"Okay. I'm tired . . . a little dizzy, but I feel good."

He was exhausted. As if he'd fought a hundred Arum all at once. Pressing his forehead against hers, he breathed in her clean scent. He couldn't close his eyes, afraid she might vanish.

Bethany trembled. "What did you do, Dawson?"

"I don't know. I honestly don't know."

She let go of his hand and cupped his cheek. "Whatever you did, it saved . . . it saved me."

Bethany was alive! She was here in his arms, touching him. His cheeks felt wet again, but he didn't care. Nothing else mattered except the girl he cradled to him.

Bethany stayed in his arms and on that damn cliff for what felt like hours, and she didn't want to ever leave his embrace. She was warm wrapped in his arms. But they had to go. She stood, surprised that she even could. There was no doubt in her mind that at least one of her legs had been broken. And by the amount of blood that had dried in her hair, she was sure her skull had been cracked like an egg.

She put the pause on those thoughts.

Right now, she couldn't even begin to think about what had happened.

Dawson looked weary as he climbed, but he lifted her off her feet, holding her against his chest. There was only one way to get back down. "Hold on and close your eyes," he said.

Bethany did as instructed and felt the change in him. His body hummed, and she could see his bright light behind her lids. The wind rushed at her face, blowing her hair back. Seconds later, his lips brushed her forehead. When she realized he was walking, she struggled in his arms. He was obviously weaker now and shouldn't be carrying her.

"Are you okay?"

"Yes," she said, staring at him. Dark smudges had already bloomed under his eyes. What he did had worn him out. "But I can walk."

"I'd rather carry you."

She smiled. "I'm not going to fall again. I promise."

Dawson didn't find the joke funny, not that she blamed him. It took a little convincing that she could walk before he set her down, but he didn't let go of her hand or take his eyes off her the whole way back to the car.

The drive to his house was quick and quiet. When he killed the engine in front of the house, he faced her. "Bethany . . ."

In that instant, she remembered what she'd heard. Him saying he loved her over and over again. A knot formed in her throat, and her eyes burned. "Thank you," she whispered hoarsely. "For whatever you did. Thank you and I love you."

Dawson leaned back in his seat, smiling weakly. "I wish—"

"I know. I heard you. And that's all that matters."

He kissed her gently, as if he were afraid he'd hurt her. "I'm going to drive you and your car home, then come back to my house."

"I'm really okay." She glanced down at herself. Her shorts were torn and her hoodie was bloodied. She was a mess.

Thank God her parents had taken Phillip to a puppet show in Cumberland and Uncle Will would most likely be in bed when she got there.

Outside of the car, he pulled her into a fierce hug that she didn't want to end. He smoothed back her hair, kissed her until she thought she'd stopped breathing again.

"You're glowing," he murmured against her temple.

"How badly?"

"You're bright but beautiful." There was a pause when he kissed her forehead. "Brighter than I've seen. I'll feel better getting you home and checking out the area first, okay?"

Oh, no. Her heart sank. All the ground they'd made with the others would be lost. "Your family and friends—"

"I'll take care of it. Don't worry."

It was hard not to worry, but right now, her brain was spinning with everything. Once inside her car, he got behind the steering wheel and smiled at her. He looked so tired; his hair was a mess of black waves and his shirt was covered in her . . . her blood. She swallowed thickly, forcing her gaze forward.

Standing on the porch was Daemon. By the brutal look on his face, there was no doubt that he'd seen them—seen her trace.

Bethany's house was dark and silent when she walked in. All she wanted to do was shower all the blood and grime off and sleep for a year. Dawson was coming back over, and she was going to sneak him in. A first for her, but she knew he honestly needed to be near her right now. Dawson was rattled, still shaky over what happened.

So was she.

In the kitchen, she grabbed a bottle of water and downed

it in one gulp. The memory of falling haunted her steps as she threw the plastic in the recycling bin. She'd fallen and the impact—oh, God—the pain had been so intense but brief. Final.

And then there had been nothing.

Bethany wasn't sure how long that nothing had lasted, but the next thing she'd heard was Dawson telling her to please wake up and that he loved her. At first, she'd been confused. Had she fallen asleep? But then it hit her.

And she was still reeling from it.

Had she been knocked unconscious? If the blood was any indication, she'd been seriously injured. The big question was—had she been knocking on death's door or had she died?

Bethany shuddered.

Somehow, Dawson had healed her—fixed everything that had been damaged in the fall. What he had done was awe-inspiring and beyond comprehension. And their hearts—they'd been beating in perfect sync. She didn't know how she knew, but she did. It had to be some kind of weird byproduct of what he'd done. Very weird, but nothing she was afraid of. How could she be?

Dawson loved her.

And that kind of love . . . It was amazing.

Still thirsty, she grabbed another bottle of water and headed for the stairs. Without any warning, the kitchen light came on.

Uncle Will stood in the doorway, his eyes blinking against the light. "Bethany, what— Oh my God, are you okay?"

Crap. "Yeah, I'm fine."

He shuffled to her as fast as he could. Over the last couple of weeks, he had been getting better, stronger. Brown hair peppered with gray covered his head now. Soon, he'd be living back in his own home again.

"My God, Beth, you're covered in blood." He put a shaky hand on her shoulder, eyeing her like any doctor would, searching for visible injuries. "What the hell happened?"

Think fast, Beth, think fast. "Dawson and I went hiking, and he cut himself on a jagged rock. He bled . . . a lot."

Uncle Will's eyes widened. "Did he bleed all over you?"

"Pretty much, but he's okay." She went past him, heart pounding. "Everything's fine, though, so there's nothing to worry about."

"Beth—"

"I'm pretty tired, though." God, she needed to get away and clean herself up. "I'll see you in the morning."

Not waiting for a response, she dashed up the stairs and closed her door behind her. Crap, her uncle would probably say something to her parents and they'd flip. But there weren't any visible injuries. Maybe she'd be able to convince them it wasn't as bad as it seemed to Uncle Will.

Not maybe. She *would*.

Dawson's secret relied upon Bethany convincing her family everything was fine.

18

Dawson was so wiped out he could barely stand. He plopped down at the kitchen table, resting his head on his hand. A steady throbbing had taken up residency between his temples. He needed to shower and then get his butt over to Bethany's. What he wanted was to hold her, to reassure himself that she was very much alive.

But first he was in for a major bitching session.

Daemon glared at him from across the table. "What the hell happened? And don't you dare say nothing. She's glowing like a freaking sun."

What could he say? He didn't have a clue. No way could he explain what he had done, and until he understood it better, he wasn't going to tell anyone. Not even Dee.

"I'm still waiting," Daemon said.

Dawson pried one eye open. "I was showing off, being stupid. I wasn't thinking."

His brother's mouth dropped open. Disbelief filled his expression. "You have to be the—"

"Stupidest guy around, I know."

"That doesn't explain why both of you look like you jumped off a mountain."

Dawson flinched. "Bethany fell . . . and skinned up her hands. It looks worse than it is."

Daemon's gaze surveyed him. "No doubt."

Dawson sighed. "I'm sorry."

"Sorry," Daemon growled. "Sorry really doesn't fix this, bro. That other Arum—he's still out there. And now you've gone and lit up your girl's ass like the Fourth of freakin' July. Again. You're going to get that girl killed."

Whoa, that stung like a bitch. "Is the other Arum really out there, Daemon?" He lifted his head, weary. "We haven't seen him or any other Arum in months. He's gone."

"We don't know that."

Very true, but he was too tired to argue. "I'll keep her away from here until it fades." If it ever faded, because he wasn't sure it would. "I'll take care of this."

Anger blew off Daemon. "You know, I've been crazy to let you keep fooling around with this human, hoping you'd eventually come to your damn senses, but obviously I should've stepped in a lot sooner."

"I'm not *fooling around* with her." Dawson sat back in his chair, meeting his brother's furious glare. "I love her. And I'm not leaving her because you don't approve. So get over it."

"Dawson—"

"No. You don't get it. My life isn't yours—it doesn't belong to the Luxen and it doesn't belong to the DOD." Fury fueled his energy now. "And giving her up is like giving up a piece of me. Is that what you want?"

Daemon's fists thumped on the table. "Dawson, I—"

"She makes me happy. And shouldn't that make you happy? For me? And without her . . . Yeah, I don't need to finish that thought."

Daemon looked away, lips thin. "Of course I want to see you happy. I want nothing more than you and Dee to be happy, but bro, this is a *human* girl."

"She knows the truth about us."

"I wish you'd stop saying that."

"Why?" Dawson ran his fingers through his hair. "I can stop saying it, but it doesn't change anything."

A dry, bitter laugh came from his brother. And then what came next rhymed with *suck* and ended with *duck*. "And what happens when you break up?"

"We aren't breaking up."

"Oh, Jesus, Dawson, you're both sixteen. Come on."

Dawson flew to his feet. "You don't get it. You know what—it doesn't matter. I love her and that's not changing. Either you can support me like a brother should or you can stay the hell out of my face."

Daemon lifted his head, his eyes wide and pupils white. Shock stole a lot of the color from his skin, and Dawson had never seen the look on his brother's face. As if Dawson had walked up and shoved a blade deep into his own brother's back.

"So, it's going to be like that?" Daemon asked.

Dawson hated his next words, but he had to say them. "Yeah, it's going to be like that."

Standing, Daemon pushed back his chair and went over to the window. Several moments passed in silence, and then he laughed roughly. "God, I hope I never fall in love."

A little bit surprised by that statement, Dawson watched his twin. "Do you really want that?"

"Hell yeah," Daemon replied. "Look at how stupid it's made you."

Dawson smiled in spite of everything. "I know that's probably an insult, but I'm going to take it as a compliment."

"You would." Daemon faced him and leaned against the counter. "I don't like this. I've never liked this, but . . . but you're right. You've been right."

Hell just froze over.

A small, wry grin appeared on Daemon's face. "I can't tell you who to date. Hell, no one can tell any of us who to love."

Man, he stopped breathing. "What are you saying?"

"Not that you need my permission, because you pretty much do whatever you want, but I'll support you." He rubbed his eyes. "And you're going to need it when the rest see how bright she is."

Struck dumb by Daemon's submission, Dawson crossed the room and did something he hadn't done in a long time. He hugged him. "Thank you, Daemon. I mean it, thank you."

"You're my brother. The only one I have, so I am stuck with you." He hugged Dawson back. "I do want you happy. And if Bethany makes you happy, then so be it. I'm not going to lose you over some girl."

Three days later and Bethany's trace was still as bright as the day on the cliff. And they had the same amount of answers to what happened as they had then. A big fat nothing. They'd gone around and around, trying to figure out what happened. Short of confiding in Daemon or Matthew, Dawson didn't know if they'd ever find an answer. The whole not-knowing and constant discussing it was driving them both crazy.

So tonight, they were doing something normal. Going to

the movies like any other normal teenage couple would. They were even doing dinner. And at home, sitting on his dresser, was a fresh bouquet of roses he planned on surprising her with. Maybe even a few candles . . .

But Bethany had only picked at her dinner.

He glanced at her as he pulled into the parking lot. Her cheeks were flushed, eyes bright when they were open. Right now, though, she had them closed as she rested in the seat.

"Hey," he said, patting her leg. "You okay over there?"

Her lashes fluttered up. "Yeah, I'm just tired."

Dawson parked the car and twisted toward her. "We can call it a night if you want."

"No. I'm good to go." She reached out, placing her hand on his cheek.

He watched her and the words bubbled up before he could stop them. "I can't believe how lucky I am. You've been so accepting of everything. I almost can't believe it."

"I love you, Dawson. I love who you are, what you are. And I don't think love recognizes differences. It just is. And we really aren't that different."

Damn if he didn't start to feel his eyes burning. If he started crying, he'd kick himself.

"We have different DNA. I don't even have to breathe if I didn't force myself to, Bethany. I'm an alien—total ET over here. That's definitely different." But he placed his hand over hers anyway.

A faint smile appeared on her lips. All of her smiles were beautiful. "So? That doesn't change the fact that I love you. And I know it doesn't change that you love me."

"You're right."

"And, yeah, we are different on a superficial level." Bethany leaned over, kissing his lips. His fingers curved around hers tightly. "But we are the same. We laugh at the same stupid jokes. Neither of us has a clue what we want to do after school. Both of us think Hugh Laurie is a genius even though we hate TV. And we've both seen *Dirty Dancing* at least thirteen times, although you'll never admit it." She winked.

He pulled her hand from his cheek, pressing his lips against the center of her palm. "And both of us are going to fail gym."

She giggled, because it was true. "And we have a love for all things sugary."

"And stupid nicknames no one else gets."

Nodding, she placed her other hand on his chest. "And our hearts beat the same. Don't they?"

God, they did. Like two halves that were split but somehow still joined. He bent his head, brushing his lips along hers. He was in awe of her—no, enthralled by her. She was his. He was hers.

Dawson found her lips, feeling his heart pick up and race, matching Bethany's equally pounding beat. He shivered as a pleasant rush bloomed over his skin. "I love you."

Bethany smiled against his mouth. "Ditto. We're going to miss the movie."

He'd rather stay in the car and see how fogged up they could get the windows, but he nodded and opened the door. The sweet, tangy spring air swallowed him. Summer wasn't too far away. Funny. Three months had changed his life.

Heading around to her side, he draped his arm over her shoulders, steering her across the parking lot.

She grinned up at him. "Everything is sort of perfect, you know?"

Damn if it wasn't. He pulled her closer and—

A cold chill snaked down his spine, exploding over his nerve endings. The feeling was recognizable. Arum.

Spinning around, he wrapped his arm around Beth's waist and pulled her against him. "When I tell you to run, you run."

"What?" She struggled in his grasp and then stilled. "It's them, isn't it? Oh my God . . ."

They were on the cusp of the protective beta quartz, but her trace was definitely visible to any Arum. His eyes scanned the dark sky and then dropped over the surrounding woods. Everything was cast in shadows.

He wanted to send her into the theater, but that would require them splitting up, and he wasn't leaving her anywhere. "We're going to get back into the car," he said quickly. "And then—"

The shadows pooled in front of them, taking shape and form.

Without saying a word, he swooped Bethany up and headed for the thick tree line. Part of him hoped he wasn't making a huge mistake, but they'd never make it across the parking lot. And he needed to be where he could defend and keep an eye on her.

Rushing through the woods, he swore he could hear her voice in his head, saying his name, but that couldn't be possible. It had happened when he healed her, but in his human form, it shouldn't be. But he had to table that.

Once they were deep enough in the woods, he set her down. Her eyes were wide and panicked as she stepped back.

"Everything's going to be—"

The Arum came from the sky, slipping through branches like a dark, tumultuous cloud. Grabbing Bethany by her shoulders, he pushed her to the ground and then switched into his true form.

Her startled gasp propelled Dawson forward. He would die before he let anything happen to her.

He leaped into the air, crashing into the Arum. The thunderous impact rattled the trees, and they crashed through the leafy branches. Several yards away, they skidded across the ground, grass and dirt streaming into the air and leaving a rough trench behind.

The Arum's dark laugh slithered through Dawson. *Don't worry*, he said. *I won't kill you yet. I'll leave you alive ssso you can watch the life bleed out of your human.*

Rage pounded through him, and he rose up, feeling energy crackle along his arms. Gathering the energy into a tight ball of anger until he was taut with the pressure, he let go and a stream of bluish-white light blasted into the Arum's center.

With a roar, the Arum reared up and expanded, tossing Dawson into the air as though he were nothing but a child. *If you give up, it will be lesss painful.*

Dawson's shoulder slammed into the ground. He rolled onto his back and popped up in his human form before the Arum reached him. Spinning out of his grasp, he avoided the thick tendrils stabbing at him.

Damn, he'd been drained once before, and he wasn't going through that again.

The Arum shifted into his human form, letting loose a series of blasts that Dawson barely avoided as he raced toward the bastard. The matter the Arum wielded left craters in the ground, destroyed the ancient oaks it came into contact with.

He hadn't heard Bethany make a sound for so long, the thought that something had happened to her made him falter without even meaning to. He took his eyes off the Arum, searching for her. The minute distraction cost him. Letting out another chilling laugh, the Arum threw his hand out.

In the last possible moment, Dawson switched to his true form. The dark matter hit him in the chest, and he absorbed it the best he could. The blast still knocked him off his feet but would've incinerated a human. Over the red-hot, slicing pain shooting through his body and the buzzing in his ears, he heard Bethany's horrified scream.

A split second later, he sprang to his feet and took off after the Arum. The Arum was nothing more than a shadow, but he was heading straight for Beth. It was like all his nightmares were becoming reality. The terror was worse than when he'd seen Beth topple over the edge.

All he could see was Beth's pale face, her wide eyes. It became his whole world. A part of him, probably the one that held all of his humanity, switched off. His vision sharpened and purpose filled him. Beth was threatened.

And the Arum was going to die.

Still in his true form, he rushed the Arum and tackled him from behind. He heard a soft gasp, but he rolled the Arum onto his back. The air around them became charged. Reaching down, he unsheathed the obsidian blade from around his lower leg.

The Arum struggled wildly under him, but Dawson clamped a hand around the SOB's throat and pinned him there. Without saying a word, he plunged the blade deep into the Arum's center.

There was a flash of golden light and then the Arum broke into pieces that hovered in the air for a few seconds, like an irregularly shaped puzzle. And then they simply fizzled out.

Shifting to his human form, Dawson stood and swayed to the right. Pain arced up his leg. He looked down and noticed it seemed off. As if his left leg was going the wrong way, bent at an odd angle. Broken. Slipping the obsidian into his back pocket, he sighed and changed into his Luxen form so he could heal. It would take a couple of minutes to repair the damage, but at least he wouldn't feel it now. And anyway, he had more important things to worry about.

He faced Beth.

She was standing under one of the scorched trees, her arms wrapped around her waist. Trembles ran through her body, and he hated that she'd seen this—seen him kill.

Bethany?

Her head cocked to the side and she blinked. *Are . . . are you okay?*

Hearing her voice again in his thoughts was a heady, inexplicable feeling. Coming back to her, he knelt and cupped her cheeks. His light enveloped her as he pressed his lips against hers. Through this new bond, he heard her saying his name over and over again. *Dawson. Dawson. Dawson.*

It's okay. It's over. He slipped back into his human form, pulling her against his chest, resting his cheek against hers. Their pounding hearts beat in unison. *I'll never let anything happen to you. I promise. You're safe with me.*

Bethany's fingers dug into his shirt as she shivered. *I know. I love you.*

He would never grow tired of hearing those three words, through their bond or spoken out loud.

Dawson? A shudder rolled through her body. A moan was muffled against his neck. *I don't feel . . . I don't feel good.*

He let go, stepping back. *Beth—*

She didn't trip, but it seemed like her legs gave out on her. He reached for her, but she hit the ground, face pale as she pushed up to her knees. Her skin looked damp and clammy.

Fear tripped up his heart as he shot toward her. Was she hurt? The Arum hadn't reached her, he was sure. "Bethany, what's wrong?"

A shudder rolled through her body. "Dawson . . ."

Kneeling beside her, he grasped her shoulders. Her moan sent his heart racing. His eyes darted around quickly. "Baby, talk to me. What's going on?"

"I don't feel good," she said, her voice weak. And then he heard her as clear as day in his head. *I think I'm on fire.*

Placing his hands on her cheeks, he found her skin to be hot. Too hot. Her lids were heavy, hiding her eyes. "Bethany, tell me what's wrong."

"Something's wrong—"

A twig snapped nearby. In a flash, four shadows swallowed them, and his stomach pitched. Oh, God, no. There were more Arum.

Gathering her close, he knew he was too drained to fight off four of them. For the first time in his life, he envied his brother's strength. Bethany was going to die, and it was all his fault. Because he was too weak to protect her.

He held her tighter. *I'm sorry*, he said through their mind link. And he'd never meant those words more than he did then.

Tensing his shoulders, he gathered his remaining strength. This might be the end, but no way was he going out without a fight. He'd take as many of the bastards with him as he could. He squeezed Bethany one last time and turned to face them.

There was a flash of intense light, blinding even him, and before he could shed his human form, something cool was placed against his neck. Then his world went to hell. It felt like the light was being torn from underneath the skin, muscles pulling, bones snapping. Red-hot, fiery pain exploded, taking . . . taking everything. Him. Sight. Sound. *Everything*.

The last thing he felt was Bethany being pulled from his limp arms. A finality of black crashed over him in waves he couldn't surface from, welcoming him into the nothingness that dug in deep, refusing to ever let him go.

19

Daemon rolled his shoulders, unable to shake the sudden tension building in his back and neck. Like he'd slept wrong, but he'd done a whole lot of not sleeping.

"Babe, you're not paying attention to me at all."

He glanced over at Ash. She'd ordered summer dresses off the Internet or something and was doing a little peek-a-boo modeling show. And by her current state of dress, he must've missed the good stuff.

Extending an arm, he said, "Sorry."

She swayed her hips over to him. Instead of taking his hand, she climbed onto his lap and started going for it. Her mouth was everywhere—his lips, cheeks, throat, lower. Normally he would've been all into this, especially since Ash had been sweet that day. But his mind . . . it was someplace else.

Over her shoulder, moonlight sliced through the window.

Ash stilled and then straightened. Her lower lip stuck out. Somehow, she was still hot as hell. "Okay. What's going on, because you are so not on the same page as me."

"I'm sorry. I don't know. I just feel . . ." He couldn't put it into words, because he wasn't sure how he felt. He shook his head. "It's nothing with you. I swear." She looked like she was going to argue, but remarkably decided not to. "Okay. Well, maybe . . . maybe tomorrow we can pick this back up?"

"Yeah, of course." He cupped her cheeks gently and kissed her. "I'll call you in the morning."

Ash gathered her stuff up and left. He lay back on his bed, suddenly exhausted. Before he knew it, he opened his eyes and it was morning. Holy hell, he'd never just conked out like that.

Pushing himself up, he scrubbed at his eyes and yawned.

The tension in his shoulders and neck was still there. Great.

On his way downstairs he passed Dawson's bedroom. The door was cracked open. From the hallway he could smell the roses he'd bought for Bethany.

Maybe he should do something like that for Ash— Wait. Daemon pushed open the door. Dawson hadn't been home. And it was obvious that he'd been planning on coming back last night. He dug his cell out of his pocket. There were no messages from him.

"Dee?" He went down the steps, three at a time. She was sitting on the couch, huddled up in a little ball, wrapped in a quilt. "Have you heard from Dawson?"

"No." She looked dog-tired. "Maybe he stayed over at Bethany's."

All night with her parents there? He doubted that. Going into the kitchen, he made Dee and himself some breakfast. They ate in silence, which was unusual. Dee always had something to talk about.

"You feeling okay?" he asked.

She shook her head. "I feel beat."

"Same here." And the weird feeling in his stomach, like a

bundle of knots, kept growing and growing. Nothing he did, even running, eased them.

Sometime in the late morning, right before he was about to go to Bethany's house and see if his dumbass brother just couldn't be bothered with letting him know where he was, there was a knock on the door.

It was Officer Vaughn and Officer Lane.

Daemon took a step back without speaking. Something . . . something awful was creeping up his throat, into his head.

Officer Lane looked terrified. "Sorry to arrive without warning, but we need a few minutes of your time." Okay, they were never sorry before. Ever. As if he were moving through water, he turned to his sister. Her pale face was tight. On autopilot, he sunk down beside her.

Vaughn remained by the door, his eyes sharp. It was Lane who sat in the recliner and clasped his hands together. "I need to ask you a few questions about Dawson."

His mouth went dry. "Why?"

"Was he with a human girl by the name of Elizabeth Williams—also known as Bethany or Liz?"

The knots had turned into acid. Had the DOD found out about Dawson and Bethany? The DOD knew that the Luxen and humans had . . . relationships, even though it was a little bit on the forbidden side of things—for obvious reasons.

"Why are you asking?" Daemon sat straighter, figuring two officers were about to disappear if they'd discovered Dawson had exposed what they were.

Lane glanced at Vaughn, then took a deep breath. "Was he with her last night?"

"Yes," Dee answered. "They're friends. Why are you asking?"

"There . . . there appears to have been an incident last

night in Moorefield." There was a pause and all sorts of horrible things rushed through Daemon. "We don't know what happened, but I am sorry, he was gone. Both of them were."

Daemon opened his mouth to speak but lost his voice. Gone? As in, they weren't where the DOD thought they were, because he surely couldn't mean gone as in *gone*. He started to stand but couldn't will his legs to work.

His sister drew in a shaky breath. "He's coming back, right? With Bethany?"

Daemon bit down on his molars. *Gone* was a term humans loved to use when they couldn't wrap their tongues around the word *dead*. As if saying *gone* somehow lessened the blow.

Vaughn's expression remained impassive. "Both of them were dead. I'm sorry."

Daemon couldn't maintain the useless task of breathing. He locked up, every muscle, every cell. A roaring sound, like a low growl, filled his ears. His vision dimmed.

"No," Dee said, whipping toward him. Hands flew to her hair, tugging erratically. "No. Dawson's not dead! We'd know. He's not dead, Daemon! He's not!"

Lane stood, visibly awkward, and cleared his throat. "I'm sorry."

There was a pressure building in his chest. "I want to see my brother."

"I'm sorry, but—"

"Take me to my brother's body now!" His voice shook the windows and the humans, but he didn't care. "So help me, if you don't . . ."

Vaughn stepped forward. "Your brother's body and the human's have been disposed of."

"*Disposed . . .*" He couldn't even finish the sentence. Nausea rose sharply. Disposed of . . . like nothing more than trash that needed to be taken out. "Get out . . ."

"Daemon," Lane said. "We are truly—"

"Get. Out!" he screamed.

The officers couldn't have left quicker.

The wooden floor quaked beneath his feet, rolling until a keening howl accompanied the movement. The house shook on its foundation. Windows rattled. Pictures slipped from the wall, shattering against the shaking floor. Furniture toppled over and elsewhere in the house, more things fell. He didn't care. He would destroy everything. He had nothing left without his brother . . .

Dee. Oh, God. Dee.

Daemon started toward his sister, but found his legs just wouldn't keep going. He stopped, bending at the waist as a wave of pain that felt so real slammed into his gut. Not his brother. He couldn't really comprehend what just happened. You don't wake up and everything is normal only to have your entire life destroyed in seconds.

"Please, no," Dee whispered. "No, no, no."

He knew he needed to pull it together for his sister, but a cyclone was building inside him. All he could think about was the day in the kitchen. Him hugging Dawson—that couldn't have been the last time he would hug him. No—no way.

Daemon racked his brain. When was the last time he'd seen Dawson? Yesterday? He was eating a bowl of cereal. Froot Loops. Laughing. Happy.

Last time took on a whole new meaning.

Lifting his gaze, he saw Dee was blurred. Either she was losing hold on herself or he was. Had he ever cried before? He couldn't remember.

She seemed to wobble, and he shot toward her, catching

her before she fell, but then they both hit the floor, holding each other. Daemon turned his head to the ceiling, letting out an unearthly roar that surely broke the sound barrier, shaking the house again. Windows rattled and then blew out this time. The tinkling sound of glass falling cut through the wake like distant applause.

And then there were Dee's sobs. Heart-rending sobs racked her slender body and shook him. The sound broke his heart. She kept flipping in and out of her natural form, falling apart in his arms.

Dawson *wasn't* coming back. His brother *wasn't* going to walk through that door ever again. There'd be no more *Ghost Investigator* marathons. No more teasing fights with Dee over who ate the last of the ice cream. And there *weren't* going to be any more arguments over the human girl.

The human girl . . .

Dawson had lit her up like a beacon—that had led the Arum straight to Dawson. That was the only explanation. The Rocks still protected them in Moorefield. The Arum had to have seen Bethany . . .

Never in his life had he hated humans more than he hated them right then.

Sorrow and rage rippled through him as his light burned reddish-white. Dee's tears poured through the bond; her whispered denials kept coming, and God, he would've given his own life at that moment to take away her pain and loss.

And to change some of the last things he'd said to his brother. *You're going to get that girl killed.* Why hadn't he said he loved him? No. Instead he'd said *that*. Misery cleaved his soul, sinking in deep like a hot, serrated knife.

His head fell to his sister's shoulder, and he squeezed his eyes shut. Tears still seeped through, scalding hot against his now-glowing cheeks. Light flickered all around the living room, casting strange shadows of the two forms huddled on the floor together.

Dawson was dead because of him—because he hadn't warned his brother enough, hadn't stopped the relationship before it got out of hand. He was dead because of a human girl. And it was Daemon's fault. He hadn't done enough to stop him.

He held his sister tighter—the last of his family—and swore never again. Never again would he let a human put his family in harm's way. Never again.

Daemon wouldn't lose his sister, no matter *what* he had to do to keep her safe.

ACKNOWLEDGMENTS

First off, I want to thank the wonderful team at Entangled Teen. Special thanks to Liz Pelletier and her mad editing skills. Thank you to Kevan Lyon for always being a fantastic agent. A huge thanks to my crit/beta partners: Lesa, Julie, Carissa, and Cindy. You guys are the fantastic four of awesomeness. I couldn't do any of this without my family and friends for being supportive.

Also, a big thanks to Pepe and Sztella for being insanely hot and making the cover art for the series rock.

ABOUT THE AUTHOR

#1 *New York Times* and *USA Today* best-selling author Jennifer L. Armentrout lives in Martinsburg, West Virginia. When she's not hard at work writing, she spends her time reading, working out, watching really bad zombie movies, pretending to write, and hanging out with her husband and her Jack Russell, Loki.

Jennifer writes young adult paranormal, science fiction, fantasy, and contemporary romance. She also writes adult and new adult romance under the name J. Lynn.

www.jenniferarmentrout.com

PERFECTED

by Kate Jarvik Birch
July 2014

Ever since the government passed legislation allowing people to be genetically engineered and raised as pets, the rich and powerful can own beautiful girls like sixteen-year-old Ella as companions. But when Ella moves in with her new masters and discovers the glamorous life she's been promised isn't at all what it seems, she's forced to choose between a pampered existence full of gorgeous gowns and veiled threats, or seizing her chance at freedom with the boy she's come to love, risking both of their lives in a daring escape no one will ever forget.

THE WINTER PEOPLE

by Rebekah L. Purdy
September 2014

Salome Montgomery is a key player in a world she's tried for years to avoid. At the center of it is the strange and beautiful Nevin. Cursed with dark secrets and knowledge of the creatures in the woods, his interactions with Salome take her life in a new direction. A direction where she'll have to decide between her longtime crush Colton, who could cure her fear of winter. Or Nevin who, along with an appointed bodyguard, Gareth, protects her from the darkness that swirls in the snowy backdrop. An evil that, given the chance, will kill her.

THE BOOK OF IVY

by Amy Engel
November 2014

After a brutal nuclear war, the United States was left decimated. A small group of survivors eventually banded together, but fifty years later, peace and control are only maintained by marrying the daughters of the losing side to the sons of the winning group in a yearly ritual. This year, it is Ivy Westfall's turn. Only her bridegroom is no average boy. He is Bishop Lattimer, the president's son. And Ivy's mission is not simply to marry him. Her mission, one she's been preparing for all her life, is to restore the Westfall family to power . . . by killing him.